Praise for Dungeness . . .

"*Dungeness* is a remarkable work. Karen Polinsky weaves a rich tapestry of fact and fiction, sprinkled with Northwest native art, language, and historical images, about the churning cultural changes of the Olympic Peninsula in the 1870s, seen through a young native girl's experiences. But even more than this, Polinsky imbues her narrative with a deep and captivating sense of mystery."
— Joe Upton, *Alaska Blues: A Story of Freedom, Risk and Living Your Dream*

"Polinsky's innovative mix of fiction and fact is well designed to hold the interest of her intended readers—teenagers and young adults—while teaching them history essential to her tale. A mystery surrounding an actual 1868 massacre of Tsimshian Indians drives the suspenseful plot. Between chapters in which the fictional protagonist recounts her experiences, Polinsky presents short factual vignettes about events, circumstances, and Indian culture and beliefs. The information is admirably accurate, respectful of cultural differences, and relevant today as increasing numbers of people are again crossing cultural and racial lines to form families."
— Dr. Alexandra Harmon, *Indians in the Making: Ethnic Relations And Indian Identities Around Puget Sound* (former chair of the American Indian Studies Department at University of Washington)

DUNGENESS

DUNGENESS

a novel

KAREN POLINSKY

Bink Books

Bedazzled Ink Publishing Company • Fairfield, California

paperback 978-1-945805-18-9

Illustrations
by
Cara Thompson

Cover Design
by
Brock Walker

Bink Books
a division of
Bedazzled Ink Publishing, LLC
Fairfield, California
http://www.bedazzledink.com

To Mary Ann Lambert and
her storytelling legacy,
and the three bands of S'Klallam:
Port Gamble, Jamestown & Elwa.

Acknowledgements

Dungeness, the novel with history, for me has been a journey across boundaries into new worlds. Along the way I have encountered so many exceptional people—with diverse talents and outlooks, from different places— united by their love for this Pacific Northwest landscape.

Here I would like to express my gratitude to a few of them:

To Marie Hebert, the Cultural Director of the Port Gamble S'Klallam Tribe, who gifted me with the collection of primary documents that began this search to rediscover the past.

To Dr. Alexandra Harmon, author of the seminal work Indians In the Making: Ethnic Relations and Indian Identities around Puget Sound. and former chair of the American Indian Studies Department at the University of Washington. Professor Harmon supported me in developing the first draft, setting a high standard, and deepening my understanding of the historic challenges of the regions.

To historians Michael Schein, author of *The Bones Beneath Our Feet*, and *Katie Gale's* Llyn De Danaan, and Pam Clise, columnist for the *Peninsula Daily News*. To all of the scholars, writers and history buffs who volunteer at the Research Center of the Jefferson County Genealogical Society, especially Ann Candioto. What a resource!

To the earliest readers of the manuscript: To Zann and Craig Jacobrown, and Katie Zonoff, who love many of the same things I do. To my friends Kirrin Coleman, Sarah Hewes, Barbara Hume, Kelly Hume, Doug McKenzie and Peter Thomson. To my friend Eric Stahl, also an attorney, who advised me on copywright; still, any errors or oversights are entirely my own. To former Public Historian of the Museum of History and Industy Dr. Lorraine McConaghy, Bainbridge Arts and Humanities' Kathleen Thorne, and Island novelist Carol Cassella for offering me advice on what to do next. To Jay Gusick and Bill Mawhinney for that final copy edit. Thank you.

For thinking outside of the box, to Michael D'Alessandro executive director of Northwind Arts Center and William Tennent, executive director of the Jefferson County Art and History Museum.

To Bennie Armstrong, the former chair of the Port Madison Suquamish Tribe, for offering his advice and support, and sharing his own stories. Without Bennie I wouldn't have had the courage to finish the book or embark upon the collaborative exhibit. To Wendy Sampson, educational director of the Elwha S'Klallam Tribe, who strives to keep the language alive.

To the S'Klallam artists, who took a risk: to weaver Cathy MacGregor, a humorous, warm, versatile artist; to Jimmy Price, whose wit and wisdom I will never forget; and to Master-Carver Joe Ives who has enspirited my life with his undaunted optimism.

To all of the families, and the entire staff at the Jamestown S'Klallam Tribe. In particular, Tribal Chair Ron Allen, his assistant Ann Saergent, and publications director Betty Openheimer, for their help with the book and the exhibit. Also, thanks to the Olympic Peninsula Inter-Tribal Cultural Advisory Committee for their support and the Suquamish Tribal Council for their support.

To my children, Lee, Cynthia, and Adam Foley. To my husband Michael Foley, who believed in me. And to Cara Thompson, the designer of the book and the exhibit. Her insight, humor, and skill made this project possible. Best of all, she is a friend.

Last but not least, everlasting gratitude to Tom and Carol Taylor and Sherry Macgregor for sharing their time, and the precious past, with me.

About this Project
By Cara Thompson

Dungeness has been the uncovering a lost trail, a legendary Indian highway, more complex, haphazard, passionate, and enchanting than this book can convey. I say uncovering because we didn't seem to have a map, or at least not one we could read. It seems we never accomplished what we set out to do, as we adventured. At times we embarked spontaneously, at times with unrealistic itineraries, wearing our bathing suits under our shorts, with bikes waving like a banner, barely strapped on to the back of her blue toy car questing to the Olympic Peninsula.

Before I came into this hurly-burly book bonanza, Karen had completed her own undertaking: researching and writing *Dungeness* for more than 10 years, calling on some magical inspiration from the curiosity, candor, and pride of one S'Klallam woman, an original. When Karen finished, the book had become more than just a work of historical fiction, but a coming-of-age story with some history, some philosophy, some native lore, some regional myth, and some-thing that had never been done before! Karen knew that sharing her story would call for more than just words, but a whole crew of imaginative people coming together to shape an old story in a new way.

At this time Karen asked me to add artwork to the story and design the text. As we struggled, now together, to assemble the pages, we fell upon the secret message of the hidden narrative, while listening to the stories of the visionary artists Joe Ives, Jimmy Price, and Cathy MacGregor; eating Indian tacos at a pow-wow at the Port Gamble Tribe; dividing an apple pancake with Mary Ann Lambert's family; and visiting S'Klallam language classes. We spent the summer of 2015 finishing the book while learning how to carve our very own portrait masks from a wise Master Carver! As we ventured further into the unknown, whether our mini-expeditions were successful or not, at the end of the day there was always a cider and a salmon sandwich at Sirens, a distinguished pub in historic Port Townsend.

The secret message: if you want to shine a light on something: look, look back, look inside, look around, and listen. What we learned on the journey has inspired the *táʔkʷt* (to shine a light on something) revisionist-history contemporary art exhibition.

However creative, unsystematic, or outlandish our project became, Dungeness kept moving forward, inspiring a collaborative, multimedia art exhibit at Northwind Arts Center in Port Townsend, a symposium led by three of the foremost women authors writing on S'Klallam history, and a series of gratitude gatherings for all those who made this project possible.

In Karen's words: "This entire project has been forged in friendship," with the Tribes, the families, the galleries, the librarians, the historians, the artists, the past, the present, and between Karen and me. Friendship has no map; friends make maps together. Dungeness is just a sappy glistening of what we uncovered. The book is our map to a place of love and chance.

Prologue
September 1900

Dear Reader—

The night is still. The waning moon illumines the white-and-black lighthouse, surmounted by a red lantern room. The universe whispers, "t-sh."

Below, on the south side of the Dungeness sandspit, a beached fleet of canoes: forty-to-fifty feet in length, honed with an axe blade to withstand a sea journey of five hundred miles or more. It's a rich fleet, pregnant with sacks of flour, sugar, and soap. In addition: three tea kettles, two sets of brass hinges, eighty used blankets; all purchased with dollars earned from the harvesting of hops in the dry heat of summer.

On top of the dune, a half-dozen canvas tents billow as if breathing. Inside, eighteen Tsimshians, hotly at rest. The men place their tough bellies on top of the sturdy hips of their wives. A small boy clasps his fingers to make a pillow for his cheek; a little girl sighs, pressing her palms in between her knees. Together they dream of the welcome they will receive in their home village on the north Pacific shore, greeted by sentry poles with round eyes and grimacing grins, fifty-to-eighty feet high.

Outside, two dozen makeshift warriors wait for a black wind to rise. The leader of the ambush—the S'Klallam call him Nu-Mah the Bad— lifts up his hand, hatchet-like. To whites he's known as Lame Jack. By any name, he's a scoundrel. Lame Jack lets the axe blade drop.

At the signal, the S'Klallam bury their weapons, splitting the flesh and cracking the cartilage and bones of the seething canvas beast. The blood of bodies far from home unfurls on top of the pebbly beach like a map. A raft of seals, their heads bobbing on top of the waves, turn their eyes into fire. It is their role to witness what happens here. From the fall to the winter, they will groan about it and roar.

On September 21, 1868, eighteen Northern Indians were transformed into seventeen corpses. Nusee-chus, a Tsimshian girl too frightened to cry, sacrificed a pair of silver pendant earrings, her life, and that of her unborn son. The eighteenth murdered body?

In this journal I will clarify how the earrings, created by a Tsimshian craftsman for his new bride, came to me. For a while the earrings belonged to my mother Annie, also a girl bride, though a reluctant one. She was never seen without them. As a baby, I can still recall reaching out to still their eerie brightness. When I was six, my reluctant mother—vexed by fear and love—branded me with the silver fish. This violent sacrificial act, the call to action of my quest, a mystic journey to unknown places across the great divide between life and death.

In these pages, I explore the events of my coming of age in the Pacific Northwest, more or less in the sequence in which they occurred. In alternating chapters, I have composed short essays about local history, in chronologic order, to brighten my passage.

Today, I am twenty, a teacher of Native American children in Kansas. More educated. Not as clumsy. Wiser, perhaps. Intuitive by nature but not as keen as some. If you question my perception or doubt any +of the claims put forth here, ask Annie.

I still have a lot to learn; not from the dead leaves of books, but from the living landscape, seeding the songs of our ancestors, who, like fossil ferns, have buried their knowledge deep within the earth. Newcomers who disembark here trespass upon their bones. The subterranean whispers of those who belong to this place—without whom this landscape cannot exist—shadow our past and light the way to our future. The story of the S'Klallam people is our story. The fate of the indigenous is our fate.

Choosing where to begin is like dropping an anchor from a random star. According to S'Klallam belief, there is no true beginning, and no end: death, merely a crossing over to a wider, deeper, brighter awareness. Still, to strip the moss off the mystery, one must start somewhere. I begin where consciousness begins: As a wide-eyed infant on the Strait of Juan de Fuca in the autumn of 1876.

I am that star.
This is my story.
It is random.
It is everyone's.

When our young men grow angry at some real or imaginary wrong, and disfigure their faces with black paint, their hearts, also, are disfigured and turn black, and then their cruelty is relentless and knows no bounds, and our old men are not able to restrain them.
—Chief Seattle
From a speech published in
The Seattle Sunday Star
1854

There is no circle any longer, and the sacred tree is dead.
—Nicolas Black Elk
The final line of his dream-vision
1932

Invariably there are three sides to any story, whether verbal or written. Herein, then, is contained a chain of stories based on facts, and having three sides: The White man's side, the Indian's side and Public Opinion's side.
—Mary Ann Lambert
From *Dungeness Massacre and Other Regional Tales*
1961

Part I

On The Strait
of Juan de Fuca

1
The Aia'nl
(From Klallam Ethnography
by Erna Gunther)

There is a tidal pool at the end of the spit where the ducks often gather. He saw a woman walk. It was strange . . .

. . . when he reached home he could not eat his evening meal . . .

She stood on the opposite side of the fire and looked at him.

He called to his uncle to drive her away.

"Don't you see her?"

For many nights she came in this same way.

His people begged him not to be afraid. They told him she would give him the power to see far off and find missing things.

Still, he did not want her, for her appearance was so terrible. She was very dark with a purple forehead and large round eyes, without corners like ours. Her eyelashes were white.

At last she came no more.

2
The Sick Fox
(c. 1876)

At high tide the five-mile spit of sand is like a bent elbow. At the tip of the crooked finger, the New Dungeness Light Station overlooks the sandbar with a shifting, uneasy regard.

A girl, restless, props her chin up on the rail of their fragrant plank house. A lock lashes at her squinched forehead. She loops it around her boney ear, a convenient oarlock. Pendant earrings shaped like fish banter in the sunlight.

She shrugs once, and then reaches for the cradleboard leaning on the sill. Beside it, a wide-weave pot-bellied oyster basket. In her arms, an infant sausaged inside a rolled cedar mat. She secures the bundle to the cedar plank. A leather strap across her forehead supports the basket, which rocks against her hip. Thus encumbered, Annie races down the oozing path in between the mucus grass to the water's edge.

Her flat right palm shields her eyes.

It's a clean morning full of sun, one made for sport.

On the horizon his bright green troller with its matchstick mast, bobbing. The old man, Charles Langlie, Norwegian sailor turned farmer-fisherman, anchored out a short distance from the Dungeness sandbar. He can't expect to bring in much, not without help. According to Carl, Jake-the-Makah ought to be here on the other end of a purse seine net. However, when Jake shows up tomorrow, Carl knows better than to question him or display his irritation. Carl may be the boss, but Jake is prideful and won't put up with much.

With or without his hired man, the next step is to deliver one or two basins of the smaller fish to the cannery at S'Klallam Bay. Annie figures, even with a modest take, he won't be back for hours.

How did Eliza-the-third, E'ow-itsa in Coast Salish, aka Seya, persuade the fourteen-year-old S'Klallam princess to wed the old Norwegian mariner?

What makes her stay?

At first, she reasoned, or at least hoped, a liaison with a white husband almost four times her age could only increase her status. Instead, she has become his near slave. Each day Annie fetches potable water from the creek, prepares fish stew, boils water to scrub his cuffs and collars, and gathers kindling from the beach. All this, before the baby!

The fisherman, with a halo of white hair and a glowering aspect, can claim one or two finer points, as well as some unanticipated talents. With no cash to pay the canoe-preacher, he managed to throw up a decent house. In the evening, Carl sits by the fire uncoiling his sleeves. On the little iron cook stove he crisps glowing ginger cookies with a spicy aftertaste. Despite his rough manners, he's never rough with her.

sé?ya?

grandmother

The story of how he netted his unsought treasure, he embellishes. In nearby Sequim—not exactly a town but instead a few signposts buried in the mud—cannery workers, lumbermen, farmers, and oystermen meet at a tavern, The Corners. Here, Carl toasts the passage of time with Hjalmar Henning, an original pioneer who makes his living hauling logs with an ox team.

At the bar, Henning coughs up the coins, which gives him the right to bellyache: about farmers who pay in kind instead of cash; claim jumpers quicker than his scatter shot; but worst of all, where are all the women? Can't find a girl—white, brown, red, or Chinese—to brand a steak, wring his socks, or measure out his whisky.

To prick him on, Carl relates a marvelous confabulation, about how a damned alcoholic snagged a princess. Carl should know by now that the term "princess," and other nomenclature of European aristocracy, increasingly offend the local Natives. These satiric honorifics mock historic S'Klallam hierarchies, a source of great pride. He's aware, but he can't help it: to Carl, Annie is, and always will be, his princess.

Henning bites his lip and squirms. No fairytale princess, but an actual blood-and-flesh woman, that's what he wants.

Meanwhile, on the lost beach, beside the big log with its medusa-like roots, Annie drops her load of bearded oysters and kneels. With her fingertips she combs the infant's wisps. The baby gurgles. Annie wiggles her index finger and recites the tale of Slap'u, wild woman of the woods. Listen: You can hear her whistling through the dank trees. Another warning sign (just in case you weren't paying attention!) she smells bad. Slap'u, with the tangled seaweed hair, steals babies from the beach, and tosses them into the basket on her back. Bad children kidnapped by Slap'u never return.

It's not that her infant daughter is repellant, but rather oddly out of place, like a true word spoken out of turn, or liberated from context. For one thing, despite her noble lineage, she's a "round head." The practice of the tribal elite—to press flat stones against the baby's brow, to flatten the forehead as a symbol of status and a beautifying feature—is now, according to the white territorial government, though not precisely a crime, a barbaric out-of-date ritual. At times, in the intimate dark of the hot cabin, the babe smells sweet enough to drink, like hot milk from a goat. At these times, Annie would like to fold her into her heart, but that wrought iron gate won't give way. At other times, she would like to swing her like a club, shattering her round skull.

The infant, roused by the salted-earth scent of the mother, nearly leaps out of her skin. Annie pries at the straps; then reverses, and pulls them down hard. Instead of loosening the leather laces, she secures a new knot. The infant attempts a lopsided grin as the vague portrait of her mother clarifies and blurs, solidifies and crumbles—

Annie takes off.

Without a backward glance.

The baby, four months old and baby nearsighted, becomes flat and stiff like the cradleboard. Something in the active air has altered. As the sand holds onto the disappearing tide, she can feel the shape of her receding. The whole world yawns.

The infant learns that *outside* is not *inside*.

Outside is peopled with a physical reality of rocks, driftwood, water, and sky. The elements vibrate with their own style of chatter. Inside begins as a mute regard for other people and the world guided by the sensations of the body. When an infant perceives the difference between inside and outside, she makes a journey from the everywhere to what we are & where we stand.

My mother, a noble S'Klallam. My father, a philosopher-king. I only wanted to be normal. To be loved. For me, the offspring of two distinct worldviews, "normal" had not yet been invented. I was like an ordinary rock turned into aerolite by conditions beyond my control. I disturb the universe. I became extraordinary, without really wanting it.

Like so many people out there.

Even you.

The baby flaps its stubby limbs. She puffs up her cheeks and rounds her lips to scream, but instead gulps and inhales a burning ball that later she will rename Utterly forsaken. However, this impression of *alone* is merely an illusion. Sure, her mother, the life force, for the moment has fled. However, the world is alive. The timeless, teeming, evolving world.

Rounding one end of the beach log, a slouching shadow passes through the reedy purple grasses.

A band of small birds curves into the air. Jostling crows consult and dash off. A great blue heron, balanced on one backward knee, lifts up, hacking out his disdain.

The shadow congeals into an identifiable shape: a creeping fox, advancing inch by inch. Its open jaw swings, unreeling translucent strings of saliva. The black tips of his sharp ears are cocked. The ill creature lifts its addled head and moves it from side to side.

It hunkers down on its white paws. The sick fox leaps. A rifle explodes, followed by a turbulence of crows. A smell like burnt coffee wafts.

Due north a quarter of a mile up the shore, Annie, meanders in-between the rocky pillars. Hopping over shore rocks like an ebullient child, she feels her freedom.

The report of a hunting rifle recalls her to reality. When she is vexed, Annie's forehead contracts into one brow of woe. She halts to listen. Then, she straightens her spine, pebble by pebble, and whirls. Her legs stretch, unfurling seaweed banners from the soles of her feet.

Now she is flying.

Meanwhile, like a pull toy, the soul of the fox is pulled back, and evulses from the grey-glove of its impermanence. The pelt somersaults and drops onto the wet sand, relocating a colony of leaping creatures, could-be-fleas and might-be-shrimp. Silently, its dead body curls up into a crescent moon-shape, the bleeding shadow of what once was.

Who shot the sick fox? No one ever claimed the deed. In the Pacific Northwest, babies die. Oftentimes, they survive. Miraculously, like this one.

To me, it was Annie who loosed me from my bonds. That day in September, to relocate past joy and escape the prison of the present, Annie escaped. Blue thunder. Annie hastened back to find: ME. She kicked aside the cradle board and lifted me UP. My head became the sky.

My mother sees me; therefore I am.

Before that moment, Annie and Carl were strangers: worse, hostile warriors, from alien worlds, with alien weapons, yet, in their own way, well-matched.

That shot married them.

But still, the crouching shadow lurked.

```
              20 February 1879
              Married

   LAMBERT, Charles
          &
      Annie Jacob

                        By J.A. Kuhn, Probate Judge




              17 August 1878
              Marriage License Issued

   LAMBERT, Mr. Charles
           &
      Miss. Annie Jacob  - (An Indian girl of the
                              Clallam Tribe)


   Extracted from the Democratic Press
                        5 February 1879




              25 January 1870
              Married

   LAMBERT, Charles
           &
      Mrs. Susie Williams

                        At the home of John C.
                        Appleton
                        By William H.H. Learned,
                        Probate Judge
```

Marriage certificate of Mr. Charles Lambert to Miss Annie Jacob.

3.
Vancouver "Discovers" The Strait
(from the logs of Captain Vancouver)

In April, 1792, Captain George Vancouver rounded the tip of Cape Flattery, the extreme northwest tip of the continental United States. Under a fair wind, the thirty-year-old navigator and mapmaker sailed east into the Strait of Juan de Fuca. Between the latitudes of 47 and 48 degrees, Vancouver entered a broad inlet. For twenty days he followed the Strait past a series of harbors with towering bluffs, rocky platforms, and sentinel firs.

In 1792, from the deck of his ship, Captain Vancouver kept a log in his own hand, noting the picturesque as it coalesced and dissolved. What he observed was not, "one uninterrupted wilderness" but instead, "in many directions, extensive spaces that wore the appearance of having been cleared by art."

What he described was a gentleman's well-groomed estate. The unfurling coast, he later wrote, presented "a picture so pleasing it could not fail to our remembrances certain delightful and beloved situations in old England." When they reached Protection Island, a sand-and-grass sanctuary for birds, "our attention was immediately called to a landscape, almost as enchantingly beautiful as the most elegantly furnished pleasure grounds of Europe . . ." Because the rolling green and purple valleys between the sheer bluffs reminded him of home, he named the curve of coastline protected by North America's longest sandspit, New Dungeness.

Along with his pastoral meanderings, Vancouver remarked in his journal on the savaged faces of children and old people marked by smallpox scars. When his ship *The Discovery* first entered the Strait, the log mentions twenty-five or thirty thriving villages. By the mid-nineteenth century, the waves of illness from explorers and colonizers had devastated the coastal tribes. Evidence of the pestilence was everywhere. Entire villages had sickened and died.

Later on, near Whidbey Island, Vancouver suffered a minor scrape. He lost the 900-pound anchor from his vessel the HMS Chatham. The pestilent iron, for two hundred years, will remain buried underneath

Juan de Fuca's Strait. A reminder to the whites: despite the centuries, the invaders are still here.

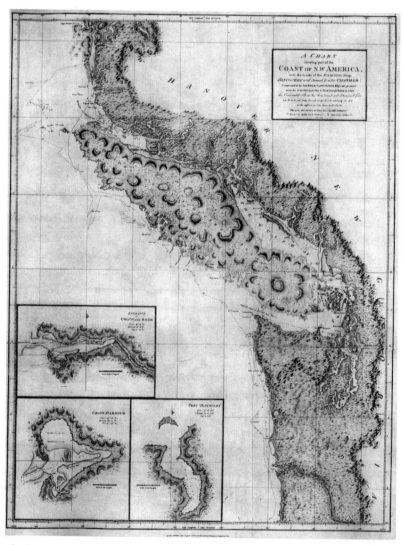

A chart showing part of the coast of N.W. America: with the tracks of His Majesty's sloop Discovery and armed tender Chatham. *Image courtesy of the Geography and Map Division, Library of Congress.*

4
Swan Boat
(c. 1880)

My father, a driftwood sailor, thumbed the cardboard globe and incised it with his horny nail on a random longitude and latitude which he called home.

The fall I turned four, Carl built a small loft for me over the entry of our cabin. A hemp ladder reached up to a loft shelf covered with a bristling sack of squeaky feathers, my bed. I propped my doll on the roof beam curtained with cobwebs. Up here I could treasure my thoughts yet keep an eye on the people I loved in the chamber down below.

At the far end, a fireplace provides heat to the bedroom alcove. Beneath my toes thrust out over the ledge, the kitchen: an iron cookstove, topped by three pantry shelves, with glass jars and clay vessels filled with flour, lard, dried berries, and spices; a slab table and two bright benches, which had somehow crawled out of a mean hunk of swamp maple; and one factory-made chair where Carl knitted or smoked his pipe. Annie's mother Eliza II—I called her Seya; grandmother in Coast Salish—had twisted, urged, and abused a colorful rag rug out of scraps. Huge and heavy, it made the two halves of my world whole.

"Millie, you're wanted," my father called.

Woozy, I slid down.

On the factory-made chair, my mother sat with her knees up. Her well-oiled locks dripped down. Not her usual self. INSIDE OUT, her essence revealed: pod and seed. Inkwell and ink. A candle guarding its own flame.

She was—alarming.

Carl, hand trembling, treated me to salted halibut in a chipped saucer. I thrust it back into his tough belly, which *oofed* in time to Annie's ache, and then went soft. I looked up; he looked down. Instead of scolding me, he traded the lump of fish for a quarter loaf of stale bread, and pushed me out. "If you see your grandmother, tell her to come apace."

As the morning mist lifted, treetops nodded on a pillow of cloud. I crushed the bread, I wound up, and let go. A bufflehead with a teal mask nipped at the explosion of crumbs. After that, I stumbled down the dry trail to our curved beach, where Carl had toppled the skiff. The nether region, a barnacled topographic map of the world. I clambered up and balanced on top of the sharp shells. Still bleary, I shielded my eyes from the Strait which glinted like a rogue's cutlass.

Not long after, Seya appeared, picking her way over the green rocks. In the white light she was easy to spot, even at a quarter of a mile, with the grey-and-white Hudson's Bay blanket tossed up over one shoulder. Striding after her, a jaunty gentleman in a bowler and powder-gray topcoat wafted. The graybeard, making his way with a cane, panted. Trailing behind them, Jacob Cook, Carl's handyman.

"Hullo! Hullo!" I wobbled on the keel of the

ʔaʔáʔmət

to be at home

upside-down boat. To my surprise, with the merest nod in my direction, Seya hobbled up to the house. The gentleman, in his mid-sixties, dropped his bruised leather satchel and held out his glove. I shook my head, leaped, and landed against the hard thigh of Jake, Carl's fishing partner, who, as usual, refused to play. The tall Indian dragged my legs through the sand until I found my feet.

James Gilchrist Swan: to me, a trumpeted name in a fairytale. Later I learned that Swan—explorer, artist, and ethnographer—even then, was famous, from coast to coast and in Europe, too. It was his pen that first described the Pacific Northwest. In the 1840s Swan served as a clerk for a shipping concern in Boston. When gold rush fever became epidemic, he abandoned his wife and two children, fleeing fusty New England to commune with cathedral trees in the final frontier. In vest-pocket notebooks he chronicled his travels: the damp winter harvesting oysters with the coastal tribes and his subsequent travels north up the untrammeled coastline to the Olympic Peninsula. These notes became *The Northwest Coast*, the first detailed description of Oregon and Washington. Later, he published articles, sketches of flowering plants and Indian artifacts, and a monograph of the Makah.

Swan eventually settled in Port Townsend. A Renaissance man, he simultaneously served as a journalist, judge, and consulate of two countries. He tried to raise funds for an expedition in the Queen Charlotte Islands to gather more artifacts. Though warmly well-respected, no one seemed all that eager to back him. A dreamer, Swan, had lost money before: attempting to build a brand new port for the outmoded whaling industry, shilling for a proposed railroad, and more. Also, he was also known to binge on whiskey, which made him a bad risk.

Addressing me as an equal rather than a child, Swan described his passage from Port Townsend to Dungeness: The mid-morning started out fine, but by mid-afternoon the weather turned bleak. As Jake's dugout canoe rounded Dead Man's Point, the wind began to shrill. With skill and fortitude, "and more luck than we deserved," the paddler maneuvered his craft in between the sea stacks.

Jake, the hero of the tale, looked bored. Either that, or he wasn't listening. As Swan gossiped with Carl, the lean and rugged jack-of-all-trades poked holes into the sand with a pointy stick. He tossed up the wet clams until they accumulated in a heap on the beach. Every minute or so, he glanced up at our plank house.

At last, the cabin door flew open on its rope hinges. My father, a scowling prophet, in India rubber boots medallioned with silvery fish scales, scuffed down over the rocks to the edge of the Strait, where, motionless, we waited.

My father cried out, "Tell me! Can she, will she, survive?"

Swan, startled, said nothing. With his kid glove he reached inside the pocket of his jacket for a bottle. Like an agate, or a sperm oil lamp, the mid-morning sun set fire to the amber liquid inside. My father received the vessel, embossed thusly:

OUR "OLD CUTTER"
AS IN 1857 SO NOW AND ALWAYS

OLD
J.H. CUTTER
WHISKY

He lifted up the bottle, thrusting out his nob of chin. Abrupt brow, deep set eyes, thin bent nose; his white eyebrows looped down, a froth of steely grey which joined the sideburns of his beard at the temples. Like the rest of him, his neck was scrawny. His Adam's apple went up and down. At last, he lowered it and declared, "What we should do now is pray." He added, sadly, "But I can't."

The seaweed steamed on top of the water.

Swan replied, "Let's go fishing."

Heave ho! Together, they lifted the rowboat and rolled it into the sputtering tide. Swan handled the oars; my father jealously guarded his bottle. Jake, the Makah, looked on with disgust. When Swan ordered him into the boat, Jake refused.

"Hey!" I chirped up. "What about me?"

Carl set down the bottle and lifted me into the boat.

Jake remained there, standing on top of the rocky beach, gazing at us steadily. As the waves pulled us back he turned taller and thinner, a burnt-black tree blending into the stepped-up wood behind the plank house.

Our skiff, off balance and anything but smooth, upset a clique of seagulls. A merganser dipped his black-feathered cap and disappeared. Here the Dungeness River collided with the salty Strait, causing the tide to rebound. Our skiff, despite Swan's best effort, turned 'round and 'round. I imagined the fish looking up at the barnacled bottom of the skiff to gaze at a spinning map of the world.

Carl, in his great misery, told Swan, "When Eliza gave her to me, I pledged to protect her. If she dies, it's my fault."

He wound up. The bottle arched and disappeared into the mystic.

He went on. "I have served on merchant ships and whaling vessels. One time, a brig. The deck all heaped up with sugar cane and casks of palm oil. Underneath, a hell: slave boys from the Congo, below the deck wallowing in filth, awash in their own fear. I'm not a good person. I've done nothing of value for others or me.

"Not until I met Annie." He squinted at the featureless sky. "Swan, do you think God, in order to punish me, will take the life of an ignorant girl?"

Swan exhorted, "Gad, man. We're not in heaven, we're in the world. We suffer enough without the help of a higher power. I love Annie, too. But, what makes you think she's less guilty, or less wise, than the sum total of humanity, a damnable lot?"

He pointed his oar at my father. "Most whites, knowing very little about them, regard Indians as wayward children. They start out trying to protect them and end up damning them all to hell. However, Indians are not children, except, of course, those who are. Their men: intelligent, sensitive, and capable. Their women, wives and mothers by the time they are fifteen, even more so. We remove from their power to survive, and then condemn them as irrationally unethical. The mote in the eye, as it were.

"For example, we condemn the S'Klallam for stealing slaves from Native villages. However, this practice can in no way be compared to the trade in human chattel from Africa, which we have outlawed but only very recently.

"Likewise, we condemn their system of justice. But why? Coast Salish justice maintains the balance of power. When a tribal member is killed, his village demands payment, in money or blood. More often than not, a settlement is reached and the goods are delivered without further ado. Overall, there is more peace than war. Can we say as much?

"The decay of the living organism," Swan went on, "the law of the conservation of energy, the transmutation of matter—to white man, these are the metaphysical theories, impractical and impersonal; to the shaman, life and death is a door that swings both ways. European men-of-letters claim that their minds are open; that may be, but their eyes are shut. They fail to take in the ample evidence everywhere in the natural world: nothing is past, and that which perishes remains."

The waves heaved against the side of the craft. A breeze edged in, side-swiping the tears that wobbled down my father's cheeks.

The clouds had descended, opened up, and vomited a pestilent rain.

"Yes, yes, I know!" Carl exclaimed. "You're a scholar, well-informed and broad-minded. I'm sure everything you say is true. But I want to know: will Annie die?"

I began to cry.

The two men looked abashed; both had forgot me, or maybe they assumed I was too little to understand.

We had ended exactly where we started. By now the scalding breeze had carried our craft back to the shore. Jake Cook, gone. Swan shoved the handle end of the oar into the mud and pried up a stream of muck. Breathing hard, my mouth was open; the grit plashed against my teeth. Carl called out, "Capsize!"

He and I leaped. Together we managed to hoist the boat up onto the beach without wetting Swan's mantel. Naturally we had hooked no fish; no one had thought to bring a line.

Holding onto Carl like fish bait on a line, we made our way up to the cabin.

Once inside, the dusty air smelled like dried grass and smoke. Our sense of relief was palpable. In the tiny dark room attached to the kitchen, against the headboard, Annie, in a halo borrowed from the setting sun. Her figure, hot and cold, red and black, encircled a pod of energy, a new star called Charley.

Annie Jacob holding her first child, Mary Ann Lambert, Port Townsend, Washington, 1879. *Photo courtest of the JamestownS'Klallam Tribe.*

5
Pestilent Spirit
(19ᵗʰ Century)

The Nu-sklaim—in English, called the S'Klallam or Clallam—also as "the Strong People" for their skill in war, survived the epidemics better than most of the indigenous peoples of the Pacific Northwest Coast. At the mid-point of the nineteenth century, the governor's assistant George Gibbs described the band as "the most formidable tribe now remaining . . . Their country stretches along the whole southern shore of the Straits to between Port Discovery and Port Townsend . . ." The territorial government described the S'Klallam as the most resilient tribe on the Olympic Peninsula, and one of the most adaptable in the Pacific Northwest.

nəxʷs°λ'áy'əm'
S'Klallam

xʷanitəm
white person

Nevertheless, at the time he made his report, their numbers had dwindled. In 1854, Gibbs in his tribal census reduced the tally of Indian villages noted by Vancouver, twenty-five or more, to just eight. Gibbs noted as many as "1500 fighting men." Just three years later, the drastic decline continued. ES Fowler, an Indian agent, counted 1,000 men, women, and children. Fifteen years later, the Strong People, still the dominant tribe on the west side of Hood Canal, numbered "something over 600," according to U.S. Indian Agent Edwin Eells. In the 1880 census, Reverend Myron Eells recorded the low tide mark: 485 men, women, and children. Of those, 290 were full-blooded.

Still, despite their perilous decline, the S'Klallam fared slightly better than neighboring tribes. For example, the same 1880 government census puts the Makah of Neah Bay, historic whalers who sold oil to the whites, at a mere 150. They were devastated by smallpox in a single year.

The What Cheer

Two days before Christmas in 1859, the *What Cheer*, commanded by Captain Thompson, departed from San Francisco for Portland. However, the ship never anchored there. Just outside the harbor, smallpox infected the crew.

Steering clear of the sand bar at the mouth of the Columbia, the ship made for Puget Sound. Instead of setting fire to the poxy debris, the sailors cast off infested tools and wares. As the current oozed in, it distributed the diseased jetsam.

In Ozette, at the tip of the continent, bedding and other debris worked its way up the beach. Within weeks, the whaling settlement was transformed into a grave of 400 corpses. The death ship traveled down the Strait of Juan de Fuca to Dungeness. Soon, packs of diseased dogs looted in the woods and on the beaches. In Washington Harbor, an Indian picked up a coat on the beach. Within days he died. Other villages fell.

The War Department, reporting on an earlier epidemic, described how in 1859 wild dogs spread the germ of illness into the interior: " . . . the Natives, frightened, left their dead unburied. These were devoured by the coyotes, who shortly became afflicted with a terrible skin disease, in which the hair fell off, and the whole surface of the body became covered by scabs and putrid sores, which, irritated by the sun, wind and sand, were a dreadful annoyance to the miserable brutes . . ."

At last the What Cheer dropped anchor underneath the towering bluffs in-between the sea stacks near Rocky Spit. The remains of Captain Thompson were burned and then buried in a dry knoll just a few yards from the high tide mark. At some point, white settlers erected a cross there.

Today, this desolate piece of shore known as Thompson's Point, or Dead Man's Point, has become a place of pilgrimage for both Indians and whites. I predict: one hundred and fifty years from now future generations will search for the grassy trail that leads to the marker of the smallpox captain. Folks from every walk of life will go there, to decorate his grave with sea glass, unusual rocks and shells, and rusty congealed lumps of iron, acknowledging the shared burden of history.

Gravesite of Captain Thompson at Dead Man's Point.

6
Shake Up
(1881)

"Breathe," I said.

Less than a minute before, I had been startled into wakefulness by screaming victims with bleeding eyes and bursted skulls. I was five. For more than a year the recurring nightmare of a massacre—what and where? *And why me?* The lightless hours of whispering rain: a deadly lullaby.

But tonight something other than *the dream* had waked me. It wasn't a sound, but the silence. On trembling knee, I made my way down the hemp ladder.

The hearthside, dim and breezy. Inside the cradle, creaking on a beam, Charley's bright eyes called for help. Seya, resting on a cedar mat by the fire, stirred. Alarmed, she pulled herself up, reached into the cradle and lifted him up.

The baby rattled.

She tossed a blanket over him and prepared to set out. Not for the white doctor: she had little faith in his methods, and no cash to pay him—but for the Sunday morning service at the Indian Shaker Church in Jamestown. A new religion founded by a modern-day prophet from Squaxin Island.

A new magic.

Reluctantly, Annie agreed.

I inserted, "Me, too."

Seya replied, "Fine. As long as we go now."

From the alcove bed Carl groaned.

The bleak path unfurled. The floating tips of the evergreen bough beckoned. Through the mossy mist, my grandmother advanced. With my heart scampering, I hurried to keep up with her. "Let me." She handed me the bundle, a tight package except for the hanging fist that bounced. By the time we reached the first full twist in the path, through a sweeping dome of Douglas fir, I drooped.

Annie rescued me. I held onto the tips of Seya's dry fingertips. Annie followed, singing lightly to the infant pressed against her chest. Every so often I tilted my head back to watch the fir canopy exhale.

Like the curtain between dream and waking, the tangled rhododendrons and the mist parted. The Jamestown Church, also the schoolhouse, erected in 1878, gleamed in spilt sunshine like the froth on top of milk. With its pretty picket fence, mission-style portico, and steep cedar shingled roof, the Jamestown church was the first on the Olympic Peninsula to sound its bell.

kʷi?núŋət

dream

Just north of Sequim, Jamestown was not a "preserve for Natives," but instead an independent, privately owned township purchased for five hundred dollars by the S'Klallam residents who refused to be removed to the Skykomish Reservation, one hundred miles south, overcrowded with near and far neighbors who were not always friends. Under the leadership of Tuls-Met-Tum, known to whites as Lord Jim Balch, S'Klallam families pooled their resources to purchase the two-hundred-and-ten-acre parcel from the white farmer Richard Delanta.

Reverend Myron Eells, a missionary from the Skokomish Reservation, serving as a local minister for thirty-three years, named the new township after Balch. The total acreage of Jamestown was a hundred acres less than the three-hundred-and-sixty acres allotted by the Donation Land Claim Act, one third of the land awarded to a married white couple. Nevertheless, Jamestown afforded the Indian villagers a chance to determine their own destiny.

First light crowned Mount Baker. The air sang: horses stamping; women gossiping; unbridled children shrieking; the yap of a little dog; the bleat of an insistent lamb. To me, a little girl who mostly stayed at home, it felt like Election Day or the Fourth of July. I wanted to shout and to clap, to stamp my feet. Then, I thought of Charley.

Without a word, Seya took the hot bundle from Annie and headed for the door underneath a portico. For more than a minute Annie remained, staring at nothing.

Absentmindedly she hauled me from the churchyard, past the whitewashed cottages, to a twisted tree on the edge of the shore. The day turned clear. She kicked off her shoes and sat down on top of her full skirt. Annie leaned back onto the prickly grass and closed her eyes, the same shape as the brittle Madrone leaves. I leaned against the tree and curled off the bark to the polished ceramic of the unexposed wood.

"It's odd," she said. "The Indian Shakers took my baby. Right now they're bathing him in holy water, palpitating him with their dirty hands, disturbing him with their bells. Maybe they'll cure him. Maybe they'll kill him."

I sucked on my muddy thumbnail.

"Don't cry. Have some breakfast." From the pocket of her skirt she retrieved a charred lump of potato, one that turned my lips and the inside of my mouth black.

She did her best to smile. "Want to hear a story?"

7
Annie's Tale: The Silver Earrings
(c. 1875)

I grew up on the south side of the Dungeness sandbar on the crooked hook known as Graveyard Spit. In the longhouse, on my mat, I would watch the maze spiraling through the hole in the rafters, like the white thread on a spindle whorl.

My cousins were my sisters and brothers. We spent most of our time on the beach. We raced hermit crabs. We speared little fish on sticks and waved them in the air, like a whirligig. Like children everywhere, we competed in everything: running, leaping, wrestling, tying knots, and aiming rocks at the birds.

In those days about the only vessels on the Strait were Indian canoes. Never refer to a canoe as a boat—as if Europeans invented sea travel. If you do, you'll be tossed into the water. Most canoes, one or two persons could handle. Others, fifty or sixty feet long, could transport an entire family to the Cape Scott Light Station, Vancouver Island, or through the inside passage to Bella Coola and Alaska.

One day a military steamship anchored inside the crook of the spit. The Hudson's Bay official delivered the news: The U.S. Army had requisitioned the harbor for military and commercial vessels, small to mid-sized, to load and unload their wares.

In contrast to the others—whispering and wailing. My mother Eliza became a stone column. The truth is, an officer in the U.S. Army named Smyth, a too-friendly acquaintance, had warned her in advance. "Do you understand what I just did? To help you, I compromised military protocol and risked my job. You owe me."

The officer handed her a paper, though he must have been aware that neither one of us could read. "Meet me in my office. If you don't come, I'll find you." He kept bobbing his head up and down and stretching out his neck, like a heron ingurgitating a fish. "Don't forget to bring your daughter."

As if to make the point, the ship's cannon fired a warning. Then, the gun on the ship's deck boomed. The longhouse smoked and flamed.

I opened up my hand and showed her soiled sugar lump inside my palm. "The army man gave me this. And kissed me, here."

"What are we going to do?"

Eliza II thought. Well, it wasn't the first time she had fled a village in flames. At last, she said, "Let's go."

"Where?"

"Where they won't look."

With a bundle and a basket, we crossed to the mainland and followed the shore. When the sand ran out, we stopped. Without speaking, Eliza stacked up drift logs and washed-up planks. Three days later, it was finished. Essentially, it's the same house on stilts that Seya lives in today.

Eliza had no real plan. Yes, we had enough to eat, but the two of us were alone. After several days, I forgot my fear. I became restless, even bored. Each day, I awoke a bit earlier, to wander down the beach. Each day, Seya noticed but said nothing.

One day, just before noon, I was standing up to my knees in the water, peeling sea urchins off a rock, cracking them open with my teeth, and sucking them out of their shells. From in between the sea stacks, a cedar canoe with a sharp beak appeared. The paddle, with its pointed tip, moved in circles to keep the craft steady. The canoe lingered, whoever was in it watching me. Without turning my head, I turned back to the shore and headed toward our secret place. Like an otter, or a seal pup, the canoe followed.

Every day I would find a new place to dangle my feet. The paddler, though not bad-looking, was not good with words. One thing: he could handle a canoe. Each day he would aim the stern in between the rocky palisades in order to get closer to me. It became a game. On top of the flat paddle, he balanced a single strip of smoked halibut or dried elk, or one time, chocolate wrapped in paper and gold foil. Within easy arm's reach, like bait.

This Indian was a Makah carver from Neah Bay. In his timid, determined way, he tried to impress me. One day, about a week after that first day when he caught me pulling urchins off the sea stack, he told me he had an extra-special gift for me. An offering. "What?" He refused to say. He told me to meet him that night, next to the twisted pine on the tip of the point.

Because it was summer, I had to wait long hours for the last embers of the sun to fade. There were so many stars in the sky that at first the moon kept its head hidden, like a loon. When it rose, it beamed. In the water about five yards from the shore, rested a soiyutl, a larger seafaring canoe, decorated with the emblem of the sacred thunderbird.

From inside the bow this odd and compelling boy sprang up. He wore a cedar band across his forehead. His black hair, unbraided, flowed down.

He stood tall.

He danced.

And sang.

I know it sounds strange but in fact it was beautiful.

I got in and he turned the notched bow to the lighthouse.

The eve was still, peaceful. Astride a plank in the stern, I watched him paddle the craft. The truth is: I knew nothing about him, not even his name. I asked how he acquired his fine canoe. A craft like this one was worth a hundred dollars, or more.

He said simply, "I made it for you."

"It would take a skilled carver at least two months. With help. Two weeks ago, you'd never even seen me."

"Not true."

"Then, how is it I don't remember?"

"For centuries; in my dreams."

I admit it, I laughed.

°ƛə́wən'

earring

It sounds silly but the words did something to me. His words, though somewhat hard to take seriously, empowered me. As you know, standing up in a dugout canoe is not the smartest idea, especially if the sole paddler is maneuvering around a point with the tide rushing in at night. For the first time in my life, I felt vital and strong. Beautiful. For the first time I perceived the song of my spirit power in the freezing current underneath the water.

He took me to Graveyard Spit, the site of my home village. It was deserted now, except for a muskrat crown threading through the water and a screaming killdeer that whirled to draw us from its nest.

The night breeze unlaced my hair.

One dry hand reached for the buttons on my collar. He clenched my neck with his scarred left palm and gathered the loose locks into the empty cup on the top of my spine.

I thought to myself, *What's happening here?*

I said not a word. For no real reason, I trusted him.

Thumb to index finger, with a fishhook, he punctured my earlobe. He inserted a wire. Next, the left lobe. Afterwards, he dabbed at the blood with a rag.

Before this, I had no idea if I even liked him.

After what he did to me that night, I felt as if we were married.

For the rest of the night we sat on the beach, knee to knee, but otherwise not touching. The air hissed with the mixed-up noise of water lapping, birds screeching, harbor seals hacking.

At sunrise, he kissed me.

8

Revenge of The Silver Earrings
(c. 1875)

"Ten months later—you."

Annie fingered one lobe. "Your grandmother says the earrings are cursed. She told me to sell them to a collector, singe them in the fire, or bury them in a hole . . ."

She unhooked one, and then the other. On her knees she leaned into the tide, which jumped and thrashed. She opened up her hand. The eager fish thrashed, but before they could escape, she plucked them from the black current. Inside her palm, the silver earrings whirled.

"Millie, shut your eyes."

Like Isaac to Abraham, I laid my head down. She smoothed the damp in the hollow at the back of my neck with her cool sure fingers. All told, the pain was not much. After, I think I must have slept, because when I opened my eyes the tide had receded. Smiling, she braided my hair and set me on my feet. My small fist inside of hers, she led me away over the dry sand, through whole villages of sand fleas, where crabs poked fun at the mottled surface.

By now, it was midday, the white church so bright that it hurt. Underneath the triangular portico, the door, painted fire engine red, opened. The crowd spilled out: The men in black coats, followed by women in puffy dresses and smocks, and little children in their burly sweaters with over-sized wooden buttons, tumbling out onto the musty grass in the churchyard.

Throughout it all, the ceaseless tinkling of bells. There was my grandmother, the black crocheted shawl on top of her grey woolen jumper, with Charley in her arms. I ran up to greet them. She fingered the collar of my blouse, studded with sapphires drops. Her eyes winced at the swinging fish.

Charley leaned way, way down. His eyes, shiny and black. He reached out a dimpled fist. Was it the Indian Shaker ceremony that cured his fever? I didn't know or care, as long as he was well.

Annie's hand rested on my shoulder. Dazzled, she eyed Charley. She studied him like an artifact, or a vision without substance conjured by a magic lantern. Little by little she began to believe. Annie lifted him with both hands. While Charley squirmed, she kissed his forehead, nose, and chin.

He squirmed. His chubby fist reached out and grasped a flickering fish. He pulled on it, hard. "Charley!"

"Charley?"

I looked at Annie, who looked at my grandmother.

He would survive, but not without cost. The fever had made him deaf.

Seya pronounced, "It's the earrings." Bitterly, she went on. "I've said it before. They're tainted. What's more, they don't belong to you, and never did." She pointed. "Or her."

She shook her finger at Charley. "Get rid of the earrings. Sell them, or bury them. If not, pay the price. Let go of the past. Your children need you now."

At the same time Eliza accused her, she forgave her. Seya threw open her shawl. Annie laid down her forehead on her soft shoulder and wept. I lost myself in the thick folds of Annie's skirt.

As I bent my head down, the fish slithered out of Charley's snotty fingers. He wailed. I suppose it was better this way. If one of us had to suffer, it was right that we should suffer together.

Charley recovered from the fever. When he could only toddle, Seya carried him to Jamestown on Sundays. When he was old enough to decide for himself, he became a life-long member of the Indian Shaker Church. Though he could never hear their bells, he felt their healing vibrations.

9
Shaker Bells
(c. 1880)

John Slocum, stubborn and taciturn, was not widely known for his geniality. Yet, after his spiritual transformation, whenever he met a stranger, Indian or white, in church or out, he held out his hand. Later, he would require his disciples to do the same.

This is the story of how John Slocum of the Indian Shaker Church at age forty died—and came back to tell about it—establishing a new religion.

In the 1880s, in Oyster Bay, Slocum lived on an isolated homestead, earning most of his pay at a nearby logging operation. He was of medium height, with a jutting eave of black hair on top of his swooping forehead, deep bright eyes, and a speckled beard. He married a wife who gave him thirteen children, only two of whom survived. Despite the hard times, Slocum refused to move his family to either the Skokomish or Squaxin Island reservations. He didn't believe in a handout. He favored whiskey and betting. His profligate habits broke his health, which made it even harder for him to support his ailing family.

One day at work he fell ill. On a cedar plank he was carried to his farm in Skookum Chuck where he died at about four in the morning.

His mother placed coins on his eyes. She wrapped a bandage under his chin to keep his jaw from dropping, so his soul wouldn't spill out. That night and throughout the following day, family, friends, and neighbors sat around waiting for the coffin to arrive.

John Slocum sat up.

Astonished kin and neighbors gathered round. Slocum announced, "If the people would convert to a new form of Christianity, renounce sin, and build a new church, God would repay them with a new medicine."

Slocum recalled his disembodied spirit, glancing down at his dead body. Reluctantly, he had come back, Slocum said, to teach the people to love one another and to be good. He then shook hands with everyone and said, "We should always be glad to see each other because, who knows? This time might be the last."

Slocum ordered the people to build him a church. Inside: an altar, with wax tapers and hand bells. Slocum also taught the people how to pray.

As news of the miracle spread, people began to refer to Slocum as a prophet.

A year later, Slocum again fell ill. Again, he died. His wife Mary, terrified to lose him a second time, began to shake all over. Again, Slocum revived. Slocum realized that he had returned from death a second time, only after his wife Mary began trembling. He thought, this must be the medicine that God up in heaven had pledged to send the people.

Prayer within the Indian Shaker Church looked a lot like a traditional healing ceremony. Slocum, never a big talker, allowed others to lead the church he had created. His bleak outlook had not improved. In his second passage to the other side, he had seen things that made him even more depressed than when he lived. When he passed away the third time, it was for good.

Though John Slocum's mystic revelation had been witnessed by a mere handful, word traveled overland and up the Hood Canal to Dungeness. The Jamestown Shaker Church, the first church in the county with a bell tower, was built in 1878. Inside, the only decoration was a cross on the far wall and a candelabra hanging down from the ceiling. On the altar, a collection of bells.

Shaker Healing

The following details come from an eyewitness account of a Shaker healing ceremony in the Jamestown Church:

A youth of eight or so had become feverish ill, sick enough to die.

In the center of the room, the sick boy stood as still as a post. With hypnotic energy, the congregants circulated around him, stamping their feet and ringing bells next to his head. Every person sought a new and inspired way to make the boy "shake." They passed their hands over him, blew on him, stroked his body, and whirled him round and round. He never moved an eyelash.

Hours passed.

Still, the boy never moved.

When one devotee fell out, exhausted, another stepped in.

Finally, the youth's feet folded and his head hit the floor.

As he came to, he began to tremble and shake. The others watched, but did not intervene. Finally, he stilled. When it was over, he scampered to his feet. In the words of one participant, the boy was "free as a cricket," completely healed.

PART II
School Days

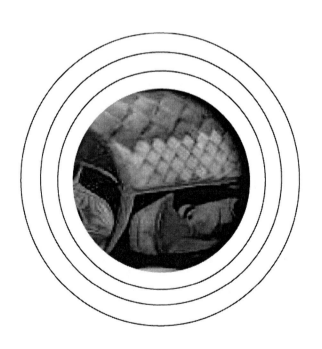

Female side of the 9 foot salmon carved by Master Carver of the Port Gamble S'Klallam Tribe Joe Ives. The Salmon People play an important role im S'Klallam culture and lore.

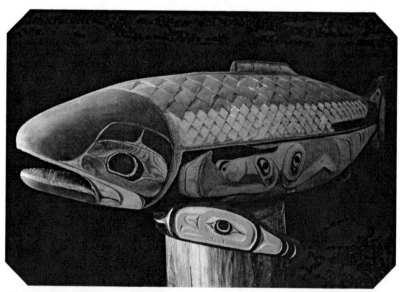

"Many years ago we (S'Klallam) used to turn our Tamanowas, or Spirit Guardians," says Joe. The flip side of the salmon reveals a young man in his Tamanowas form.

10
Spirit Canoe Paddle
(c. 1884)

Little girls and boys are naturalists. At seven, they become philosophers. By the time they are ten, they have derived half a dozen theories to account for the multitude of questions they generate daily. Those with exceptional courage spend the rest of their lives exploring ideas that, years before, their childish minds intuited. One summer's day, when I was seven, nothing happened.

Nothing changed my life.

I awoke at daybreak. By mid-morning I was leaping over the scattered sticks, combing the beach.

The oily rocks glinted in the beaming air. Salty suds polished my naked feet. The frothy advance overtook my father's skiff stranded upside-down on the rocks. For a moment the whole world appeared to hold its breath. Then, the sky whispered, "Hush-sh-sh." and the black current fell back. It was then that I perceived the rowboat sliding up the beach. One moment later I realized my mistake. The rowboat, hunkered down in the wet sand, had not moved an inch. The sand slide created an optical illusion. I realized: What we perceive looks different depending on where we stand. Nothing is true or untrue: Everything depends on one's point of view. Reality, implacably rooted in time one minute before, all at once became as slippery as eelgrass.

Every so often, my father's taciturn hired man, Jake Cook, would bring his half-brother George to play with me. Jake could do it all: fisherman, logger, handyman, guide, and carver. He worked for little or no pay. We relied on him to survive. This was a fact that no one ever mentioned. Jake lived alone in a trapper's cabin in the woods. His father and mother were Makah. His mother died when he was small. His father remarried a S'Klallam. His stepmother Jennie allowed George to tag along if he had no schoolwork or odd jobs to do.

George dressed in overalls, with no shirt, whether or not it rained. He had boots but not shoes. At the Jamestown school, inside the Shaker Church, he excelled in every subject. He adored science, old and new. When he was nine he notched a pine beam to use the run-off from the roof to irrigate his European vegetable garden with native herbs. At twelve, he was curious and clever as a Steller's jay, and just as irritating.

One morning, George appeared, toting on one shoulder a mysterious object; flat, and about a meter long. He held it up for me to see. The object was a hand-carved cedar plank crudely hewn. Powdery white. In the center, a bold and inky sketch of a dancing skeleton, his right hand lifted up. Encircling the figure, inky black dots spiraled upward. According to George, these black spots and dashes represented the shaman's spirit power. In the center of the wide end of the paddle, near the top: A big round eye, with lashes springing out in every direction. Just above the eye, which looked like a black-and-white sun, a carved feather, bent over.

Cautiously, I turned it over in my open hands. "What is it?"

"A paddle."

"I can see that. What is it, really?"

"A portal, for the energy of the dead. It's used in a ritual unknown to whites, that few S'Klallam have witnessed. It's a spirit board for the spirit canoe ceremony."

"Did you make it?"

"Don't be dumb. I whittle, but I'm no carver. Not like Jake. I found it, believe it or not, up in a tree. Inside a dugout river canoe, wedged in between the branches."

In the woods, on islands, and other remote places, the S'Kallam, and other local tribes, too, buried their dead in the trees. My grandmother—who believed that objects were magic, blessed or cursed—considered the relics of the dead untouchable, except by a shaman.

George explained, "The spirit board is used by a medicine man to heal people who are ill. It finds things, like unloosed souls. It can save you, even if you're dying."

"How does it work?"

He furrowed one eyebrow. "Certain materials—for example, metal and water, conduct electricity. Wood does too, but less efficiently. Maybe the spirit board is a conduit for energy fields in the environment. Who knows? I ought to design an experiment—"

"Give it back. I'll show you how to do it—"

But George refused and held firm.

The root ball of a nearby drift log tilted upward like a palace stair. George ascended. With both hands he raised the paddle. The sun, which glinted all around it, touched the blind eye. George began to sing. He chanted the same syllables, over and over again, until the line changed until it echoed.

In the sand I found a lump of charred wood, the debris of a beach fire. With the piece of coal, I added stripes and dots to my belly, arms, and legs. Still not satisfied, I climbed up the root tangle, brandishing my black crayon. "Decorate my face." I pointed to the shamanistic eye on the spirit canoe paddle. On my forehead George drew a big circle.

I danced, and laughed, and danced.

Suddenly the game seemed wrong.

George climbed down and crouched in the sand as he rewrapped the spirit board. He set it up against the log, and then waded into the water. After grabbing handfuls of sand, he scoured his chest, his arms and legs.

He yelled, "Millie! A sea cucumber vomited up its guts. Want to see it?"

"No! The water's too cold."

We scrambled up and down the driftwood logs in our usual way. Hungry, I bolted without a backward glance, heading for the bleached white cabin. Slathering in anticipation, I could taste the saliva—salty and sweet—inside my own mouth. Delicious.

Inside, next to the slab table in the manufactured chair, Carl smoked his pipe. He scowled. "What the devil? Look at her, Annie. Scrape the black off her. The little heathen needs a bath."

"What, now?" She shrugged, lifted up both hands, and opened up her fingers, laced with stringy guts. On the table, a flayed salmon, so large it almost covered the slab. At the moment Annie was prying out entrails with her fingernails. Leaning over the fish, peering up at me, she grinned.

My father squared his jaw. "Go ahead, laugh. I've said it before: I want her brought up proper."

She wiped her hands on the apron on top of her big belly. She crossed her arms on top of her painful breasts. "What does that mean?"

"Look at her. Sure, she can split firewood, peel off cedar shakes with a chisel and mall, and tend the kitchen garden. She's the only one who can command that goat, her namesake. However, she's entirely without education. She reads: books for boys, like *Treasure Island*, the logs of Captain Vancouver, or Swan's pocket notebooks. To what end? What's more, she's stubborn as hell. That reminds me. When was the last time you took her to church?"

Annie stared at him opaquely. Dead silence: a bad sign. Her anger could be triggered by *nothing* or *anything*, most often by me, though usually I had *no idea* why. When she was angry she stayed that way, until bitter rage became a trenchant sorrow. In these moods, Annie fled.

She disappeared for a day, or even a week. At times for a month or more.

Though I looked nothing like my mother, Seya said I acted like her: enthusiastic one minute, intractable the next. Carl, wringing his gnarled fists, almost always gave in. Her black moods frightened him. I think he was afraid she might leave him for good.

I inherited the strongest tendency in each. Like Annie, I would become petulant over the most trivial detail. Like all wayward children, I often refused to obey without really knowing why. At other times, I traveled far out of my way for to give in. Just like Carl. I ask you, which is worse: To turn from those you love, or sidestep your own needs to please others? Growing up, neither one is viable. Like a netted fish, I flailed.

Carl with his pipe stem pointed. Again, he said, "Look at her."

Nervously, I twisted my sunburnt elbows striped white and black.

Carl stood up and emptied his pipe on the kitchen table, mixing the spent tobacco with the fish guts. "If we cleaned her up some—sanded off the rough edges, and rubbed her with a polish rag—Millie could blend in."

"Huh," said Annie.

She didn't seem upset, or even surprised. As if, she had been expecting these words—for a hundred years or more.

"What about Charley?" She looked down at her protruding apron, smeared red. "This one?"

I suppose, at this point even Carl knew that he had wandered into hostile territory. For one thing, in a war of words, even in her adopted language, Annie would win. Words: arrowsheads or buckshot on the battlefield of culture. The high ground: determined by social standing and political power. Carl raised the bowl of his pipe, which matched her belly curve.

"Charley. Raise him up your way. That one, too. If not Christian, then decent. But this one's mine."

"Christian. Decent. I suppose they're not the same?"

"You laugh. Tell me. What happens to you and Millie when I'm dead?"

On that eve in summer when I was seven, in the kitchen end of our one-room plank house, my mother Annie Jacob Langlie bartered her daughter, a lanky girl with brown eyes, a square forehead, and bad timing, for her adorable son and her unborn child.

I suppose, families everywhere negotiate treaties. That afternoon Annie appeared to give in. However, like the signers of the 1854-1855 Treaties, she never renounced her claim.

Beneath the leaves—fire.

At night, underneath the quilt, she told me stories. Meanwhile, in the room below, ravaged by his own demons, my father muttered, grumbled, and sighed. To prevent Carl from hearing us, Annie spoke in a low voice, which deepened the darkness by shades. I loved and hated her weird tales, terrifying and true.

In the feathery darkness, Annie whispered, "I was only ten . . ."

11
Annie's Tale: The Winter Ceremony
(c. 1871)

I was only ten.

If I stayed up all night, I could never sample all the aromas inside the busy longhouse: roasted sea anemone, sweet cakes made of corn, barbecued oysters, salmon, pork, and mustard greens. But I could try. I planned to drum, dance, and play games until the sun came up, or I fell down.

From behind a pole I noticed: a group of half a dozen men, with cedar headbands and fringed armbands: the Black Tamanowas. Glaring at one and all, these fiendish fellows never mingled but instead stole in between the scattered parties and, now and then, disappeared into the dark trees. Rumor had it that any person who revealed even one word of the rituals of their cult would be murdered in the night.

A frantic boy, about my age, from behind a post regarded me like something nice to eat. He wore a cedar headband; his brow was slashed with red paint. Looped round his wrist, a braided leash, collaring a skinny dog, which nipped at the back of its own legs, and whimpered. The boy tugged at the leash.

Seya hissed, "Stick to me."

I lay down on my belly on top of a stack of stiffly creased blankets. In the red glow, in between the dancers, the shadows writhed.

I think I slept, because when I woke up someone was screaming.

It was the boy I had noticed before, blindfolded. Striped and dotted black and streaked with blood. Bound by a rope and wildly attempting to break free. The dog's leash, still tied to his wrist, was frayed black with gore. While his limbs flailed, his frantic eyes went this way and that, seeking a way to escape to the dark forest for all time. The spectators remained perfectly still. The wild boy bared his teeth and snapped his jaw at an old woman in red, who shielded the bundled infant in her lap. The other male dancers pulled back on the rope hard. A spirit doctor, in a thick shirt fringed with tiny wood paddles, shook a sheep horn rattle as he whispered in his ear. Little by little, the boy's gyrations became less frenzied. In the rhythm of his footfalls, a pattern emerged. The rhythm, complex and deliberate, grew stronger. Controlled. Little by little, his handlers slacked the rope. Little by little, they began to follow his lead.

He had subdued his spirit power and now it belonged to him. This unseen force would strengthen and protect him for the rest of his life. No longer a boy, but a man.

The beat of tough feet on hard earth went on and on. A plaintiff song stirred. I stood up and shuffled my feet. Hands, many hands, reached out for me and pulled me into the circle. I danced harder. Seya reached inside. I used my belly, arms, and legs to resist her but it was no use. She lifted me up and carried me outside. The red-hot glow inside the longhouse was extinguished by the cold emptiness. It was a clear night with stars.

You might think that I was grateful to Seya for rescuing me before the spirit took over my body. Wrong. In-tranced, I was afraid of nothing; I felt I could do anything. For example, I might have torn open the little wooly dog, scooped out his heart, and consumed the grinding organ.

"Let me go." I resisted her until we arrived at our place in the village longhouse and she threw me down on my cedar mat. Retrieving the crucifix from in between her panting breasts, she asked Jesus to save me.

From that moment on I rejected her, inside and out. Wrongly; I see that now. Back then I was not old enough to grasp how complex life really is.

To receive one's song, or spirit power, is to discover your place in the universe. One does not achieve this—or any lesson worth knowing—without pain. Seeking a *tamanowas*, or spirit power, is like agreeing to exist inside your own worst nightmare until you have vanquished it. To return to this world, you must subdue it. This takes skill, courage, and determination. Have you noticed that those who have learned how to handle their spirit power rarely succumb to anxious feelings or depression? That is because the mind, the body, and the spirit have been cleansed, and revitalized. The spirit power protects you, in your journey through this world and the next.

12
Siwash
(c. 1886)

When there was no real opportunity, I begged Carl to send me to school. After a while, I stopped asking. I had learned to love my freedom more.

In the early 1880s the only school within reach was the Jamestown School, which had opened its doors to about thirty or so Native children in April of 1874. A decade or so later, enough white settlers were "proving up" claims to justify about half a dozen new schoolhouses, establishments with names like Lost Mountain, Bear Meadow, and Happy Valley. Carl had somehow managed to save up the cash to pay the fee at the new Burrowes School, two miles through the dark woods over a footpath with mossy dims.

Up to that point I had been homeschooled. "Home fooled," as Carl put it. At four and five, he used whatever dime novels were on hand to teach me to read. Page turners like *The Pirate of the Gulf* and *Buck Taylor King of the Cowboys*. A week or two after my seventh birthday I received a package from Swan—although off collecting in the Queen Charlotte Islands he had managed not to forget me—a copy of *Little Women*.

Who knows how many times I read and re-read the cheap volume with the peeling cracked cardboard cover? True, I had never braided the mane of my show pony, sipped tea through a sugar cube, or fainted into my bodice. I had little idea how a person who looked like me, or anyone in my family, would fit into that fine and fusty world.

On a hot morning in late August, Carl took me by the hand. More curious than afraid, very soon I was pulling him along. After a little while, we came upon the fresh-hewn school kneeling in a knoll.

The Burrowes School, more like a barn, was named for the farmer-logger who donated the lumber. The name captured its dank darkness. My father bowed his head slightly under the vestibule.

Adjusting to the brown light, I faced the class shyly. A dozen or so classmates, of both genders, of all ages, giggled. My sweater, too big and too warm, made me doddle like a fat duck. They pointed at my slippers, which they called moccasins, a Canadian Cree term, one that I had never heard before.

The mistress of the school, Miss Susan Brown, peered at me through the spectacles straddling her needle nose. With a jerk of her salt and pepper bun, she declared, "Beads and other baubles are not proper for children at school."

Carl knuckled my shoulder. "I've paid the fee." He scratched his sparse beard. "Why not? Are you afraid that she'll turn out vain? Aren't little girls supposed to be cute? So why strip her of her confidence?"

Never before had it occurred to me that Carl was someone you might call a character. A speechless Miss Brown nodded and pointed at an empty desk in the center of the schoolhouse.

As I made my way down the center aisle, a big boy in oily overalls whispered, "Siwash."

In Chinook, the local trade jargon created for commerce with the Bostons, the word meant savage. Here, white kids with no shoes considered themselves one cut above Indian or mixed-race brats in leather slippers. In Jamestown, of course the reverse was true. There, if an Indian kid looked white, she had better charge up her knuckles.

I found my place next to a girl with plaited yellow hair. She wore a red blouse with buttons on the cuffs, a lambs-wool cardigan, a pleated skirt, and real leather shoes. I stared and stared. I couldn't stop; I was sure that I had seen her before. It hit me. Here before me, the girl from the Royal Baking Powder tin.

Sullenly she rejoined, "You smell."

Congenially I answered, "You smell."

I bathed a lot. I mean it. At daybreak we were dropped into the icy current of the Strait. When the sun was out we bathed in the evening too. My mother claimed her cruelty would protect us from illness. It did, mostly.

In contrast, most white settlers bathed once a week at most. To compensate, their wives used copious amounts of powders and scents. One of the most costly perfumes, from ambergris, is gleaned from the intestines of whales. Indians deplore bottled scents, and, in general, considered white people unhygienic; therefore we pinched up our noses whenever we noticed a lady approaching. How astonished was I to see a yellow-haired girl react to me in the same way.

Like all children we believed our teacher never left the schoolhouse. Without a doubt we knew she would go on teaching the same lesson day after day until the end of time, and never stop teaching until she breathed her last breathe. But at the end of my second year at the Burrowes School, the wholly unexpected: Holmgren's wife suddenly passed on. For the sake of his three daughters and one son, our Miss Brown married and left us.

Without delay a handful of parents hired a teacher for the fall term. She was twenty-five and highly qualified. Better still, she accepted the meager salary without qualms. After they sealed the deal, the eager committee discovered: her sister was Miss Laura Hall, the founder of a communitarian experiment in nearby Port Angeles. As such, Miss Delia Bright was marked as a dangerous radical. Well, wasn't it true that in their own classrooms the Puget Sound Cooperative Colony had banned the use of the Bible? Without it, what was left? Darwin, Marx, and Freud? The socialist Eugene Debs? Worse, the suffragette Abigail Scott Duniway?

Gasp! Upstanding citizens, sound the alarm: revolutionist in the schoolhouse.

S'Klallam School at Jamestown near Dungeness,
Washington, ca. 1905.

S'Klallam group portrait inside the Shaker Church, Jamestown, ca. 1903.

13
Brave New World
(1886-1900)

At the turn of the century, white settlers on the Pacific Northwest Coast embarked on a series of communitarian experiments. The first, the Puget Sound Cooperative Colony, inspired a radical trend. The utopian experiment in Port Angeles promised a culturally rich atmosphere, founded on equality, where workers would receive their due. Though white workers were treated with respect and women were allowed to fully participate, people of color—African Americans, Asians, and Natives—were kept out.

Peter Peyto Good, a Harvard graduate who had visited a worker's collective in Guise, France, introduced the concept. He arrived in Seattle to discuss the notion with a family relation Laura Hall. In the fall of 1886, at a series of events sponsored by the Knights of Labor, Good began to agitate against the Chinese miners and railway workers in order to whip up support for an all-white workers utopia. In November of that year he was arrested, charged with conspiracy against the federal government, and imprisoned for ten days. The following winter, perhaps as a result of the ill effects of his time in jail, he died suddenly.

But his grand scheme did not. Seattle city attorney George Venable Smith, enthralled by Good's maps and models of an ideal community for working men and their families, became the new spokesman for the cause. Laura Hall became editor of a newspaper created to articulate the goals of the worker-owned collective and to fend off attacks by those who considered the members dangerous radicals.

The Puget Sound Cooperative Colony (PSCC) selected a site in Port Angeles, a fertile river valley with a deep harbor protected by a curved sandbar called Ediz Hook. Decades before, Port Angeles' founder, entrepreneur Victor Smith, convinced the territorial government to remove the customs from the older and more established township of Port Townsend to this pre-platted city. In 1865 Smith drowned in a shipwreck, and the Custom's House returned to Port Townsend. Without him, Victor Smith's dream of a thriving farming, whaling, and logging town perished.

Three decades later, PSCC introduced five hundred new citizens from as far east as Ohio and Chicago to this remote outpost on the Strait of Juan de Fuca. Right off they built essential industries that would support their new lives on the edge of the wilderness: a sawmill, a brick factory, and a dairy. Later, the colony added a store and a hotel, a lecture hall and a library, and even an opera house.

Already, the first wave of white settlers had removed a nearby S'Klallam village from the teeming shore to the far side of Ennis Creek. When this second wave arrived, the Natives provided fish, game, and other supplies. The utopian theorists blithely accepted these supplies while trespassing on the property of the local S'Klallam, without extending to them what they claimed were the basic rights of all workers.

The original aim of the colony: to provide working men and their families with a secure future through the efficiency of their co-owned industries; however, profitable land speculation by PSCC, which began as a means to end, compete with the Cooperative's more lofty goals. Everyday practical problems caused the leadership to overturn their principles, which led to the charge of hypocrisy, and riled up the community. For example, though the colony was supposed to be controlled by the workers, originally all eleven board members were well-educated social theorists. Eventually, men of more practical accomplishment replaced the board. Despite these changes, however, the experiment broke apart. In November of 1900, the last assets were sold at auction.

Nevertheless, in the decade and a half that the utopia lasted, the Puget Sound Cooperative Colony had a lasting impact on the culture of the region. Early on, the community established equal rights for women, for example, on the PSCC board. Minerva E. Troy, the daughter of the colony physician, became one of the first women to make a run for the U.S. House of Representatives. Respect for women, independent thinking by laboring men, as well as commitment to the arts, continue to define Port Angeles today. Collaborative projects, for example the steamship Angeles and the West End Opera House, instilled a can-do attitude that is the legacy of the PSCC.

In 1889, as the newest state in the union peered ahead to the turn-of-the-century, PSCC became the model for other social experiments in Washington. For example, the Equality Colony in Skagit County aimed to provide a working model of shared wealth that would eventually convert the entire nation to socialism. Though most did not linger long, utopian experiments such as the Puget Sound Cooperative Colony encouraged newcomers to think big when they imagined the region's future. Another word for this: Hope.

14
Socialist in the Schoolhouse
c. 1887

When Delia Bright became our teacher at the Burrowes School, more than a few families bolted. I'd never met a Socialist, but it was common knowledge that their wiry hair concealed horns as their cloven footprints scorched the earth. I couldn't wait.

On that first day of the fall term I arrived early. The schoolhouse was empty, except for the wood cutout of a tall woman chalking tall letters on the fresh coat of bright green paint. Bustle wagging, she added a final dash of lightning to the quote that later on in class she ritually repeated, like a mantra.

"All life is an experiment."
—Ralph W. Emerson

She turned round.

Miss Bright might be called handsome, though her features—enormous eyes, wide mouth—were too large for anything finer. Straddling her broad nose, a pair of urgent eyeglasses. Both her aspect and her personality were robust. Her mingled curls, trimmed around her big head, fitted her like a helmet. She had an incisive way of lifting up one delicate, feathery eyebrow—her eyebrows were her only feminine feature. When she spoke, her cheeks flushed with color. When she got excited, she sweated. A lot.

Exactly two minutes before class commenced, Miss Bright rang a brass bell. For our first lesson, she ordered us into the cold gold of autumn, the Northwest's finest season. She led us into the forest and stopped at the hollow stump of a Doug-fir to assign us a new task, and bend us to her will: this day, to trap insects. Our pulse ticking inside our cupped palms, we would carry the specimens back to the classroom to study them.

Miss Brown had never allowed us to step outside during class except to use the outhouse or gather kindling. I guess she thought if she flung open the door and let the copper light and green rain pour in, we would all run away. If so, she would not have been wrong. Miss Bright knew how to stimulate our curiosity. She expected us to ask questions and learn, so we did.

skʷúkʷəlixʷ

to teach in a school

ʔaʔkʷúst

to teach how to

I wandered into a nearby glade and crouched down to examine a moldering swamp maple leaf, bigger than my head. I examined the bark of a winnowing alder, which newcomers from the East Coast sometimes mistake for a birch. Like a magician's spotted hanky, the bark lifted up—and then, poof! Exploded into monarch butterflies.

ʔaskʷúkʷəl

learn how to

kʷənúɫt

learn by watching

I clapped my hands, and then leaned in to observe the insect's compound eyes calculating my wherewithal. The satiny black body covered with white dots tickled my palm. Exhilarated, I stiffly walked back to the schoolhouse.

"Oh, oh!" exclaimed the perspiring Bright.

Miss Bright shared one or two facts as she wedged into my fist a hanky treated with ether. "The caterpillar stage of the monarch has eyes at both extremities," she remarked. She pointed out that for a predator the marking would resemble the eyes of an angry bird. This adaptation, as she called it, protected the butterfly in its migratory journey of over two thousand miles to Mexico.

I pinned my specimen to the plank and painstakingly penned a label:

Danaus plexippus

How many butterflies can one fit on the head of a pin? At first I felt happy and proud; by transforming the luminous creature with wooly feet into an artifact, I had joined the ranks of well-known Western naturalists like Lewis and Meares.

And Swan.

I drew back.

I had murdered an exquisite child of nature, but it was not only that. By stapling it to the two-dimensional plank, I had trapped its spirit, thus preventing it from crossing over. This is what men of pure science do: trapped in their two-dimensional view, they pin themselves to the wall until their wriggling souls expire. Acidic tears burnt my eyes.

This was not heaven. The dead butterfly had become as two-dimensional as paper. What had I done? I was a *murderer*. The dead butterfly raised its forelegs and began to sing lugubriously.

In Miss Bright's schoolhouse, we studied all subjects: science, mathematics, and literature. She drew us into the tales and journals of the Transcendentalist writers of New England. History became the art of storytelling. Many of us had grandparents or parents who had not been born in this country. As the cold rains began and the days darkened, Miss Bright asked, "How does your family celebrate Christmas?"

One eve, as I sat on a mat near the fire, fashioning a doll for Charley out of scraps, I put the question to my father, who was smoking a pipe in his rocking chair. He smoked, and reminisced, sharing memories of boyhood Christmases in far, far-away Norway. He described the celebration of St. Nicolas, which featured a Christmas tree with lights, marzipan, butter cake with strawberries and cream, and coins and candy hidden inside tiny shoes placed outside the door the night before. In lieu of a colorful festival of plenty, from my perspective, a dream.

Next to the fire, Seya, in the spindly chair, cradled Julia, two years old. She listened without speaking as my father recollected the fishing village of his youth. On this particular eve I didn't ask her to describe our S'Klallam traditions—for example, the traditional potlatch. Some part of me also knew that, even in the schoolhouse of Miss Bright, there could be no mention of feasting, the bone game, tug-o'-war, barefoot dancers, and epic speeches. Native rituals were likely to be seen as savage or pagan, even inside Miss Bright's radical classroom.

I asked Carl, "How old were you when you left home?"

"Eleven. 'Bout the same as you are now."

"What happened?"

"I set off after my father died. He drowned fishing. I was the oldest. I decided I could do better on my own."

What, leave home? "How?"

He coughed a little, and began.

15
Carl's Tale: Norway, Away!
c. 1836

I was not quite eleven. One eve, after school—me and the young gents—had a smoke. We philosophized and rhymed until day climbed into night.

In Norway, in wintertime, the daylight lasts less than a minute. I looked up at the sky. The night winked like quicksilver. For one instant I felt a flicker of my father in that North Sea of stars.

When I got home that night, my mother scolded me, unremittingly and without mercy. When my father died fishing, I never shed a tear. Now, just listening to her—the defeat in her voice—made me want to cry. Instead, I laughed.

The next day, when I woke up, my mother was sitting in the kitchen holding her cup and saucer. She asked me to sit down. All night, she stayed awake, thinking. With my father gone and children to care for, Mor had resolved I should quit school and go to work.

Though more than a little distressed, out of boy-mannish pride I turned away, as if I didn't care. Certainly, I did care. So, why didn't I tell her? If I had, everything might have been different.

"Fine," I coldly replied. "Just let me tell the schoolmaster."

"Fine, but it's your last day," she said.

I left our little cottage at the usual time. The sky, as dull as a nail, opened up. Each snowflake was the size of my eye. My mother, noticing that I had left my cap on the table inside, brought it out to me. I can see her still, in her cutout housedress leaning out over that pretty porch rail to hand me my father's old fisherman's cap, floppy as a pancake. When my mother handed me his cap, the dry snow was blowing all around her.

As I turned to go I noticed, underneath the lace curtain, the innocent eyes of my brothers and sisters eagerly beseeching. Would they get enough to eat? Keep each other warm? I pretended that it didn't matter. I imagined that they didn't belong to me as I strolled down to the quay, whistling.

My mother hoped that I would find as a job as a farm laborer, a butcher's boy, or a blacksmith's apprentice. Anything that would put milk and meat on the table. Her words meant nothing; all I knew was the bitterness in her voice.

Stepping off, I felt almost cheerful. A chunk of snow slid off one of the rooftops, cracked my head like a flowerpot. I didn't curse; instead, I laughed. Nothing bothered me. I was that eager to get away.

By noon that day I had signed onto a British merchant ship, departing for the Greenland Sea at high tide. The captain took me on as a cabin boy. I was not yet of age, so, when I signed the papers, he wrote in his own surname, Langlie. Like a father, he taught me the trade, and also how to make vodka from potatoes, but that's another story.

Pappa's name is lost.

A winter's tale is a sad tale. By and by I learned to rue that day. It's not the weepy eye of Mor that keeps me up at night, oh no. It's the moaning of the little children who, by and by, had not so much as a crumb to eat.

I had wanted to be free, so I fled.

16
S'Klallam Fishing Weir
c. Fall 1888

Annie observed, "It's getting colder. The fish are running early this year."

In the fall the rainy curtain rises on the drama of the leaping fish. Each year I looked forward to the long walk along the high bank of the Dungeness River, to a mountain lake, a winking eye in between the wispy peaks. There, we fished and picked berries and harvested camas.

However, three weeks into my second season at the Burrowes School, my father delivered the news: "Millie stays. So as not to fall behind."

What? My Jamestown "cousins" big and small absented themselves for a week or more and no one said a word. I gaped at Carl, but before I could speak he stopped me. "Don't say nothin'. I'm in a dark mood." His silver-plated molars bit down on the stem of his pipe with a sharp clack that made my jaw hurt. My mother, chafing her hands on her apron, remained silent.

Sun up on the following day, Carl went fishing. With Julia strapped to the cradleboard, for the first time Annie strolled with me to school. In between the boughs, at once several meters ahead, or behind, Charley danced. To my mother, I said nothing. As usual she had refused to stand up for me, and so I hated her.

When we reached the clearing, there was Miss Bright, shrub-like, in the vestibule of the Burrowes School. Right off, she spied Annie in a hand-stitched gingham blouse topped off by Carl's plaid work shirt, the hem of her long skirt trailing behind. On her feet elk slippers: durable, waterproof, and flexible for climbing. Miss Bright, giddy, must have forgot that Indians hate to shake hands (except, of course, the Shaker zealots). To evade her virile grip, my mother adjusted the strap on her cradleboard. Nodding, she set off, Charley skipping over her heels.

"Is that your mother? You don't resemble her. Where is she off to?"

I bit my lip. "They're headed up to the autumn camp near the lake. To harvest berries and smoke fish."

Miss Bright asked, "So, why are you here?"

Dumbfounded, I stared at her.

"Ahh," she said, "the spelling bee.' Evidently bored, she added, "No doubt, you'll win."

I won first prize: a pencil. Huzzah! My goal had been to impress Miss Bright, but since she didn't care, neither did I. Somehow or other I had let her down: a most familiar feeling.

Pondering, I recalled her words: Life is an experiment. I could still impress her. At noon, I stepped out of the schoolhouse into a solid downpour. I had a plan. I would track Annie, east on the Dungeness River, then up the steep trail to Marmot Pass. If I made time, I might stumble into camp before dark.

Thirty minutes to cross the Sequim prairie to surmount the first foot-bridge. My thin pink hair fell down as I leaned over the handrail to watch the water hobble over the rocks, which glittered in the afternoon sun like heaped-up treasure. All at once, a barnacled rainbow, with a hooded brow and hooked snout, leaped up. It had to weigh twenty-five or thirty pounds. It landed on a rock, spewing sperm and blood. Before I had time to appreciate the stunt, another fish—a meter in length— followed. This fish fell back as well, and disappeared into a black pool underneath the bearded bank.

I counted the swift shadowed fish, hemmed in on all sides, layer upon layer, until the numbers became a cascade. The Dungeness was no longer a river but a churning salmon byway. One tired fish, scraped a rock, unfurling in his path a bleeding ribbon of loose flesh. Others, less lucky, marinated belly up in the hot sun. In the shallows, between the flat rocks, pink pearls peppered with sand. At any moment these eggs would hatch. The emerging redds would feed on the salty flaking flesh of their spent parents. As the timeless murder of Kronus reveals, even the gods can't stop the inevitable: youth consumes old age.

The course of a river, inscribed on rolled maps that travel the world, armchair travelers regard as fixed. Navigators know the truth. A river is a narrative that evolves. A river, for as long as it survives seeks the most direct route to deep water. Even a historic river in a well-established channel may suddenly change course. When the first whites settled the flood plain, the Dungeness River leaped up, and broke free, abruptly jogging to the southeast. Some blamed the new farmers who engineered dikes and canals to feed their fields. Perhaps it was just nature's way. These days the river, once boiling with fish, tends to run either too fast or too slow. Though a flood to some, the salmon run is a trickle compared to what it was.

I threw a twig into the water, and then jumped to the north side to watch it reappear. Underneath the bridge, anchored to the supports, I saw a S'Klallam fishing weir. Inside, a dozen or so mazy fish. In the old days, a trap such as this one, made of sticks, would have waylaid enough fish to feed an entire village. Whenever my father Carl noticed an un-manned weir, he would lament, "It's the lazy man's way." He used a cork line, a lead line, and three different types of net—not to mention the muscles in his arm—to capture salmon.

My mother disagreed. "It's smart instead of stupid. Why go after the fish when the fish will come to you?"

I returned to the trail and went on, slapping at mosquitoes, once in a while angling to escape the stench of dead fish, an aroma which fortunately quelled my hunger and thirst. I carried on in this way for some time. But, after about three quarters of an hour, I realized my mistake. The river, refreshed by the summer melt that tumbled down the mountain, thrummed. Annie, I was certain, observing the thrashing water, had crossed over to the steeper trail on the south side.

I contemplated my dilemma: to return to that place and lose the better part of an hour, or to tempt the gnashing current? To get to the other side, I would have to leap from rock to rock. If I removed my stockings and my skirt, there was a chance I could make it. However, if I dropped my clothes in the river, or even if I didn't, a hypothermic chill might addle me, and cause me to lose my way.

What to do? Take on the mad river, or go back and lose time?

A reply from just behind me, a blowy distraught moan.

The breeze lifted up the tasty stench of wet dog.

I whipped around.

Black bears—hooded in their brown fur—are shy, reluctant to sound off. This one sounded out until its saturated lips vibrated. In response, a bellowing sob, like that of a human baby. On the opposite side of the fast river, a shiny black cub clawed at a slender pine. The mother studied me with dull eyes.

A pregnant bear-momma carries its offspring for about the same amount of time as a human. Once the cub is born she'll care for it for a full year and more. If the cub is male, in late summer or autumn of his second year he must strike out on his own. To the female cub the mother bear cedes a portion of her territory. The mama continues to track her, risking her own life to save the adolescent should the need arise.

Fate had sent the she-bear, to teach me how to deal with Annie. Nature's textbook; if only I had paid attention to the lesson. I didn't, so she and I suffered.

Back to the more pressing problem: confronted by a bear, what is the proper response? Advice abounds: Grab a big stick. Wave it, and shout. (No such weapon was available.) Take five steps back. Turn, and run. (With the river behind me, and a wall-of-bear in front of me, not an option.) Lie down and play dead. (Would you?) Never, ever look a bear in the eye. (Too late.) Her eyeballs had penetrated mine. I had entered the Brain of the Universal Bear. Until she was prepared to let go, the Universal Bear owned me.

Madam Blunderbuss fumed from side to side, slapping her feet on the soft sod. Her matted winter coat, decorated with a potpourri of seeds, twigs, and blossoms, made her to look even more enormous. With a stony expression, more evil for its emptiness, she stood on her hind legs. When she clacked her teeth, I could smell her fossilized breath. Her tongue looked like a bleeding wound.

The bear dipped her paw menacingly in my direction. Not quite so demure, I plunged into the rapid river. The current, which a few minutes before appeared an impregnable barrier, welcomed me like an eager dance partner.

I scrambled up the opposite bank. Nose to snout an under-sized river monster, the chary bear cub began to bawl. Head first I hit the brambles and wormed my way inside. Through the sticky boughs I observed the she-bear shake her hips and rise up. Her chuffing grumble—terrifying to me—little by little pacified the cub, who worked his way down the tree. After that a shuffling plash, followed by a piddling scramble. Something—or someone—had provoked the filial pair to move on.

Through the thorns I spied a pair of spiked boots. How was it that in every crisis Jake-the-Indian-tracker materialized? I crawled out of my hole on bruised bleeding elbows. I was only half right. It was Jake Cook's half-brother George. He seemed more miffed than concerned, not enough to unpack the hunting rifle strapped to one shoulder.

He looked down at me, studied me, and remarked, "Dzunuk'wa."

The mythic cannibal woman of the north. Forest dweller, without a mate. Loveless and unafraid. No doubt, I appeared otherworldly. The berry branches had coordinated a hostile campaign, replacing the freckles on my arms and legs with overripe berries. In a cloud of gnats, covered in all manner of natural debris, I deserved the label: wild woman of the woods.

I asked George, "Did you see that?
"What?"
"A momma-bear. Mad to save her cub."
"Not just one bear, but two?"

Dzunuk̓wa

mythic northern wild woman

Later on he confessed that it was the deeper rumble of a bull that caused him to leave the trail to investigate. If the male bear hears an infant cry, he will track it and destroy it, along with anything else in its path. George, sliding down the bank, arrived in time to see the mother bear and the glossy buttocks of the baby crashing through the brush. He lied, to tease me? To downplay his heroic intervention? I meant to feel grateful, but—

I rinsed my wounds in the cold copper current. Together we scrambled up the steep bank, gripping onto anything without thorns. Over his shoulder George carried a sack of twisted apples. Up on the trail he offered me one. He inquired, "Aren't you supposed to be in school?"

"So?"
"I used to think you were smart."
"You quit school to work at the lumber mill."
"I did it because I had to."
"They pay you three dollars a week."
"So what?"

I moved past him, to take the lead. His hand on my shoulder reined me in. "Jennie needed cash for her cubs. As soon as I can find a way out of here, I plan to go to trade school to become an engineer."

An Indian at college? Is that possible? I wondered.

"One day, I'll be in charge." He touched the flat of his bent thumb to his heart. "One day I'll be the boss. One day I'll be rich."

I stared at him. "You're crazy."

"Dzunak'wa."

He let me lead, up the trail, winding and steep. After a long while, we arrived at a felled log with a view of the Sequim valley, the Strait, and Vancouver Island. On a bandana George unfurled dinner, which included two more apples and a hunk of smoked trout.

I hoisted myself up onto a large stump. George re-tied his cleated boots. I recalled how at first I had assumed it was his brother Jake who had appeared out of nowhere to save me.

"Your half-brother Jake is quite a bit older than you—"

"Nearly twenty years older. Jake is from Jennie's first marriage. After Thomas Cook, she married my father. My father died when I was small. Maybe that's why I look up to Jake. He's more a half-brother. He's brother-father-uncle. I know I can rely on him."

"Where does he sleep?"

Tossing his apple core, George replied, "In a cabin in the woods. Maybe he built it. Maybe he found it. Who knows? Usually he stops in for dinner but he never stays. He prefers to live alone."

George helped me down off the stump. He pointed out the trail.

I remarked, "Your brother Jake is weird. What's the matter with him?"

George said nothing for a long time. I was pretty sure that my rude question had put him off. I was about to apologize when he asked, "Millie, how old are you? Almost twelve now?"

He went on. "When Jake was younger than you, he was there. The massacre at Dungeness. How he ended up there, I don't know. He doesn't talk about it. I suppose he wanted to be with his father. When Thomas, along with the others, was sentenced to hard labor on the Skokomish Reservation, Jake went with him. Two dozen men cleared more than a hundred acres by hand. Jennie believes it was the backbreaking labor and rough treatment that eventually did Thomas in. By the time the father and son returned, Jake was also ill. Thomas died. Jake recovered. At least, he seemed to. In another way, he didn't."

With a frond he wiped away the smear of mosquitos that hovered over us. "What Jake needs is—a girl. According to Jennie. Each time he drops in, she drops a hint. The last time, Jake left and stayed away for a month. Jennie says in the past he did something—bad." George paused. "Apparently, his waywardness makes him even more attractive. More than one women has gone fishin' for his lost soul. I have a different theory. I think he's already taken."

"Jake's always, always alone."

"Maybe he can't be seen with her because she's off limits. Jake won't give her up, even if it kills him. That's how he is. When he decides to stick, no man-made law, or force of nature, can move him."

Of course I wanted to know more. I was about to demand a name— or a list of names—when, in a branch above our heads, a Douglas squirrel with a flame of orange on his belly shrieked. He chased a smaller female squirrel round and round the braided trunk of a fir. The female squirrel eluded him. She leaped, dropped, and ran vertically down an adjacent tree. The irate male clicked out a command: Stop. In response, she whirled, not to heed but to mock him. She laughed. Then, suddenly, without warning, and for no real reason, she gave in. He leaped; she met him half way. The two squirrels mated violently.

I looked at George; ashamed, he looked down.

The last rays of the sun cut through the cedar forest.

"Let's go," he said.

As the trail climbed, the scrubby pines that curled up from the vertical slopes became more and more sparse until the twisted shrubs gave way to a meadow carpeted with alpine flowers: hanging bluebells, a whorl of magenta, the yellow slipper with wide-open lips.

I stood there on the edge of a waterfall that boomed. Icy drops leaped up. I became part and particle with the gushing green that raked its furry fingers across the spongy meadow. For an instant I had the urge to toss myself over the edge and become one with the flow of nature and time.

Down below, in the center of camp, my mother looked on as Jake unjacketed a coho with his carving knife. He leaned in to hear her laugh. She smiled broadly, and then absently lifted her gaze to inspect the horizon, searching. For something stolen, lost, something that was never really hers? Me?

I tumbled down the steep path. George, not far behind, hissed, "Be careful, slow down."

By the time we arrived at the camp, the sun was down, the night air, cold enough for snow, polished the breeze. The sky fell.

Annie tossed me a blanket. Rather than scold, she asked, "What took you so long?"

Jake Cook, without a word, handed me my dinner blackened on a stick. Near at hand, he seemed a less romantic figure. A stalwart, Carl's partner. By the time he handed me the clay mug—weak, with sugar—I had already ceased to notice him.

In the Land of the Salmon People
A Skokomish Tale

It has been said, "When the salmon disappear, the S'Klallam will disappear." Salmon hold a central place in their lives and their lore.

"Sammon"—as these fish are called in Chinook trade jargon—hatch in freshwater, mature in the current of the rivers, and journey to the saltwater where they grow large, at last returning to the site of their birth to spawn and die. The eggs, implanted in the shallows, are called redds. One fish may bury up to 8,000 of these waxy pearls. When the alevins escape their transparent sacs, and grow bigger than a pine needle floating, they are called fingerlings. One year later, after they have fully matured, the salmon fry begin their journey to the ocean. This adventure lasts three to five years, after which these fish return to the gravel of their birth to die.

How do these fish negotiate the currents and tides of an average distance of 1,000 miles, or sometimes three times that? Some claim the salmon use their sense of smell to find their way, or, perhaps, taste the water. Others insist that these fish navigate by the stars.

In the Land of the Salmon People

On the Dungeness River lived a youthful warrior, a seer, who had received his powers from the Winter Ceremony. He wore a cedar band, dyed red. He carried a stick with a leather string and a sharp bone. If someone teased him, he stropped that person with his weapon. That did it: he or she stopped laughing.

One time, an old Indian told him, "An old salmon never dies but instead returns to the place where he started."

Curious, the young man hiked up the Dungeness River, where the fish spawn. There, he discovered a worn-out salmon. The young man lifted up the fish and cradled it in his lap. He removed his cedar headband and tied it around the old salmon's tail. Sure enough, the next autumn, when the youth returned to the river, he noticed a leaping fish, its sides a reflection of the rainbow, with twined cedar round its tail. Suddenly, the young man knew the old story was true.

All the people came to see the fish.

The young man warned them, "If you see a fish with cedar bark wrapped around its tail, don't touch it. Let it be."

The following fall, the youth again went up river to see the fish spawn. This time, the old salmon, in the last throes of its life, spoke up.

The fish said, "Get ready. This time, we're going to take you with us." Instantly, the astonished youth found himself inside the river, thrown up and thrust down against the current. At last, he arrived in the Land of the Salmon. Here, he wandered. This wide-eyed warrior met all types: humpbacks, silvers, kings, and dog salmon with crooked eyes. He realized there exist as many types of fish as there are Indian nations.

há?nəŋ

thank you

sčánnəxʷ

salmon

The next autumn he returned to Dungeness. He looked okay, but something was not right. He felt dizzy; he couldn't stand up. On the bank of the Dungeness River he kneeled. The people gathered round him.

He announced, "I have been to the Land of the Salmon. The chief salmon told me to tell you this: When you catch a fish, don't toss it down. Cut it up on top of a cedar mat. After you eat the fish, throw the bones in the water. As you do this, say, 'Thank you, salmon.' If you do these things, the salmon will always come back."

My life is over, the young man realized.

His body was too weak to sustain him. He knew he was finished. He died, but the people still tell his story. As long as they remember, the fish will return.

Part 3
Zones In-Between

Fresnel lens used at the Dungeness Light Station
from 1857-1976.

17
Leaving Dungeness
c. 1889

And so I became a Transcendentalist.

And a truant.

Really, what's the difference?

Actually, I never decided to stop going to school. Each day I set off with the best of intentions. Somehow, along the way, I was waylaid by an impulse. On good days I followed the shore. When the shimmering rain turned from grey to green to white, I stayed dry exploring the forest. One day I hiked for most of the day, following the Gray Wolf River to Moose Lake, another to Sequim Bay where I mingled on the mudflats with starfish and migrating terns. I even considered an overland journey to the New Dungeness Light Station but then ruled it out. It would take two to three hours wobbling over the rocks at high tide to get there. Plus, without the cover of trees, the stately fir, shimmering alder and blushing swamp maples, my father in his fishing boat might see me, which would put an end to freedom.

In late October, on a trip to sell our goods in Port Townsend, Carl chanced upon an acquaintance, the bereaved Episcopal minister Paul Mathieson. His feeble daughter Edith needed a girl. The labor shortage was widespread; a servant that could do it all for the pay of a scullery maid was not easy to find. Though Mathieson had never even seen me, he offered me the job. Carl accepted on the spot. Later, he suffered doubts, but Carl could not go back on his word. White or Indian, in the wilderness or in the city, a deal is a deal. A man's word is his oath.

No one asked me.

I dropped my traveling case down into the cradle of Jake Cook's canoe, wedged in between the bloated baskets overfilled with potatoes, mollusks, and goat cheese for the market in Port Townsend. First, Carl would deliver supplies to the lighthouse, where we would stay overnight. The next day, Jake and George would paddle the canoe to the farmer's market in Port Townsend.

Like crows on a drift log, my family had gathered to see me off. Annie looked out at the white sky and remarked to no one in particular, "She never received her Indian name. Up north to the potlatch on Village Island, they still perform the Winter Ceremony. Millie should go there."

My father, rearranging the bundles inside the canoe, paused, and stood tall to glare at her. "Don't you get it? Are you stubborn, or stupid? That's why I'm sending her away." He tugged at his beard and added, "Damn it."

Seya asked, "Why wasn't she baptized?"

No one seemed pleased. Carl openly regretted his decision. Annie stared at me with sad tired eyes and looked away. Seya, like a bauble-eyed bottom feeder, a flounder or a halibut, stared at me sideways. Sensing disaster, Charley molded himself to me like a starfish on a piling. Seya and Annie embraced me. Even baby Julia reached out her spread fingers. Eight arms lifted me up on my toes, blistered from the shiny boots purchased with cash from the city. The traveling ensemble, altered from the cast-offs of a neighbor lady who hired Annie to do laundry, chaffed my skin and my heart.

Of course it was my fault. If Carl found it necessary to banish me, it was because I had let him down. Humiliated, I climbed into the canoe, and seated myself behind the thwart, and hunkered down in between the baskets. With false cheer I waved.

George, prying the mud with his tapered paddle, remarked, "Lucky you. For getting out of here."

That undid me.

As the salt pillar of women and children melted into the weepy fog, I began to cry, gently at first, until, all at once, the tears stormed. The minute I left this place, I would become a stranger, even to myself. What hurt most: it was Carl, the one who called me "the pearl of Ostrea Lurida," who had exiled me. Proud of me, or so he claimed; then why did he want me to change into someone else? If my own family rejected me, how would I succeed with the Reverend's ailing daughter?

As I sobbed, the gentle rhythmic sounds all around me—the slap of the paddle against the shushing water in the rising fog—gradually consoled me. By the time I had stopped crying long enough to look back, my grandmother and Annie had piled a heap of charred firewood on the smoking sand.

Steamboat Girl
S'Klallam Folklore

Day breaks on the Strait of Juan de Fuca.

At the edge of the shore, a girl, ten years old, stands erect, straight as a stick. She sheds her robe. Frothing up in between the seaweed grasses, the copper water feels almost tepid. Elated, she leaps and dips.

Reemerging, in between her feet she notices a stick. Her feet begin to stamp out a rhythm on the hard sand. The stick keeps time in the air.

Instantly, she freezes.

From out of the belly of Mount Baker, a steamer appears. The churning monster advances, belching black water.

The girl peers at it through her spread-out fingers.

The moment she looks at it, she collapses.

Dead.

This could be the end of this story.

But it's not the end.

This is the beginning.

Her spirit peels off and lifts up. For a time, her soul hovers, peering at the scene below: At the edge of the water, her naked body, curled up on the sand in a crescent moon. Beneath her, two stacks coughing steam. The side-wheel, grinding. The black stack on top of the ship sucks in the vapor from a bilious cloud. Six seconds later, the chimney vomits out her soul.

The steamship is a carrier of disease.

This only adds to her power.

Not long after, her spirit returns to her body. The lids open; her eyes collimate the light. After a minute, she is able stand up. One more, and she can dance. In her fist the black stick leaps up, like a piece of iron animated by lightning.

This girl has passed from one world into the next and survived. Now she can do anything. From then on, with the skill and strength of a warrior, Steamboat Girl protects her people.

For example, in winter a group of children, including a baby as portable as a stick of firewood, disappear. Kidnapped by a fierce tribe from the North. Soon to be slaves.

The girl blackens her face with fish oil. She tracks down the culprits, saluting them with a SCHWACK! from her bone club. KER-ACK! The sound of her weapon on top of their skulls invokes the thunder. Her older brothers, out fishing, note the surge of white lightning through the billow of clouds. By the time they return, the children are playing a game with shells and rocks on top of their cedar mats.

That night, in the dim of the longhouse lit by a central fire, the village celebrates the safe return of their children. The girl-warrior dances like never before.

Next to the smoldering fire, she thrusts her straight black stick into the earth. Instantly, in its place, grows a noble cedar, a center post for the longhouse.

Her kin, old and young, gather round.

The girl declares, "This is my power."

She adds, "This is my last dance."

She collapses. The girl stretches out her body on top of the hard-packed earth. Softly, she sings, hour upon hour.

Then, she sits up.

Steamboat girl announces, "Invaders are on the way. They mean to end it all. I have seen them. Stop them."

And dies.

Of course the people believe her. But what can they do? The girl is gone. Her power remains, yet no one is sure how to use it.

18
To the Lighthouse
c. 1889

Jake and George leaned, dipped, and pulled. The beak of the canoe, a wolf's head, bobbed. Yet for the best part of an hour the lighthouse remained an unchanged marker in the distance.

On the sandbar a sea lion barked. Seagulls and terns wheeled and screamed. Once, I leaned over the side and laid my hand on top of the water. A cloud of herring boiled up. If I had grasped quickly I would have held one in my fist. George noticed too.

Out of the mist stood the black-and-white tower of the Dungeness Light Station. The steely rain towered above us, a seemingly insuperable wall between our shallow vessel and safety. As we struggled to capture the beach, a wave ripped up the shoreline and swamped our canoe.

Jake shouted, "Jump!"

We salvaged the·cargo, tossing out baskets and rolled cattail mats, dragging them up onto the sand. Jake and George emptied out the canoe and shoved it up onto the beach. Meanwhile, the rain soughed.

We made our way up to the lighthouse. Hunkering down, shouldering the wind, we opened the little gate and stumbled through the kitchen garden. On the bright green door I dropped the brass knocker, a bearded Celt with a thick brow and pursed lips, homage to the North Wind. As I waited, buried in my father's sweater, out of the corner of my eye I glimpsed a bent form with a dark headscarf hunching behind one corner of a little shed.

Just then, the lighthouse keep William Blake opened the green door beneath the striped tower. "Hullo! Have you heard? The Indian Wars are over. Geronimo is captured!"

News from the East Coast of the Unites States, and Europe, and even as far away as China, traveling by schooner or merchant ship, reached William Blake first. An eager storyteller, not one to save the best for last, Blake announced this tidbit while we shed water in the vestibule. My breathless father nodded.

Blake directed us inside past the winding stone stair up to the tower, through a pantry, and into a hot, steamy kitchen that smelled like

cinnamon, yeast, and fresh coffee. After we had draped our wet togs on
the back of the kitchen chairs, he showed us down a tiny corridor to two
small bedrooms, one for Carl, the other for me. He commanded us to
strip off our wet things and return to the kitchen for a hot supper.

The lighthouse kitchen, with bright tile from Mexico and pretty rag
rugs, was spacious enough for a thriving household. Blake lived there
alone; not due to the melancholy temperament oft attributed to those
who tend the light on isolated shoals. His father Henry Blake held the
post for decades. After the eve of the massacre in 1868, Blake's mother,
a spritely woman of Mexican descent, preferred to live on the mainland.
Since then a generation had passed, and still Blake could find no bride
who was willing to pass the long bleak winter on the tip of the spit where
the cruel wind still remembered. While the sociable Blake, confined to
his post, courted solitude, his imagination wandered.

While Carl and I change out of our sea-sponge woolies, Jake and
George moved the rest of the cargo inside the shed. Steaming by the
stove, they stirred sugar lumps into the hot coffee that Blake poured.
Blue plates on top of a black tablecloth, served black beans, cornbread,
clams, and a smoked breastbone of goose.

My father asked Blake, "The petition for statehood?"

"Haven't you heard? President Harrison agrees. There's a new star on
the flag. Count them: forty-two. In Port Townsend I've been told the
people are drowning in drink and women. It's well known, in the Key
City, the men never set down their mugs, except to call for more. And
oh, the notorious massacre here at Dungeness: that harrowing tale now
has an epilogue."

I knew from George that Jake Cook, as a youth, had witnessed
the murders at Dungeness. Though I begged them to describe it, no
one would tell me, not even in whispers. Carl considered the topic
unfit for mixed company (i.e. naïve girls and grown-up Indians). But
the unabashed lighthouse keeper, desperate to tell, refused to take
the hint.

Blake remarked, "About two weeks ago. I got up at the usual time.
On the beach, just over the picket fence, I saw a dugout canoe. Stretched
out inside, a fellow of about twenty, in a plaid shirt, with a red bandana.
Curled up on top of his chest was a little wooly dog."

Eagerly, I nodded.

Encouraged, the lighthouse keeper went on. "I asked the young man,
'Who the heck are you?' He rubbed his eyes, but said not a word. I

shook my fist. His dog leaped up. It yapped. I tried once more. 'What you hanging 'round here for? What? Did you lose something?'

"The fellow replied, 'My past. My mother was here. According to my father, after that she was never the same. Anyhow, I need to get it back.'"

Blake paused dramatically. "Suddenly, a light went on inside my head. I asked him, 'You ain't Tsimshian?'"

Like sand, silence filled the tiny kitchen.

I piped up, "Go on."

Blake peered at me keenly. "How much do you about the murders that happened here?"

"About a kilo more than she needs to know," my father inserted.

I begged, "Mr. Blake, tell me. You must."

My father's brow flared.

Oblivious, Blake exclaimed, "I will, I will."

However, his account was once again rudely interrupted by the rasp of a wood leg on a ceramic tile. Jake's chair. Apparently our paddler and guide had no desire to hear the bloody tale. Rather, he'd take advantage of the break in the weather to move in the kitchen supplies from the shed. He motioned for George to follow.

But one set of avid ears was enough to fire up the keeper of the light. In the glow of the lamp, his swarthy face looked luridly handsome.

Blake embarked upon his tale—

19
Blake's Tale: A Cry in the Night
c. 1868

In September of 1868 a band of Tsimshians headed north after harvesting. With their pay, eighteen northern Indians landed on the spit. That night, my mother Maria, sat in front of the bedroom window uncoiling her black hair, peering at a dying ember of a Native campfire on the south side of the spit. For a moment she thought she heard a murmur and a wail. Then, nothing. "Do you see anything?"

Henry collapsed his spyglass.

"Nothing," he said, "nada."

They turned in.

"A few hours later, a rapping at the front door.

Henry roused himself to open it.

The girl standing at the mat, shedding blood like rainwater, had been stabbed at least a dozen times. He gasped; she fell into his arms. She was pregnant, and ill; her teeth were chattering. He tried to hold her up. She thrust out a bloodless fist, which wretched open to reveal—a gold coin. To purchase her life. Of course, my father and mother refused.

My mother removed her dressing gown and tore it into strips to staunch the girl's wounds. At the same time she called out to my father, "Lock the children in their rooms. Quick!"

It was too late.

My brother Richard, four years old, standing in the cold hallway in his bare feet, detailed in his waking mind and dreams every detail of the scene.

My father lifted him up and carried him into his room. He kissed him on the brow, and turned the key in the door. Today, twenty years later, Richard is still plagued by the image of that girl bleeding on the tiles. That night, in his small bed, he did what he could. He prayed—

20
Scritch-Scratch
c. 1889

While Blake blasted us with his tale, the heave of the little kitchen door rattled the china. A large sack entered, followed by a crate. Next, a pot-bellied basket, topped off with a waxy cheese wheel, bumped over the threshold.

George entered with my satchel. "Where do I set it?" He nodded with his chin in the direction of the little hallway that led to Richard's chamber. Obviously he had something to say to me. Not wanting to miss a word, unwillingy I followed.

Through the pantry behind the central staircase that spiraled up the tower, a small unlit passageway. At the end of the hall, the tiny bedroom—Richard's room. I half-expected to see him: a pale shivering boy, bloodless fingertips gripping a wooly blanket up for dear life. Rather, a feather mattress topped by a merry quilt. I sat down. From underneath stretched a lithe cat. Striped black and white like the lighthouse tower, Blake's cat Maldita. When I reached out for it, it slipped beneath the bedstead, but not before leaving me with a scratch on the back of my hand.

George threw himself down beside me on the bed. Here was his grievance: earlier, Blake had announced, "Indians sleep in the shed." I was there, too, but it didn't bother me. Honestly, I was surprised at George. Though wrong, the arrangement was standard. White settlers extended hospitality to other whites but treated Natives like servants, or worse. It wasn't merely the injustice of it, George said. The shed featured large gaps between the planks. On a night such as this, it barely slowed down the wind. He added, "I noticed a scratching sound. In the rafters or walls, tunneling beneath it?"

"A family of raccoons?" After a moment, "Anyhow, you can't sleep in my bed."

George grinned broadly. "I'm going to build myself a shelter out of driftwood. Warm and dry. And safe, Millie. Tonight, meet me on the south side of the spit. Look for my campfire. I need to talk to you. This could be our last chance."

.

"To do what?"

"You'll find out," he stammered. "Later on, tonight."

We went back into the kitchen. Right away George pitched in, arranging jars large and small on the shelf. All of a sudden, I recalled the odd figure I had noticed slipping around the back of the shed. I asked Blake, "How is your mother?"

"In the glory of her declining years. As you know, she lives in town with my brother Richard. Why do you ask?"

"Does anyone else live on the spit?"

"Nadie, nobody. Why?"

Jake looked at me. My father openly stared. George tried not to look at me.

I slurped scalding coffee. What was it that I had seen? A raccoon? An optical illusion in the driving rain? Too vexed to pursue the matter, I asked, "Mr. Blake, what ever happened to that Indian girl, sole survivor of the massacre?"

"Not so. That girl was pregnant, which is perhaps what made her so determined to live. As soon as she was well enough, my father saddled his mule and brought her back to the mainland. Later, the territorial government put her on a steamer and sent her home with trade goods worth twice the value of what had been lost."

tá?k'ʷə́ŋ

smoke from a fire

"What about the others?" I knew how the tragic tale ended. Frightened, I was desperate for Blake to drop the final curtain.

"Eighteen Indians—men, women and children—ambushed inside their tents by the S'Klallam. Those who fled were crushed into the sand."

Blake handed Jake a plate of heaped-up pastry. Sticky juice leaked over the edge. The blackberries, fatly purple, pulpy, and glistening.

Jake set it aside. "No thanks," he said.

Carl, in spite of himself, had been drawn in. "That Indian, in the plaid shirt, with the little white dog, what happened to him?"

"Yes, yes. I almost forgot."

Blake loaded up his own dish with steamy juicy pie. "Just as he was about to shove off, that Indian said to me, 'A long time ago, my mother came here. Something bad happened to her. The white family who lived inside the lighthouse station helped her.'

"I asked, 'You ain't Tsimshian, are you?'

"He nodded.

"Eureka! I shouted, 'Go directly to the house of my brother Richard. Believe me, it would change his life. Believe me, he would be a new man.' I guess he had other plans. After he shoved off, he headed due north to Esquimalt.

"Did he find what he was looking for? Who knows? At least, now we have the epilogue. The unborn son of that sixteen-year-old Tsimshian girl survived to become a man. On the night of the massacre, my mother Maria saved not one life but two."

But why then eighteen bodies on the sand?

Between Life and Death
S'Klallam Folklore

For the S'Klallam, and other Northwest tribes, the boundary between life and death is not final, but a permeable border that can be crossed and re-crossed. To put it another way, in this philosophy, death is not the final departure from the railroad terminal, but instead a door that swings both ways.

This is why, according to a popular legend, the Suquamish leader Chief Sealth, was not insulted but relieved when whites misappropriated his name for the gold-rush city of Seattle. After losing their loved one, friends and relatives refrained from saying his name, since the pronouncement could induce his spirit to return. Sealth preferred to remain at peace in the Land of the Dead.

This is also why Christ's mythic transformation from life to death and back again is not all that surprising. It may be the reason that so many Pacific Coast Natives are ready to convert. Like Jesus, a mystic, or shaman, increases his strength by traversing the boundary between the living and the dead. When the shaman's spirit power is enhanced, the village grows stronger. I have heard it said that one can visit one's dead relatives—by traveling up the Dungeness River.

A S'Klallam Funeral

The girl, not more than six, contracted smallpox, rapidly declined, and died. Her coffin was a canoe, which her father and her uncle carried to the beach. Her cousin placed the dead girl's body inside the vessel. Her mother covered her up with a coverlet of calico. Her father and his brothers set the canoe on legs made of crooked sticks.

They worked together to construct a makeshift hut around her.

Next to her burial hut, the women built a fire and tossed into the flames all of the things the little girl loved best: a doll, two or three oranges, a ball woven out of grass that made music as it rolled across the floor. Each object as it burned made its own kind of smoke: a column of white, a gray or black cloud, an amber fountain.

The father leaned into the flames and captured the smoke inside his clasped hands. The wet grey smoke writhed against his palms. He cracked open the palms and breathed in deeply. After that he poured sugar on the fire, which created a pillar of thick smoke.

The mother of the little girl, agitated one moment before, suddenly became tranquil. "We can go now," she said.

For that family, the little girl was not dead. They often visited her at the burial hut, to tell her a joke, or a story, or to deliver some little thing they had saved for her: an orange, a button, or an unusual rock or shell.

Life comes from death. As the rotting stump of the cedar provides a nursery for the spring sapling, and as the crumbing body of the adult salmon is the first food for the fingerling. Death is not final; death is not even death.

21
Beneath the Shed
c. 1889

I dashed from the sheltered entryway above the tiny green door of the lighthouse, through the garden, and out the front gate. The polished soles of my new boots surfed the slimy grass. The next instant I found myself sitting in a puddle just outside the shed. Muddy, chagrined, I managed to find my feet. Pressed up against the woodshed, I pondered my next move. At least for the moment, I was protected from the wind and rain by the miserable little outbuilding.

Panting, I hovered there.

In the gaps between the planks of wood, a homey scene materialized. Jake's kerosene lamp browned the interior like a sepia photograph. On top of a pile of discarded sacks he sat cross-legged, stripped down to his long lean waist. It was freezing but he showed no sign of it. Intently, he stared at a small piece of cedar inside the palm of his hand. He bent his wrist, twisting the blade of his carving knife. He seemed relaxed, at peace.

No doubt George had overreacted. If he wanted to pretend he was an original pioneer and build a house out of scrap in the wintry rain, that was his choice. I preferred to get out of the weather and into my goose-down bed. I was just about to give it all up and make a dash back to the lighthouse when a scritch-scratching vibration in the plank pressed up against my palm stopped me.

A bandit raccoon?

Could it be the old woman with the headscarf, the one I had seen slip away behind the shed?

Nearer to the water, I noticed the cheering flames of a fire in front of a squat heap of driftwood. With my head down, I ran at it pell-mell. When I reckoned I was near enough, I hurled myself at it.

"D'Zunakwa," said George. He was sitting inside under a two-toned blanket, his knees up. He stretched out his arms. "You're shivering." He lifted up the blanket. "Quick, get in."

I tumbled in.

"D'Zunakwa," he whispered again fondly. He dabbed at my wet face with the tail ends of his shirt. Inside, his shelter with its front porch roof to shelter and ventilate his fire, didn't look so chaotic.

I was freezing, and drenched. I removed his broad arm and placed it behind my shoulder so that I could feel his rib cage move against me. I pressed up against him until the heat from his body seeped in. When was the last time I had cuddled with George? As a little girl, I sat on his lap.

Looking back, I can see that I was flirting.

A little.

George seemed to warm to my act.

Putting his head outside the shelter and pointing, he said in his knowledgeable-older-boy voice, "Do you see those poles standing up in the sand in a V? Those are traps. In winter at night you paddle your canoe into a flock of ducks. The ducks startle up and get tangled in the nets. For some reason the trick works only on ducks. The geese know better."

"That's mean," I said.

"Are you a duck?" he teased.

"Be serious," I said. "Annie mentioned something just as I was leaving. How do kids get an Indian name?"

"It usually happens at the winter ceremony. Boys, and sometimes girls too, receive their spirit power."

"Then, why not me?"

George shook his head. "The territorial government banned it. On the beach in Vancouver and Port Townsend Indians perform the ceremony for tourists, but that's not real. They do it for money. To me, that's embarrassing."

"Oh," I said, disappointed.

George, looking thoughtful, stared into the fire. "Well, there is another way."

I waited.

"You allow it to find you."

"How?" No answer. I tried again. "Tell me about your spirit power."

"You're not supposed to ask." He hesitated. "It's personal. Not something folks talk about. It's definitely not something I like to talk about. A few years ago, I was tested." He looked down at his bent knees. "I failed."

"What happened?"

George took my hand, and told me the story of his spirit quest.

22
George's Tale: A Rotten Fish
c. 1889

I had reached the age when a boy discovers his spirit power and becomes a man. That same year, the white government prohibited the winter ceremony.

Uncle Lyle felt bad about it. Around the time of the summer solstice, he took me to a remote beach; I won't say where.

Together we built a tall and narrow shack made of cedar planks. Then, Lyle disappeared. For three days I prayed. Each day at sunrise, I would walk into the water. And then meditate inside that sweat lodge. I listened to the wind and the murmur of the tide, waiting for my spirit power to find me.

At first, it was boring. What's more, I wasn't completely sure I even wanted to be there. I had nothing to eat but mussels and a few handfuls of berries.

I spent a lot of time pacing over the dry drift logs. At the edge of the water lay a fallen tree, wrapped in eelgrass, hollowed out by the tide. Mid-morning of that third day, out of curiosity, I bent my head down to look inside. Inside the black heart of that tree, something slimy moved. I reached way in with my fist, withdrew it, and opened my palm. Something moved. It wriggled, wetly. I dropped it.

A moldering half-decayed herring.

The herring spoke to me. "Do you want to become a man? Hold me in your hands. Lift me up, speak to me. Tell me the one thing you want most. Whatever you want most is within your power to achieve."

I felt something . . . rising up out of the earth, swimming into the core of my being.

It frightened me.

A lot.

I dropped the moldering cold lump. And ran.

I reached the line of trees and kept on. The drooping curved boughs of the Douglas firs scooped up the sunlight and thrust it underground. What happened next, I can't say. I blacked out. In my eagerness to escape whatever it was, I must have torn through at least one spider web;

when I woke up my entire face—lids, nostrils, and mouth—was covered in a ghastly residue.

That evening, my uncle returned, with his big grin and an even bigger steelhead trout. We stacked up the firewood and grilled that fish.

At first, I was too hungry to do anything but eat. After I had slaked my hunger and thirst, I told Lyle what happened.

Lyle, slowly, chewed the pink-and-white square of fish on the sharpened charred stick. Slowly, he replied, "It's too bad you rejected that spirit power. A herring, now that's protection. Not just for you, but for the whole village. Anyhow, don't feel bad. You weren't ready. I misjudged. It's my fault. On the other hand, the spider web: that's positive. It means that you will achieve every ambition."

Mouse Woman, a shape-changer who moves between the spirit and human sorld. She often appears as as wise old woman to guide youth when they need her advice the most. Transformation mask by Craig Jacobrown, demonstrated here with a Haida button blanket worn by S'Klallam Dancer Chenoa Egawa.

23
Be Careful What You Wish For
c. 1889

"I never told anyone. Not my mother, Jennie, or even Jake."

George concluded, "Two years later Uncle Lyle was crushed by a float of Doug fir. That means: you're the only living soul except for me who knows. And, maybe, one ugly fish."

He was still holding my hand.

"Anyhow, I'm glad I told you. It's something you should know about me."

My fingers, minutes before stiff with cold, were now beginning to sweat. "Lyle said you would achieve your dreams. What is it you want most?"

He gave me a long look. "That's easy."

You, Millie, you. That's what I hoped he would say.

George answered, simply, "Money."

Earnestly, he went on. "Well, that's not it, not exactly. What I want is power. To get it, I need to make others (I mean: whites) respect me. I want to be the one in charge. The boss. I want to be revered for my acumen and skill. I don't know how I'll get there. It may take more than passing through a spider's web."

He stared at me intently. "What about you, Millie? What do you want?"

"For something like that to happen to me. Really, really, really weird." Childish, I know. But, if I had a spirit power to protect me, my father might allow me to chart my own course. Annie might learn to love me. "Afternoon tea with a talking fish."

George winced. "Just recalling it makes me sick." The hot tip of his finger moved a lock and jangled one earring. "When they catch the light, they writhe. They look wet. When I notice them I feel nauseous. I hate them—"

He shuddered.

His aversion to the earrings bothered me. I took it personally. The earrings were a souvenir from Annie; the only relic I had left.

I felt betrayed.

Which is better: friendship or romantic love? I was enjoying the intensity of his attentions, but was it for me, or the girl he wanted me to be that attracted him?

"I have to go," I muttered.

He sighed and studied my eyes searchingly.

Deeper and deeper.

I stayed.

Shuddering, for reasons too complex to analyze, I asked, "Is it true? That eighteen dead people are buried here?"

"That's what folk say, but I don't believe it. The culprits were forced to return the stolen items, down to the last cake of soap. Yet, the authorities recovered only one canoe. What if the killers stacked up the bodies inside the canoes, and then drilled a hole or two in each hull? The murdered Tsimshian: fish food."

A seal coughed. A hard rain beat time to a whimpering wind, which brought to mind familiar dream visions of murdered children with their arms and legs splayed. I shivered and moved closer to George.

What happened next, I suppose, was my fault. I put both of my hands around his neck. He leaned down, I reached up.

He leaned down.

The heat from his mouth felt—like?

Honey-butter on burnt toast.

He looked smug, satisfied.

I was not.

How do I put it? A queasy hunger began to claw at the inside of my belly. I felt hungry—no, starving. At the same time, sick. As if I had eaten the whole loaf and wanted more. I wondered, is this love?

George leaned back on his bent elbows. "Now, Millie, pay attention. By this time tomorrow, you'll be a servant in a big house. When you're polishing their silver, or emptying the nightjar, remember, you're in it for *you*. Don't work too hard. Do just enough to keep the job. Also, I want you to wait."

"For what?"

"Me. What else?" He took my hand. "You don't need to know the details. I've got it all worked out. Don't worry, I'll find you. Okay?"

"Uh. Sure. All right."

How long? A week? A month? More? George was seventeen, I was twelve. Surely, he didn't expect me to keep my word for more than—a season, or two?

"Yes," I said, "I promise."

I tipped up my chin, hoping that he would kiss me again.

He didn't.

Lifting the blanket off of my knees, he said, "It's time for you to go." He arranged it around my shoulders with care. "Shall I go with you?"

"Why?"

"To make sure you're okay."

Now that he liked me, was I suddenly less tough and more fragile?

"What, I'm not a baby," I whimpered as I crawled out of the shelter on my hands and knees.

Outside, I stood. An aural mist sheathed me. Though the rain and the wind had ceased, there was a death chill in the air. Rafts of wet driftwood covered the beach right up to the garden gate. For balance, I thrust out my arms.

An owl said, Ku ku kkkk ku.

A shadow—cold, swift, and terrible—passed over one shoulder. No, not a shadow, but something else with weight and heft and sharp claws.

I screamed.

Talons scratched at the blanket that I threw over my head to stave off the attack. I tumbled back onto the piled-up driftwood. The thing, whatever it was, stepped on top of my chest. It flapped its shawl. A claw reached down and lifted me up by the roots of my hair. Up and up, into the bleak night.

Was this the vision I had prayed for? The spirit I invited to enter me? If so, I rejected it now, with all of my heart and soul.

I had nothing. No one to protect me. No weapon to lash out and defeat the thing. Still screaming, I fell. Through the blanket I noticed a flash of fire, the stars popping—or was that the sound of hollow driftwood against my skull?

When I came to, one cheek was pressed up against the piece of driftwood. The cold wet wind gnashed at my scalp. When I touched my cheek, my fingertips came away bloody. The right side of my face was incised by two slender lines. I found my feet, and made for the garden gate, which was wide open.

Once more, I felt a certain vibration; then, a terrible sound: *scritch scritch scratch.* I turned around. There she was.

An old woman with a purple forehead. Round black eyes and white eyelashes. With or without hair, I couldn't say. Wrapped around her head, George's wool blanket with the single red stripe. One curled claw held it in place. With the rusty tip of her index finger she beckoned to me to come nearer.

Entranced, I complied.

Then, as if to say "stop!" she held up her right hand.

When she unfolded the fingers and flattened her palm, what did I see?

Through a hole in the middle of her right hand, a silver dollar of daylight.

Her spell, for now, was broken. I whirled and fled, passing through the gate to the sheltering eave of the mystic lighthouse that glowed candle-white. I seized the latch. My last chance to save myself, bolted shut.

The next instant, the green door creaked open.

Blake.

"Oh, sweetness and light," he exclaimed. "What has happened to you? You're bleeding."

I was about to concoct a fib, something imaginative, when, just then, knee-high, something from outside roiled my skirt. In the crotch seam of my pantaloons, a claw raked the tender flesh of my inner thigh.

I shouted like a demon possessed.

Blake, like an apocalyptic preacher, chimed in with, "Maldita. She-devil with claws. Beelzebub."

Had Blake, in the deepest, darkest weather, the only living, breathing human, witnessed her too: the crone with the purple brow?

Just then the lighthouse keeper's cat dashed out from under my skirt. She wound herself around Blake's wool trouser leg until he scooped her up and pressed her to his chest. Delighted with the mayhem she inspired, the cat purred.

"This scratch on my cheek? Last night in my bed I was ambushed by your cat. After that account of the massacre at dinner, and the surprise attack by your adorable feline, I couldn't sleep. At dawn I went out to see the sunrise."

"A creepy dark tale," Blake rejoined, "but, unfortunately, not true. A little after midnight, I noticed your bedroom door ajar. Up in the tower, with my spyglass, I've had an eye out for you . . ."

Would the lighthouse keeper tell Carl? If my father realized that I had left my bedchamber to meet George, there would be the devil to pay. I had had my share of supernatural encounters for one night.

Blake, no fool, nevertheless, was an incurable Romantic. I concocted a lie more to his taste, and in doing so (as novelists will tell you) discovered that it was absolutely true. "Actually, I went out to meet . . . a boy. I know it was wrong. But it was my very last chance to uncloak my heart."

I held up a scraped palm. "Returning to the lighthouse, I slipped. In more than one way. Mr. Blake, take pity. Don't tell my father."

Fondling his cat, Blake pondered. Finally, he grinned. "Go inside and wash your face. I'll make coffee."

Good fellow. I thanked him.

A new thought occurred. From the lighthouse tower, I might be able to glimpse the old woman in her rags lurking about the shed. I doubted I had enough energy to make it up the fabled 74 steps.

I pointed. "May I? One last look at the sunrise on the day that love dawned?"

Blake shrugged. "Why not?"

I was so tired I could hardly lift up my boot sole. I can't recall climbing the seashell stair, only the weird sensation that its mirrored light was calling me.

Third order of a Fresnel lens. Like an underwater diving helmet, with a magnified eye in the middle of its cut-glass body. I touched the magic lantern; it was hot. A genii's lamp, I could see why the romantic Blake had dedicated his life to its care.

I made my way around it to the east side of the round tower, and, leaning on the island rail, looked down.

Up in the tower, I took in the view from every angle.

Across the twinkling Strait, the British city of Victoria. On the tip of the spit, an elephant seal in repose. On the south side, in a hectic pile of bleached drift logs, I re-discovered George's hut. Inside Cline's Spit, an infantry of great blue herons guarded the bay. Turning to the northwest, the mercury of the Strait, unbroken.

I had returned to the place where I began.

Of the old woman, no sign. Perhaps she had crawled back into her muddy lair underneath the shed?

Then, I noticed something.

On top of the flat water, in the distance, a streak of black, dashed with red. A canoe, perhaps? More than one? A fleet of five canoes?

The first canoe crested on a wave. It lifted, tipped up. And went down.

Raise an alarm. I was about to cry out for Blake and stopped. The scene shimmered. It vibrated, so that I began to doubt my senses. For one thing, not one canoe in the fleet created a wake. They seemed to float above the water. Also, just one minute before, when I had studied the water from the exact same angle, I had not seen even one canoe.

An optical illusion? A fold in time? Vision of the past? Waking dream? I noticed Blake's spyglass on the sill. The lens misted and then cleared. What is it?" I asked out loud, to no one.

Nada, as Blake would say, nadie.

No one. Nothing

The fleet of canoes?

IMAGINED?

DEAD?

BOTH?

The 100 foot tall Dungeness Lighthouse tower taken in 1898. *Courtesy of the New Dungeness Light Station Association.*

Part 4
Whiskey City

View of Port Townsend from the Bluff. *Photo courtesy of the Jefferson County Historical Society.*

24
Carved Doll
c. 1889

About twenty-feet long, painted red on the inside and black on the outside, the Nootka-style canoe clung to the current. Jake's paddle was made of big leaf maple. It had a crosspiece on top and a bell-shaped bottom. The narrow tip made it easy work to shove off, pry the canoe from the mud, or glide through the water without making a splash. A weapon for the S'Klallam warrior, a pointed paddle stupefied victims.

Wooden figure of a man with European overcoat carved in the 1800s from the Myron Eells Artifact Collection owned by Jamestown. *Photo courtesy of the Jamestown S'Klallam Tribe.*

Below the bow, I squatted on top of a rolled cattail mat, amongst the bulging baskets and sacks and crates tumbling over with red, yellow, and brown vegetables destined for the Port Townsend market.

I couldn't take my eyes off him.

I leaned forward slightly, to catch his profile: his broad brow, strong nose, and raised chin. His hands were scarred from work at the lumber mill. The scraped knuckles seemed an essential part of him: *we are what we experience.*

As the bluffs and shoreline slipped by, I watched his smooth and muscular shoulders dip and pull, dip and pull. Each pull of the paddle, like a firm handshake, was a deliberate assertion of character.

I realized, physical attraction, like a plummeting piece of shooting star, breeched the clouds and entered my world. For the first time in my life, I felt a warming surge of desire, both thrilling and calming, ease through my veins like a rising tide, filling me up, and teasing my nose, my ear lobes, and my fingertips. I shivered, but not from cold.

I had been raised by two Native women, humorously direct about everyday biologic need, including sex. So, it wasn't that I hadn't been aware of the contortions of humans and other living creatures; I simply wasn't interested.

Even at age twelve, I was far more eager to reach my hand in between the rocks of a whirling tide pool to pry out a burnt orange sea cucumber, cocked and ready to ejaculate its sticky insides, than curious about that secret male part to which it is so often compared. Often while exploring I happened upon a geoduck, like a pricked thumb. I might prod it with my big toe to make it squirt saltwater. I never pictured its long, leathery erect neck as other than what it was. To me it was just a clam.

That day, something inside of me changed, not just my thoughts, but also my senescent connection to the world. Suddenly, I wanted to touch that divet at the base of his skull and the top of his neck that gathered sweat. No, I wanted to lick it. Weird.

When it seemed that my fixed gaze would burn a smoking hole through his flannel shirt, he turned round. For one wing-beat his eye met mine. His gaze traveled to the train-track incision beneath my right eye and remained there for a full second.

George and Carl worked together to lift up the canvas sail, a trapezoid on a frame made of sticks, like a Chinese fishing junk, though smaller and less elaborate. Our wake spread out like wings. The day warmed and the fog lifted; the air, hard and delicious, scoured clean every rock, shrub, and drift log that hurried by. Meanwhile our canoe pursued the bluff coastline, with its rocky outcroppings known as Dead Man's Point for the sea captain buried there.

My stomach thrummed a drum roll. I thought, "At this very minute Annie is simmering a stew. For the eleventh time Seya is reciting the tale of how the mink tricked a princess into marriage. It's Charley's favorite. He gets it, even though he's deaf. Julia's listening, too. So what am I doing here?"

I couldn't envision Charley, baby Julia—for that matter, Annie or Seya—away from our half-crescent of purple marsh on the shoreline. I couldn't imagine the people I loved the best in any other setting. I wondered if from time to time, my mother would mention my name aloud. But, after a few days, or a week, there would be no practical reason. When the family mentioned Millie, they would mean the goat.

The awful sense of loss was not just personal. It was both more and less than that. As I threw back my head to take the full measure of the crumbling bluffs, as I watched the periodic pocket of pines go by, I understood: *nothing is permanent*. Everything dies, and yet it lingers. Not long before, twenty-five S'Klallam townships dominated this waterway. Now, a village here and there, with ten houses at most. In the wind I could hear the laughter of the spirit-children who were no longer there. This mystical sensation made me feel sad, but also reassured and less lonely. The ghost fingers of the breeze twirled my braids and played with my bootlaces.

My father, with his white hair blowing about like a wet twig that had picked up a few strands of seaweed, had the air of an aged prophet. Carl, wiry but strong, might provide an artist's model for the Norse god of the sea. This afternoon, however, even in the crisp autumn sunshine, he looked weary and old.

Did he regret his decision to send me to Port Townsend?

I moved closer. "Tell me the story of Njord. To seduce Skadi, he showed her his beautiful feet. But in the end she discovered that she could not love him . . ."

"Not now, Fishbait. Some other time."

"Like, when?"

He could not mistake my desolate tone. I wanted to hate him but he looked so glum. I put my hand on his knee.

"At sea. What's it like?"

Carl glared at the sun. He leaned over and stared down at a rust-colored jellyfish that hovered in the water. Finally, he said, "A ship is a kind of church. In a storm on deck you can shout into the wind a prayer, or a curse. You toss out a wish, float it on top of the water, and watch it disappear. It requires a fathomless courage for a man who shouts out his truth in the rumble of a storm not to throw himself in. Not just the dissolute ones. Sober men, too.

"At least once in a lifetime each person should embark upon a quest to find someone—as unlike yourself as possible—to love. Old or young, high class or low, Indian or white; it doesn't matter, as long as he or she is nothing like you. A lover, or a friend. Either way, as long as its love. If you do this, no matter what your past decrees or what the future holds, you will find out: Inside of you is something good."

I curled up near to him, awash in a wistful affection for this peculiar man. Very soon he would no longer be there to protect me: from the silence of nature, the violence of man, and the destructive logic of my imaginative mind. A gust lifted up a flap of water. A salty droplet landed on the bridge of my nose, leaped, and skittered off my chin. I thought of Annie, pressing the baby to her hot cheek. Charley, hiding his face in Seya's apron.

Swallowing tears, I reached for his dry hand. "Papa, why do I have to go?"

Carl sighed. "It's not exactly a 'have to.' It's a choice." He added, "The most diabolic one in my life."

He spread out my fingers and, like a fortune teller peering at the future studied my open, empty palm. "I'm not articulate, or well-educated, like Judge Swan. How do I say it, Millie? Life used to be simple. No, that's not true. Things were more complex, but people preferred it. Then we became a nation. The government registered us, in order to show us where and how to live. The church does it, too. Now there's a rulebook for who belongs, and who doesn't."

Carl's gaze, opaque under dull skies, stared at mine until two sets of eyes became one. "Before, if a fellow—white, black, Mexican, or Native—took care of his brood well, folks asked for nothing more. If his wife, Indian or white, helped the family to prosper, she was deemed worthy. Now the church calls a marriage between a white and an Indian 'unholy.' Tell me, what has changed? Has God filed a land claim?

"These days, a fellow can mail order a European girl of the servant class, suitable to his wants and needs. These days, if a white man marries an Indian, instead of 'wife,' his neighbors will call her mistress, concubine, or worse. If the fellow beats her in the middle of the street at noon, no one will lift a hand. If the two of them are legally wed, he can beat her to death."

Our paddlers pretended not to hear. At the end of each and every phrase Jake and George pulled. Their paddles steered our craft as Carl's words filled the sail that carried us forth.

I pictured myself married to George. Could this ever be? In society's view, if I became his wife, would I be viewed as his "property?" Or, because I could pass as white, would I "own" him? Is all romantic attraction a form of slavery? Did I want that?

Carl continued. "With training, you'll become a fit companion for the preacher's daughter. With minor education you'll find a place in society. You can get a job. Or else, marry up. When you do, marry white. For your own protection."

He lifted up the heel of the left boot. "Remember that time you tripped on that rusty hub of wagon wheel? You broke your ankle. After five weeks Seya removed the splint. You wept because—"

"—I was afraid my ankle would not take my weight. But Seya said because it was a clean break, the bone would be stronger than before."

"Exactly."

According to Carl, my future relied on one over-simplified choice: White or Indian? To what extent can a person choose his or her identity? If I pretended to be white, was I even pretending? If I chose to "blend in" I might thrive, but at what cost?

On the spit George had urged me to hold onto the past. Was he right, or Carl? Meanwhile, inside my mind my mother's voice insisted, "Whatever you do, don't take off the earrings."

The day aged. Steadily Jake and George paddled across Discovery Bay, named after a British captain's ship. Here, Vancouver noted shrunken heads on sticks, a S'Klallam warning to keep out. In the direction of true north, Protection Island rose up like a fortress wall. Both Natives and whites have tried to make a go of it on this lump of sand, awkward as a waving thumb. Both failed. Protection Island, one of the few local sites where seabirds nest, has no fresh water.

But here, birds prosper. Flocking gulls, cormorants, and terns vie for a place on the beach. An eagle, perched on a drift log, resembles the sculpted head of a king. Tiny holes pocked the steep wall of the bluff. The rhinoceros auklet, named for the small horn on top of its orange bill, drills a tunnel fifteen to sixteen feet long into the bluff walls to incubate her eggs. Hatching, the chicks face the back wall. This forestalls premature adventuring, worrisome to any parent, even those who recall their own youthful pranks.

The female auklet travels a hundred miles or more in a day to find food. When her craw becomes too weighed down to handle the wind off the water, she unloads her catch. From time to time these regurgitated fish have been known to rain down on top of the feathered hats of the ladies strolling in Port Townsend.

Hungry, I opened up my satchel to rummage for crackers.

"Ahhh."

With a hollow klonk a weird object tumbled into the bottom of the canoe. I held it up to examine it. A cedar figure six inches tall; a crone with a wincing forehead, stained purple. The right arm is extended. Her wrist is flexed, fingers outstretched like the petals of a flower. The center of her right palm harbored a tiny hole. From all respects a terrifying toy, tenderly worked by a skilled craftsman.

"Ahhh," I cried out again and dropped it.

Jake scooped it up with his paddle from the bottom of the craft. Peering at it, he remarked, "It could be a shaman's fetish. Or, maybe a paddler wasting time at the lighthouse, waiting for the currents to change or the tide to come up, carved it to pass the time. It's an Aia'nl."

"What's that?" I asked.

"A folkloric figure, not all that well-known. A spirit, in the shape of an old woman, who can simultaneously observe the past, present, and future. See her peering through that hole in her hand?"

Jake handed it over. I held it out at arm's length. With a thrilling jolt the object communicated all of the terror of the previous night into my singed fingers.

"Let me see it," said George.

He leaned back on his haunches to examine it on top of his knee. "It's hard to say. A well-preserved artifact? Though it might have been carved this morning. Where did you get it?"

"How should I know? I opened my bag. It fell out."

My father remarked, "It's evil. Quick. Toss it over the side."

I retrieved the doll from George. I brushed his calloused palm. Usually so cool, but now it was burning. "No." I said. "I'm keeping it."

I wrapped it up in a handkerchief and stuffed it inside the satchel. Who was the old woman with the purple brow? A vision, or real? With three salty fingertips I touched the three incisions. Jake called her the Aia'nl. She seemed to be searching for me. Why? To kill me? To save me? The weird doll whispered, "I am yours." Like the lamp on top of the lighthouse tower, the Aia'nl would illuminate my quest.

Two Views of a Massacre
c. 1828

The first massacre in the history books is not the violence at Dungeness, but a revenge mission by white soldiers hired by the Hudson's Bay Company, or HBC. At Diamond Point, on the extreme northwest tip of Discovery Bay, the HBC murdered at least two-dozen men, women, and children. The attack was a punitive strike against the S'Klallam, retribution for the killing of a Scottish fur trapper. Ironically, after the incident, leaders on both sides defended their actions in nearly identical terms: HBC Chief Factor John McLoughlin and the S'Klallam chief both claimed that a violent reaction was necessary to keep their people safe.

Just the Facts

The murdered fur trapper Alexander McKenzie, chief trader for the Canadian Northwest Company, should not be confused with Scottish Sir Alexander MacKenzie the first white to successfully cross the North American continent.

This less fortunate and long-forgot trader with the same name had business in Victoria. On foot he made his way to Port Gamble to find the S'Klallam chief to hire a canoe to guide his party across the Strait to British Columbia. The chief appointed his son, and one other boy, to convey the group of five to the British outpost.

The crossing, delayed first by a storm and then by the shifting tides, took two days. In Victoria, McKenzie went about his business. A little more than a week later, when the canoe shoved off for the return crossing, it held one more passenger: McKenzie's wife, a Chinook. The Native woman had been waiting for McKenzie in Victoria. At first, the S'Klallam youth, afraid that the Chinook might see them as accomplices in a kidnapping, refused to take her. When McKenzie insisted, they agreed. Without further mishap, the canoe returned to Port Gamble.

However, once the canoe party returned home, McKenzie, displeased with something the boys had done, refused to pay. McKenzie and his men departed. That night, S'Klallam warriors ambushed and killed all five white men. Their bodies, clubbed to death, were left in a clearing. McKenzie's Chinook wife was captured.

That summer, HBC's chief factor McLoughlin ordered his men to get the girl and punish the tribe. As a result of the HBC mission, up to twenty-seven S'Klallam villagers died. None of those killed played any role in McKenzie's murder.

The S'Klallam Version

The chief never denied that S'Klallam warriors, at his urging, ambushed and killed McKenzie. When the fur trapper refused to pay, he felt he had to act. The chief believed that if he allowed the insult to stand, the S'Klallam would continue to be exploited by the white traders. In his mind, a show of force was required.

McKenzie and his men, wearing backpacks, appeared in the S'Klallam village. They asked to be conveyed to Fort Langley in Victoria. The chief agreed to find two dependable boys.

Then, according to S'Klallam witnesses, McKenzie demanded, "Do you have any food? I'm so hungry I could eat a dog."

As a joke, the chief offered to sell the white men an emaciated beast sniffing the fur-trapper's boot. To the chief's surprise, McKenzie assented, and the dog was killed, skinned, strung up on a tree limb, and flayed.

The chief, astonished but still attempting to be cordial, remarked to McKenzie, "Looks like venison." The chief was even more surprised when the white men refused to eat it. Was the dog killed to impress the Indians with the cruelty of the white men, or merely as a crude jest? On this point the chief's curiosity was never satisfied. The next day, when the men left, the sad corpse of the dog, untouched, dangled from a bent bough.

About two weeks later, the whites and the two young men returned, this time with an added person in their party, McKenzie's Chinook wife. McKenzie told the chief, "These boys are worthless. I don't intend to pay."

After McKenzie and his men departed, the boys displayed their bruises. One of them had suffered an injury to the lower spine when one of McKenzie's men kicked him with his boot to make him work faster.

That night, the chief convened a special council. He asked, "What would the Bostons do if we had done this thing to them?" He told a group of S'Klallam raiders to track McKenzie. At nightfall, they followed him to the dark edge where the trees bleed into the shore, and hunkered down into the shadows.

One of McKenzie's men, still awake, noticed the ducks rising, how they seemed to carry the light of the moon on their wings as they lifted up off the Strait. The man remarked aloud, to no one in particular, "Ducks don't fly at night. Except, for a reason." Without troubling to take off his boots, he laid down and tossed a blanket over his head.

The Indians crept up. In the silvery light, the blades of their hunting knives, which had been pressed up against their thighs, came to life. The screams of the first victim woke up the others, who raised a ruckus, but not for long. McKenzie was overtaken with a club, his wife captured.

The White Point of View Takes Over

HBC's Chief Factor, McLoughlin, put together a corps of sixty employees, government soldiers, and volunteers to avenge McKenzie's murder. When asked why, McLoughlin gave the same reason as the S'Klallam chief. He explained to his soldiers that if their expedition failed, not one of his people would ever feel safe again.

One of the soldiers, a Hudson's Bay clerk named Frank Ermantinger described the mission in his journal on the seventeenth of June as "a fiasco beset by quarrels." For example, a last-ditch effort to keep the incursion secret turned out to be "a burlesque," to use Ermantinger's word. On July 1 when the soldiers arrived, a US gunboat, The Cadboro, called in to support the HBC mission, sounded a greeting with its gun. Because the S'Klallam, mostly women and children had no previous contact with white soldiers, were ill-prepared for what happened next.

At daylight white militias in canoes stumbled upon two S'Klallam longhouses on the edge of the village at Diamond Point. One soldier, and then another, perhaps believing that the village harbored those who had murdered McKenzie, fired. "Two families, I believe, were killed. Three men, two or three women, a boy and a girl." According to Ermantinger, these Natives believed that HBC blankets, soaked with water, were impervious to HBC lead. They crawled underneath the blankets, and died. In the opening foray, one white soldier was injured in the crossfire of company guns.

Chief Trader McLeod and his officers could not agree whether the real objective of the mission was to punish the S'Klallam raiders, or to ransom McKenzie's Indian wife, known as the Princess of Wales. Either way, the expedition would have to negotiate. Very soon, the tribal leaders arrived in their painted canoes. They climbed aboard the Cadboro. In the middle of the talks, two Indians, fearing for their lives for reasons unknown, leaped off the ship. When they ignored the order to halt, the canoe on the deck exploded. One Indian died instantly; another, wounded, was seized.

A moment later Captain Simpson appeared on the deck. Furious, he informed HBC Chief Trader McLeod that no one but the ship's captain could issue the command to fire. But . . .

"Since this business has begun," Simpson said, they might as well "make the most of it." By this he meant that McLeod should issue the order for The Cadboro to fire on the S'Klallam village. McLeod agreed; the village burned.

An estimated twenty-seven died. McKenzie's killers were never identified. The following day, McLeod traded the wounded warrior for McKenzie's wife. He declared the mission a success. Later, the action was reviewed and found wanting. As a result, McLeod failed to achieve a promotion.

25
Port Townsend
c. 1889

As the night clouds tumbled by, the silver-dollar moon illumined the sheer cliffs rising to a height of well over a hundred feet. Jake and George, perspiring and sighing, pulled around the tip of Point Wilson. The sandy embankment, edged with fir, suggested a vast wilderness rather than the thriving port with brick fronts, pastel cupolas, and white steeples, just around the bend. For now, nestled in the tree line against a bluing sky, a single man-made feature emerged: the square top of a tiny castle.

Six years previously, Episcopal pastor John B. Alexander erected the brick tower to impress his bride-to-be. He failed. By the time he returned to Scotland to fetch her, she had married someone else. A remote mini-castle with a view of the San Juan Islands was not enough to persuade her, or any other lassie, to linger long in that lonely landscape.

Rounding the tip of Point Hudson, the Strait enters the Puget Sound. Jake maneuvered our canoe over and around square boulders and other glacial erratics dropped by the mile-thick ice sheet that retreated 15,000 years ago. After another ten minutes of paddling, the bluff dropped down to a beach, where canoes of every length and width fronted the tent-like shelters of the itinerant Indians that stopped to trade or repose for a while.

As we passed by, an elder wearing a broad-brimmed felt hat, with a blanket wrapped around her shoulders, crouched down to poke at a rack of blood-red salmon. The night wind fed the dancing flame. Two small boys urged a white dog to leap through a steel hoop. A firecracker, or maybe a pistol, exploded; one man swore and several others laughed. The scene on the beach was an altogether festive one. By now I was starving; I pestered my father to order Jake to put in at Point Hudson. But no, he told me, our goal was Union Wharf.

In a weeklong bash the port city was celebrating the Act of Congress and rubber stamp by President Benjamin Harrison that established the state of Washington and an international boundary with neighboring

Canada. But as Blake had observed: Port Townsend, also known as the Key City, didn't need an Act of Congress to throw a party.

Port Townsend Bay hosted half-a-dozen two- and three-masted schooners, naval ships, steamships, and tugs. Half-a-dozen brigs had dropped anchor in the harbor. At the beachfront docks, a clutter of sailboats, rowboats, and canoes created a chaotic scene. Water Street, the entry to the downtown's commercial area, featured in brick, granite, and marble all of the enterprises required in a settlement with development potential: hotels, banks, cafes, and saloons. The Hastings Tower, with its ornate front, wedding cake trim, and a toothpick rail, looked as if it would be more at home in Paris or London than in a western town on the rim of the continent. Up on the bluff, the cottages and more stately homes of the well-to-do, punctuated by two church steeples, staunchly held their ground against the burbling up of sin from the teeming waterfront.

As Jake Cook eased the canoe onto the beach alongside the base of the busy dock, Carl readied the sacks of potatoes and onions. I could do nothing but maintain an upright posture in the creaky canoe and stare. The glitter and throng, horns and bells, hooves and boot heels, howling hounds and sailors singing, the stars and the firecrackers, were so distracting that I forgot to be afraid.

Drunken mariners and street boys in scraves pressed past gentlemen in frock coats teetering on top of their canes. A bobble of plumage caught my eye. Parrots cloaked in satin, trilling and teasing, one in royal purple, the other emerald green. In the twilight, the ladies laughing loudly, slid by.

"Don't look," Carl ordered.

"At what?" I yelled back.

A brilliant POP, followed by an astringent whiff, made Carl leap.

I giggled.

As Jake handed up my satchel. The festive atmosphere seemed to make him more serious than ever. To Carl, he said, "I'll take the canoe round to the beach below Point Hudson. Meet me there. It won't take thirty minutes for you to deliver her uptown." Jake treated me as if I were an errand of the most trivial variety; once dispensed with and promptly forgot.

Carl said nothing and rubbed his chin. He didn't have to say the word for me to guess what he was thinking: "Whiskey."

Standing alone on the dock, George knew not what to do or say. He wiped his palms, blisters oozing, on his thighs. I stepped up, seized his injured hand, and kissed it with a healing tenderness. Well, not exactly. Licked it, more like. An awkward gesture, but at least it was something.

"Goodbye, George." I stated.

I lifted up on my toes and rubbed my forehead, nose, and chin on his hard hairless chest, while my severe father looked on.

With his index finger George lifted up my chin.

"Don't forget."

"What?"

"You know."

His driving ambition? My past? Our future? The weird doll? Blinking back tears, I nodded, as if I knew. George, attempting to smile, instead grimaced and turned away.

Carl had agreed to meet Judge Swan at a bar for sailors known as the Blue Light. I held tight to the cuff of his greatcoat as we stepped away from the pier. I had no parting words for Jake, though I doubt that he noticed or cared. He was too busy taking care of business.

We shoved past the drunken crowd. Halfway there, I stopped. Obstructing the foot traffic, a young man, exceedingly pale and slender, stood on a wooden shipping crate gesticulating madly. His glistening top hat made him look leaner and taller, like a slash of black ink.

With a bow he announced, "The Ballad of Harriet Hastings. A classic verse, composed on an unpaid bill on top of a bar last night by me."

"Look, father," I said, tugging on his sleeve.

"What?" asked Carl.

"It's a poet." Actually, his silk scarf and stagey style reminded me more of an actor. He was, without a doubt, the most handsome man I had ever seen. Agog, I waited to see what he would do next.

"Millie. Come away. A scammer and a con, that's what he is."

I refused.

Carl sighed.

The poet-actor announced an original verse, very fresh, entitled: Hattie, She Did It for Daddy.

A frowzy woman, whirling a soiled silk parasol though it was dark outside, cackled. Curious, the frenzied crowd drew in. Two weeks before Hattie Hastings from Port Angeles had been cuffed for smuggling drugs across the Strait. The young miss at the center of the scandal was excessively attractive. In addition, Hattie Hastings is "no dope," the poet punned.

According to the Port Townsend Morning Leader, Hastings, though caught with the goods, at the hearing convinced the judge (Swan, I found out later) that she was, in fact, no criminal, but instead a dutiful daughter doing all she could for her impoverished family.

The poet declaimed:

> *Too pretty for jail*
> *Too purt to skip bail.*

The paper called Hasting's testimony "gushing and sloppery," Judge Swan released her into the custody of the Deputy United States Marshal Lee Baker:

> *With a price on her head,*
> *Marshal put her to bed.*

with a flourish, the poet concluded—

> *The cop and the smuggler*
> *snuggled.*

The crowd guffawed.

"Not bad," remarked Carl. "Then again, not good."

Then he noticed the tears on my face. Apparently, I wasn't immune to the poet's craft. "It's sad!" I exclaimed. "She wasn't a bad girl, not really. If she committed a crime, she did it to please her father. In the city anything can happen. Oh, Carl. I promise, no matter what, I'm sticking to the straight and narrow."

"Don't fret." Carl laughed, wiping my face with his cuff.

When the poet-actor passed the hat, the happy mob slid away. I begged Carl for a nickel but he would not give way.

We turned to go.

"Stop. A word."

He leaped down off his box.

To my astonishment, his long pale fingers—well-groomed but without gloves—seized my own. He showed me his empty hat. "I'm Thomas Astor. If you refuse to help me, I'll be shanghaied by pirates. Or worse, the military." He straightened up. A black lock dripped over one eye. "Kidnapped by sailors, and then bled to death in the hold. You don't want that to happen to me, do you?"

I didn't see the profit in capturing boys with no other aim than to slaughter them underneath the deck, yet, there was so much that I didn't know. Tugging on my father's sleeve, I averred, "Father, we must help him."

"I'd rather kick him to the next corner." Carl growled. "Oh fine. I'll sponsor him for a hot meal, but that's all."

A dirty wind from the north blustered. We hurried on to the Blue Light. Through the lavender cigar smoke we managed to find Swan. On this special day the proprietor, a lady wearing a square felt hat with one tall black feather, had reserved his usual corner table for him. We discovered him sipping "the usual," a glass of clam nectar, "with a kick."

"It's a great day," he extolled, "for Washington State, the last stop on the transcontinental rail."

Using his walking stick with the coiled snake, he pried himself out of the booth. He clapped Carl on the shoulder and pressed his ermine whiskers to my forehead. He didn't have to bend down, as I was now nearly the same height. The poet Thomas Astor curtsied. Swan, one eyebrow cocked, offered him a drink. Astor without hesitation, accepted.

Inside the booth, I pressed against the paneled wall. My father pulled in next to me. Thomas Astor sat across from me and next to Swan. We ordered the special: soup. Lifting their beer mugs to toast, my father and Judge Swan celebrated the economic opportunities that statehood would usher in. This topic, so lively for them, was of little interest to me, and even less to Astor, who devoted himself to his plate of chowder.

The tavern was named after the blue light on the street end of the wharf. Whenever the double doors opened, a winter breeze made the kerosene flames flicker. Other than that the place was airless; we were like mussels steaming in seaweed. The floor was black with grime; covered with a layer of dirty sawdust. The cigar smoke, body odor, and scent of drying wool made me feel seasick, a sensation curiously absent in the canoe.

The piano plashed out "The Old Settler's Song." All around mugs clacked. Identical twin sisters, hatless and sweating, in twin frocks thrust out their hips and moved their matching pleated skirts this way and that. A woman in purple satin leaned over to wipe something that looked like melted tar off the ruddy beard of a man who laughed so loud that he howled. With a shot glass Swan toasted, "Health, success, and good fortune—to me." Those near enough to hear laughed, and also promised themselves the best of everything. Astor, who had polished off the last of his fish stew from his crusty pot, and mine as well, stood up suddenly, and almost passed out. He steadied himself, and for the pleasure of all, belted out a then-popular tune, "Malarkey."

The public house applauded. Astor bowed and collapsed onto the bench. He reached across the table and touched the wound on my cheek. With lifted eyebrow he inquired, "What happened? Girl fight?"

I resorted to the fib that had failed me before. "Cat scratch."

"Minx." He studied me. "Hm. How old are you, anyway?"

"Twelve," I announced bravely.

"Hm. Despite your girlish appearance, something tells me you're more than ready to experience the world. There are things I could teach you. After all, one good deed deserves another; one misdeed deserves two."

He drank. He brushed crumbs from the elbow of his jacket. In a more serious tone he advised, "Trust me, if you ensconce yourself up on the bluff, jamming scones for the mistress, you'll die of ennui; either that, or consumption, though I wager that the boredom will do you in first. If you're seeking an education, stick to the waterfront."

Words of wisdom: the last thing I can recall. The previous night I had not slept at all. The canoe journey—though not hard work, at least not for me, though Jake and George might hold the opposing view—had fatigued me. Thirsty from the salted breeze and sun, I had been stealing sips of black beer from one glass, and then another. My lids creaked shut, as if weighted down with silver dollars. If that had been the case, I'm sure that the poet-actor would have palmed them. The last thing I noticed before nodding off was Astor siphoning the barmaid's tip into his coat pocket off the corner of the table.

Next thing I knew, my father had tossed me over his shoulder like a sack of meal. The mud of Adams Street sucked on his boots—one of several parallel streets named for the American presidents, and, coincidentally, corrupted by filth. We began climbing the tumbled-down stairway; a seeming ladder of opportunity, oblivious to class, creed, and color. The wooden stair swayed. The night whispered, "Fly. Fly away." Nothing—not a wing or a prayer—could rescue me now from the next step up: scullery girl.

As we gained the full height of the bluff, a hundred feet, a gull shrieked. In the dim light of evening, I noticed Carl's quavering jawline. I knew then, the Blue Light had never been part of the plan.

Miserable, he exclaimed, "Go in. Now. Without me. I don't want the Reverend to see me like this. It's not decent."

I yoked my arm around his neck. "Papa, don't go. I'll be good, I promise. I can help you fish Please, please, please. Don't leave me here. How will I ever find my spirit power?"

He held me in his woeful gaze. "You're a wonder. What you lack is spit and shine. Here, you have a chance to improve yourself. In church, a front row seat with a leather-bound bible with your name on it. Understand?"

No, no, not a word. "Papa, when will you come back for me?"

His spirit was drowning in a sea of regret. "When the time is right. I'll come, or send word. Somehow, by crook or by hook."

"Do you promise?"

"As well as I am able, I do."

Inside a lamp brightened. The lace curtain lifted and fell. The back door creaked and spilled out a pail full of warm light.

"Hello? Who's out there?" The melodious voice of a bell-shaped silhouette called out in a voice, low but insistent. "Millie Langlie, is that you?"

I peered at her through the black boughs of an apple tree. When I turned back, Carl had disappeared.

City of Dreams
1851-1902

Port Townsend, aka the City of Dreams, for the visions it inspired in the first pioneers of this northeastern-most outpost of Washington's Olympic Peninsula, and those today who keep that dream alive.

Originally, it was the placid harbor and fertile valley capped by the castle bluff that attracted the new settlers. West of the cliffs, shimmering lagoons and brilliant meadows were dotted with elk. The first settlers used chalked strings and the nubs of pencils to calculate the exact value that the lumber, fish, and farmland on this corner of the Olympic Peninsula would yield. When one scheme failed, the collective imagination of the town, arriving in a canoe, a sloop, an ox-cart, or a train, replaced it with a new one.

On May 8, 1792, Vancouver's ship—not *The Discovery*, under repair in an adjacent harbor, but one of his smaller vessels—exited the Strait for the headwaters of Admiralty Inlet. At that moment, Vancouver became the first European captain to enter Puget Sound. As he rounded the point, he noticed a sheltered harbor topped by a bluff with sparse trees. He noted the cove as an ideal location for a settlement and named it after his friend and patron, the Marquis of Townshend. The Marquis, a commander of the British forces, never set foot in the town.

In 1851, Port Townsend was declared a city, a full six months before Seattle. By that May, Port Townsend boasted fifteen bachelors and three complete families, a demographic breakdown typical for frontier towns in the Washington Territory. East coast pioneers established the first private and public institutions: Plummer, Pettygrove, Fowler, Clinger, Hastings, to name a few. Decades later, at the end of the century, a stiff photo captures four men, original pioneers, posing in front of a trade blanket. Perhaps it's fitting that this symbol of the coercion and corruption of the Indians should serve as a backdrop for a portrait of the venerated founding fathers.

Whiskey sapped what strength the Natives who'd survived the epidemics had left to rebel against the new social order. Three decades before, in order to harvest beaver and sea otter pelts to sell to European haberdashers and overcoat manufacturers, the Hudson's Bay

Company established forts throughout the region. HBC Chief Factor John McLoughlin strictly forbade the trade or sale of liquor to the Indians. However, when American settlers arrived in the region, these restrictions could not be enforced. Over the years, as the northern-most outpost on Puget Sound, Port Townsend was an international gateway, with its gambling dens and brothels drew eager sailors in droves. In the gold rush epoch, and in the decades after, hard liquor was the easiest commodity to come by. Rumor has it that even the great writer Jack London spent a night in jail here.

"Whiskey built a great city." These are the words of J. Ross Browne, a government inspector. In 1857, in two accounts in a San Francisco newspaper, Browne's witty descriptions of Port Townsend made him an enemy of the civic-minded. Browne wrote: "With very few exceptions, it would be difficult to find a worse class of population in any part of the world. No less than six murders have occurred there during the past year. It is notorious as a resort for beachcombers and outlaws of every description." Browne called those who objected ungrateful. When news of the Frazier Gold Rush hit, it was Browne's colorful pieces that attracted prospectors in need of supplies . . . and in want of the high and low entertainment that he'd advertised. As Browne himself predicted, his reputation eventually transformed from detractor to benefactor. A few years later, when Browne landed on the wharf, he was greeted by a delegation of prominent citizens and a brass band.

In the 1860s, as diplomats from the United States and Great Britain clashed over possession of the San Juan Islands, loyal American citizens dropped the "h" in "Port Townshend." This period of tension with England, which lasted twelve years, is sometimes called The Pig War. On San Juan Island, a Berkshire boar, property of the Hudson's Bay Company, triggered an international crisis when it trespassed into the garden of an America farmer. After the pig was shot, diplomacy prevented further bloodshed. On October 21 of 1872, Emperor William I of Germany, acting as arbiter, appointed a commission in Geneva. One year later, declaring the boundary with England to be the Strait of Haro, they awarded the islands to the United States.

In the next several decades, as the city continued to thrive and grow, so did its notoriety. The Key City's seamy reputation may have played a role in the decision to move the customs house to Port Angeles in 1862. One year later, the righteous might of God, made manifest by a melting glacier, washed the new building into the Strait of Juan de Fuca.

President Lincoln took time out from the Civil War to authorize the return of bureaucratic functions to Port Townsend, where the customs house remained a bastion of corruption for decades to come. Trade in opium, the smuggling of illegal workers after the Chinese Exclusion Act in 1882, and routine murders of every description added to its scurrilous reputation.

Citizens hoped and lobbied for the Northern Pacific Railroad would name Port Townsend, as an emerging national and international center of trade, the last stop on the trans-continental railroad. This scheme, like so many others, inspired and ultimately disappointed.

The citizens of Port Townsend: committed to the dream, even if they knew it couldn't last. "The Old Settler's Song" by Francis Henry captures a popular conviction: in the long run, it's better to be contented than rich. In the 1902 semi-centennial celebration, original pioneer B.S. Pettygrove led the crowd through to the final verse:

> . . . *no longer the slave of ambition,*
> *I laugh at the world and its shams,*
> *as I think of my pleasant condition*
> *surrounded by acres of clams.*

26
Up on the Bluff
c. 1889

"Quiet. You'll wake father."

This from a young man with a beakish aspect like a hawk, or a preacher, and penetrating dark eyes. His large head looked larger thanks to his curly brown hair. He attempted to comb the wiry locks down on his forehead . . . unsuccessfully.

Over his shoulder, a girl, slight and fair, in a dress with pink piping, so diaphanous it looked white. Later I learned it was her nightgown. I could not see her feet but this didn't surprise me; I expected a beautiful ghost like her to float.

"Millie Langlie, at last." She knelt down beside me. "How eager I am to at last meet my companion. Another girl to talk to! So, why are you crying?"

"Edith, for pity's sake. She's entirely undone. Filthy and exhausted. In the morning you can ply her with questions. For now, wipe off the mud and put her to bed." Bitterly he added, "So the rest of us can get some sleep."

As the petulant lad scolded, the girl's colorless lashes fluttered. The back of her hand covered her mouth as she coughed. Feathery curls fell down on her delicate collarbones, as fragile as a bird's. She wavered, as if too frail to stand. I ached to place her in a chair.

But the young gent was not finished with her. "Fetch a blanket, a good thick one. She can stretch out here, next to the stove."

"She'll fry, or freeze. She had better sleep with me."

This miffed him. "She's here to care for you, not the reverse. If you coddle her, she'll follow you like a pull toy, with about as much practical use. I'm pretty sure that's not what the Reverend had in mind when he sent for her. For tonight, do what you want. In the morning, he and I will teach you how to manage the household staff."

Household staff of one: me.

The battle won if not the war, Edith turned to go. "Goodnight, brother."

Not husband, but brother. That made sense. Only a few years older than me, she seemed too frail, too kind and good, to be married to a husband, least of all to this scoundrel. I noted his white skin and slender figure. There, the resemblance ended. They two were as similar as a lamb and a timber wolf.

She guided me past the formal dining table next to the glowing brick hearth and up the stairs. I peeked into the stately parlor with its creamy walls and its green-gold drapery, which covered the front windows from the ceiling to the floor. It was a good room, the best I had ever seen. Our lit taper passed by standing lamps causing heavy maple chairs and carved end tables to cast intricate shadows.

As I followed her up the narrow stair, she remarked, "You mustn't think my brother harsh or cruel. Quite the opposite. If anything, Chris is too sensitive. Ever since mother died, I've been ill. My father dedicates all of his energy to the parish. So you see, it all falls on Chris. It burdens him because he cares."

The first door in a little hallway opened up to a bedroom, with a pink aura, like the mist at sunrise. Perhaps it was the wallpaper, with its swirly floral pattern that, in the candlelight, created this impression. The room, not large, was dominated by a huge bed on a wooden frame, covered by a gauzy pink canopy and a ruffled valance all around it. Pink pillows, trimmed in green, floated on a sea foam quilt, lavender with green trim. A lamp hung on the wall on either side of the bed, each an upside-down glass jar. Next to the enormous bed, a tiny table made of a shiny black wood with a white marble top. The legs of the table were bowed, as if they could hardly withstand the weight. The left-hand wall featured a wardrobe with two wide doors and a full-length mirror built into the center panel. There were three small Persian rugs with opulent blues and greens, swirling pink, and black.

On the wall opposite the wardrobe, a large window, with side-by-side doors and glass panes, stepped out to a tiny balcony, the only view of the town and the harbor, the coastal range, and the peaks of Mount Baker. In the center sat a little wooden bench behind an iron rail. From this seat a girl could track the street life below, the slow glide of a brig, or the illumination of the stars. A girl could dream.

However, as I would soon discover, life lived small—regarded from the compressed end of the telescope—can satisfy for only so long.

Above the bed, next to a slender crucifix, there was a large charcoal sketch of a determined woman with a piercing stare, not unlike her sons.

Without really wanting to, I continued to study it as Edith removed my wrap and untied my soggy boots. I kept my little satchel, with everything I owned, pressed up against me. Finally, I put it down in order to peel off my damp bodice, which clung.

"Quick," Edith cried. She lifted up the stitched coverlet. She threw it over me, and nestled into the bedclothes from the opposite side.

I began to cry.

Edith asked, "Do you miss your mother?"

"Yes," I cried.

Edith nodded. "I miss her, too. I mean, Adele . . . my mother. That's her in that drawing you've been admiring."

"How did she die?"

Her eyes burned, in the pale light of the moon coming through the window. "Do you really want to know?"

"Yes, please."

With a sigh, she commenced her tale.

A final act of generosity did my mother in. As the Reverend's wife, she devoted herself to good deeds. She volunteered at the Marine Hospital. Once in a while an entire ship's registry falls ill. That's what happened when a passenger, an Irish servant girl named Mallory O'Quinn, with an infant on her breast, attracted Adele's special pity. Mallory had traveled by ship from Ireland to New York. Her prospective employer had turned her away; they'd not advertised for a maid with a baby. In compensation (and to get rid of her, fast) the mistress offered her a train ticket. Mallory, to take fullest advantage of the opportunity, booked passage as far west as one can go by rail. From San Francisco, she took a schooner to Port Townsend. By the time she arrived, she, along with most of the other passengers and crew, was delirious with fever. She was carried from the dock to the nearby Marine Hospital.

About a year before, at an Irish estate where she scrubbed, and mended, and cooked, and baked, and ironed the sheets, she had become well-acquainted with an American, a youth of artistic sensibility, from the upper-crust of New York. Sharing many personality traits—wit, vivacity, and joy—the two entered into reckless liaison; after a month of uninhibited passion, he disappeared. Mallory, optimistic and self-contained, chalked up the affair to a lapse in judgment that she didn't intend to repeat. However, she soon realized that sometimes women are forced to account for their adventures in ways that men are spared. She wrote a letter to the young man, disclosing all. She sent it to his New York address. She received no reply. Unfazed by this, and every other obstacle, she used the wages that she'd saved to board a clipper ship to the New World.

Her son was born at sea.

In her epic journey Mallory O'Quinn contracted a fever and collapsed. My mother hoped that she could nurse the girl, and her child, back to health. Thanks to a strong constitution, she recovered. Her baby son did not. Adele, of course, ordered a proper marker for her child, who knew no joy and only suffering in his tiny, short life. In Mallory's mind, this final act of kindness intensified her debt. As soon as she recovered, the Irish girl, who was just twenty-years-old, fled, pledging never to return until she had found a means to recompense my family. Soon after that, my mother succumbed.

Edith concluded her tale. "Taking care of mother, I contracted the same illness. Even now, as I retell it, I find it hard to catch my breath. I never go out. I'm sorry for you. You're sure to find me dull."

Inside I shouted, Never! I was already enamored. "What about Mallory O'Quinn's lover? As my father, Carl likes to say, The rogue ate the oyster but left the pearl."

Edith studied me. "What does that mean?"

I replied, "Hmm, I'm not sure. The saying seems to suit the circumstance."

She went on. "Last winter, a youth in a good suit, slightly worn, hair dyed black, called, looking for Mallory O'Quinn. At the time no one was at home except our cook Harriet, who has since up and married. Poor Harriet delivered the sad news to him: Mallory's baby was dead, and Mallory had disappeared. Before she left, Mallory let fly that she might 'strike out for the silver mines of the Caribou.' If so, I hope her bad luck has turned to sterling."

With aplomb I replied, "I hope she died."

Edith looked even more shocked than before. "Millie. Why?"

"Because she's too ungrateful to live. To abandon Adele, after all she did for her. How could she?"

"How quickly you condemn. Adele succumbed to the fever about a week after Mallory departed. Had she known, I am certain she would have remained at her side until the end. Be charitable. Every night I ask the Virgin to help Mallory find a way to use her womanly insight and skill to benefit others and herself."

Did the Virgin respond to Edith's prayer and guide Mallory? Later, I wondered. At the moment, I remained perplexed. Was the Irish girl in the story bad or good? What fate did she deserve?

Edith, distracted by her own thoughts, added, "I am in no position to judge her. My mother was devoted to sacrifice. But until Adele fell ill, I never gave a thought for anyone but myself. When I look back, I realize I should have died in her place."

Now it was my turn. "Don't say that."

Edith looked up to the little crucifix nailed on the wall above her head, next to the portrait of her mother. She pressed my palm to her heart. "From now on I will try to do better. I'm happy that I'm ill. God sent me the fever to test me. And you. He has sent you."

How good she was. And lovely, too, like a painting. But odd. After all: *she said she was happy to be sick.* Edith's striving after virtue without a doubt outran my own search for self-improvement by half a mile. Nevertheless, she did appear to go to an extreme. Where did she get the idea? Her father's preaching? From the charitable Adele? Or was it her natural purity, which made her so unfit for the world, and caused her to look so like an angel?

Edith continued to gaze patiently at the crucifix.

From the very first, I was dazzled by her light, as if I had tumbled inside a magic lantern. Just being near her filled me with the desire to be good. Later, I learned: The wish to become angelic may be deadly. Like Icarus, Victorian girls who leap off the wrought-iron rail fly too near to the sun, or clip their wings on the palisades of the waterfront hotels. Either way, they drop into the sea and drown.

A Sunbeam in the House
c. 1887

Most Victorian literature portrays females as holy or wholly corrupted. Why are there no in-between categories, such as somewhat-slutty-but-with-potential-to-improve, the partial slattern, or a-bit-of-a-trollop-but-with-a-heart-of-gold? When comparing Port Townsend's "fallen women" to "the virtuous ladies," it's hard to say who was more free.

The Cult of Domesticity

A handbook for Victorian housewives exhorts: "a virtuous woman proves her worth in the role of a wife and mother." For middle to upper-class women, there really was no alternative to marriage. Even women engaged in the handful of respectable professions—teacher, nurse, and governess—were expected to find a husband before the age of thirty.

That notwithstanding, in a pioneer town like Port Townsend, even for ladies living on the bluff, "marital bliss" was no vacation. The manor is paid for, not with a dew of perspiration, but with actual sweat. Truly, as Louisa May Alcott declares in the eleventh chapter of *Little Women*, "Housekeeping ain't no joke!"

In the City of Dreams, as elsewhere, keeping house was the opposite of child's play. The majority of the households on the bluff couldn't afford servants. Therefore, the lady of the house rose before daybreak to stoke the hearth, fetch the water and the wood, and bake the bread. All of this, before breakfast. She could study the latest fashions in Paris, but when it came down to it, she was her own dressmaker and often sewed her husband's shirts. On washday, she scrubbed his clothes and her own, as well as the array of household linen; then, passed it through the wringer and pinned it up to dry. In the evening, if she reposed by the fire, she kept the mending in her lap. In addition to the daily chores, there were the seasonal ones: tending the vegetable garden in spring and summer, putting up jars for winter, and salting down the meat in fall, to name a few.

To get all of this done, a housewife ought to be as beefy as a butcher in a meat locker. Yet, to appeal to the "the stronger sex," she must always appear frail. According to the ad for Joy's Vegetable Sarsaparilla in the *Port Townsend Morning Leader*, "the common afflictions of women are sick-head, aches and nervous disorders." Her pallor, shortness of breath, and tendency to faint might be the result of a corset drawn too tight, or a side effect of laudanum, the opium compound her doctor prescribed to numb the aches and pains so that she could sleep at night. Or maybe her wan complexion was merely a sign of her very real exhaustion.

Weary, or seriously ill, a proper wife was expected to maintain her cheerful attitude. As the Reverend EJ Hardy suggested in his guide to good manners, which would see seven editions: "Sweetness is to woman what sugar is to fruit. It is her first business to be happy—a sunbeam in the house, making others happy—" A woman who showed signs of illness might be suffering from a nervous disorder known as hysteria. In this case, her husband could send her for a rest cure, or have her locked up indefinitely.

Many husbands believed that in order to keep a wife smiling, she must be protected from worldly matters. But this could never be. Economic realities were as much a part of a woman's life as any man's. For example, a mother would exhaust every avenue to keep her child from the pangs of poverty.

Helga Estby Accepts the Challenge

Take the case of Helga Estby, a Norwegian who finally settled in Spokane. After her husband's construction business failed, when the mortgage and back taxes threatened the family farm, Helga learned of a challenge from a mysterious benefactor. As a promotion, a bicycle brand offered $10,000 to any woman who could walk from coast to coast.

With her daughter Clara, who carried in her purse a curling iron and pepper spray, Helga Estby covered fourteen states, passing through gold rush towns and Indian reservations—and rain, dust, and snow—evading hobos and robbers till at long last she made it to New York City. Mrs. Estby proved: Victorian women may have looked delicate, but appearance isn't everything. Helga Estby defied society's expectation for one reason: to feed the kids.

Fallen Women

Shortly after I arrived in the Key City, this headline appeared: "A Queer Freak; Depravity Worthy of the Pen of a True Zola." *The Port Townsend Leader* described a scandalous divorce, with a follow-up story the next day.

An electrician named Charles Duncan married "a pronounced brunette with snapping black eyes and uncertain features—" as if her moral confusion had somehow blurred her face? According to the piece, when Duncan offered to marry her, he "had thought her pure," though later he learned, "she had not been what she should."

This is what happened. Shortly after the wedding, Duncan came home a day or two early from business in Anacortes. His wife was not at home. When he went out to look for her, he discovered her in a "house of ill fame" on Adams Street. As it happened, she was "the favorite in Viola Garnett's establishment." Though less than pleased with his wife's accomplishment, Duncan, a forgiving sort, agreed to overlook the lapse, but only if she agreed to quit her job.

His wife said no.

The electrician testified, "She flatly refused, saying that she had tired of married life and wanted to be permitted to enjoy herself in her own way."

Needless to say, Duncan's divorce was granted.

PROSTITUTE or PRISONER OF THE BLUFF?

Which would YOU choose?

27
Home Schooling
c. 1889

A tweedy stout figure poked at the musty fireplace. He wore a somber long coat with woolen trousers awkwardly humped up inside his patent leather boots. He turned to greet me, his unkempt bristle, big forehead and hawkish nose revealed a blunt likeness to his son. Unlike Christopher, whose cheeks were parchment, the Reverend wore muttonchops on either side of his ruddy face.

In his fist, a doughy ham hock, a large brass key.

Of all the wonders in Port Townsend, there was not one more astonishing than the Reverend's Waterbury clock, by Benedict and Burnham. The frontispiece, made of solid brass, featured numerals in ivory. Inside the polished mahogany cabinet, a tall glass door revealed the inner workings of a pendulum and chains, a system of weights that caused the clock to chime on the half hour. This clock, modeled on a Swiss timepiece, one that would have cost ten times more, had been shipped inside a crate from Waterbury, Connecticut. That morning, and every morning before breakfast, the Reverend would wind up the lovely clock with his special key.

The good Reverend claimed he was "ecstatic, elated, and overjoyed" to meet me, not just because I was the daughter of that "old parsnip" Carl. Even more so because he had "to beat the devil around the stump" to find a housemaid for Edith. To start the fire he bent low, blew hot and cold until his eyes watered, then regained his feet in order to rub his bruised knees. I lit the fire with a single match.

Delighted, eager to discover other skills, the Reverend pointed at the arched doorway to the kitchen. "Fetch me a cup of tea. Put sugar in it. Not too hot, mind you. I don't want to be scalded. I like it weak, milky and tepid."

Those three words more or less summed him up. He was good at heart but not reliable. When fate took his wife Adele, his character folded; yet he hoped never to lose his belief in tomorrow. Peace, until the day he died, was what he prayed for.

However, this was not to be.

Edith, inside the kitchen, was already pouring. Her brother, in a severe black long coat, leaned on the pastry table, adding up figures in a book. His manner the night before had put me off; I was nearly too nervous to look at him. However, by light of day, to my astonishment and his chagrin, he seemed as bashful as I.

In daytime, the Mathieson's house seemed less luxurious but more livable. The downstairs, with its high ceilings and ornate decor, less stuffy. Upstairs, the little bedrooms, careworn yet charming.

After handing off the china cup and saucer, I hurried upstairs to launder my raggedy underthings. I tried to tidy Edith's room but her bedclothes befuddled my best intentions. The satiny sheets dallied and danced and refused to lie flat. As a housemaid, I had a lot to learn.

Nervous, I stepped out onto the balcony.

To my right, the capacious front porch of our nearest neighbors, the McCurdy's. Just beyond that, on the edge of the bluff, the fire tower with its brassy bell, matched in height only by the wooden cross on top of the Methodist Church. Beneath my feet, a sheer drop to the waterfront. Assorted tea-tray rooftops spread out before me. On Front Street, I saw the upper story of the clam cannery, with its symmetrical windows and fire porches, black against the red brick. Best of all, the wedding-cake ornament on top of the Hastings hotel. While in the harbor, a fast cutter was waving farewell. To my untraveled eye there was more delight here, than to the jaded tourist looking down from his hotel balcony in Florence, Italy.

I readied myself, and went down.

In the kitchen, the conversation had turned crusty. I lingered at the threshold. When I stepped over it, all conversation ceased. After an awkward pause, the good Reverend resumed, "But, I made a pledge to her father."

He went on. "In two years Millie will earn a diploma from the new secondary school. Along with six other women, she will distinguish herself as a member of the very first graduating class. She will set an example for future scholars. This is how I convinced my old friend to relinquish his daughter. I can never go back on my word."

Chris rejoined, "Father, we all know you are the best of men. But how will we afford it? Since you refuse to consider the dollars and cents, I must. To go to school, Millie will need a quality coat, shoes, and other supplies. We could deduct her expenses from her wages. However, what if she doesn't suit us? Surely we can't fire her, and then ask her to pay us the wages she has not yet received."

Edith handed me a mug of tea and white bread with butter. No jam. Apparently I had not earned it yet. The hot brew, dark and smooth, revived me, though I missed the tangy sweetness of Annie's cedar-bark tea.

Christopher ran his fingertip down a column of figures. "Now that I've been hired on as a clerk at Rothschild's, who will look after Edith? At the moment she seems well enough, but who can say? What if without warning the fever returns? What happens if Millie is off at school—"

Edith interjected, "Millie may be uneducated but she's not deaf. It's unchristian to talk about her as if she's not here. Look. Now I'm doing it, too."

She turned to me with a melty smile. With or without marmalade, my knees turned to jelly. "Millie, what do you want? To go to school in town, with rude children half your age? Or to stay here with me?"

Edith was ill, and so good. Unlike the father and brother, she cared about my feelings. Selflessly, she left the decision to me. Still, I knew what she wanted me to say. For one full minute, I nibbled a crust and pondered. "Why not both? I can help Edith with the housework and receive an education. She can teach me here."

They studied me with astonishment.

After a long moment Edith replied, "Though I consider myself quite useless, I do have one or two skills: China painting, beaded bags, miniature landscapes, and floral designs made from braided hair. I could teach her Romantic poetry, and a phrase or two in French. Christopher could handle the more advanced subjects. I think we've hit upon a plan of improvement for Millie, in accord with my own needs and wants."

Christopher added, "If Edith and I were to tutor her, Millie would receive a better education at a lesser cost. Without exposing her to the waterfront riff-raff, which, given her background, might tempt her to delinquency and other crimes." Sensing the advantage, he pressed on. "How would you like to write a letter to her father explaining how she caught typhus playing rochambeau"—their name for the children's game of rocks, scissors, and paper, I later learned—"with the daughter or the son of a Chinese grocer? A Russian sailor? A Canadian cowboy? What's more, she's no longer a child; her womanish traits are emerging. Look to the future. How would you like to introduce Carl to the fiancé: an Irish journalist, a German grocer, or worse yet, a British pirate turned government official? Is it not better to keep her up on the shelf on our bluff?"

The Reverend dropped his cup; it sounded in the saucer. "You're right. I promised Carl that I would, keep Millie safe. Also, that I would provide her with the best education available. Therefore, that's what I shall do. Millie will study at home. You two will tutor her."

Edith clapped. She leaped up to kiss her brother, as if the idea had really been his, not mine.

The amiable Reverend waved his cup. My alacrity merited a pat on the head, though I calculated that three short steps by the minister to the soapstone sink would have saved me nine. Welcome to the servant class.

Chris did not smile, or seem glad. Constitutionally nervous, anxiety seemed to be his prolonged response to any situation. He warned Edith, "Let's not forget that Millie must earn her keep. Therefore, her first lesson will be splitting the firewood. Second, making a neat stack. Third, keeping the fire lit. And so forth." For the first time he seemed eager, almost cheerful. "I know. I will help you, Edith, by writing out a to-do list for Millie."

He reached for the ledger. Edith stopped him. "No, no." She laughed. "You will be late for your new job at Rothschild's Emporium. Papa, you promised to review next Sunday's service with the Ladies Auxiliary. Hurry, both of you, to your manly occupations. Leave the household tedium to the women."

The Waterbury clock, as if to make the whole scheme official, tolled eleven times. Chris, noting the late hour, hurried off. The Reverend, thrusting the buttered heel of the bread into the pocket of his waistcoat, did the same. Edith laughed, added a packet of sausage, pecked him on the cheek, and pushed him out the door.

After we swept up the breakfast, Edith showed me how to prepare the dough to bake half-a-dozen loaves, enough bread for the rest of the week until Sunday. It was work, but also fun. Edith was sixteen, old enough to run a household, but still a girlish friend and companion. After we arranged buttered lumps that we set in pressed metal loaf pans on top of the wood stove to rest and rise, Edith said, "Tomorrow, I'll teach how to say How are you? in French. Today you're too tired. Let's go up to my room and find you proper clothes."

Upstairs, I stripped down to my cotton slip. I skipped to and fro to keep warm, while Edith rummaged through a heap of discarded clothing. Altogether the morning had sapped her. With the clothing laid out, she leaned against the pillows.

I pranced around half-naked on tiptoe, trying to amuse her; I put on this and that: a velvet jacket, a stacked-up skirt, a silk hat. With a wicked laugh, Edith offered up a playful name for this charade: "Female Boarding House." At the time, I had no idea what that term meant, or "den of iniquity," or "cat house," or "brothel," all names for the enterprise that was a keystone of the Key City's economy. When I recall her brother's determined effort to keep me from the waterfront, it strikes me as ironic that one of the most corrupt elements of city life was introduced to me by my coy mistress that first day.

The fit of giggles turned to wet hacks, which could not be soothed. I prepared for Edith a hot brew of Oolong tea and honey. Sipping it slowly, she recovered herself enough to ask, in a pleading, teasing way, "Well, are you going to stay here with me, or not?"

"Don't you want me to?"

Impatiently she piped up, "Then, unpack your bag. I want to see your things. But first remove those earrings. For here they're too bright and too different. I'll keep them safe for you."

I shook my head. She shrugged. I spilled out my satchel on top of her lavender quilt. The weird little doll tumbled onto the bed.

"An Indian artifact. Where did you get it?"

"I found it. Rather, it found me."

"Where?"

"On the Dungeness spit. Seventeen people were murdered there."

"Good heavens. How did you ever manage to escape?"

Now it was my turn to smile. She knew more about the city, but I knew more about the wilderness of Dungeness. "The ambush happened twenty years ago. At nighttime, in a storm, they say you can still hear the people screaming."

"Who did it?"

"S'Klallam Indians."

"Oh lord. Are they fierce?"

For an educated girl her ignorance astonished me. During the day, tribes from California to Alaska traded in the marketplace and shops. At night they camped on the beach at Point Wilson. Locally, the S'Klallam outnumbered them all. The esteemed S'Klallam Chief Chetzemoka, who had died quite recently, long before had prevented an Indian uprising to wipe out the white settlers. All this was news to Edith, who listened with perplexity, as if I were speaking in the S'Klallam dialect of L'Kungen.

I replied, "My mother Annie is S'Klallam. She gave me the fish earrings. As far as I know, she's never killed anyone."

"Praise God," Edith exclaimed. Though I meant my statement as a jest. I suddenly began to feel like a weird Indian artifact. Would Edith, now that she had seen my "savage" side, send me away? Actually, Edith made no sign that she was about to reject me. Quite the opposite, if the twinkle in her eye was a telltale sign, then I had improved in value, like an unusual and most-excellent toy.

After a moment's thought, she declared, "As we all know, there are two types of Indians: the good and the bad."

I asked her, "What do you mean?"

"For example, you are good because your skin is fair. Not as fair as mine, of course. I know everything about it, because—" With guilty delight, she declared, "I've read James Fenimore Cooper. Please, don't tell Chris. He's read it more than once himself, and doesn't find it suitable."

Fenimore Cooper's *Last of the Mohicans* did more than any other work to burn diametrically opposed images of "good" and "bad" Indians into the minds of white Americans and Europeans. In 1826, the year the novel was published, Jefferson's decision to remove Eastern Indians west of the Mississippi still excited hot debate. Contrasting stereotypes, of the Noble Savage and the Wildman of the Woods, made Indians appear ill-adapted to life in the industrialized Northeast. In fact, Indians, especially those with land, very often thrived, even if the wealthy ones did tend to give more of their money to kin and community than the average white person. That aside, white liberals and conservatives never tired of debating what to do about Indians degraded by poverty, exploring every solution except the restoration of their acreage. Thus, in the next decade, the forced removal of 16,000, aka the Trail of Tears, was carried out by Presidents Jackson and Van Buren with nearly genocidal results.

I would like to say these exaggerated images did not affect me. The truth is: the moment I stepped onto Union Wharf in Port Townsend, my idea of the world, and my place in it, inverted. Back in Dungeness, my natural pallor indicated ill health, especially when contrasted with Annie's vigor and good looks. Now as I looked down at my own freckled hands, I wondered if heritage would exclude me. If indeed I did prove acceptable, as my father Carl hoped, would this new identity prompt me to renounce half of what had made me?

Meanwhile, Edith, "the good," seemed lost in her own pastoral meanderings. With a faraway look, she said, "How romantic."

"What?"

"You, Millie, you." Enthralled, she went on. "My brother is one year older than me. He wants to be a missionary to the unenlightened. Don't you see? That makes you an ideal partner for him. However, we need to make him believe the idea was his own."

She grasped my wrist. The sudden motion caused the little carved figure on top of her lap to commit suicide over the edge of the bed. It hit the floorboard with a thunk. I knelt to retrieve it. The crone glared at me through the hole in her palm. But, except for a tiny dent on the back of her skull, she looked all right.

"As the earrings are a gift from your mother, I will permit you to keep them." Edith pointed to the trunk at the end of her bed. "But you must stash the doll. Though my brother is a paragon of empathetic understanding, I can only imagine his reaction. No doubt he will call it 'a false idol.' Bury it. If you do as I tell you, soon you will become my grateful little sister."

Good and Bad Indians
c. 1854-1858

In the history of the Washington territory, as elsewhere, the newcomers' lust for land led to minor violence between the new white immigrants and indigenous land-dwellers. As more incidents occurred, testy government officials called on the settlers to "take down their rifles." Despite the rising tensions, white farmers, manufacturers, and merchants still relied on Indians for food, transportation, and labor. Therefore, in this new "call to arms," it became expedient for white settlers to distinguish "good Indians" from "bad ones."

Locally, this attitude is best exemplified by the white response to two famous Indian leaders: Chetzemoka, a S'Klallam, and Leschi, of the Nisqually.

Chetzemoka: A Good Indian

In 1854 the first settlers of Port Townsend arrived to find the site of their future town occupied by the S'Klallam. The tribal leader was Lach-Ka-nam, who became known to whites as Lord Nelson. Wary, the old chief abdicated in favor of his son, S'Hai-ak, or King George. Soon after, S'Hai-ak drowned. His brother Chetzemoka, aka the Duke of York, succeeded him.

To assess the impact of whites, Chetzemoka journeyed to San Francisco in the brig *Franklin Adams*. There he met James Swan, back from the gold rush, with nothing to show for it except his pocket lint. Swan offered to take the S'Klallam leader around. In return, Chetzemoka invited Swan to be his guest in Port Townsend. This exchange of hospitality altered both of their lives.

In San Francisco, Chetzemoka concluded that the whites—with their superior numbers, technology, and government troops—could not be vanquished by the coastal tribes, diminished by disease. Like Chief Seattle of the Suquamish, Chetzemoka cautioned his people not to resist, but instead to accommodate the newcomers. As if to demonstrate the point, after he returned from the Gold Rush city, Chetzemoka favored

Western attire: a navy suit with red stripes ripping down the sleeves and trousers, topped off by a sailor's cap.

When territorial governor Isaac Ingalls Stevens proposed a series of local treaties, he declared Chetzemoka the chief representative of the S'Klallam and the Chimicum. Negotiations took place on a sandy point north of Port Gamble called Haud-Skus. The 1841 Wilkes expedition renamed this arrowhead of land on the northeast extreme of the Kitsap Peninsula "Point No Point." It was a fit name for the coercive agreement which over time made little attempt to compensate tribes for their stolen property. Chetzemoka detected little benefit in the treaty, but believed that any attempt to resist it would only accelerate the demise of his people. For this reason, he did his best to persuade the leaders of the other tribes from the Olympic and Kitsap Peninsulas to sign it.

Skokomish Chief Hool-hole-us was not persuaded. "I don't want to sign over my right to the land. All the Indians have been afraid to talk . . . It makes me sick . . ."

For Chetzemoka, who had witnessed the future in San Francisco, the S'Klallam must cooperate in order to survive. Not only did he sign the Treaty of 1855, he argued for other tribes to do the same. He said, "Before the whites came we were always poor. Since then we have earned money and got blankets and clothing." He added, "I hope the Governor will tell the whites not to abuse Indians as they are in the habit of doing, ordering them to go away and knocking them down . . ."

According to one account, Chetzemoka "saved the day" with his well-timed words. White historians have lauded his role in the Treaty negotiations.

In fact, Governor Stevens never doubted that the Indians would comply. Really, they had no other choice. In the 1855 Point No Point Treaty, the signatory tribes were offered $60,000 in exchange for 438,430 acres of land, paid out over the next twenty years. The Natives of Puget Sound were also guaranteed schooling and medical services, and the right to fish in their "usual and accustomed places." The majority of these promises were never fulfilled. As a result of the document signed at Point No Point, the S'Klallam and half-a-dozen other tribes were reassigned to a reservation representing less than one percent of their original territory, located southeast of Port Townsend at the mouth of the Skokomish River.

Governor Stevens' son and biographer, Hazard Stevens, called the treaty negotiations of 1855 one of his father's proudest achievements. Yet his account shows the negotiations occurred at a time when the tribes were weakened by illness, overwhelmed by the weapons technology of the whites, and divided. Hazard Stevens wrote: "The success and rapidity with which he carried through these treaties were due to the careful and thorough manner in which he planned them, and prepared the minds of the Indians . . . Besides, the Indians realized their own feebleness and uncertain future . . . when they understood the wise and beneficent policy and liberal terms offered by the governor, they gladly accepted them . . ."

Chetzemoka's wife, See-Hem-Itza, an eyewitness of the treaty, offered up a different point of view. When was asked what compensation she received, she replied, "About three yards of calico, some beans, some molasses, but no money."

Soon after the 1855 Treaty council, outraged local Natives made a plan to rout the whites. Chetzemoka, once again, stepped in. He convinced the rebels to put up their arms, and then climbed a hilltop above the city to signal to the whites that they could stand down. For his support of the treaty, and his intervention after, Chetzemoka was called "the proven friend of the Whiteman."

According to the white view, Chetzemoka qualified as "a good Indian." The record recalls Chetzemoka as an astute leader dedicated to the survival of his people.

A Bad Indian: Leschi

In the treaty negotiations of the mid-1850s, and the period of tension that followed, whites hoped that "the good Indians" would exert their influence over "the bad," but many feared the reverse. In the autumn of the year of 1855, rumors spread of a Native insurgency against the broken promises, displacement, and starvation brought about by the treaties. Settlers, dramatically outnumbered, worried that Indian leaders would call upon their tribes to rise up against local whites and the territorial government in Olympia.

The captain of *The Decatur*, a government ship docked in Seattle, warned his white friends that "every tribe is more or less connected, that is, every tribe has friends or relations in the adjoining ones, and the bad Indians are trying to corrupt the good ones." He said that the Nisqually, southwest of the Hood Canal, had allied with other hostile tribes to resist the expansion of white settlement. The leader of this rebellion:

Chief Leschi, an Indian so "bad" he would have to be executed as an example to others.

Ironically, not long before, Leschi had been considered one of the good ones. Due to his wealth—he owned more than one hundred horses—his height, and his calm demeanor, people looked up to him. For this reason, Governor Stevens appointed Leschi and his brother Quiemuth to represent the Nisqually in the treaty council in the winter of 1854. No one knows if Leschi signed the treaty or if, as one witness alleged, his "X" was a forgery. At the treaty council, Leschi rejected the proposed reservation, two square miles on top of a rocky hillside. With no direct access to the Nisqually River, the tribe would starve. Leschi went to Olympia to file a formal protest.

In mid-October of 1855, with tensions on the rise, some members of the Yakima tribe killed an Indian agent. As a precaution, then-acting Governor Charles Mason ordered Chief Leschi and his brother Quiemuth into "protective custody." The two men vanished. When officials came to arrest them, all that remained was their plow, set up in the field where a moment before they had been seeding their crop. Chief Leschi organized a rebel band of about three hundred men. However, he soon realized his attacks on the local militias would delay but not prevent the expansion of white settlement in Nisqually territory. He pursued peace talks; his overtures were rebuffed. Eventually, Leschi was charged with the murder of a volunteer militiaman, Colonel Abram Benton Moses, and arrested.

His brother Quiemuth was also apprehended. While in custody, Quiemuth was killed.

The case against Leschi relied on the testimony of a single witness. Leschi denied killing Colonel Moses; however, he did admit to engaging in acts of war against the territorial government. Leschi testified, through an interpreter. "I went to war because I believed that the Indian had been wronged by the white men, and I did everything in my power to beat the Boston soldiers, but, for lack of numbers, supplies and ammunition, I have failed. I deny that I had any part in the killing . . . As God sees me, this is the truth."

At Leschi's first trial, the jurors considered any violence by Leschi as an act of war. The verdict split. In the second trial, Leschi faced a simple charge of murder. This time, he was found guilty. On February 19, 1858, Leschi was hanged at Fort Steilacoom.

If the jurors' decision intended to demonstrate the American justice system to Natives, it failed. While the majority of white settlers opposed a pardon for Leschi, many prominent citizens, for example, the well-known pioneer Ezra Meeker, were belligerent in their attempts to stop the execution. The arresting sheriff put himself in jail to delay the execution of the Nisqually leader, in his opinion, an innocent man. The controversy around Leschi's death sentence undermined the idea that the white system of justice had delivered an indisputably fair verdict. Indeed, many Indians said they had no idea why Chief Leschi was even arrested. According to the Indian system of justice, even if Leschi had killed Moses, the murder of the volunteer militiaman had been repaid by the murder of Leschi's brother Quiemuth.

Some claimed that Leschi never really died. Others said that he was killed, but came back to life. A Nisqually warrior named Wahoolit, Leschi's grand-nephew, explained:

Just before the execution, Leschi told Wahoolit, "As soon as they hang me, loosen the rope from my neck and put me on my horse, and take me home quick. I'm not going to die. My power is going to help me."

So that is what they did.

After Leschi was killed, the Nisqually set him up on his horse, and drove the beast home. When they took that rope off, Leschi came to, gasping for breath. That's when Leschi sang his spirit song. His people helped him sing. Leschi had come back to life.

Afterward, some of his people became afraid that the unconquerable Leschi would encourage a new rebellion against the US Army. This time, they would all be killed. Afraid, the spirit doctors conspired to deprive Leschi of his "big power." In doing so, they ended his life, once and for all.

28
Swan Returns
c. 1890

Springtime on the Olympic Peninsula gusts like winter. At least once a day, the windows are shrouded from the outside by sheets of rain. When the clouds part and the sun breaks, the sudden heat pops the poppies and glazes the salmonberry. I, Millie Langlie, a housemaid, rarely had time to experience the healing, harmonizing care of the sun.

I went to church and market, through the drizzle the parted ferns, doubling in width and breadth overnight, unfurling in the morning. In Dungeness the shifting of the seasons inspired a calm feeling of pleasant anticipation. In the wilderness, the seasons blended. Here, in the city, the seasonal change, although pleasant, felt more jarring, like the curtain rising on the next act in an unknown drama; I wasn't sure what to expect or even what to feel.

During the day Edith trained me in the household arts, and in French literature and art. At night, Chris tutored me in history, the physical sciences, and math. Of these, history interested me the most.

Like all history lessons, Christopher's were biased. Blatantly so. As we studied the "unfolding drama of the American experiment," Chris insisted, those who occupied the land before the explorers arrived had no alternative but to assimilate. Land-owning Natives ought to settle down and till the land. Perhaps one day they would even be granted citizenship. Those who resisted would die.

"What if—?"

"What if—nothing. History is a river to the sea."

I asked him, "To me, it's more like a spreading estuary. If we could open up our minds."

"Wrong," Christopher interrupted. "Once you have been properly schooled, you will see that I am right. Progress is progress. No one can stop it and nothing can alter it."

Over time I learned to question Christopher's ideas. He maintained an unshakable faith in the Trinity: money, power, and war. I argued for the capacity of everyday people, with their everyday stories, to revise our understanding of the past and remake the future. Rejecting his theories helped me to clarify my own. For this, I owe him a debt.

His math lessons, due to no fault of his, made less of an impression. One evening in spring, as I labored over a simple geometric proof, Christopher happened to remark to Edith, who was mending his stockings, "Who do you think came into Rothschild's? Lieutenant Smyth, that ne'er-do-well. The one that nearly tossed me in a jail cell when I was just a child of seven."

I looked up from my slate.

Edith remarked, "After so many years, I'm surprised that you recognized him, the rogue."

"Though he's no longer an officer, he was still wearing his uniform. I wonder, is that permitted? The dirty fellow looked as if he hadn't washed or slept for three days. Longer than his cheap bottle will last."

This chapter from Chris' boyhood had more to offer me than the equal acute angles of a triangle. "You nearly went to jail? What happened?"

Seya used to say: the storyteller owns the story. Each detail in the story is like a jigsaw puzzle piece stamped out of his or her soul. I fully expected my tutor, who took his role far too seriously, would refuse to share his. To my surprise, he folded his arms, gazed at me, unfixed the phlegm in his throat, and began. I think he was even smiling a little.

Imagine: a hot day in summer. Chris, and his schoolmate, Mack, two years older, came upon a washed-up dory. The craft had seen better days. Next to it, buried in the sand, a damp, shiny sack. Inside, a small round tin. Together, they pried open the lid and found a tar-like substance. Just the right stuff for sealing up a leak in a boat.

At that moment a petty officer appeared.

Smyth, and three soldiers, had been sent out that day to put down a pack of wild dogs, a few of them diseased. While his men took on the snarling pack, Smyth wandered down the beach to investigate the truants.

When Lieutenant Smyth happened along, the two boys were busy working the goo into the gaps. He seized the tin, unfolded the blade of his pocketknife, and dipped it in. Smyth pondered, and then demanded, "Does this belong to you? If so, you had better produce a stamped receipt from the customs house, or it's my duty to arrest you."

The baffled boys shook their heads.

"This time, I choose to believe you. Next time, I won't. So take heed and mend your ways." He pocketed the tin. "You can keep the skiff."

The officer hurried off. How could he know that the contraband he had remanded would lead to his unraveling?

Chris concluded, "I could never understand why he traded a jar of glue for a boat. It took me a whole year to figure it out."

Opium! The local market for the Chinese import was too lucrative for the drug to be outlawed; instead, it was heavily taxed. Those who failed to pay the bill of lading could end up in jail. If they were lucky, corrupt officials would seize their precious cargo. That afternoon, as Christopher relived an adventure of his boyhood, I began to feel a very real affection.

I had now served the Mathieson family for nearly six months. On that first day I accepted Edith as my sister; I believe she felt the same toward me. The Reverend, though not always sensitive to the demands of our daily existence, was nevertheless a genial gentleman, and likeable. His son Christopher, less so.

It's true, he fretted over Edith and the household finances. He dedicated generous amounts of time to my education. Yet, his arrogant manner, combined with his relentless anxiety and lack of humor, put me off. Besides, though his manner was always correct, he seemed to derive a certain satisfaction from needling me. Edith nurtured the hope that one day I might learn to love him. For now, I aimed to feel something more positive than an active dislike.

Shortly after, Chris noticed me by the fireside, sketching a plan for a proper English garden, like those I was studying with Edith. It was just an idea; our yard was small and we didn't have the means. He stole up behind me. Teasingly, he snatched the pencil right out of my hand. When I reached for it, his fist disappeared behind his waistcoat. Though I was a bit miffed, I tried not to show it. An overreaction would have pleased him.

A few minutes later, bored with his jest, he gave me back my pencil.

His tone turned serious. He took a long look at the overworked page of my notebook. On it, out of my imagination, a drawing of a fountain with a female nude entwined in a flowing veil that covered her exactly where it should, two cupids at her feet blowing on shells, to the entertainment of two gold carp frolicking in the suds. Frivolity. (Little did either of us know this idle sketch was a future premonition of the Haller Fountain, a Port Townsend landmark.) Blushing, Chris reminded me that the hour had arrived for me to prepare our evening meal. No doubt, I had sufficient chores to fill up the time to overflowing.

Chris, recalling this fact, admonished, "Too much studying can be unhealthy for a girl."

After six months in Port Townsend, Christopher had no reason to fear I'd destroy myself with too much education. In the well-ordered house of the Reverend, I was perpetually exhausted. Each night I went to bed with Edith but awakened hours before her to light the stove, empty the chamber pots, and prepare porridge from the cast iron kettle for the two men before they set off. The rest of my day, until nighttime, I labored.

My goal was to spare Edith so that she might recover her health. Though she improved, her progress came in fits and starts. Even when her blue eyes brightened, and her lips and cheeks blushed pink, the shattering cough never quite left her.

The following autumn, a little less than a year after I had entered the household, Swan called. Since that first night in the city I had glimpsed him once or twice. His scholarly work kept him occupied. In addition to other enterprises, Swan had been busy negotiating with the Smithsonian for a major display of Northwest artifacts at the Chicago World's Fair, still two to three years away. He was also working hard to attract new support for an old idea, Port Townsend as the proposed terminus of the cross-continental railroad. Also, he still believed that Port Angeles could revive the whaling industry. With all of this, in addition to his posts as judge and Hawaiian Consul to the United States in Port Townsend, it had been some time since he had stopped by. He said he was sorry; he hoped that I would forgive him.

Instead of a reply, I curtsied.

Swan, who had been acquainted with me for all of my life, seemed astonished at the change in me, though not pleased. Without one word to anyone, I served a hearty meal and cleared away the dishes, with a neat little bow every now and again. I was proud to exhibit my self-improvement. Little did I know how foolish I must have appeared.

After supper Swan and the Reverend retired to the dining room. The gentlemen reclined in facing armchairs mixing up the smoke from their cigars. Edith, a parakeet, perched on a tiny three-legged stool. Chris warmed his long legs by the fire. I re-entered with a tray of shortbread stars with marmalade. I was about to withdraw when Swan stopped me. He offered me his own chair. I declined, so he stood up.

Tapping his cane, back to the hot fire, he addressed me thus: "You have not asked about your home in Dungeness. I'm sad to say we've had a rough time. I waited to come until I had good news.

"After you left, Annie disappeared. Carl tried to find her, but his efforts failed. What's more, he had Charley and Julia to look after. Jake Cook offered to find out. He learned that a family of Northern Indians had camped overnight halfway to the point. Apparently, Annie paid the paddlers three dollars to carry her to Cormorant Island on Alert Bay up in Canada. She wanted her unborn baby to receive his Indian name in the Winter Ceremony."

This was the first I'd heard of my mother's disappearance, as well as her fourth pregnancy, yet all I could blurt, "That's illegal!"

"The practice has been discouraged by the Canadian government. Still, there are tribes who refuse to give in."

My mind raced to multiple places simultaneously. If I traveled north, might I discover my spirit power? I could not ask, not in front of the Mathiesons. Fearful for my mother, I stored the information for later.

Swan went on. "As soon as he heard this news, Carl told Jake to go after her. George, too. At the last moment, Miss Bright added herself to the search party. She argued a woman would know what to say to convince the distraught mother to come home, though Miss Bright is not an Indian, a wife, or a mother. As soon as they landed on Cormorant Island, the three were directed to a cedar-plank house, which they entered through a round opening, the giant eye of a whale. Inside, Annie greeted them. They dined on cubes of toasted halibut dipped in fish oil. When they had finished and washed their hands, Annie said, 'I'm ready to go now.' And that was that."

"So, the incident concludes happily and without cost to anyone."

"Not quite. Miss Bright was fired. Really, she brought it on herself. Jake tried to warn her. Of course," Swan grinned, "once she's made up her mind, nothing can stop Delia Bright, from paddling a canoe, peeling the shell off the back of a live crab, or sniping at a wildcat with her rifle."

"Is she sorry?"

Swan replied, "I doubt it. Whatever she was looking for in Dungeness, I hope she found it. Now she's off to sketch in Paris, skirt bulls in Pamplona, purchase cloth and art in a marketplace in Morocco, and navigate the Nile. After that, who knows? She's quite a remarkable woman."

I drew in a quick breath. "And the new baby?"

"In English, he's called James, after me. In the S'Klallam dialect, Ste-tee-thlum, after a legendary chief. Since her return, Annie seems peaceful. More willing to compromise. Less restless. Almost happy."

I had one final question, but I was afraid to ask. For months, I had been waiting for my father to visit me, or at least send word. Why did he choose to stay away? With so many tumbling offspring to care for, perhaps Carl had no time or energy for me. Or perhaps he felt that any contact would create pain for both of us.

I ventured, "And Carl?"

"He's an old man, like me, and easily distracted. The harder he works, the smaller his catch of fish." He chuckled. "And you, Millie? How is school? Top of the heap, or under-water?"

The Reverend fiddled with the brass key to the Waterbury clock. He was about to reply, when Christopher blurted, "Millie doesn't go to school. I tutor her, right here in this parlor. Edith has taught her how to keep house. See how she has improved."

"Yes, I see."

Swan's ironic tone could not be missed.

I dropped a second curtsey and rushed to tell him of my improvements.

"Judge Swan, look at me. I can keep the house free of dust, maintain the oil lamps and hearth, rub down the woodwork till it gleams, remove smudges and prints from nineteen windows—that's over a hundred panes—and untold mirrors, and fix a decent meal in under an hour. When the Waterbury strikes four times, tea is on the sideboard. How the herbs in my kitchen garden thrive. Edith revealed to me the beliefs and the habits of a pastry pin, yet my crust is flakier. The linen that I unfurl is brighter. Every Sunday I go to church to listen to the Reverend's sermon. So far I am not converted but perhaps one day the spirit of Christ will enter me. Why do you frown?"

"Millie, tell me the truth. Are you happy here?"

I turned to Edith. She remained silent. The question was for me, and me alone. Defiantly I declared, "I think so. Yes."

Swan did not seem persuaded.

To the Reverend he said, "I will report back to Carl. Meanwhile, she can remain, with one condition. Once a week you lend her to me to sort the collection. I'm hoping that the task will revive her curious mind."

The Reverend, relieved, chirped, "Of course. I agree to everything."

Christopher interjected, "Father, take a minute to think it through. Edith is still not well. What if she takes a turn for the worse?" He glanced quickly at the Judge. "Consider Millie's reputation. Who will escort her? And, how will it look, hour upon hour alone with him in his quarters?"

Swan chuckled as he twirled his cigar. "You ninny. She'll visit me in my office, not in my boudoir. Gad. What are you thinking? I could be her grandfather."

Christopher remarked, "I've heard that one before. About Dolly Roberts."

The Reverend startled, spilling his port, exclaimed, "Christopher! That will be enough," in sharp rebuke.

Later, Edith explained. Amelia Roberts, fondly known as Dolly, was the daughter of the founding pioneer FW Pettygrove. Several years earlier, when Dolly was a cheerful, spry girl of sixteen, Swan at fifty-seven had courted her assiduously. Dolly rejected Swan to marry his old friend, a gentleman of some means. Though all this had transpired long ago, it was cruel of Christopher to mention it now.

"You arrogant seal pup," Swan said seething.

He was like a teakettle left on the top of a stove to cool; he whistled long and low. No doubt it crossed his mind to depart for the last time, slamming the door. Despite the affront, out of loyalty to the Reverend and his deceased wife Adele, no offense could provoke him to reject the son or daughter—or me, though what had forged this iron link, I never thought to ask.

Calmer now, Swan inquired, "Son, do you remember how Dolly and Adele formed the whole of the church choir? Those Sunday sessions were a delight during my most desperate hour; when I'd recall my son and daughter back in Boston. When a parent and child go their separate ways, that gaping hole is hard to fill."

He frowned, and then went on, speaking directly, and pointedly, to Christopher. "Often those who mature too fast are hard on themselves, and hard on others. Allow yourself to be a child, for a bit longer. I haven't quit; though, as you mentioned before, I'm too old to dally with girls."

Christopher turned away, not in anger, but to smear away a tear. Though he deserved the chiding, I could not help but pity him.

In the days after the Judge's reprimand—or perhaps because of it—Christopher changed for the better. He became less critical and began to act more spontaneous and open.

I began to feel something very like affection for my adopted brother.

Cha-tic, The Painter
c. 1818-1900

When he was five, James Gilchrist Swan's sea captain father disappeared at sea. He was raised in Medford, Massachusetts by his mother Mary Tufts Swan. Despite the loss of his father, he thrilled at the tales of his uncle, William Tufts, a world traveler, who, in the first decade of the new century, shipped to the Pacific Northwest coast.

When he came of age, Swan became a businessman and married to please his mother. However, the California gold rush gave him the chance to escape the society of the proper New England parlor, a life that never felt quite real. Swan invested in a ship, and said goodbye to his wife Mathilda, his son Charles, seven, and Ellen, his daughter, just four.

After a short-lived, half-hearted attempt to find gold, Swan became an "oyster entrepreneur" at Shoalwater Bay. This enterprise, as in every subsequent half-cocked business venture—a whaling station, the Port Townsend railway, a new type of factory that made paper out of seaweed—turned into nothing. Each new venture, no more profitable than the last, gave him one more excuse to stay on.

Yet he was educated, articulate, curious, and affable. Such that in the last half-century of his life, Swan served as an Indian agent, a justice of the peace, and as a member of the Hawaiian consul.

In the end his greatest legacy would be the forty-one years he passed inside his notebooks. The journals—in tan, maroon, or black leather, one with a marbled cover, small enough to fit inside a jacket pocket, to balance on his open palm—capture the real James Swan. As a scientist, a stickler for accuracy; always counting, classifying, and measuring. Not just an observer, he was keen to sample new things: for example, tea made from the bark of a young hemlock, a salve made from bear fat and spruce gum, or an eyewash made from salal, all "excellent," according to the explorer. Above all, his journal reveals him as a sensitive appreciator of this rugged, yet oddly agreeable, altered reality.

In his sketchbook, Swan documents a world and a way of life. In the early days he sketched flora and labeled each specimen with the Indian name, for example, the delicate white flower known to the Makah as tsit-sit-tsao-up-quimp, as well as with the English name, trillium. A little later, he captured the facades in a Makah village as well as the interior of a S'Klallam longhouse. Swan drew tools—a halibut hook, a chisel with a handle carved from a whale rib—and other everyday objects, for example a shallow dipping dish or a basket for steaming clams. As his artistic ability developed he became more and more fascinated by the various pictorial styles of the tribes, as well as the nuance of individual craftsmen. With the same precision he applied to the botanical sketches Swan preserved the art styles of the indigenous. The Makah called him cha-tic, "the painter."

An astute ethnographer, in all of his work Swan eschewed stereotypes that failed to note the diversity of the Native peoples. Nevertheless, he felt compelled to address the prejudices of white readers. For example, he refutes the view expressed by frustrated missionaries, that West Coast Indians were immune to religious thinking. In The Northwest Coast Swan asserted: most Indians, when interrogated by whites, refuse to discuss their beliefs. The relationship between an individual and his spirit guardian is complexly personal, and not easily put into words. However, anyone who bothers to look and listen will discover in daily practice a deeply-rooted spirituality. To Swan, the Makah openly shared the details of their daily lives: how to prepare whale meat, or make red paint from saliva and salmon roe; as well as more weighty matters: courtship rituals and burial ceremonies, and even their most sacred precepts.

Swan also acknowledged the increasing pressures of white settlement. Like the majority of whites at that time, he believed that the Indians of the Northwest coast must assimilate or die. To the Smithsonian's Spencer Baird, who published *The Indians of Cape Flattery* and later paid for his expeditions to Alaska and the Queen Charlotte Islands, Swan wrote, "The time is not distant when these tribes will pass away, and future generations who may feel an interest in the history of these people will wonder why we have been so negligent." Swan made it his mission to document a world in flux, so that the know-how and wisdom would endure.

His Makah friends believed that by writing these things down, Swan was dabbling in a dark sorcery that could only do them harm. Maybe they were right. While his journals did explain the customs of the Makah and other Natives of the Pacific Northwest, his work did little to mitigate the threat to their land and their lives, and may have even encouraged white settlement of the Pacific Northwest.

All said and done, I cannot help but admire the unusual determination of this nineteenth-century journal writer to explore without prejudice a distinct, and often opposing, worldview.

From the Journal of James G. Swan.

Tamanowas of the S'Klallam Indians returning on canoe to Port Townsend beach, May 1, 1859. *Image courtesy of the Franz R. and Kathryn M. Stenzel collection of western American art, Yale Collection of Western Americana, Beineke Rare Book and Manuscript Library.*

Photograph of James G. Swan and Johnny Kit Elswha, 1890. American Indians of the Pacific Northwest Images. *Photo courtesy of the University of Washington. Special Collections Division.*

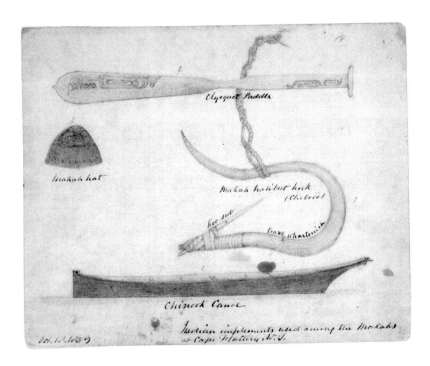

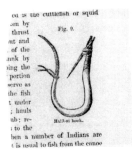

Indian implements used among the Makah at Cape Flattery. October 18, 1859. *Image courtesy of the Franz R. and Kathryn M. Stenzel Collection of Western American Art. Yale Collection of Western Americana, Beinecke Rare Book and Manuscript Library.*

Interior of a Makah Lodge, Neah Bay 1859. *Image courtesy of the Franz R. and Kathryn M. Stenzel Collection of Western American Art. Yale Collection of Western Americana, Beinecke Rare Book and Manuscript Library.*

29
What is Happiness?
c. 1890

The old post office, now Swan's two-story, white-clapboard house on Adams Street, with its office on the first floor, answered all of his needs both public and private. To the left of the entry, a totem, thirty feet high, capped off with a seabird, a type of gull. *Larus occidentalis* served as a fit symbol for Swan in those days, who, after a lifetime of exploration had become more or less contented to survey life from on high while preening his wings.

Once a week, on the appointed day, as I entered his lair, Swan, with one eyebrow cocked to greet me, leaned back in his swiveling captain's chair. The eccentric explorer, now past seventy, had not lost his vivacious curiosity.

The office spilled over with so much treasure, both natural and handcrafted, a visitor found it hard to sit down. Stacked up on shelves, on top of tall cabinets, climbing the walls, Swan's sacred objects: inky sketches of a dogfish, a whale, and a thunderbird; carved masks; a small bow with an areola of arrows; a twisted cedar headdress. Hanging on the wall at eye level behind his big desk: a polished pair of mountain goat horns. On top of his desk: toothy seashells in a line; a sculpted figure, part man and part frog; a ten-inch welcome pole fashioned out of argillite from the Slatechuck Quarry on Graham Island in the Queen Charlottes. Draped over the back of his chair, a Tlingit Chilkat blanket skillfully created with a distinct design on either side.

The cluttered office was scarcely large enough for two, let alone three. Swan's professional quarters proved even more awkward on the days when his other assistant, Johnny Kit Elswa, turned up. Elswa, a Native Haida tribesman, rented a room in Port Townsend, was a painter and jeweler. He was also one of the first Native artists to transfer the bold, mythic creatures that appear on totems, hats, and carved boxes to paper and canvas in red and black ink, thus helping to establish the region's characteristic art style.

About six years previously, Johnny Kit Elswa accompanied Swan on a collecting mission in the remote Queen Charlotte Islands. At the age of sixty-five, Swan, with his guide, embarked upon his most ambitious and risky expedition. To persuade Spencer Baird from the Smithsonian to finance the trip, Swan wrote, "I know the importance of making these collections—and writing the Indian memoirs now, while we are among them and can get reliable facts—The time is not distant, when these tribes will pass away."

Baird hired Swan, who hired Kit Elswa.

Fifty years before the journey, in the weather-torn archipelago known to locals as Haida Gwaii, a population of six thousand had been reduced by illness to fewer than a thousand. Swan described the township of Masset as "sixty-five houses old and new nearly all of them with carved column or pillar in front, covered with heraldic devices . . ." He also took notes on the local flora, collected tools and art, and netted a specimen or two for the U.S. Fish Commission, which he kept alive in a copper tank. Finally, after a series of mishaps Swan met Chief Edinso, still energetic at seventy. The chief introduced Swan to his nephew Charley, a carver.

Swan, the enraptured collector, was captivated with Edinso's nephew's work. "Two beautiful canes nearly finished, each representing a serpent twined around the stick which was a crab apple sapling—on top of one was a clenched fist. He asks $10 each."

I picked up Swan's walking stick. "What a marvel."

That afternoon, as I took notes for the catalogue, on the other side of the desk Kit labeled a series of sketches, first in English, then in Haida, thus: Raven (Hooyeh); Whale (Koone); Cirrus Clouds (Tekul). With his tweed jacket specially tailored for his broad shoulders and barrel chest, his deep-set eyes, and wide scowling smile, Kit overwhelmed me, just a bit. He looked up from the portfolio and nodded. "It's the work of Edinso, nephew of the old Haida chief. Collectors call him Edenshaw."

He rummaged through a cigar box until he found an etched silver bracelet. "Here's one by Edinso. Note the split thunderbird design, with the two curved beaks nodding off in opposite directions. Two sets of round eyes gaze into the future and the past at the same time. Simple yet profound. The genius of Edinso."

He held it out to me. "Put it on."

He fastened the bracelet around my wrist. Was it the artistic design, or the brush of his fingers, that murdered my heart with a lightning bolt?

Stunned, I removed the bracelet.

Kit wrapped it in a square of flannel and replaced it in its cigar box.

Over time Johnny Kit Elswa introduced me to the work of two-dozen Native artists. He showed me how each tribe or band had developed its own style, distinct and bold. He patiently explained how the various designs communicated a fundamental belief, practice, or myth. His black hair and eyes, his fiery spark and dry humor, made me think of George.

Each day I spent in the office I tried my hardest to impress him with a quick mind. Yet I knew nothing. To Kit Elswa I remained a ridiculous girl, less than half his age, who kept asking the same nervous questions.

One afternoon, right after he summarily dispatched Kit on an errand, Swan inquired, "Millie, is something the matter? Either you talk too loud, or say not a word. You overfill the teacup, then set it aside until it grows cold. You stare at me in an intense, searching manner, simultaneously ignoring everything I say. It's irritating as hell. Tell me, what's the matter? Or should I just beat you about the head with my walking stick?"

"The matter? Nothing. Except—well—it's that I'm just so happy to be alive."

"Don't be a ninny."

Truly, I wanted to tell him. But how could I confess my passion for the Haida artist without humiliating myself more? In a scholarly tone I inquired, "Judge Swan, can an Indian and a white marry?"

"Hmm." He gave me a long look. "A theoretical inquiry, I suppose. Let's see. The government used to support the practice. Now they discourage it. If one can find a Justice of the Peace, or a priest to do the deed, well, why not?"

"What I mean is, will they be happy?"

"Define happiness."

"Safety. Permanence. Something to rely on."

"Ha." Swan was in one of his dazzled melancholy moods. "No place is safe. Nothing is permanent. I left my wife in New England. Many years later, she died. I still miss her. My black-haired boy, and my girl, a towhead. Yet I tossed it all away. Why? To see the northern lights shimmer on top of the ocean. To feel the grit of a live oyster between my teeth. To aim a rotten apple at the butt-end of a rampaging she-bear. To pass the night arm-in-arm with a tree in a killing rain. Why did I abandon a life that was permanent, safe? I had my reasons, which I can no longer remember. Still, I don't regret it."

He went on. "What about Carl and Annie? To me, the two best people in the world. Do they fit? Are they unfit? To love themselves, and love one another, in this plaguey lifetime? How should I know? Why should anyone listen to me?"

For a man of no opinions, he had an endless amount to say. "Notice my exceptional assistant Johnny Kit Elswa. Never mind, you already have. Johnny reminds me of a man, a Makah named Jimmy Swell. Without the friendships of these two men, I would not exist. Permanence and safety? If I had stayed in Boston I might have achieved contentment. But happiness? Never."

"Who is Jimmy Swell? I've never heard you talk about him."

Swan dropped a cube of sugar into his cup of black tea. "He was from Neah Bay, the place they call the Beginning of the World. In Qwiqwidicciat, the Makah tongue, he was called Wha-laltl Asabuy. The most talented fellow I have ever met, he could fight, farm, hunt, navigate by the stars, and pluck a whale. His greatest gift: memory. If he had lived, he would have become one of the great men of our time.

"Our friendship was an honor. I wanted to express my gratitude. In a tablet of red clay I carved the words 'Ha hake to ak,' which in Makah translates to the creature who illuminates the earth and the ocean with his lightning. The esteem I felt for Jimmy Swell inspired a masterpiece, however, I never got the chance to give it to him. Just two days after I completed it the S'Klallam murdered Swell. Six months later, eighty painted Makah warriors in twelve canoes landed on the beach where Swell had been killed and decapitated two hapless S'Klallam who were out hunting seals. I suppose, justice was served."

"Do you really believe that?"

"Certainly I do. However, as I said before, it doesn't matter what I believe."

I tugged on a silver fish flashing on my earlobe. "What about the killing spree on the Dungeness spit? After several months of hard labor, the culprits went home. Were they punished too harshly, or not enough? Was justice served?"

Swan shrugged. "The S'Klallam paid up. The Tsimshian accepted the blood money. Justice? It depends on your point of view."

He sighed. "One thing I do know. Lame Jack, the instigator, was no Jimmy Swell. His own people referred to Lame Jack as 'Nu-mah,' the Corrupted One. He served the whites and sold his own people. For that the settlers paid him well. The tribes were ill, starving. Warriors watched their wives and children perish. Perhaps those men followed Lame Jack's war cry because they had no one else. Jimmy Swell had been murdered; Leschi, executed by white justice. The so-called chiefs, hereditary leaders with skill, wealth, and honor, were all dead."

Trembling, I cleared away the tea things.

When I returned, Swan had pulled on his greatcoat. Anticipating a dinner invitation, he offered to walk me home. I handed him his walking stick. Of all the magic objects in his collections, this was the one he cherished most.

"Alive or dead, Edinso outranks them all. A Western philosopher once said that two figures can't occupy the same space at the same time. Edinso exposed the shallowness of that idea. In a nutshell, that's his contribution."

So, that was it. The two-dimensional designs and three-dimensional sculptures of Edenshaw and other Coast Salish artists depict humans and animals as they change shape, defying physical barriers.

Suddenly a new idea occurred to me. If two objects can occupy the same space, can one mind grasp two realities? For the first time I realized how Swan had journeyed. This ship chandler who had left proper society to explore the wilderness dwelt in two worlds at once.

Nothing ever came of my childish infatuation with Kit Elswa. Several months later he disappeared, never to be seen again, not by Swan despite his relentless inquiries, or anyone else in Port Townsend. Perhaps he died, or returned to Haida Gwaii.

Once in a while I still think of him.

Katy, Makah Slave Girl
c. 1865

In the winter of 1865, while collecting for The Indians of Cape Flattery, Swan, in his late forties, hired a Makah slave girl named Katy to cook for him and clean his cabin.

When she died from fever, Swan buried her on the beach just above his schoolhouse. Later, when her grave was disturbed, by a dog, or a skunk, Swan covered it with a plank.

In his journal, Swan reported: " . . . as she was a slave I wished to show the Indians that we considered slaves as good as free persons . . ."

Might there be another reason; a bond between the two outside of what his social class and the broader white society condoned?

Friendship?

Love?

30
Alexander's Castle
c. 1890

Heart, we will forget him,
You and I, tonight!
You must forget the warmth he gave,
I will forget the light.

As I maneuvered the dust cloth, Edith reclined on the sitting-room couch, declaiming a stanza, with a sigh so deep I turned around to look at her. The dark circles around her luminescent eyes made them brighter still. On her pale cheeks, two livid spots.

I went to her. "Edith, are you feeling ill?"

She coughed. "What I want to know is, will I live long enough to know what it feels like?"

"What?"

"To love and be loved."

I removed the book from her mealy grip. "The Reverend loves you, and Christopher, and mother up in heaven. I love you, too, even if I am paid to say so." Though I say it ten times more often than I'm actually paid, I refrained from adding.

A volume by Emily Dickinson. Her poetry, and for that matter all Romantic verse, for under-stimulated girls like us was like whetted knives to schoolboys.

Edith flushed.

"And you, Millie, aren't you curious? What it's like to be kissed?"

Two years older than me, she could only assume that I knew even less. Little did she suspect, though she was the beauty, I was the expert. What if she knew about my clandestine encounter with George underneath the eye of the lighthouse? How would she react?

How does one describe it? Like the sun when it blisters your lower lip? Like, sweat on your lids? An itch you can't scratch? Running headlong, you stop short at the precipice, sigh with relief, and then leap into the abyss. Out of the corner of your eye, you glimpse a color that no one has ever seen before. Love. I could talk about it, but not in a way that made sense.

While Edith and I fantasized in verse, the men dreamt of dollars and cents. While Edith and I darned their wool socks, embroidered her trousseau, baked bread, and wondered aloud about love, the Reverend and his son occupied themselves with weightier matters: God and real estate in Port Townsend where land values were rising sharply. Chris engineered a trip—the only outing he ever suggested—to assess the opportunity for speculation along the proposed rail line.

Our versifying in prose was interrupted by a knock on the kitchen door. Without bothering to remove my apron I hastened to open it. Dripping from rain, only partially sheltered by the kitchen porch roof, a tattered boy with muddy hands held out a folded paper. I took it, fished out a nickel from the jar, and sent him away. On the front, penned in a precise hand: Millie.

In two years in Port Townsend, I had not received one letter, and exactly one visitor: Swan. Neither Carl nor Annie had a penchant for letter writing, Swan rationalized. What's more, Carl, on market days, had all he could do to complete the journey and the return in a day. Probably my father believed any contact between us would undermine my opportunity to succeed in Port Townsend.

Then, what was this? Most likely, bad news. My fingers shook as I pried it open. An accident or sickness. Worse?

"Millie, what is it?" Edith called out to me from the parlor.

I replied, "A half dozen eggs. The delivery boy was late. No tip for delinquents. In the future he will know to deliver the order before noon."

I don't know why I lied.

In the dim pantry, darkly aromatic, I squinted at the one-liner:

"At 4 o'clock meet me Alexander's castle."

Unsigned.

There was no need. I knew who it was from; one rub of the paper told me.

An Episcopal cleric, John B. Alexander, erected a castle up on a bluff for his bonnie bride-to-be from the highlands. When Alexander went to fetch his betrothed he discovered that she had married another. Alexander traded his Romantic ideals and his castle for a reliable government post in Tacoma. Ever since, the red-brick tower endured as a monument to thwarted love.

I leaned against the jars of pickled peppers, pondering. My clever playmate never lacked a plan.

His current gambit?

And, what about Edith? Should I tell her? Or lie to her, and shoulder the responsibility for whatever happened next?

A moment later, I was kneeling beside her.

I confessed all. For once, Edith attended to me. For a long while after she looked into the fire. Finally, she said simply, "You must get ready."

"But you're not well, and I may not be back for hours. If Christopher finds out—"

My objections were far from genuine. Perhaps she noticed. Edith tossed down the letter. Her face was pale, her blue eyes bright. "Changeling. I often think of that night when you materialized out of the mist. You were greener than springtime. You needed to be taught how to set the table, shine the silver, and de-grease a linen tablecloth. You were either too innocent—or too rude—to exist. I made it my mission to improve you."

She went on. "Stupid me. From the first moment, it was I who learned from you. Ever since that day, the gap between us has only increased. You've read every book in father's library. By assisting Swan you've learned about people and places that I never knew existed. Once a week when the Judge dines with us, after our meal, rather than clearing away the dishes, you converse with the men. During his last visit, you put up your boot heels, just like a man. When you lit father's cigar, I half-expected you to take a draw."

Edith continued. "When I was a little girl I spent happy hours in the garden. Adele—not for want of trying—could not keep me indoors. Then, she died. It was as if she were testing me. Before she died, I flitted like a fairy, after dull as lead. I stayed in my room.

"Then you came. Suddenly, I recalled, the windswept town beneath my iron balcony is only steps away. I want to open my wings, to receive the sea air; at times to strive against it. But I know I never shall, because each night the fever returns. Each morning I am roused by a killing cough. My life is over. Yours has just begun. Pluck the day. Step outside. Go now."

There were tears in my eyes. "What if—you need me?"

"Don't be a ninny. You'll be back before nightfall."

She added, "Do it for me, Millie."

A fit of coughing stopped her. When she could speak again, she said, "Now, hurry upstairs. Out of my things we'll dress you up, like we did that first day."

We were halfway up the stairs when I stopped and turned round to face her. "What about Chris?"

She replied, "Millie, you are my sister. Nothing you can ever do or say can ever alter that fact. Marry—whomever you want—or don't."

Downstairs, the Waterbury clock struck twice.

With her arm around my shoulder for support, we climbed the stairs together.

Edith, propped on the pillows, acted as my wardrobe consultant. Over a pair of bright bloomers I wore her purple dress. With Edith's toilet set, I combed my hair and fixed it with her tortoise-shell comb. I borrowed her straw hat with the wide brim, too summery for the season. Over my shoulders I flung her mustard-yellow cloak and fastened it with Adele's heirloom broach. I scrambled for the pair of kid gloves she had tossed on top of her dressing table. In my haste, without being aware, I had appropriated all of her favorite things.

Edith drowsed. Now and then, she hacked.

At last, when I found that I was ready to go, I could not. Instead, I went to her. I removed one glove. With my fingertips I smoothed her brow, perspiring yet cold. What if her fever returned?

If I stayed, I might never see George again. It seemed an awful choice: my adopted sister, feverish and real, or a cherished figure from my past? Tenderly, I covered her. Her last words echoed.

"Go," Edith said. "Do it for me."

I went.

Though button blossoms dotted the salt grass, a winter breeze buffeted the bluff. I descended the wooden staircase and headed down to the beach, which served as a pedestrian highway from Port Townsend to Point Wilson. I arrived there in less than five minutes. From there, Alexander's Castle was two miles west, about forty-five or fifty minutes at a brisk pace.

Along the beach wound a line of dugout canoes, as various folk wandered the mudflat with its tide pools and filmy grasses. Higher up, a scattered village of tents propped up on sticks and tied down with ropes. Itinerant Indians, mostly S'Klallam. As I traversed this lively scene, no one took any particular notice of me—a lanky red head in unaccustomed finery, holding up her purple satin skirts as she scrambled over drift logs. Stepping on top of the round rocks, I became hobbled after only two to three steps. I removed my boots and stockings and tied them to my waist. In the sand the hem of Edith's mustard cloak now trailed after me.

I walked on. After a while I noticed an old woman. Behind her the Point Wilson lighthouse, which signaled every thirty seconds. In her fist, a curved canoe paddle, blunted at one end. She wielded it like a walking stick. Strapped to her back, a basket of firewood.

In Port Townsend, at night and in broad daylight, destitute Indians like sad ghosts wandered the streets and beaches, begging for a coin or a crust of bread. On an isolated stretch of beach, the last thing I wanted was to find myself face-to-face with a beggar. But what could I do? There was no way to go around her, and I was not about to turn back.

As the distance fell away, I noticed her cloak made of doggy wool, the bundle of kindling strapped onto her shoulders with a hemp rope. When we were near enough to grasp hand, she peered at me through her wrinkled lids, offering up a gap-toothed grin.

I nodded once, lowered my chin, and pressed on.

All of a sudden I recalled the old adage by Seya: "Never pass by an old woman without offering to carry her bundle." Not so very long ago, one glimpse of the spirited crone might have evoked a homesick tear. After just two years in the city, I hurried by, loathe to greet her, unwilling to even look at her, lest she pick my pocket. How practical, how fearful, how far from home.

A gull scoffed.

I stopped, turned around, and stood there for a full minute. Meanwhile the crone picked her way over the slick rocks. I thought about calling out to her, but what would I say? Shout out a greeting, offer to assist her? That would only startle or frighten her. Besides, I had places to be. By now the spry beggar woman had all but disappeared. With daylight waning and no option that I could see, I trudged on.

Before long I reached the winding trail that climbed the steep cliff to Alexander's castle. I put on my boots and laced them up tight.

At the top the wiry shrubbery opened up onto a field teeming with elk. A male with wide shoulders lifted up his heavy head. He rolled his round eyes. His black nostrils twitched. This bull was so stately I might have passed underneath. After a minute he lowered his muzzle to nibble the salty yellow grass.

Just beyond the herd, a square brick tower lost in English ivy. I noticed that the arched windows of the bridal suite at the very top overlooked the pasture and the stick trees, but with no view of the

Strait. Perhaps John B. Alexander feared that the dismal sky and grey water might inspire his bride to take the plunge. If so, his anxiety was, excuse the pun, ungrounded, because she'd refused to come. Married to the familiar, solid and dependable, she preferred to stay at home. Or perhaps she was like me; someone who had traveled far, but could go no farther.

Underneath the roof of the little side porch, a tiny door esconced in greenery. Recently forced, the door opened easily. The floor plan was modest but with an airy ceilings. In between the kitchen and parlor, a wooden stair, steep as a ladder. I reached the top and paused there to rest.

The chamber door leaped.

George doffed his hat. "Dzunak'wa." Crazy forest creature.

Not the reaction I craved. Like a prim partridge, I strutted, assessing the accoutrements of the empty room. Ludicrously, as there were none; the bridal suite had no furniture, no decoration of any kind. On the north wall, two tall windows and open sky. The floorboards, fir, stroked by the fading sun. The cedar panels on the ceiling were painted milky white.

There was nowhere to look, except at him.

Though tempted, I was afraid. I turned away to face the sunset window. Sick at heart, I asked myself: Why had I come?

After more than two years, would he like me?

Did I care?

Answer: Yes.

Unsure what to do next, I unpinned my hat. To be more precise, Edith's. A straw hat with black ribbon and a pale yellow songbird wired to the brim. Flat as a dinner platter, unwieldy as a breakfast tray, I tried to rest it on the sill. It teetered and fell. My gloved hand reached out. Inside my clenched fist, the little bird's crushed skull.

George looked concerned. And then laughed.

I did not.

Despite his too-familiar manner, it was undeniable that both of us had changed.

George, no longer a boy, or even boyish. He was taller, broader. His lips and cheeks, ruddy. The scar on his chin from a boyhood mishap had faded to the merest trace. In other respects he had not changed. He was still ruggedly handsome and supremely self-confident. In fact, he seemed more intensely determined than ever.

In Edith's attire, I felt a fraud. Why not a plain jumper with a clean apron, or better yet, Chris' old coveralls for splitting wood? I nearly apologized. Almost. My pride would not allow it, and if it did, what would I say?

If I looked fancy, George was even finer. His neckline looked as if it had been traced in white chalk; apparently he had just paid a visit to the Port Townsend barber. He wore a tweed coat with a brown vest on top of dark trousers. A white shirt with a club collar, with a black tie. All this topped off by a brown derby. In a word, George looked smart.

That afternoon I committed a series of missteps, not one of them serious, but taken together, irretrievable. In dreary days and weeks that followed, I could not help but ask: What if? What if Edith had been reading Machiavelli, instead of Romantic verse? What if I had worn my own attire? What if I remained at the side of my mistress? What if I had carried the basket for the crone? Maybe the one act of contribution would have somehow freed me to vibrate to the heartbeat of my old friend.

What if?

Instead, I coldly offered him the fingertips of one glove.

Not mine. Edith's.

For an instant, he cradled my hand inside his palm, like an injured bird. Weighing it. Testing its warmth and its grip.

Then, he dropped it.

And looked away.

Clearly, George was not attracted. That seemed, well, unfair. We were both well-dressed; in fact he was gadded up even more than I. The difference was this: while I appeared every inch the fine young miss in the city, even in his best clothes, George could not pass for a white gentleman. Instead, he looked like a well-tailored Indian. Unlike me, his past became him.

Stiffly, I remarked, "How pleased I am to see you. Tell me, what is your business here in Port Townsend?"

"I'm here to outfit myself for a job. Judge Swan got me a low-level post with the Geological Survey. I'll be toting the heavy equipment until I learn how to use it. We'll map the major and minor tributaries, from Spokane to Missoula."

"How fortunate for you. Where are you off to now?"

"East of the mountains. Tomorrow I'm traveling by oxcart. This waistcoat cost me everything. I have just enough for my transport and a few meals along the way."

Proudly he added, "Water turns the wheel of industry, irrigates crops, and nourishes livestock. Potable water settles whole townships. Those with the legal rights to water will rule the land. I want to be one of those men."

"You're ambitious," I said. I didn't add the words, "for an Indian." I didn't have to. Both of us knew that George would have to surmount the bias against him to achieve his goals. All at once I recalled the tale of the rotting fish, the spirit power that George had rejected. What did George desire most in life? Respect. A chance to use his talents. To defy the odds.

I replied, "I'm sure you will succeed—"

With or without me?

What was George to me? A paid babysitter, as I was to Edith? Friend? Lover? What did he want from me?

What did I want from him?

If he asked me, would I drop everything and go? Toss up my satchel onto the oxcart, and clamber up after it? Cross the mountain passes in a blizzard, to suffer the bitter winds of the Northwest's high-desert plains? His boss, and the other roughnecks who came from all parts, what would they say about George the engineer with his bookish, freckled, redhead wife?

A doomed scheme.

I prayed, a little, and waited for him to ask.

In silence.

More silence.

He did not.

Instead, he observed, "You seem different."

He rubbed his smooth chin and gazed out the window. He made as if to go, and then turned. His calloused thumb scratched my cheek as he reached for the silver fish. "At least you still have these."

"You hate them. I remember you said so, the last time we were together." If I stirred up the past, maybe I could rekindle a connection between us. More likely, after the sun went down behind Protection Island and Mount Olympus, he would disappear forever from my life.

"That night on the spit, I sensed you were holding back—" (the affection I craved. Since I could not say this, I went on.) "—information. What do you know about the silver fish? How did Annie get them? Tell me about the Aia'nl? Who carved it, and how did it end up in my satchel?"

He frowned and then grinned. "That's more like it. The girl I used to know, with so many questions, no one has time for an answer." He glanced at the tinted window panes. "It's getting dark. You should go. Besides, I'm not the one to ask—"

"Jake?"

He nodded and put out his hand. "Goodbye."

The demands of daily life pluck away at the past. Long after the moment becomes ancient history, we discover we have allowed what is most precious to disappear into the sucking sand. As the sun sets, in a flash of lustrous brightness on a window pane, we recall what we have lost. That evening, in the tower, side by side but without touching, gazing out the window of the virgin bridal suite, we watched the gilded edges of the clouds turn black.

Whatever had happened between us was over. George bent over to retrieve Edith's hat, discarded on the floorboards. When I reached out to receive it he took my wrist. He grinned. "You're a stupid kid, but I still admire you, and here's why: you're curious. You don't stop asking until you find out. That's brave."

His hand moved down my wrist. He played with my fingers.

George continued. "Cowardice, or courage? Sometimes it's not so clear. You escaped a ravening bear; I ran away from a talking fish. Not every moment is a great one. Forgive others for what they can't do. You can start off by forgiving yourself."

He didn't kiss me.

It took me years to forgive him for that.

One day, his words would save me.

The Murder Trial of Xwelas
c. 1878

For half a century, liaisons between mature white men and Native girls were run-of-the-mill. In addition to the basic human need for companionship, white settlers partnered with Native women for practical and political reasons. Pioneers relied on local tribes to survive and to do business.

Like their white counterparts, often Native girls had little or no say.

Suddenly, in the second half of the nineteenth century, the landscape changed. Mail-order brides of Europe descent began arriving daily by ship or rail. Suddenly pious whites argued that liaisons between Natives and whites, in fact, had never worked. Just like that unions between white men and Native women were seen as dangerous and ungodly.

Wifely Revenge

As a cautionary tale, local folk might cite the true story of Xwelas. Also known as Mary Fitzhugh Phillips, in 1878 the S'Klallam mother of five was charged with the murder of her white husband.

Xwelas was part of the last generation who grew up on the Strait somewhat sequestered from white influence. As a girl, she imagined that one day her marriage to a warrior would create an advantageous connection for her band. By 1850 the marriage of her sixteen-year-old niece, E-yow-alth, proved that times had changed.

Though the partnership was proposed to achieve the traditional aim of creating an alliance, E-yow-alth, the highly eligible daughter of a S'Klallam noble and an elite Samish family, was offered to a white soldier, business man, and Indian agent named Edmund Clare Fitzhugh. E-yow-alth's father, a respected Indian leader who later gave his name to the town of Sehome, initially opposed the marriage. At last, he relented and allowed his sixteen-year-old daughter to wed Fitzhugh, more than twenty years her senior.

The match was a respectable one. In the town on Bellingham Bay, Edmund Fitzhugh served as the superintendent of a coal company. With no legal training, he also acted as a territorial Supreme Court justice. Once, while gambling, he shot a man to death; afterward, he tried and acquitted himself. Fitzhugh, if not widely admired, at least had money. True to S'Klallam custom, after the wedding Xwelas paid a call on her niece in Bellingham Bay. Fitzhugh took her in as a second wife. Later, he abandoned both women to become a Confederate commander. After that, he disappeared. Two decades later on November 24, 1883, he was found dead in a San Francisco hotel.

After that, E-yow-alth and Xwelas both remarried white men. Really, they had few options. Both had children to support, and no viable means. Any hope for a Native husband was compromised by their first failed marriage to Fitzhugh.

Xwelas, by now in her thirties, married a gold-rush profiteer from Alabama named William King Lear, who kept a shop and dispensed land titles. To her household she added a third son, Will Jr. Lear received word of a relative's death and returned to the East Coast to claim his inheritance. Possibly Lear returned later to follow the Alaska gold rush. It's unlikely that Xwelas or his son Billy ever saw him again.

At forty, with three sons by two different white men, Xwelas returned to her relatives in Port Townsend. In the winter of 1873 she married George Phillips. This third and final liaison with a white husband would prove intolerable.

Phillips, a laborer, was well-known for his bad temper. Once, an eyewitness saw Phillips strike Xwelas with a canoe paddle. On the night before he died, Phillips and Xwelas attended a party at the house of their neighbor William Shattuck. Phillips gambled and drank while Xwelas tended to their baby Maggie. At the time Xwelas was pregnant with a second child by Phillips.

According to witnesses, when they left, both were intoxicated. When they reached their home Phillips broke down the door with an axe. He grabbed two rifles off the mantel and loaded them. He then called her names and threatened to kill her. At that point, Xwelas told the court, she decided it was safer to sleep in the woods. With the infant Maggie on her back, she left, taking with her a double-barreled shotgun. According to her testimony, Phillips, still inebriated, went after her.

Xwelas testified that she had acted in self-defense. The fact that she ambushed him while hiding in the brush undermines this claim. The range and direction of the shot suggests that Xwelas had, at least to some extent, premeditated the decision to put an end to her ordeal.

Xwelas never denied shooting her husband. This admission alone could have earned her a death sentence. Instead, the white male jury accepted her plea of insanity.

They may have believed that Xwelas, a Native American woman—and violent, to boot—was not mentally competent to stand trial. Perhaps they subscribed to the popular view that any marriage between a white settler and an Indian was destined to go bad. Or they felt the circumstances mitigated her crime. Maybe, they just pitied her.

Xwelas probably did not spend more than a few months in jail. What became of her and her five children after the trial is unknown.

31
Chinese Medicine
c. 1890

"Edith! I'm back!"

Though long past suppertime, the kitchen stove stood grimly monolithic and cold. The parlor hearth, colder. I threw down Edith's cloak, speckled and streaked with mud. Without stopping to unlace my boots hurried up the stairs.

Her head had fallen forward on the pillow. I lifted the stringy curtain of hair. With trembling hand I soaked my hanky (hers.) with cologne and pressed it her forehead, cheeks, and chin.

Not a word, a cough, or a sigh. I shook her, kissed her, and cried out.

I moved the lamp nearer. Through her white blond hair, parted with sweat, the white glow revealed the curve of her skull. For an instance it seemed as if I had glimpsed her corpse. A dark thread of blood crawled out of her nose.

I shut my eyes, squeezed out one tear, and lifted my gaze to the cross and the portrait beside it. "Don't let her be dead. Save her, Adele."

On the top of the night table, a round mirror. I held it up to her gently parted lips. Nothing.

With my thumb I pressed down on her wrist.

Nothing.

Then, a faint throb.

My own heartbeat, or hers?

Help was required and quick. At this hour, what to do?

The Reverend and Chris, on their real-estate tour, would not be back until the next day. I could go for the doctor who was a member of the paris, and a near neighbor. I rejected the idea. The doctor would surely ask, "How long has she been like this?" Also, "Where were you?" Eventually, the truth would come out. If Edith died, the Reverend and Chris would believe, rightly, that I had murdered her.

I'm not proud of what I did.

Sometimes the selfish desire to survive is not brave. Sometimes you're required to go the whole way, to confront the essence of the fear. What that meant for me was to expose my true self to those who were sure to judge me. I wasn't ready. One day, I would be called to account. That night, Edith would pay the price.

Unwilling to call the doctor, I knew of only one place that I could go for medicine. Open for business at all hours, in stacked canisters and jars behind the counter of the Zee Tai Company, on the waterfront, with goods and wares from the Far East, with the cure for every ill, including those inflicted by the addictive narcotics available at Zee Tai.

I'm ashamed to admit, I was afraid to ask a Chinese person for help. I had been taught to distrust our Asian neighbors. Though Port Townsend relied on its Chinese workers—merchants, farmers, cooks, and handymen—the truth was that in two years, except in shops and in passing, I had no meaningful interaction with any Asian person, no real firsthand experience. Christopher referred to our neighbors from the Far East as "Orientals" or "Celestials." According to the Reverend, the heathen Chinese also belonged to their own order of Masonic lodges, and prayed in Taoist or Buddhist temples, called Joss houses. But from what I could see, the Chinese were like everyone in Port Townsend, including me: trying to get by, and get along.

From the frying pan to the fire, I had to try.

For the second time that day, I descended, this time down the rickety stair to the murky maze beneath me. When at last I reached the street, rain, mixed with garbage, vegetable scraps, and equestrian and human waste, climbed my skirt and over-spilled my ankle-high boots. Peering into a flickering gaslight, which taunted me with more shadow than light, I careened into a sailor with a feathered escort, twice his age and half as tall, who corkscrewed her filthy neck rolls to scoff at me. A crowd of street urchins, in an evening match of "kick the can," nearly knocked me in to a gutter. As I was about to fall down, I managed to grab onto the ornate brass handle that led into the magnificent portal to the Asian market. Saved by Zee Tai.

Inside, the Chinese market was pungent and sweet. In the back, through a curtain, I watched as ghostly gentleman—many with brims and scarves to cloak their identities—went up in smoke. Nearer to me, a polished counter, long and wide, served as a barrier between the casual customers and the passage to the nether regions below, passages that smuggled drunken sailors, escaped convicts, and contraband to ships in the harbor.

Behind the gleaming counter, a Chinese clerk, in a blouse and wide black cotton trousers. When I opened my mouth to speak, he turned away. Feigning not to notice me, instead he saluted a tall woman, dressed entirely in pink, who had just entered the shop.

"Madam, as usual we are here to serve you, with medicinals from the Far East. Time-tested. Potent. Whatever you want, we can get it."

"Thank you, Bobby. I know I can depend on you."

Of a medium height, her proud aspect made her look taller. Though her wavy ashen locks were interrupted by white icicles—a premature frost in her—she could not have been more than twenty-five.

She set down her little beaded purse. Her glove removed a folded packet of bills, old and new. "You know what they say: 'One night with Venus, a lifetime on Mercury.' One of my girls is down for the count. I sent for the doctor. He prescribed a powder. Potassium iodide, I think. She's been vomiting for a week. And no better; the rash has spread. What can you give me, Bobby?"

"Sarsaparilla root. Wait here while I make an herbal reduction for a poultice. Ten minutes or less, I promise."

He was about to disappear behind a lurid curtain when I piped up, "That's not fair. I was here first."

His chin trembled. The Chinese herbalist stammered, and shook his fist. "Hooligan. Do you know who this is?" What I didn't know then, and later learned she was known from Baja to Vladivostock. Her house attracted mariners from every corner of the globe seeking love. "Urchin . . . get out . . . and don't come back."

The lady in pink, not at all perturbed, laughed. "Bobby, give the kid a chance." In a low voice, she advised, "Don't go at him that way, with hammer and tongs. Quickly now, Millie Langlie. Tell me. What is so urgent? What do you need?"

I confided, "My mistress is ill. This winter she caught a cold, which in the past day has swept her poor ravaged body like wildfire. There's blood on her pillow. At this very moment, she lies in her bed with no one to soothe her. If she doesn't get help soon, she'll die. It may already be too late."

She reacted warmly and at once. "It's consumption. I'm sure of it. Don't ask me how I know. Bobby, get her some medicine. As soon as it's ready, deliver it to the Mathieson house. Hurry, Bobby, do it."

Instantly, he complied. From out of her purse she handed me a little package, wrapped in brown paper and tied with string. "Take this, Millie. Brew it up, strong, and make her drink it down, even if she chokes. Now go."

I clasped the package to my heart, and raced up a hundred-and-one rickety wooden steps that seemed to go nowhere, winding their way upward through that circle of hell reserved for the worst sinner of all: one who gives up a friend to save herself. I threw my whole weight against the front door, which I had left unlocked, and flew up the stairs.

She was alive; just. On her chin, the pillow, and the coverlet: streaks of blood that went from bright red to gummy black. Her perspiring body shivered.

I built up the fire in her bedroom. I placed a small chair next to Edith at the bedside, and waited for the kettle to steam. Soon the water was hot enough to brew the special tea. Try as I might, I could not get Edith to take enough of the scorching, bitter liquid. Edith's face was an alabaster mask of her face.

Frightened, exhausted, I stretched out beside her. Details of the eve threaded through my addled brain like ticker tape. The lady in pink at Zee Tai had called me by my Christian name. She had ordered Bobby to deliver his concoction uptown to this house. How did she know?

I did not wonder for long. I dozed. Thirty, maybe forty minutes later, I awoke to the neighbor's Boston terrier yapping frantically and a rapid knock at the front door. I roused myself, hurried down the steps and opened the front door.

Shock of black hair and jet black eyebrows, cocked quizzically. Elegant features, including a straight nose, rosebud nostrils and delicate lips. He wore a silk scarf round the collar of his blouse with white sleeves that billowed in the breeze, on top of brown velvet trousers. Absurdly, he wore no coat.

He bowed, so that the stray lock fell down. He had no hat to doff.

"Oh," I said, "it's you."

The actor Thomas Astor.

However, this was not the moment to get reacquainted. I showed him the way to her bedroom.

Edith's face was white, her lids swollen and bruised. Her aural gold floated on top of the white pillow. Astor grasped the thin, breakable shoulders. He lifted her off the pillow and shook her hard. The chalky lips parted.

"Quick," Astor urged. "Hand it over."

The bottle was midnight blue.

I cried out, "If it's poison?"

"So what? If she's dying, she'll die. The elixir will quell the pain as she sachets off to the great inevitable. It might even cure her, but who knows?"

Edith gagged and fell back on the pillow, insensible. He dropped the spent bottle on the end table and strode out.

What could I do, except follow him? Looking back: a harbinger. In the future I would always follow Thomas Astor.

Down in the parlor, with trembling hand I rekindled the fire as he fell into a chair. Now that we had a chance for us to talk more, neither of us had anything to say. Both of us were exhausted. The scene upstairs, appalling.

I collapsed onto the sofa.

The actor mused, "What was it that Bobby said? A few drops, a tablespoon, the entire bottle? I can't recall."

I replied, "You have killed her. Or rather, I have done it, with your help."

He arranged his face into a pitiable expression. "Really, whenever I go out of my way to help, someone cries bloody murder. Why is that? Less than one hour ago I was up to my chin in a game of Double Ten. About to scoop the kitty. Instead, I was ejected from that pocket of warmth, into the cold night, in order to save lives. That's not my style."

siyá?əx̣

poison

As he spoke, he rose and began pacing to and fro as if the hearthside were a stage. "Heroic exploits are not in my line, except in the climax of the drama. Though fine speeches are easy to memorize, they mean very little in reality."

He threw himself down on the camel-colored sofa beside me and sighed. "Why complain? You and I both know: what Mallory O'Quinn wants, Mallory O'Quinn gets."

Of course. The Irish servant girl, whose life had been saved by Adele. By tragic circumstance, transformed into the lady in pink. Once, long ago, I had called her ungrateful and wished her dead. All of a sudden I comprehended why she had stayed away. A lady of the night cannot leave a calling card at a minister's house.

From a respectable distance Mallory O'Quinn kept watch. Later I learned that Mallory knew everything about everything: in particular, the ups and downs of Edith's illness, the exact minute I was called in as a housemaid and companion, as well as the dubious state of the Reverend's finances. A word from Mallory O'Quinn had established Christopher in his clerkship at Rothschild's Emporium. Now she had used her influence to procure rare and valuable medicine for Adele's daughter, and called upon Astor, the New York gentleman who had ruined her, to save Edith's life in payment for destroying hers. I could see how Mallory O'Quinn turned love into a commercial enterprise, but she still had a heart.

As I pondered, Astor searched through his vest pockets, an assortment on the outside, half a dozen more stitched into the satin interior. Finally, he extracted a folded piece of red cloth or paper and tossed it onto the sofa.

"What's that?" I asked.

"Mallory again. It's a paper lantern, to cover the lamp, so that the brightness won't hurt Edith's eyes. See?"

He slipped the red paper over the kerosene fixture, which hung like an upside down jar, on the wall. The lantern made the parlor look like a bordello on fire.

Astor took a pipe out of his pocket, as well as other apparatuses: a miniature oil lamp, a tin, and a golden needle, like a hat pin. He opened up the small metal box, and with the pin removed a gummy glob, which he began to turn inside the sputtering flame.

"What is that? It reminds me of a toy. I know. A magic lantern."

"Better, and why? Instead of a translucent image on a plaster wall, you see only what you wish to see. Now that I think of it, what a perfect way to describe the actor's craft. We all have nightmares. We all have dreams. My talent is to conjure waking visions and teach you to believe in them."

I nodded fiercely, though I wasn't really listening. What I wanted was for Astor to stop talking. My head hurt. I was exhausted. Was Carl right? Was he a flim flam? The revelation about Mallory chastened me not to rely entirely on first impressions, on the other hand, hadn't I seen enough to call him a cad?

Yet, he had cast his spell on me again. As I mused, the sticky blob on the end of the pin began to squirm and then bubble.

Astor put the pipe in his mouth. "Come. Next to me."

Outside the first hint of day was misting. My tired brain registered him sitting there, back straight and knees crossed like a yogi. I slid over next to him. He raised his pipe and handed it to me. I drew it in and coughed. His elegant hand gestured: Again.

The sharp edges of my astute intellect blurred, submerging all anxiety and fear. All at once, I was a child, standing on the edge of the rocky shore at Dungeness. I curled up next to Astor. "Tell me a story."

He turned, and nudged me with his nose. "Okay. First, let me check on the monster in the bedroom closet."

I closed my eyes, drifting. A few minutes later Astor returned. "Don't worry." Obviously I wasn't; I was dreaming. "If anything, her fever is worse, but at least she's still breathing."

He fell down beside me. Using a taper with the flame from the fireplace he relit the pipe. "A story? How about The Tale of the Magic Lotus Lantern?' Know it? Of course you don't."

Astor's Tale: The Magic Lantern
From the Song Dynasty

On a mountaintop sat a perfect little temple dedicated to the Goddess San Shengmu. The deity, famed for her compassion, is often shown brandishing a magic lotus lantern.

The young scholar, Liu Yanchang, journeyed to the capital to take his exams. On the way, he decided to divert his course in order to pay homage to the goddess. The journey took two days. At night, to stay warm, he piled leaves on top of himself. When at last he arrived, he went inside the temple and approached the altar. He bowed down until the tip of his nose met the cold stone floor.

Yanchang asked the goddess, "Tell me, will I pass my exams?"

No reply.

The goddess of compassion was off, salvaging a village suffering from plague. Thus, she gave no sign. The youth sprang to his feet. Simultaneously he leapt to the conclusion that the goddess was a fraud, therefore he vandalized the temple wall.

When San Shengmu returned, she was enraged to discover that her temple had been defiled. She pursued the young man down the mountain paths and unleashed a sudden wind that made the trees double over, depriving the youth of all shelter.

Yanchang—cold, wet and tired—crumpled to the ground.

Several days later, cruising down the mountain pass, the Goddess of Compassion discovered him, on the side of the stony path. Thinking that she'd killed him, she gently put a feather to his lips. He lived. Relieved and grateful, the goddess built a hut for him, carried him inside, and cared for him tenderly. Over time, she learned to love him.

Yanchang recovered. As soon as he could speak, he asked the goddess to marry him.

San Shengmu found herself confronted by a paradox. Without the youth whom she loved she could not exist. However, if she agreed to marry him, she would have to trade immortality for her love. When she died, her love would die, too. But while she lived, her love would live—

Astor paused. He closed his eyes and sighed dramatically.

"What did she do?" I demanded.

"She married Yanchang. The Chinese goddess chose lusty youth over timeless virtue. An instructive little tale, don't you think?"

Astor clapped his hands. "I'll stage it at the Palace Theater. I'll play the role of the youth who violates the inner sanctum of a goddess and de-mystifies her. If you're good, I'll give you a free ticket. Or, a minor role. Why don't we call this the undress rehearsal?"

He leaned over and peered into my eyes. "What. Actual tears?"

"I thought the boy had died. Foolish though he was. You don't need to be a Goddess of Compassion to feel sorry for a stupid kid who's lost his way—"

He pinched me.

Emboldened, I asked, "Mallory O'Quinn, who's that?"

"She holds the key to finest brothel in Port Townsend. I should know." He nibbled the tip of my left ear as he spoke this. Whether it was the smoke, or the attention to my lobe I felt as though I was floating . . . weightless. "Mallory has asked me to spare no effort to help Edith Mathieson to recover. She's paying me, of course, but that's not why I'm here. We go back. The fact is there's nothing I wouldn't do for Mallory."

Astor turned thoughtful. "Edith is not bad looking, in a trampled lily-of-the-valley sort of way. Edith's a familiar and lovely cliché. You on the other hand . . . you're different. Something about you—original, resilient, and daring—attracts. The contrast between you is alluring. It calls for a closer examination."

He pulled me nearer. Still feeling weightless, I let him. He put the pipe to his own lips again, and then pressed them to mine. As before, a mellow warmth enfolded me in a smothering embrace. My forehead, temple, and neck began to perspire. Astor kissed me there, and there, and there. I shivered. Like a snake charmer, he put his tongue inside my mouth . . .

. . . geologic epochs passed . . .

The front door opened and closed. A freezing gust rattled the panes in the parlor windows. I cracked open my granite lids to the milky light of a new day, with the foreboding glare of Christopher and the Reverend Mathieson, looking down at me. Raindrops somersaulted on the brims of their matching black hats.

The Reverend stared at me quizzically. Chris, with an expression of grim reproach.

Above us, the red lantern, askew, mashed in on one side, pathetically whirled. Where was Thomas Astor?

The Celestials
19th Century

Port Townsend's Chinese district, in its day, represented one of the most thriving Asian communities north of San Francisco. At its height, the Chinese population, according to widely divergent estimates, accounted for between five to twenty percent of the population. Some whites accepted the Asian immigrants as neighbors and friends. Others referred to the Chinese as "Celestials," ascribed to them supernatural powers. Still others called them far harsher names and openly persecuted them.

These attitudes were not confined to Port Townsend. In the 1880s, up and down the West Coast, with fewer jobs in railroads and lumber, the hostility toward Asian workers steadily increased. The Chinese community in Port Townsend managed to hang on longer than in other towns. However, by the end of the decade, the Chinese neighborhood in Port Townsend vanished, with only a hint left of the aroma and color the Chinese added to the daily throng.

The first workers from China arrived on the West Coast around the same time as the railroads were being built. They fled hard times at home, caused by overpopulation, land shortages, and famine, and the political uprisings caused by the British opium trade from China to India. Decades of strife inspired thousands of poor farmers to travel to the land of opportunity, known in Chinese as Gam Saan, "the mountain of gold." Throughout the mid-nineteenth century, Chinese laborers streamed to the American West to mine gold and silver, fell lumber, and sink iron spikes.

From the start, the Chinese were targets of discrimination. In Washington Territory, a person of Chinese descent was required to pay a $6 quarterly tax. Jobs became more scarce, as the population rose. White workers began to fear that the estimated 150,000 Chinese laborers, willing to put in long hours for low wages, threatened their own jobs. Street corner agitators from the Knights of Labor increased tensions with the slogan, "The Chinese must go!" Rhetoric of this sort was employed to attract new members to the Port Angeles workers' utopia, a successful experimental community on the Strait of Juan de Fuca which excluded all non-whites.

In 1882 Congress passed the Chinese Exclusion Act, which prevented Chinese immigrants from entering the U.S. In the mid-1880s, Washington's legislature barred Chinese residents from owning property. These laws, rather than staunching the anger of white workers, only seemed to inflame them. On February 7, 1886, a mob ushered three-hundred-and-fifty Chinese residents down Main Street in Seattle to an Elliott Bay steamer. The ship had the capacity to safely hold a hundred and fifty. Two hundred Chinese were shunted aboard. To protect the remaining one hundred and fifty, forced to wait another six days, from being mauled, a deputy fired into the crowd, killing one white protestor. President Grover Cleveland declared martial law. The city finally quieted down, but only after every Chinese resident in Seattle had been expelled. Earlier, in Tacoma, Washington, a similar drama had unfolded; violence also occurred in Idaho and California.

By that time, in Port Townsend, the Chinese had put down roots. Aptly symbolic, the Chinese "tree of heaven," between Polk and Taylor Streets, became a local landmark. The story goes like this: The Chinese emperor uprooted two of the most beautiful trees in his garden as a gift to the people of San Francisco for hosting his son. On the way to the Golden Gate City, the ship was blown off course by gale winds. The crew washed up in Port Townsend. These wayward sailors were received by the downtown "ladies." In gratitude, the captain gifted one of the pair to the Key City. The other tree still thrives in a public park in San Francisco.

The first Chinese immigrants on the Olympic Peninsula worked in canneries and mills. A majority were single and male, employed as cooks, servants, and gardeners, and laundrymen. The Chinese merchants provided goods to those hoping to make a new start in town, as well as to seasonal fishermen and those just passing through.

In Port Townsend, the Asian Colony, as it came to be known over time, added an exotic flavor to the city. The vendors offered rice, silk, tea, and spices that were not available elsewhere. The Chinese farmers delivered fresh vegetables weekly. On fence posts they inked Chinese characters to keep the household account up-to-date. In February, during the celebration of the Chinese New Year, any person passing by on the Waterfront might receive a coin or an exotic gift. Every July Fourth, disc-shaped kites filled the sky, followed by the fireworks displays.

Boosters of the local economy understood the vital contribution of their Chinese neighbors. Since the federal laws excluded workers, but not business owners, the local government allowed as many as twenty partners to claim one enterprise with a net value of a few hundred dollars. Overnight, every laborer became a trader or shop owner. Since Great Britain had no laws limiting Asian immigration, after the Chinese Exclusion Act Victoria, B.C. became a gateway, Port Townsend a portal.

If illegal workers (and opium, smuggled in tax free) made it by the Coast Guard, who were not above a payoff, the contraband was ushered through a network of tunnels underneath the streets. Geoduck Kelly was the nickname of one notorious smuggler. It was said that if the authorities boarded his boat, the illegal workers, chained together, along with the opium, would be tossed over the side.

In the 1880s the Chinese in Port Townsend, as elsewhere, became targets. Resentment took the form of harassment rather than outright violence. Children were taunted or pelted with eggs. Other kids pulled on their pigtails. White workers plied the doorknobs of the Chinese houses with printer's ink or tossed rocks through the windows. One Chinese man was arrested for "stealing water."

By the end of the decade, those opposed to the Chinese presence in Port Townsend became more outspoken. The Immigrant Aid Society, whose mission was to assist newcomers from Europe, in 1889 declared: "Chinamen have gradually come among us until their name is legion; and in their numbers, white laborers and the country have suffered. They are not of us, from us, or for us. They room together in filthy, disgusting crowds, without furniture or similar comforts, importing the most of what they eat from China while they hoard their earnings until an amount is acquired which, in their Native land would be considered opulence, when they gather it up and return to heathendom forever, to give place to others who come to repeat the operation. No person of American or European birth can begin to compete with these leprous creatures, because they cannot, will not, and ought not live as they do."

On September 24, 1900, a fire would decimate the Chinese colony. According to a rumor, it began with "a woman of the town." Mona Hervey, in a spat with another prostitute, hurled a lighted kerosene lamp. A sofa ignited the conflagration that consumed a square block. Next morning, all that was left was the exposed network of tunnels underneath the street. Miss Hervey died from her burns. Some accused the fire department of allowing the Chinese quarter to burn. They said that as the fire was fought only after the flames crossed into the white commercial district.

Whether or not the neighborhood could have been saved, the Chinese colony was never rebuilt. Today, in the tunnels underneath the street, buried in the walls or scattered on the ground, shards of pottery and tarnished coins, and broken jade remind us of the legacy of the "Celestials."

Chinese neighborhood September 24, 1900. The corner of Madison and Washington Streets. The fire leveled a square block occupied by Chinese residents, including two rooming houses sometimes used by "ladies of the noght." *Courtesy of the Jefferson County Historical Society.*

32
Women are Frail but Love Prevails
c. Spring 1890

To the Reverend and Christopher, I declared, "Edith is sick. I went to the Chinese herbalist but it was too late. I killed her." Hot tears spilled onto my cheeks.

It took a moment for the holy Reverend and his more pious son to grasp the ill tidings. Chris rushed upstairs. The minister, humping and wheezing, followed, with me trailing. But what deadly debauchery would the cleansing light of day reveal?

There was Edith, reposing here on pink-and-black embroidered cushions, her eyes blue as squid ink, or the small vial on the nightstand that nearly murdered her. However, the blush on her marbled cheeks and her pointy chin presaged a romping return to health.

Revered Mathieson, out of breath, turned to face me and inquired, "Millie, for the love of God, what happened?"

I stalled. "Indeed, what? I'm very eager to explain. Just as soon as I tend to my patient, recently returned to the land of the living."

Father and brother embraced darling Edith.

I poured water into the glass beside the blue bottle and paced. As I passed by the balcony window, I lifted up the drapery. Just beyond the front gate, with a flutter of his top hat, Astor spun to blow me a kiss. With the dexterity of an acrobat, or a con, Astor had slipped out the front door while the Reverend and Chris were peeling off their boots in the kitchen. Now he cascaded over a hedge and down the bluff stair.

At least now I could pocket the fear that he would suddenly emerge from the armoire, a hijinks more suited to the Palace Theater than the bedchamber of a minister's daughter. However, this was no time for a catnap. To prevent the Reverend from tossing me out, over the bluff edge and into downtown's running gutter of prostitution and piracy—since, without a reference, I would never work again in a respectable home—I needed a cover story, an alibi that would dazzle. But what could I say?

The Reverend occupied the chair by the bed. Chris leaned against the wall.

Both waited.

Haltingly, clasping my hands, I began. "I was sentinel at her bedside, yet her fever rose. Since Swan often described the Chinese healing arts as more ancient and advanced than our Western ways, I had an idea. But I was loathe to leave Edith . . . and filled with dread at entering the corruption of downtown district. Still, I could think of nothing else except to force my way past the drunken sailors and their brazen ladies, to find an herbal remedy in the Chinese market."

Chris picked up the blue bottle and peered at it suspiciously. "See how your time with Swan benefits us daily. Of course, you might have called a proper doctor. Tell me, what is contained in that concoction that you poured down her throat? Do you even know?"

Miserably, I shook my head. Of course, he was right. Once again, an action I deemed clever was really rash selfishness.

Angelic Edith. Tired dove, she intervened. "See how much better I am. More awake, more alive, than any time since mother died." She turned to the Reverend. "Father, is that wrong?"

His sad eyes went to the dreamy image of Adele on the wallpaper above the headboard. "No, my parakeet, no. Nothing you can say or do is wrong."

He patted her hand and then turned to me. His tone became grim. "Downstairs, in the parlor, I noticed a red paper lantern. And an odor like singed rubber boots. Millie?"

My mind raced. "We burned jade incense. To purify the atmosphere, according to the clerk Bobby at Zee Tai."

The Reverend looked doubtful. "The red paper lantern?"

"So that the light from the oil lamp would not hurt her eyes."

"Sensible girl." A half-second later, he asked, "But who exactly is 'we'?"

Blast! In dishing up a lie I had provided a side serving of the truth. Calmly I explained, "As Bobby-the-clerk prepared the medicine, I became more and more agitated. All I could think of was Edith, delirious, possibly dead. A gentleman, who happened to be, uh, sampling the offerings at Zee Tai, noticed me. He rescued me by offering to deliver the medicine as soon as it was ready."

The Reverend was appeased, but not Chris. "Let me see if I understand you. Out of a concern for your well-being, this so-called gentleman left that den of iniquity to assist you in your plight?" He laughed a little. "A wolf in sheep's clothing, and Millie, stupid girl, flung the door wide open."

The Reverend guffawed. "Chris, you imagine the worst in everyone. This gentleman, I will struggle to repay him, though I know I never can. What's his name? Who is he?"

"Thomas Astor."

His name, that part was easy. On the East Coast and in the West, a distinguished one. Though the frontier had little use for leisured fops, even a dandy without a job was better than an actor. And though I had never seen a single advert playbill, I had a notion that the entertainment at the Palace might be a bit too artistic for the Reverend. "Oh, he directs family shows: musical revues and melodramas, and the occasional opera. Once in a while, but only if the script is morally-improving, he might take on a role—"

"In this case, an heroic one," the Reverend rejoined.

Chris interrupted, "Or villain. Or both. To some, notoriety is as good as fame."

Edith clapped her hands. "What fun. An actor?" She knit her brow. "When I shut my eyes, I recall: his black hair, bright gaze, and soft touch . . . Thomas Astor saved my life. Oh Millie, do you think he will return?"

I sighed. "I suspect he'd find it difficult to stay away."

The Reverend gave her a quick peck. "Edith, you need sleep. Christopher and I need breakfast. Millie, please prepare some eggs and toast for us. After that, send a note to the opera house. I want to see this Astor fellow, to express my heartfelt thanks."

Christopher frowned. "Mark me. This fellow is not to be trusted."

He bent down to kiss Edith, a tender lingering kiss.

The two men, at last, retired down the stairs.

The moment the hasp and latch clicked, Edith, grasped my chafed, freezing fingers. She exclaimed, "Millie, I had the oddest dream. And frightening. Do you want to hear it?"

The night before, I had not slept, at least not much. Ahead: ten hours of hard work, or more. On top of that, all of Edith's chores. Yet, how could I say no? Her wan smile reminded me that if she survived no request could irk me.

I fell down beside her. "Yes, do."

She creased her parchment brow. "In my dream, I died. A crow-like bird, with a cap of black feathers and bright eyes, alighted on my chest. With his beak, he pried open my chafed and bleeding lips. Into my open mouth, he dropped a gold ring. I thought I would strangle, but then again I was already dead. However, the next minute I was winging my way into the night—" Her hot hand gripped mine. "Millie, what does it mean?"

Wearily, I offered, "Edith, last night you nearly died. Today, you are alive. So, act the part. Open your mouth and say, 'Ahh.' Swallow the gold ring. Even if it hurts. Your only other choice: withering away from want. Nestling, fly. That's what your dream is trying to tell you. At least, that's what I think."

The Play is the Thing
c. 1880-1890

Port Townsend, the City of Dreams. An illusion. The first two-story structure in town was a courthouse, constructed out of granite quarried from the bottom of Scow Bay. However, even before the project was completed, the building was converted into a theater and dance hall, demonstrating the local preference for the spectacle over reality.

Fowler's Hall, named after the owner Captain Fowler, a schooner pilot, provided wholesome live entertainment. Families came, with their babies in laundry baskets, to dance a reel. But even so, the excitement could lead to unseemly displays. Once, on the first-floor stage, a local lass in traditional Scottish garb pounded out a Highland Fling. One woman exclaimed, "She is barefoot." To which the Episcopal rector replied, "Yes, and bare-legged, too." And added, for any parishioners in the house, "I'm shocked."

In 1887, an upturn in the economy brought an influx of new residents, which drove up the cost of real estate. W.H. Learned, an early settler of Port Townsend, built a new opera house, with drop-down scenery, boxes on either side of the huge stage, an orchestra pit, and gallery. Here, in an atmosphere of gilded elegance, the rough pioneers of the port city were entertained: the light opera *The Mikado*, the stage version of *Uncle Tom's Cabin*, and novelty acts of the traveling Negro minstrels. This was the first theater in town with fold-down seats. The eve they were introduced, the chairs thrilled the audiences more than the play.

If a fellow craved something stronger, the Palace Theater was the place. Here, on the west side of Madison, on pilings above the harbor, the house drink was called "a boilermaker's delight." The rowdy audience, not excluding prominent citizens from the uptown, was kept well-plied as they took in a medley of risqué musical entertainments, or even the occasional boxing match. In 1889, the Palace changed its name to the Standard. The standard at the Standard sunk even lower, until it drained through the cracks between the floorboards like the mud and the blood and the beer.

The City of Dreams, with its array of theaters for men and women of all classes, glittered like a magic lantern picture show. Theater helped to keep alive the dream of a luminous future.

Interior of the Learned Opera House in Port Townsend, WA. 1915. *Courtesy of the Jefferson County Historical Society.*

33
More Love Medicine
c. 1890

A few days later, Thomas Astor returned. Not by chance, at dinnertime. From then on, the actor showed up two or three times a week, just in time for a hearty meal prepared by this hand. Day by day, Edith's health improved. As winter turned to spring, Astor charmed Edith into submission.

Not that it was much of a challenge. She had never really been courted before. His knowledge of Romantic poetry served him well. He memorized the couplets she loved best and declaimed them with winsome innocence.

As the beach roses bloomed, Edith, herself a hothouse specimen, decided she preferred flowers-of-the-field to dollar roses from the uptown florist. This suited Astor: his free spirit and his wallet. Regularly, he traipsed a painful thicket to trap an errant blossom. When she was well enough, Edith went with him on his blowsy walks to the perimeter of Port Townsend. She leaned against him as he shouldered the breeze. Like foxgloves, they cupped their blossoms and reached for the sun.

Throughout the sunny afternoons and evenings, while the two played cards in the parlor, I served a brew made from fresh lemons, or on the grey days milky oolong, to keep Edith from catching cold. When Astor desired a cake, or a plate of toast, or anything at all, he would shout, "Millie, get a wiggle on."

Astor purchased a mah jongg set for Edith in a tooled leather case. At the time the "ancient" Chinese game, less than a half century old, was all but unknown in America. Mallory came up with it to amuse Edith in her convalescence. What if Edith only knew that Astor's gifts were financed by prostitutes.

In front of the fire the two lovers would sit for hours playing with the pieces. Edith preferred the red archer tile. She said Astor, in a million and one acts of devotion, "hit the mark." However, even as she turned up the orchid, symbol of lasting summer, I shivered, for the north wind tile clacked as it was played, it whispered in my ear: nothing good lasts. What would happen when Astor's true character was revealed?

Astor pledged a love that would not die. But was he in earnest? Could he be trusted? One part of me believed that he was sincere. A devious voice inside of me suspected—even hoped—that Astor was deceiving her. From my place in the wings, I became deeply—too deeply—involved. Often at night, alone in my bed, I imagined that I was the object of Astor's affection, instead of Edith.

However, I should assert here, from day one of his campaign to win Edith, he remained perfectly proper in his comportment toward me. His cool courtesy nearly made me forget what he really was.

tq'áw'e

love medicine

Until one afternoon in late July. As Edith was prepared for their walk, Astor paced at the bottom of the stair. As I scrambled downstairs to search for her gloves, he pounced.

"Millie the Minx," he whispered, saying the joking nickname he'd begun using for me. "Quick. Come here. Tell me the truth. These days, how do you find me?"

"Handsome," I replied.

"Thank you. But that's not what I meant. How do I seem with Edith? A rogue? Or in love?"

He twisted the brim of his hat, repositioned it, and then dropped it on the floor, and crushed it under heel. "Damn it. I want her to make her believe that my heart is true. But I feel I mustn't overplay it. Relaxed is good. But then again, I mustn't appear bored." He seized both of my hands. "For you she is a familiar territory. Therefore, show me the map of her heart."

He hurt my work-calloused and blistered palms. Ashamed to have him touch my rough skin, I put my hands inside my apron.

"All right, I will," I replied. "But before I do, tell me this: Do you really care, or are you in it for the cash?"

For an instant he looked troubled. "I admit, at first, it was all in a day's work. I liked the idea that I could satisfy Mallory by making love to Edith. The notion suited me."

His bemused smile faded. "That first night, when I fed her the elixir inside the little blue bottle, it was like resuscitating a corpse. She was worse than anything I had ever imagined. The sight of her was so horrifying, I think I really meant to poison her."

He shuddered, recovered himself, and went on. "Lately, a change has occurred. I've stopped playing the charlatan and have moved on to a more serious role."

"Pray, what?"

"How can I be sure? I'm acting without a script. If I do say, brilliantly. All I know is this. Making Edith happy makes me happy. Pretending to care has made me care."

He retrieved his hat and put it on. "I have been typecast as a gentleman. I say this: If the half-boot of suede and patent leather fits, so be it."

"Well?"

"The problem is, by acting like I pity her, I've actually begun to feel that way. If Edith were ever to experience real pain, or even the slightest discomfort, as a result of the deception that I've perpetrated upon her, I think I would feel terrible."

"I see."

"Do you?"

"Yes."

"What should I do?"

For her sake, I made myself say the words. "Marry her."

"If only I could. You say you comprehend me, but it's obvious you understand nothing—" With that he threw up his hands in a gesture of despair. Feigned or real, I could not tell.

"I shall try again. Mallory O'Quinn pledged to pay me a substantial sum to make Edith happy. If marriage is what it takes, I'm her man . . . Mallory's, that is. Which is why I can never be Edith's husband."

He declared, "Therefore, any earnest attempt to express my real feelings can only come off as a contemptible act of deceit. The more sincerely I love Edith, the less likely it is that I can ever confess my love."

Poor Astor. Trapped by his own deceit.

He lamented, "As you know, I have few scruples. But this contrived version of myself, the one that pretends to love Edith, and really does, is determined to act with uncompromising decency. Therefore, if marriage is my heart's most earnest wish, then I must keep that desire hidden, even from myself. This is the minimum requirement if I ever hope to raise myself up to the level of the one for whom I have counterfeited a love most sincere."

He paused. "Now do you see?"

Yes. I nodded my head slowly.

And no.

Still, I could not help but pity him.

"Poor Thomas. Really, your intentions, aside from the baser ones, are commendable," I gently offered. "It's true that your connection to Edith started out as a despicable intrigue. Thomas, you are, after all, an actor. Use your talent. Simply convey no more or less than what you actually feel. That will give leaded glass its crystal ping."

For nearly a minute, Astor remained downcast. Then, his countenance lifted. "Millie, how can I ever repay you? Your insight and your command of syntax has shown me a way forward. To persuade Edith of the truth, I must lie so earnestly that she'll, in fact, believe me. That's it, isn't it?"

I nodded.

"Here it is. The only way to persuade Edith of the truth is to lie to her so earnestly that she will in fact believe me. Is that it?"

I nodded in affirmation.

Astor gave me a squeeze, then a peck. I tried to make it last, but he had more to say. "Millie, one more thing. She may yet die of fever."

I thought a moment. "That's so. But if the pretended love is real, she might be saved. Let her believe that for as long as she lives; for if Edith ever experiences the slightest doubt, I suspect she'll perish."

"One night long ago, you and I lit a lamp, an opium lamp," I recalled. Astor placed his hand upon his heart. "That ember still glows. I—"

Just then, at the top of the stairs Edith appeared in a diaphanous white dress. The gauzy fabric clung to her shoulders and enveloped her like crystallized frost. And me? Hard work had made me brawny as a boy. I had sprawled like some weird vine while Edith had emerged from her chrysalis a midnight moth, or a fairy. How could I compete?

Edith silently slid down the steps and pulled him out the door, without a backward glance in my direction. With Astor around, she had no need for me. The two departed arm in arm.

If Edith forgot my lessons, Chris did not.

One warm Sunday afternoon, back from church, I studied with Chris in the parlor. An hour or so before, the lovers had gone on a ramble. They reappeared in time for tea. Somehow always managing to show up in time for their afternoon tray. Though they most often forgot to say thank you, they devoured the morsels I prepared for them. They were now seated on the front porch swing, dangling their feet over the bluff, like twittering finches.

Chris offered, "For frivolous types, every morning is like a dozen muffins hot off the rack. Teatime lasts all day, and every eve is Christmas." His eyes were bright with irritation. "We're different. Our lives our guided by a discipline and logic derived from the pursuit of a higher principle."

At the time we were kneeling on hearth rug, studying a map of Africa. To my surprise, Chris, seized my hand.

He declared, "Millie, you are making remarkable progress. In the quiet moments I find myself dwelling on your good points, rather than otherwise. From now on, you may think of me as someone who approves of you, instead of the opposite."

Though not exactly elated, I felt some satisfaction at his earnest declaration of—what? Friendship? Teacherly pride? Brotherly affection? The fact is I was lonely and hungry for affirmation. Edith, on fire for Astor, had thrust me out into the cold. Though Christopher's praise was tepid, a shivering person will happily accept a rag if no blanket or overcoat is proffered. If love is a hot blueberry muffin, I pecked at the crumbs.

As summer wore on, Thomas Astor anxiously pondered, consulting with me often if and how he should propose. Maybe he was stalling, yet I could not help but sympathize with a soul in crisis, praying for all he was worth to withstand the very real temptation to do good.

In the end, his riddles, rhetoric, and rhymed couplets gave way to a simple heartfelt appeal. One clear fall eve, our little family was assembled on the front porch to swoon over the alchemy of a rose-scented sunset that had transformed the harbor into gold brick. Edith, seated on a low stool, feeling a bit chilled, had gathered her full skirt all about her. Astor tried to find enough floor space to get down on one knee beside her. When this failed, he tumbled into her lap, holding her awkwardly about the waist.

He fervently declared, "Edith, I love you. I don't deserve a goddess like you. But I want to make you happy. At least I want to try . . . will you, darling Edith, consent to marry me?"

His address was so simple and to the point that for once I almost believed him. Almost.

Edith, unable to speak, simply nodded her assent. The Reverend, without hesitation, blessed their union. At the same time he asked them to postpone the wedding until she was fully recovered. In the background, I noticed Christopher's face darken.

Summer dallied, until autumn, like a roused honey bee, bumbled in. Inside our house on the bluff the wood stove in the kitchen glowed. Edith's engagement to Astor brightened the atmosphere as the evening shadows grew longer.

That summer, the first spur of the rail line, from the downtown to Lake Hooker on the Hood Canal, finally opened, spurring hopes that Port Townsend one day would serve as the terminus of the transcontinental railroad. High hopes inspired a fever of land speculation. Chris, never without his leather portfolio, came home for meals and to rest for an hour. After that, he was off to pursue the next real estate tip. Often he would disappear for days.

According to Edith, unselfish Chris wanted only to secure the family's future. "And yours, too," she added significantly.

Christopher criticized me less, and even boasted to others of my modest gains, attributing the majority of it to his skill as a teacher and moral mentor. At times, his gaze lingered. At times, the intensity of the critique suggested something more than a fraternal regard. Though my feelings for him had not changed, I'm sorry to say I encouraged him. A lonely girl far from home, I still preferred condescending compliments, dropped like breadcrumbs, to disapproval.

I justified my actions one other way: Christopher's antipathy toward the actor had only increased. If I sometimes allowed Chris to flirt with me in his insinuating way until my mistress married, it might distract him from other matters close at hand. The more attention I paid to Christopher, the fewer questions he was apt to ask about Astor.

I was convinced that no matter what his flaws, if Astor really loved Edith, nothing really bad could happen. But, of course, I was wrong.

"Sir, There Shall Be No Alps!"
c. 1890

In the latter half of the nineteenth century, in America, prosperity rode the rails.

The Almighty, a paper founded to promote the city of Olympia, confidently decreed that "any great terminus of the north continental railroad should terminate on Puget Sound." Through the 1880s before Tacoma, Seattle, and Portland, and even tiny Port Gamble, the Victorian logging port on the other side of the Hood Canal, competed with Port Townsend for the chance to make their city a world capital.

In the early 1870s, James Swan was commissioned by the Northern Pacific to shill for the rail. He called upon the citizens of the Key City to support a line from Port Townsend to Portland, which would link with the transcontinental line proposed to terminate in Tacoma. For a time, the scheme seemed viable. Real estate prices shot up; some properties changed hands more than once in a week. However, in 1873, due to an economic downturn, the Northern Pacific Rail rejected the transcontinental line to Tacoma. Recent arrivals to the City of Dreams, who had been attracted by the vision of the transcontinental rail, packed up and left on a steamship or a mule but not on a train.

Despite this reversal, men who had staked their reputations and cash on the Port Townsend railway refused to let the dream die. Nearly fifteen years later, local leaders, many of them original pioneers, founded the Port Townsend Southern Railroad (PTSR). The PTSR proposed a line from Port Townsend to the state capital in Olympia. By the end of the decade, a fever of land speculation swept the Pacific Northwest. Eager to capitalize on the new optimism, the PTSR raised funds to lay down its first six miles of track. After just one mile, the cash ran out. Still the mile-long run of wooden ties and steel, this as a public relations ploy by Swan and others, did help to promote the scheme to the railroad tycoons.

In 1889, the Union Pacific named Port Townsend as the final stop in its Northwest line. A jubilant editorial in the *Leader* celebrated the decision: " . . . Port Townsend will be the shipping point and supply station of a vast fleet that will bring to it the commerce of China, of all

Asia and Western Europe and the world . . ." Within a week of the decision, the PTSR met with Union Pacific officials to create a subsidiary corporation known as The Oregon Improvement Company (OIC). To seal the deal, the PTSR offered their land deeds and assets along with $100,000 in cash.

That fall the new line was christened in a ceremony that attracted seven thousand, the largest public gathering in the region to date. A photograph shows an assemblage of citizens, old and young, in their Sunday best. In the lower right-hand corner, two harnessed plow horses appear to be representing the technology of the bygone era.

If so, it was just another sign of the runaway hopes of the crowd that day. One of the orators that day, Reverend D.T. Carnahan, likened the proposed line to one of Napoleon's military campaigns. "When Bonaparte's lieutenant asked how he would cross the Alps," according to Carnahan, "the little emperor replied, 'Sir . . . there shall be no Alps.'"

It was a heady time.

On Valentine's Day of 1890 the OIC stockholders pledged twenty-five miles of the new line by fall. The contract was signed on April Fool's Day. Almost immediately, the OIC called for six hundred horses and two thousand men. The company established eighteen construction camps, with warehouses full of provisions. A lagoon was drained. Two hundred tons of steel were shipped in. By July a Port Townsend Leader headline exclaimed: RAILROAD WORK BOOMING. That same month the railroad opened a ten-mile run from Port Townsend to Quilcene. The train took fifty-five minutes each way, with round-trip fare: $1.50.

By the autumn of 1890, on the west side of town, better known as the swamp, a depot and a roundhouse were erected brick by brick. Next to the train yard, other new businesses temporarily thrived: J.J. Hunt's hotel and saloon and the McNeil Hotel. Of Hunt's hotel, the *Leader* reported, "He has about 35 rooms in all, a nice parlor, 16 x 26 feet, elegantly furnished, a large dining-room 22 x 80 feet, and a barroom of some dimensions." The buildings' facades gleamed like the freshly painted set of a staged drama.

It almost looked real.

Then on November 25, 1890, it was as if the drunk finally suffered a black out, when Joseph A. Kuhn, a trustee of the railroad, opened a telegram: Due to the failure of several key banks in London, the Oregon Improvement Company had applied for court-ordered receivership. Local investors in real estate, and businesses owners, were advised to get out. A worldwide economic crash would dash the dreams of Port Townsend.

Three years later on January 6, 1893, the Great Northern Railway completed its trans-continental line to Seattle. Swan's vision of Port Townsend's railway had dispersed in a puff of steam. Once again, hopeful newcomers packed their bags and moved on, a few of them in pursuit of the Klondike gold rush.

However, a city can no more reinvent its character than a person can. The City of Dreams lost its railway, but preserved its capacity to imagine.

34
The Lights Go Out
c. 1890

On the morning of Tuesday, November 25, the most prominent men in the city convened a public meeting at the opera house. The implosion of the investment banks would cause the railroads and other related business concerns to go bust, putting thousands in the region out of work.

The Reverend Mathieson, a simple heart, not always astute, proved to be a worthy spiritual guide in a crisis. That evening in his sermon he quoted Luke. "Blessed are you who are poor, for yours is the kingdom of God. Blessed are you who weep now."

The impact of the crash of the London banks on Port Townsend lasted well beyond the first shock waves. In fact, the financial panic would provoke violent labor unrest and create a Populist outcry against the dramatic gap between the rich and the burgeoning poor, their numbers constantly increased by new waves of immigration. This quake created a tidal wave of unemployment that crested at ten percent, remaining nearly at that level, nationwide, for the next five years. It was a sustained period of hardship worse than any time before. In the next half-decade, Port Townsend would see a mass exodus of those who had wagered everything on the rail.

The Reverend did his best to console the baffled, downhearted, and dusty men, the mothers with their distraught babes, and the dutifully downcast children who really had no idea what had happened. The Reverend urged all of us to count, not what we had lost, but instead our assets. These he listed: a fair city with productive farmland and a deep harbor. Most of all, a diverse community, if only we could put aside differences.

To the Cuban kitchen maid beside me in the pew, who had forgotten to take off her scorched apron, I handed my used hanky as she quietly cried for her future. Before the catastrophe, I doubt that I would have bothered. In the days of prosperity, I had little to do with the other hired girls. Though outwardly we appeared to be the same, I was sure that I was different, and meant for something better. No doubt they felt exactly the same way about me. Now, at the touch of my fingers on her wrist, she threw her arms around me. We embraced and quietly consoled one another as we wept.

The crisis was the Reverend's finest hour. I realized that, to lead us, he must remain fortified. I decided to go home to prepare him a sandwich and some strong tea. If he could not get away, then I would bring it to him in a jar inside a basket.

The wind was gusting in the street, throwing up bits of muddy late autumn. Clutching my hat, I made my way. Our house on the cliff's edge looked like a lone boat tossed about on an irate sea of storm clouds.

Through the back door I entered the bleak, chilly house. The atmosphere complemented the mood in church and in the town. On the hearth I lit a match, which immediately went out in the drafty room.

A flat voice said, "Everything has gone black."

In the Reverend's armchair by the hearth, there was Chris, twisted up like a discarded bootlace. "It's over."

I went to him and knelt. All across the carpet, the contents of his notebook. The scattered pages told the sad story of his destroyed real estate investments, the result of days and weeks of careful research, now rendered completely worthless.

"Poor Chris. After all your hard efforts. At least you're not alone. Up on the bluff, or down in the muck, we're in this together."

"You compare me to the riffraff on the waterfront? Not so. I am more miserable."

His voice was bland, his forehead was damp, and his mouth quivered. Chris described what he had witnessed. He had lost more than money.

That morning Chris went to the shop, assuming his place at the little desk in the corner. No one else showed. The black rain outside made Rothschild's emporium filled with a colorful collection of bright tins and jars and fabrics feel like the inside of a damp closet. No customer appeared.

A few moments later Henry Rothschild came in tapping his cane across the floorboards. In person. This had never happened before. He had a weak forehead and a curved snout complimented by a lush mustache—a cross between bulldog and beagle. Slowly planting both fists upon the counter, he drew himself up and pronounced the economic crisis in a cool, factual manner. He barked, "Everyone, go home. And don't come back."

In a hushed tone that required me to lean in, he said that he'd been frozen in shock . . . bolted in place. He didn't move as he watched, in horror, as Rothschild lifted a shotgun from below the counter . . . rested it on the floor . . . pointed it at his skull . . . and pulled the trigger. Chris was the only witness.

Chris took down his overcoat and circled round the shadow of his former employer, who was still bleeding, on his way out.

He thought about checking in with his pastor-father, but instead spent what was left of his shattered morning, and a sharp slice of the afternoon, wandering the waterfront, tossing old bricks at vermin who celebrated the disaster in deserted streets. Finally it had occurred to him that it was time to head home. As he climbed, the strong winds made the stairs seem to detach themselves from the towering bluff side and float. He paused for a moment and looked down at the once-enchanted city below. The bitter wind whipped up a cloud of swirling leaves, needles, and debris, and dashed it in his eyes. He reached for his hat and missed.

Dizzy, blinded, little by little he wended his way around to the front porch and entered through the front door.

Right off he sensed it. "Edith? Edith."

Disaster apparently stepped upon the heels of disaster. He hurried up the stairs. Her bedroom empty, he frantically searched everywhere: upstairs, downstairs, and even the cellar. Perhaps, in the moment of crisis, though she had not attended a service in some time, his sister had made her way to her father's church.

Somehow, he knew better. Edith was not at church. She was not anywhere.

Here, Chris, overwhelmed by emotion, broke off.

Listening, I had not removed any of my outer garments. I was still wearing Edith's mustard-yellow cloak, which Christopher had specially designed for her. It was made of a handwoven Falkland wool that had been lined in black satin. Very recently she'd handed it off to me. It was a small thing, still I couldn't help wonder at the pain it might cause Christopher to know that she'd so carelessly cast off his thoughtful gift. Under the circumstances it seemed a trifling thought.

"Oh, Chris. How you must be suffering." I took off my gloves and the cloak and set them on the end table. I seized both of his hands.

He seemed reassured, until his empty eyes found the pages of his portfolio disturbing the swirling floral pattern of the carpet.

Bitterly, he said, "In a way, I'm grateful. From the start all of my efforts to make money were no more than a means to an end: to secure a future for my sister. For you, too."

Christopher laughed. "No matter."

"What do you mean?"

"Edith has disappeared. With Astor."

I reached for my gloves and cloak, worriedly exclaiming, "At any time her fever could return. We must find her."

He replied coldly, "It's too late. Even if we could stop the marriage, her reputation is ruined. Between us, nothing can ever be the same. I will never forgive her. She has betrayed me."

"How long has she been missing?"

"Less than a day."

"Then surely she will return."

"No, Millie. I know that's not the case. You see, not long ago I learned the truth about Thomas Astor. He's a fraud . . . a low-rent actor . . . and an opium addict on top of it. I confronted her. She said she intended to use her inheritance to open up a new theater in town for Astor. One fact she had forgotten: Until she's twenty-one, that money can't be touched, not without father's consent. She made me promise not to say a word to him until she had a chance to consider what I had said. I agreed. Now she's gone."

"How do you know?"

"When I entered this house tonight, it was as if I had gone to my grave. The door at the top of the stairs was open. Her wardrobe, rummaged. The locker at the end of her bed, ransacked. On top of her pillow, this . . ."

He turned to face me and held up a soiled bundle.

A stillborn swaddled in putrid rags.

I'd completely thrust it from my mind. The Aia'nl. From out of the silk rags, one tiny hand thrust out. All at once I recalled Edith's warning. If Chris ever found the weird doll, his pious sensibilities would be so appalled that it was likely he would simply turn me out.

My alarmed gasp confirmed what he knew already: the doll belonged to me.

Before I knew what happened, he tossed it into the dying embers of the cold fire.

Like an angry idol, the little doll fumed and flared. The head of the little figure churned purple smoke. Suddenly it burst into flames.

With a searing sense that part of me was burning away with the Aia'nl, I cried out, "No!" And thrust my right arm into the flames.

Christopher seized me from behind. He caught my hair where the base of my skull met my spine. Was he seeking to save my life? Or was he trying to keep me from rescuing the hellish doll?

"Millie, I know that you've betrayed me. You lied to me . . . and my father. Just what did you know about Astor that night you invited him into our house?"

I replied, "I knew nothing that was in his favor. But I trusted he could cure Edith in her dire moment of need . . . and ultimately I believed his love could make her well."

I could smell the Reverend's brandy on his breath. Chris pulled my head down. His trembling mouth breathed into mine. "This morning, someone came looking for you. An Indian. Tall and lean, with a foxy face. He wanted to talk to you."

"Jake Cook," I exclaimed "It can only mean that my grandmother, or Carl . . . or perhaps Annie, is ill. What exactly did he say?"

"Nothing. I ordered him to tell me but he refused to say a word."

"Home. Christopher, I have to go home . . . now."

I tried to twist free, but Chris held firm. All the while he stared at the flame, I sensed that he had detached from the reality of the moment, as he wrestled with the realities of the day. The little doll cackled and turned black. At last, he withdrew his cold gaze from the wrathful fire.

"Go home? Leave me?" he asked in a faraway voice. Then in a different tone, he said, "It's true, everything is different now. Without Edith you can't stay here. I may as well tell you. Several months ago, father wrote to a teaching college in Kansas. He felt he owed you and wanted to make good. I asked him to wait. I felt that you needed more time. To accept God into your heart and into your body."

He eased his grip, just enough, to turn over my wrist. He searched my blistering palm, as if there were a message written there. "Does it hurt? I can see that it does. This injury is a sign. Before I fetch a healing salve, let me tell you what it means. You were sent to me from Heaven so that I might protect you. Until the day you and I are married, I must safeguard you . . . keep you free from taint."

So. Christopher wanted to marry me after all. His angry criticism, though irrational at times, proved that he cared. Chris was also right about another thing: the wound truly hurt. Its throbbing pain sapped my power to resist him.

"Your wife? First I must go home. I need to go back to Dungeness to find out who I am. I need to recover the life and love I have lost before they're gone from me forever."

"This is your home," he said as the tips of his fingers he stroked my cheek. "I know who you are. I know everything about you. I know that your mother and your father are not really married. It doesn't matter to me. I'll have you anyway. Tonight, you become my wife. My way. Later, according to God."

He held me fast as I struggled.

"You say you know me? How could you? I hardly know myself. I was just a little girl when I arrived, I've spent the past three years chopping, churning, polishing, and scrubbing. Maybe that's why I thrust my poor hand into the fire. Along with that Aia'n—" I pointed to the fire with my free hand "—these are all I had left of my childhood." I touched my silver fish earrings.

"Yes, Thomas Astor sinned on his way to her, but don't you see that Edith forgave him, with arms wide? Why can't you be as generous to a future wife? I'm not an angel, but I'm no slattern. If you're my friend, why do you want to change me?"

He bit his lip and grimaced. "You say you care. Then, don't abandon me. I've lost everything, not only our scant savings, along with Edith's trust fund, but the wealth of the entire parish. Edith is delirious or dead. Or engaging in unspeakable acts with the actor in a seamy hotel. My eyes are boiling. My head is exploding. Millie, I need you. Do you understand what I'm saying? Are you even listening? To stop you from leaving, I would do anything, even commit murder. Shall I beg you on my hands and knees?"

His sweaty palms reached for me and salted the oozing pock on my palm. "No. You say you need me, but my real family in Dungeness needs me more. Goodbye. I promise I will write to you."

Christopher fell silent but there was something in his eye I did not like to see there. Swiftly he swaddled up the scattered pages. With studied care, he lined up the edges of the pages and set the pile down on top of an end table.

"Goodbye," he blurted.

I gathered up Edith's cloak and gloves.

Suddenly and emphatically Christopher said, "Not now. Tomorrow you must go. Tonight, the Reverend will require a hot supper. See there. The wood box is empty."

Whenever Chris became distraught, it soothed him to order me about. No wonder he craved a docile wife. Well, why not play along? In the morning, I would leave this cursed house, never to return. For now, I must take the necessary steps to restore peace and calm. I owed it to the Reverend, to Edith.

I folded the cloak. Tears singed my cheeks but I made no move to dry them. Head down, I went out.

Outside, a bitter wind scrubbed clean my mind. The humped-up shed reminded me of the raccoon-infested shack next to the New Dungeness Light Station. I passed through my drowned garden, creaked open the rusty door, and propped it open with a wedge of bark. Inside, the little woodshed smelled of fresh cedar and mice: musty, humid, and peaceful. Clumsily with my left hand I reached for a log.

A white light plashed. The basket on my elbow grew heavier as I added pieces of fuel until it was almost filled. Just then, a rusty spring wheezed. I turned round. The little door, like a wood trap, cracked up against the doorjamb, extinguishing the moon.

"Black. It's all turned black."

"Christopher?"

He extended his arm. To locate me in the dark?

My basket dropped.

With nowhere to go, I sprang up like a trapped deer.

Between us sat an ancient round of Doug fir, with two-hundred-and-fifty spiraling rings protected by three inches of deeply crevassed bark. We used this cross section of log as the surface to split kindling. On the wall, within easy grasp, an assortment of tools, including a small hatchet. Chris's hand reached out. To deal me a blow?

No. His hand shot past my skull, ear level, to grasp for a buried bottle. His teeth removed the cork. He tilted the brandy back, parted his lips, and let it flow. I squirmed, as he gripped me strongly with his other hand. The whites of his wide, wild eyes twinkled in the black half-light of the shed. My resistance was pathetic. He found it amusing. He put down the half-drained vessel, having satisfied his thirst . . . and laughed.

Softly, he reminisced. "I remember the night Adele died. I was sixteen. Do I need to say it? A virgin. Overwhelmed by grief, I confessed to my father an evil urge inside of me so deplorable it made me want to die, yet at the same time, my one and only reason for living: a passion for my sister."

"My poor father. How he wept, for his wife, his son, and Edith too. He told me to plead with God, and never stop praying, until I was free of the need to have and to hold her. I tried, good Heavens, how I tried. My fervent urges to give her up only increased my desire. I knew I would never feel it for any other woman."

He squeezed me in his vise grip. "Then you showed up, Millie. Really, I hated you. Each time she petted you, or touched your hand, or combed your hair, I despised you more. But something odd happened. Through you I began to feel the touch of Edith's fingertips. When she whispered in your ear, I felt her breath on my neck. Little by little, observing the two of you together, I began to feel real pleasure. Once in a while, I would wait for you to go up, then crack open her bedroom door to watch the two of you giggling and embracing. Tonight, the thing changed again. As we stood by the fire—when I twisted your arm, hard—for the first time I experienced a surge of desire, not for Edith, but only for you. She betrayed me. But you are not like her. Millie, you must never, ever leave. Not for an hour. Not for five minutes. Not ever."

A deep, primal instinct inside me warned, if you hope to survive, don't let him smell your fear.

I smiled. "What makes you think you can stop me?"

ʔasyáwá

seer, fortune teller

Disconcerted, he pondered. The pressure of his fingers became almost gentle. Then, once more, the pressure increased.

"I'll nail the door shut. One night in the shed will make you see the light. In the morning, after you've had a change of heart, I'll free you. One whole night inside this shed, and you'll learn. Even *you* can learn—"

I imagined baby spiders emerging from their nests and felt my skin crawl. An inner terror gripped me. If I failed to contact Jake tonight, at daybreak he would leave without me. Trembling, I asserted, "Don't be an idiot. You can't keep me here. This woodshed is a rotted heap. I could take it down with my big toe—"

Christopher sighed and made a sudden motion. An open jar with brads and tacks hit the floor. In his clenched palm, a nail. He seized my forearm, with his thumb badly bruising the tender flesh of my inner bicep. With all of his weight he pressed down on me, pinning my hand to the stump. He transferred the nail from his right hand to his left. In his right fist, the hatchet.

He lifted it up.

And laughed.

The hatchet twisted, and then fell with dull smack.

There was a crack from the blunt end of the hatchet.

Next time, I'll opt for spiders.

You can consult a medical diagram. Or, examine your own hand's palm pressed flat against a flat surface. When the fingers are flexed, at the carpal, the metacarpal, the columns of bone underneath the skin, form a "W." At the base of the W, tender cartilage is wired together by live nerve endings.

Hearing a long, terrifying scream . . . which I realized was my own . . . I opened my eyes. There was no need for me to look down to see what had happened. I had felt it. That was enough.

Besides, the shed was like pitch.

I suppose it was the pain that caused Christopher's profile to glow like the gold crown 'round the head of the baby Jesus. His expression: beatific. The next instance, a look of pure terror.

Before, to intimidate him, I had scolded him like a child. That's how he seemed to me now—a frightened school boy, who'd lost a shiny penny through a hole in the pocket. Or, peed himself.

Chris dropped the hatchet and with a mangled cry, fled without bothering to fix the latch or shut the shed door.

The situation: ludicrous.

The pain: beyond comprehension.

I lifted up my right arm. The nail that had penetrated the center of my right palm pulled out of the stump, easily. When I spread out my fingers to examine the wound, my hand leaked clear fluid.

With the fingernails of my left hand, I pried.

You might think this a neat operation. It was not. Finally, the nail fell away. The injury, on top of the burnt blister, flowered. With my left hand I felt around the half-drained whiskey bottle. I poured until the icy liquid over-filled my right palm and lifted the bottle to my lips.

After that, nothing.

Protohistoric nail uncovered in the early 1990s, along with many other tools and artifacts, at the Sequim bypass site on U.S. Highway 101, a seasonal S'Klallam village over 2,800 yers old. *Photo courtesy of the Jamestown S'Klallam Tribe.*

Mary Ann Lambert standing next to her scrapbooks, Blyn, WA, ca. 1955. *Photo courtesy of the Jamestown S'Klallam Tribe.*

The Only Safety is in Marriage
By Mary Ann Lambert

It was either marriage or molestation from the riffraff of that wicked little town of Kaw-tie, then rife with drunken sailors and soldiers from every clime on earth. The raping of Indian women was a common occurrence of the day.

"Watch your step" became the slogan for Indian women and white women alike.

Just before Annie and Charlie were married, an Indian man was seen running toward the house of local police officer Louie Stevens. He nearly fell in the open doorway of his house, crying, "Come quick. A drunken white man is molesting my wife."

Without waiting for the police officer to follow, the Indian dashed off toward Point Hudson, where he found his wife in a bad way.

Louie Stevens reached in to turn the flap of the tent open. The frightened Indian, thinking the drunken white man had returned to repeat his offense, fired a gun. Louie Stevens fell to the ground, shot through the head—

Part 5
Return to Dungeness

Annie Jacob Lambert, mother of Mary Ann
Lambert, in a field near Dungeness, Washington.
Photo courtesy of the Jamestown S'Klallam Tribe.

35
Daisy
c. 1890

No sound.

I listened.

To nothing.

I existed, but I did not exist.

My soul hovered above my body.

Little by little, my spirit returned. It entered through my toes and moved upward until it filled my whole body. Folded over the stump, in the lap of the warm, wise wood, I discovered peace.

Inside the palm of the universe. I was a mote in space. But part of something larger.

How much time had passed? At any time my master, brother, friend, lover, my god, might return.

Using the stump, I managed to lift myself up onto my elbows. I tried out my feet and somehow managed to stand. My only desire: to escape the shed.

The night air cooled my burning cheeks. Half of the moon was sheared off by the clouds that hurried by. I thought about running. Since I was unable, I quietly reentered the house and prepare my departure.

The moment of my greatest peril had passed. Or so I thought.

I entered through the kitchen door. Soiled dishes were stacked up on the table next to the ice-cold stove. In the parlor, and upstairs, all was chilly and silent. The Reverend's overcoat, and Chris' cloak, absent from the hooks in the entry. No doubt they were scouring the waterfront dives for a waft of Edith's whereabouts.

I climbed the stairs. In a porcelain bowl on her nightstand I bathed my injured hand. The pain made me nauseous and wobbly. I scrubbed the red-purple puncture wound with caustic soap, determined not to cry out though no one was inside the house. After, I wrapped it up in a strip of a linen pillow cover.

I didn't bother to look for my satchel. Nothing in that chamber belonged to me; I had no possessions, except the mustard yellow cloak—a gift from a soul-sister who had fled. I pulled the house keys from my apron pocket, slipped off the apron, and laid it carefully on the seat of the umbrella tree in the front hall. Then I walked out the front door, pulling the cloak around me tightly, as I locked the door and slipped the skeleton key through the mail slot.

I will not describe my descent to the waterfront or my stumbling retreat through the empty streets of the sad city. What if I couldn't find Jake? What if he had already departed? How would I get home? Despite the throbbing in my hand, or perhaps guided by it, I made my way to Point Hudson.

At the top of the dunes, I halted. Was that Jake Cook's tent, rippling in the breeze. Beyond that, the dugout canoe that would carry me home to Dungeness. Real, or a mirage? Excited, I began to run. The rush of the wind met the swell of the Sound as the heel of my boot snagged on as greasy beach log.

Automatically, I put out my wounded right hand to break my fall. The pain took my breath away. It was as if grit and salt had been injected directly into my wound. I didn't pass out. But I can't remember if I cried out or not.

Climbing up onto the log, I pressed my left thumb hard against the wound to staunch the fresh flow of blood that oozed from it. An icy rain began to fall. As the freezing droplets slid down my spine, they pricked at every nerve. I felt light-headed. If I lost consciousness? Salvation was near at hand, yet somehow out of reach.

"Can I help you, miss?"

The ex-officer, about forty-five or fifty, might have been handsome. He reached out. "Are you hurt? You poor hand. Let me see it."

At one time a fellow of exceptional strength, now his physique was wiry, undernourished. His greasy hair fell down his stringy neck. A disease in the red left eye made it weep. He had an incomplete beard that started on his upper lip and disappeared into the collar of his degraded uniform.

Suddenly I remembered. Was this not the same fellow who had pocketed an untaxed tin of opium? And nearly tossed Christopher in jail? Was ex-officer Smyth a fellow I could trust?

I had no one else.

I opened up my right fist.

Ex-officer Smyth drew back. "Shall I take you to the marine hospital? Never mind. If you try to walk, you'll faint. I'll go for a doctor—"

"No! It doesn't hurt—well, not much. Besides, I haven't a cent."

If Smyth called a doctor, I'd end up back in the Mathieson parlor. Add to that, I might need the coins in Carl's purse, tucked into my pocket, to survive.

Smyth winced. "No money?"

"No," I lied.

He peered at me, hard. His injured eye oozed blood and pus. He sensed that I was not telling the truth. I sensed that he badly needed a drink.

A flutter next to my right shoulder.

Feathery fingers.

An Indian girl, eleven or so, perhaps younger. Her thick hair in braids, her face smeary. She wore a black silk Chinese jacket, with elaborate scarlet-and-gold trim. Fancy, but not warm. She had no shoes.

Timidly she stroked my arm. By the light of a small campfire the black satin lining of Edith's cloak shimmered. Mesmerized, the girl fingered a brass button.

I asked Smyth, "Is she yours?"

The ex-officer nodded.

"What's your daughter's name?"

The girl replied, "Daisy."

Smyth sneered, and said, "She ain't my daughter."

It took me a minute to comprehend his crime. Was it possible that her parents had agreed to this arrangement? No, not possible. If she were older—a sad marriage contract—but not this.

Daisy beseeched me with round eyes. My pity turned to rage. What courage. Despite the abuse she had suffered, she had not lost her capacity to respond to the pain of a stranger. My hand throbbed. For one instant I recognized my mother Annie at the same age, equally vulnerable, just as brave.

"Git," Smyth commanded.

The little girl did not move.

He raised up his fist. He pulled back and aimed. Then, comically, like the blackguard in a melodrama, he stumbled back.

Daisy, a mere shadow on wing, condensed into darkness.

The tent flap fell.

Smyth repeated, "No money, not even a penny? A working girl like you?" Inconsequentially he added, "You think you're better than me?"

Was I? Daisy, a child, felt my pain long minutes before I noticed hers. If I refused to help her now, how much better or worse was I than this scoundrel Smyth, so eager to get by that he inflicted suffering on others without really noticing or caring?

"Here," I said.

With the fingers of my left hand, I pulled. The fish emitted flinty moon sparks.

Smyth folded the earrings into the pocket of his greatcoat, much better than Daisy's. One or two waterfront pubs might still be open, to sop up the loose change of folks who had lost everything.

Smyth set off, shoulder against the wind. His brute form became one with the hunkering dunes.

Using my injured right hand to grip the wool, I managed to undo the mustard cloak. I checked the pocket for Carl's little purse. If I had not distracted Smyth with the silver fish, in not very long he would have found it and pilfered it.

I fell to my knees and squatted next to the flap.

"Hullo?" I whispered. "Daisy?"

No answer.

"Do you want to go home?"

Silence. Then the tent fluttered.

"Yes." She sniffed.

I laid down the bundled-up cloak in front of the tent flap.

"Go. Now."

I stood up.

The stars swirled.

I had lost everything: The Aia'nl, the earrings, Edith's cloak, and Carl's purse. For the sake of a little girl. In exchange, I had acquired a mite of her courage.

Down the beach, half a mile, I discovered Jake Cook's tent. I lifted the flap. Stretched out, Jake's lean figure, still wearing his boots. Next to him, a youth. No doubt, the second puller. If Jake trusted him, so did I.

In the narrow place between the sleeping boy and the rippling canvas, I eased in. I propped up my throbbing right hand on top of his muscular shoulder. I pressed my muddy tear-streaked cheek into the small of his back.

My little brother Charley.

He smelled clean, woodsy, and peaceful.

Feverish, I slept.

36
Dead Man's Point
c. 1890

The whirling ghosts streamed, uplifted, and vanished, leaving in the air a rotten odor, a fetid stench that pricked my forehead. I craved cold clear water to remove the bile from my throat. When I tried to move, my stiff shoulders ached. In the center of my bandaged hand, a red-and-black dot.

What wilderness was this?

Help, I thought, help.

Charley, crawling into the tent, grinned. He shimmied up to me. And smirked shyly.

A music box inside my head tinkled:

Rub a dub dub.
Three men in a tub.
How do you think they got there?

The lyrics belted out by a straw-headed lass. In her lap, a mini-version of the same, wiggling and giggling to her vibration. Bouncing, laughing, plucking away at her heartstrings.

'twas enough to make a fish stare!

Already a skilled paddler at twelve, Charley had been sent along with Jake Cook to fetch me.

With my uninjured left hand, I reached up to spin a silver fish. The gesture was automatic, a nervous habit. Instead of their cool craftsmanship, I was confronted with the unpleasant memory of Smyth's slippery fingers on my neck. Lost. Annie had ordered me to stick to the fish. In that task, as in everything, I had failed.

Suddenly I realized how completely I had botched Carl's scheme to better me. I had nothing. I had become nothing.

I'd have to start again. But how?

Charley handed me a jar of creek water swirling with pine needles. With two fingers, he gestured, "Drink it slow." How he made it known without speaking, I can't say.

In a way it's not all that surprising. In general, words are overrated. Words distort the truth, bend belief, mock justice, and massacre the weak. Without words, there'd be no language barrier. As John Slocum said, "Shake the hand of every man, woman and child that you meet for tomorrow we may die." The prophet was a man of few words. Charley, my deaf brother, had mastered the skill of reading the current underneath the surface and communicating his grasp and empathy without words. Over time, Charley, though four years my junior, would pass on this wisdom to me through his example.

He unwrapped my bandage and smeared on a greasy ointment made from a mash of feverfew and lady ferns and other leaves and twigs. With a clean strip of fabric—a cuff button proved that not very long ago it had been a sleeve—he bound the wound. After a while he folded up his knees, put down his head, and went to sleep.

The hours rattled by. A steady rain played on top of our tent. A wet wind shivered the canvas. When I awoke, Jake Cook was kneeling beside me with a tin cup of hot broth, still steaming. It smelled like duck.

"Loon," he clarified. "You don't look so good."

"Better than you," I replied.

Jake was not amused. He took off his slouch hat, folded up the rain inside it, and shook it off outside the tent. He looked older, harder. Broad nose, shiny bridge pulled to one side, as if it had broken, more than once. Pursed mouth. The braid, salt and pepper, grizzled like the fur of a mean old dog. The quiet atmosphere around him like a drum stretched too tight. A hollow man.

Three years ago on Union Wharf I had turned from him without so much as a goodbye. That day, waving him away, I was a child. Now, an adult, I could sense the hostility on both sides. A confrontation moldered, I felt sure. The thick air inside the too-small tent was barely breathable. Not a great place for friends, and no place for enemies.

I inquired, "Where are we?"

"Dead Man's Point."

That explained the fetid stench that pervaded everything.

The *What Cheer* had anchored here. Captain Thompson and most of his crew perished here from the smallpox their vessel carried. The survivors buried their captain's body in a grassy wedge. Ever after, Rocky Point would be known as Dead Man's Point.

Weirdly, his grave now serves as a place of pilgrimage. Indians and whites, drawn to this evil place for no other purpose, mark the spot with round pebbles, gigantic pine cones, shells, and the rusty slabs of iron associated with the smallpox virus.

Jake explained: "We put in to wait for the tide to come up. You got worse, so we stayed."

He knelt. Folding in his elbows to conserve space, from his pocket he removed a piece of yellow cedar to whittle. "What happened to your hand?"

Chief Joseph of the Nez Perce once said: "It doesn't require very many words to tell the truth." Which is why a detailed answer often draws attention to the lie. "I fell down and punctured my palm on an up-turned nail."

Was I trying to protect Christopher? If so, why? His brotherly attempt to redeem my Christian soul had nearly cost me my life. I pitied him. What's more, I could see no reason to relive the scene. After all, what could Jake possibly say to ease the pain and make sense of what had happened to me?

I changed the subject. "You came to fetch me. Why? Is someone ill?"

"Your grandmother. She's better now. I'll drop you off at the point. You can visit her first, and walk home after."

I nodded.

At Dungeness, the first visit goes to the oldest member of the family. We offer our elders the respect they deserve. That's just what we do. It felt right to be returning to a place where rules served a purpose.

Jake held up his carving and blew on it to clear the dust. "That's not why I was sent to fetch you."

Perspiring I waited.

"Your father is dead."

From my cramped toes, creeping dread oozed upward to my heart, poisoning my brain. I wasn't surprised because I already knew. How? In a dream-vision, in the delirium of fever.

Carl was the person who kept me safe. Even in Port Townsend the image of his green troller out on the water reassured and sustained me. As long as I could picture his little boat rocking, I felt safe. He was my guide on the mountaintop. Without him there, how could I climb to the top?

I wanted to sob.

But not now.

Not with Jake watching me.

I asked, "How did it happen?"

"We were out gill fishing. Carl was cleaning the net. He hurt his hand."

With his penknife he indicated my injury, almost as if one thing had to do with another.

"It bled a little. He didn't think much of it. Odd accidents like that happen every day. The doctor offered to amputate. Carl said: 'Who wants to be a man with one hand?'"

Jake took a long pull at the canteen. "He had a show-down with a dead starfish. And lost."

"That's funny?" It was becoming more and more difficult to hold back the tears. "You were his partner. His friend."

Jake whittled. "Carl and I had an arrangement: I did the work and he spent the cash profits." He smiled piercingly. "Friend? Not by a mile."

He paused. "Carl was Carl."

I pondered this.

Charley, wide-eyed, perceiving the charged atmosphere inside the tent, stared at us with an addled expression akin to disbelief. He opted for some fresh air, though in this dank place there was as little outside as within. He gathered up the empty cups, with a few metal spoons rattling inside, and crawled out. Through the tent flap I watched him drop a log on top of the fire. Charley grabbed the canteen and headed toward the black trees to fetch potable water for our camp.

As the rainy day became a stormy night, the heavy air inside the tent browned.

Jake had more to say. "I have more bad news. Ready?"

I nodded.

"As you know, your father hated paperwork. Bureaucracy, he called it. Swan pestered him to file a land claim, but Carl kept putting it off. Said he didn't have the cash. Hjalmar Henning offered to do it for him. His best friend registered that land in his own name, not Carl's. That means that now according to the law, Hjalmar owns it. All of it."

Throughout this narrative, he never once glanced up. The death of my father, the loss of our land, the demise of Annie's children, apparently meant very little to him. Did he have a heart, or was he a hollow drum?

Jake went on. "Henning needs a wife. He offered to wed Annie." He hesitated one instant, then smiled. "When she refused, he generously offered to take you."

Me? With Hjalmar? That rusty tool? An ox had softer hair, and better breath and social skills. If I refused, did that mean my mother . . . ? I was about to object, when a black-and-red piercing pain in the center of my hand caused me to inquire: "Where's Charley?"

"At the creek—" And stopped. He realized it, too. Charley had been gone too long. Without a word, He threw on his boots and disappeared.

For the first time I noticed that I was wearing his wool socks, from Jennie, his only pair. I recovered my own boots from underneath a heap, laced them up, and followed. Until now I had not stood up on my own accord.

Dripping boughs opened up to a trail that was greasy with mud. As we entered the forest, a mossy silence gave way to the murmur of a waterfall, half-a-mile away. Jake looked back to see me chasing him and kept on. Underneath lifting boughs with their swinging beards of reindeer moss, over roots and rocks, I followed the paler elbow patches on his dark wool shirt. A barn owl, surprised, let a mole go. Berry bushes clutched at my skirt. In the rain the mud pulled me this way and that.

Suddenly, as if the grasping hands of a spruce had tossed him, Jake veered, and slid into the creek. He shouted. A cry for help, or a warning? His words were stifled by the wet wind. The pool beneath the waterfall served as a spawning ground for salmon; the moist air smelled like rotting fish, even more putrid than at the camp. I gulped, and followed.

There was Charley, sitting with his knees up in the stream. His stiff black hat at a bemused angle. Forehead muddy, his lips and chin bleeding. Between his scraped knees the overflowing canteen.

It was clear what had happened. Leaning over the creek, Charley had slipped. The toe of his boot lodged underneath a rock, badly bruising his left ankle. Worse, he could not dislodge his foot. Now he grinned, in a goofy, hypothermic way.

Jake, in the current up to his thighs, was prying at the rock. He found a flat stick. The rock budge. Liberated. But Charley could not stand up. His numb right leg refused to take his weight. He sat back down in the water.

Jake had had enough. He slid his hands underneath his armpits and heaved. Charley cooperated, feebly. Somehow or other, he pushed Charley up the bank. I shoved Jake. The three of us, a mud creature.

At the top of the bank, as Jake set him down, Charley tossed his right arm over my left shoulder. Jake on his left. Without further mishap we made it back to our tent.

Jake hustled Charley inside. He peeled off his outer layers. With my loosely-bandaged hand I removed my boots to salvage the wool socks Jennie had knit for Jake, the only part of me that was still dry. I handed them to Jake. Charley needed them more than I did.

As he stripped him down, Jake ordered me out. "Get a bucket of cold, clear water from the creek. On the way, put a few sticks on the fire. Go quick. Be careful."

I crawled out.

Who was Jake to boss me? The truth was that I was afraid. (I'd just learned that Carl was dead; now who would protect me?) If reentering the forest meant saving Charley's life, I had to try. The wind babbled. (Leap up. My spirit said, Follow your body.) The rain abated. Without socks, my frozen feet would follow my instructions for only so long. Step by step, I made my way to the creek. I filled the canteen and ran back to the camp. With my bandaged hand I managed to balance a pot on top of the blaze.

Trembling, I rolled into the tent.

sq̓əyəŋ́ács

the hollow of the palm of one's hand

Jake was transformed. Naked to the waist, with his braid hanging down his long, lean, muscular back. His trousers were rolled up over his burled knees and knotted calves. He wore a woven-cedar anklet. If he noticed me, I could not tell.

Inside his blanket, Charley shook violently. Jake crouched down. He leaned in, and spread out his fingers on top of Charley's iron chest.

Slowly, quietly, rhythmically, Jake sang. Though the words were strange, the melody was oddly soothing. As Jake chanted, Charley began rocking. Little by little, his breathing eased, rising and falling with the rain.

Just when his condition seemed improved, he collapsed. Charley rested, for a minute or less. Again, he gasped. In pain, worse than before.

Jake removed his hands and sealed his cupped palms. He ordered me to retrieve the blackened half-filled steaming pot on top of the fire outside the tent. Without spilling much, I set it down by his knee. Jake plunged his fists into the hot water. When he opened up his fingers, a tadpole current sizzled.

One more time, he placed flat palms on top of my brother's chest. This time, he raised his cupped palms to his open mouth, breathing in deeply. Swallowing the deadly force inside of Charley would augment Jake's ability to heal others. Either that, or it would kill him.

Never before had I witnessed a healing ceremony. Though not exactly illegal, the white government discouraged the practice of Indian medicine with vague threats and random arrests for unspecified crimes. Annie, true to her pledge to Carl, kept me away from the secret nightime rituals. In Port Townsend the Mathiesons had warned me off of Indian cures, as well as Chinese herbs. Swan, however, believed that the laying on of hands, shaman, and the medicines in the Far East, had the power to relieve pain and save lives.

sxʷná?əm

Shaman

Jake Cook saved Charley's from deadly hypothermia. I know because I was there. The color returned to his cheeks. He breathed deeply. Though once in a while he shivered, or restlessly tossed, mostly he just slept.

Jake put on his shirt, crawled out of the tent to roll a tobacco cigarette and smoke. I dropped the flap, removed my drenched outerwear, and nestled in beside Charley. Though I tried not to disturb him, even this small movement waked him.

Now it was my turn. I spooned up huckleberry tea from a tin cup. He finished it, and nodded off. While he slept, I stayed close.

Meanwhile Jake returned, his shirt steaming from sitting so close to the fire. He kicked off his boots. He stretched out and turned over to face the canvas.

Our muddy tent ebbed and sighed.

Though he spoke not one word, I sensed he was still awake. After what had happened, neither one of us could sleep. In a sense, Charley's near-miss was nothing unusual, a typical camping mishap. Still, something between us had changed.

"How did you learn to do that?"

He opened one eye. "What?"

"You know."

Jake slowly rolled over, opened one eye, then shut it.

I sat up, folded my arms on top of my knees. "The morning we left Dungeness, I found that weird wooden figure inside my satchel. You carved it and put it inside my satchel. Why?"

Jake shrugged—not easy to do when one is lying down.

"Wasn't me. Guess again. "

"I know it was. George told me."

"Want to know what he said about you?" He sat himself up, reached for his carving knife, and unfolded his blade. "You're like a house-snake.

You look innocent, but if you bury your fangs, you don't let go. But I didn't need George to point that out."

Sighing, he began to whittle.

"The crone with the purple stain on her forehead? Some say she lives underneath the shed near the light station." Jake made a scritch-scratching sound with his knife, "Yeah . . . I may have carved it. But then George hid it inside your satchel. To help you remember where you came from. Did it work?"

I felt a throb in the center of my right hand. "What about George? Did he ever make it to the east side of the mountains?"

"Yup. George is a full-fledged engineer in charge of an irrigation project in Eastern Washington. White men work for him. He may not be rich but give him time. One day, maybe, he may even find his way back home . . ."

With or without me, I was glad that George was on his way to achieving his vision. "One of the last times I saw George, he told me that you were there. At Dungeness." Now or never. "What happened that night?"

His shoulders slouched. Silently, he reached and slid his hat onto his head, and pulled it forward. This was the old Jake, the one I knew so well, the one that wasn't saying.

What he said is true: once I get a hook in it, I don't let go. I had to know: how was my mother connected to the silver fish? I persisted, "How old were you? Twelve, thirteen? It's not your fault. You were a kid, like Charley."

He eyed me, and inquired bitterly, "A kid? What does that feel like? Because I'd really like to know. In Neah Bay? Half out of her mind with hunger, yet coldly aware that her kids were dying, my mother did what she could. After that, Dad and me, we wandered: the unholy ghost and his unholy son."

"Jennie took us in. For no logical reason, she saved us. Why? That's just how she is. She opened up her world to us so that we could all starve together. I was just shy of thirteen. It was my time to become a warrior. When Lame Jack gave the signal, I brought my club down."

I felt cold all over. "And then?"

"Are you sure you really want to know?"

"Yes."

Jake complied. "Asleep inside a canvas tent, a Tsimshian boy. A year or two younger. not as tall as me, but huskier all over. In a wrestling match he would have crushed me. It wasn't a fair fight. Afterwards, I rubbed down his corpse with both hands. He was a kid. Like me, he owned nothing of value. See this? I still wear his cedar bracelet around my ankle."

Jake, a carver and a killer, flipped open the blade, shut it, and snapped it open again.

"What about the silver fish?"

"I fought my way to the water's edge. I tripped, and nearly fell on top of her. Half-covered up in sand, I thought she was dead. I grabbed her wrist, to check her pulse. Inside her cupped hand, swimming in blood, the earrings. Payment for her life."

I cried out, "Not as a pay-off, but because you saved her. The girl, and her unborn child."

Jake laughed. It was an angry sound. "Believe what you want. But remember this: it's my story, not yours."

That's not true, I thought. It's my story, too. "Why did you give the earrings to Annie?"

"Why? Because they were valuable. To prove that I was a warrior. I had no doubt that Annie wanted to be with me. But she was afraid. The earrings were the only way I could prove to her that I would keep her safe and never, ever let her starve. Let our children die. I would protect her, by any means necessary."

He carved. "A day or two before, I offered her my canoe. The work of my hands. Not only useful. Elegant, too. Her reaction? She wasn't impressed."

"When I gave Annie the earrings, she stopped laughing. For a while, I made myself believe that she would stay."

He bowed his head.

The rain had stopped. Through the tent flap, the dangling sickle moon, like a fox curled up in the sand.

After that night, Jake had never left her side. My brother and my sister, for all I knew, baby James, had a tendency to look like him. A voice inside of me said: This man—a killer—could be your father.

Jake was right; I didn't want to know.

Impulsively, in a menacing tone, I commanded him: "Stay away from Annie."

Jake pulled down his slouch hat. Suddenly he seemed ordinary: a thin, weary laborer, trying to get by. He smiled, just a little. "Sorry, can't. Too late."

He slipped his hat off his head, and put his knife into its leather sheath, pulled the blanket over one shoulder, rolled over, and went to sleep.

When I opened my eyes the air was white.

Through the tent flap I noticed Charley tending the fire. He looked pale. For breakfast, we had burnt coffee. Jake untangled a line and prepared a hook. If we dangled it over the side of the canoe, we might have a meal at midday. If not, we'd sup at Dungeness.

As Jake and Charley decamped, I wandered down the bleak shore. I hoped to revive in the fresh air but there was no life to be had, not there. The fetid atmosphere oozed up from the sticky grass. I made for the black tree on top of a bald hill, the site of the plague-ship captain's grave.

From the top of the rise, I lifted up my injured right hand to peer through the morning mist. Against the backdrop of Protection Island appeared a square-masted schooner, the ragged sails blowing in the wind.

A minute later, the vision turned to mist: the ghost ship disappeared.

Then I knew. The legend was real. Captain Thompson of the *What Cheer*, buried here in the putrid mud, just as the S'Klallam elders had described it.

A mottled rock, a moon snail shell, an iron hinge, tributes to the smallpox captain, marked the grave. Carried here by vengeful Indians noting the ironic justice of their fate? Or by folks—Native, white, or both—who understood that all suffering is shared suffering because it's part of the human condition?

Little by little the tide crept up as I walked up to greet it.

The waves bubbled up over my bare feet.

Further along the beach, Jake raised his hand and waved.

My hand throbbed.

I had witnessed the past. How, I could not say. This time, I had no doubt.

It was time to leave this awful cove, a place of paradox, where, like merging rivulets of fresh and salt water, secrecy and revelation, sickness and healing, murder and love, all seemed to converge.

Fatal Injury By Starfish
By James Swan
c. 1890

A fisherman at Port Discovery, named Charles Lambert met with a singular accident which resulted in his death. A starfish got entangled on his hook, and while taking it off one of the sharp little spines or prickles pierced the skin of his left hand between the fingers. He paid no attention to it, but soon it festered, his arm began to swell, blood-poisoning ensued, and then died in the Marine Hospital here yesterday. It is the first time I have heard of such an instance. I know that the spines of the sea urchin will produce sores if they are broken off in one's flesh, but for a flabby starfish to injure a person in such a manner seems unaccountable.

—James G. Swan,
Port Townsend, April 10

37
Lost and Found
c. Autumn 1890

Somehow, while in Port Townsend, I had consigned the childhood memory of my grandmother's birdhouse shelter to the mystic realm of the long-dispersed past. As we drew near, the scene before me took on a more determined outline. Instead of front steps, an inclined plank. The front door, not a door, but a cedar panel. The house on stilts was sturdier than I had remembered and assumed. Even with Annie's cooperation, she could not have constructed it without the assistance of someone strong enough to lift a beam.

Inside, one large room, with a tiny wood stove in the corner. Above it, shelves with various things, mostly dishes and tools. Against the right-hand wall, a low table. In the center of the room, but slightly to the left, a checker-board platform overlaid with cedar mats.

Stretched out on the platform bed, my grandmother. The only part of her I could actually see were the untrammeled soles of a new pair of sequined slippers. A gift from Swan, I later found out.

She was at the center of a unique ritual; surrounded on three sides by people in somber suits. On her right, a tweedy woman with big hips, swaying. To the left, a little man in a vest and shirt sleeves, his right hand cupped under my grandmother's elbow. With pursed lips he was blowing on her wrist. At her feet, an oversized fellow with wide shoulders in a shiny vest and a stiff collar. When he turned around to greet me, I noticed his cornflower-blue necktie. He was ringing a bell.

Posted at the head of the platform, back to the wall, in a glowing white robe, the Shaker deaconess, brandishing a candelabrum. As the other three joined her in song, the little house-on-stilts uplifted.

My grandmother tossed off her blanket. "Granddaughter, home at last. What took you so long?"

I wanted to throw my arms around her. I would have, except that there was barely enough room to shake hands, which of course we did, all round, for these were Indian Shakers.

As soon as she noticed me Seya sat up, and ordered the parish claque out. As they went, they seized our hands for one last pull. They interpreted her feistiness—one might say, rudeness—as a sign that their prayers had worked a miracle. The deaconess, no longer a figure of awe but instead a hearty Jamestown matron, threw the door open.

As soon as they were gone, my grandmother stood up. Her new slippers made her dainty. As she fussed with the kettle, her eyes shined. "Look at you. Not too bad looking. Your hair is not so blond. Reddish, like your great-great-grandmother. You want tea? Take down the cups. Look, I have sugar."

She handed me a chipped cup in a mismatched saucer with a tarnished tablespoon. After that she filled her own cup and stretched out her legs on the cedar mat. She blew the steam off of the top to cool it.

It hit me: I belonged.

Maybe it's true for everyone. Like a seedpod we need to see what it's like to float unattached. Only then can we land in the place we call home.

Over the top of our rattling cups, we gossiped, as if I had never left, only better than before, since now my grandmother regarded me as an equal: a woman, with knowledge, one part sacrifice and one part suffering. Probably she credited me with more wisdom than I deserved. It was several minutes before I realized that she was speaking to me in her own Coast Salish dialect of Lkungen.

I mused, "Your great-grandmother had red hair? I thought I got it from Carl."

"They say she was a white." She acknowledged this with some embarrassment. "The Makah rescued her from a shipwreck near Ozette Village. A S'Klallam paid for her. She was stubborn, hard to handle. Once he had had enough, he gave her to my great-grandfather. Well, she wasn't bad looking. He took her in. Not a slave, a wife."

What did it all mean? For one thing, this: My straw hair and light complexion no longer proved that Carl was my father. Or that Jake, the skull-crusher, wasn't.

Seya studied me. "You're not the same. Better looking than before. Older, yes, but something else is different." She squinted. "Oh, I see. Well, you look better without them."

The tears, which heretofore I had managed to hold back, now flowed freely. With my bandaged hand, I reached up to expose a freckled lobe. "I lost them."

Seya laughed. "When it comes to bad luck, I'm the expert. One thing I've learned: It never stays away for long."

She pulled herself to her feet, and shuffled over to the small cook stove. On the shelf, next to a jar with a spray of white camas, a brown paper package tied with string. It jangled.

I pulled on the cord. Inside, a thick letter with a wax seal. Underneath: a pair of silver fish.

Seya explained, "After Carl died, Jake hurried off to tell the Judge. Swan promised to come, as soon as he was able. That same night, guess who shows up at his office door? It was that corrupt army guy asking, do you want to buy a real Indian relic? Swan paid him, all right. He tossed him into a jail cell."

She waved her hand at the earrings. "So, I guess you're one of those people. Lost things come back to you."

As I slid the posts into my ears, the slippery metal reminded me of Daisy, her cool caress in a world that failed to protect her. Recalling her vulnerability made me mad. It emboldened me to ask, "Seya, why did you give your daughter Annie to Carl? A white man, more than four times her age. You knew she loved someone else. How could you be so cruel?"

She shrugged. "What do you know about it?"

Seya shut her eyes and refused to say more. Her blunt fingers played with the bent spoon inside the cup.

I felt it keenly—my stupidity and arrogance. I went to her, and knelt down. I took her hand and gently worked her knotted knuckles. "You're right. I know nothing. Forgive me, if you can."

At last she lifted up her chin.

"Why did I do it? To protect her. Annie is like me. Stubborn. That can be a good quality, in the right situation. At other times, fatal. Annie disappeared. The next day, when she came back, she was bleeding. I had to do something. Carl turned out better than most."

With great dignity, she pulled herself up. "Granddaughter, help me. Take down the dishes. Cups, plates, bowls. Everything." Sensing in her an underlying ire, repressed for half a century, I imagined her outraged command. "Smash them, smash them all." Instead, she solemnly announced, "It's time for me to serve my guests."

I called in the Shakers and helped my grandmother distribute the tea. We sipped and chatted for a time.

Suddenly, one of the men, tiny like a dollhouse undertaker, began to chant. The larger, broader fellow sounded his bell.

The stout woman in the black withdrew a flame from the fire and touched the top of a towering taper. She passed it over to the deaconess.

Holding it aloft in her palm, the Shaker priestess whirled, in a counter-clockwise direction, to greet us one by one.

The afternoon sun pierced the cracks in the plank walls. At the very same instance, the Shaker priestess raised her arms. The wide sleeves of her robe spread out, like the wings of an Alaskan tern, or an angel.

Reeling, I shut my eyes.

The deaconess silently stole up behind me. She dropped her palms on the top of my shoulders and lengthened and uplifted my arms. With her belly pressed up against me, the vibrations of her song entered my body, and wriggled down, until they took root in my core. A shard exploded there. My hand stopped throbbing and began to heal.

There were streaming tears on my face.

Seya embraced me, her eyes shimmering with tears.

But not for long. She disliked physical touch. To signal I was free to go, she gently scolded, "Millie, your mother is waiting for you."

I ran down the ramp, lifted my skirt, and leaped down onto the wet sand. The fish earrings danced. I was about to set off, when I turned round and noticed the design carved into the square panel in the center of the salvaged door.

A swan.

No Safe Haven
c. 1906

In January of 1906, on Port Discovery, not far from the homestead where Mary Ann Lambert grew up, Mary Sadla Tunmer was brutally murdered.

Mixed-Race Marriage

Mary's mother Tam-moy was married to English settler James Woodman; first in a traditional Indian ceremony, twenty years later again in a civil ceremony. Woodman ferried passengers from the sawmill to a dock at the head of the bay, also known as Woodman's Landing. In a harmonious partnership that lasted sixty years, Tam-moy assisted him in this and other commercial endeavors.

Mary Sadla, Woodman's stepdaughter, was the result of Tam-moy's earlier marriage to an Indian youth who had died. At fourteen, Sadla left the Woodman home, which she never felt was hers. She became involved with a number of dubious characters, including the gambler Henry Quaile, aka Poker Jack, later killed in a knife fight. In her teens she gave birth to two daughters.

In 1878, Sadla, about twenty-four, met a cook on a side-wheeler. Nelville Tunmer was the son of a tailor from Suffolk, England. After his father died, Ned used his inheritance to purchase a piece of land in America. When he arrived he realized that he had been swindled. Broke, he enlisted. Described as accident prone, Ned realized a military career was not in the cards. He headed west. There he met Sadla, and built a farm for her in Fairmount.

In addition to Sadla's daughter Elizabeth (her other daughter was adopted by Poker Jack's East Coast relatives) the Tunmers added a son, William. Ten years later, Ned became the captain of the steam launch *Fannie*. Not all the cargo on board was legal; according to the *Morning Leader* on October 20, 1893, Ned was jailed by a custom's official for smuggling twenty pounds of untaxed opium.

Yet by hook, or by crook, the family of Mary Sadla and Ned Tunmer managed to get by—weathering their tempestuous marriage until Tunmer's death more than thirty years later.

Yet, after three decades, Sadla was denied the proceeds of Nelville Tunmer's estate, including his military pension, ostensibly because Sadla could not provide either a legal record of their marriage or a substantial witness.

In recorded testimony Sadla asserted, "Yes, Soldier and I lived together continuously from the time of our marriage until he died. We were never separated nor divorced."

In her deposition on April 24, 1908, before Special Examiner M.M. Brower, Mary Sadla Tunmer was asked if she could produce the name of the clergyman who officiated at the wedding on the Port Madison Reservation. She could not. She explained, "He traveled around." However, she did recall one honored guest at the Indian wedding ceremony: Chief Seattle.

What Special Examiner Brower wanted was a white witness. "White people of this country only take about as much interest in the doings of the Indians as the Indians do in the actions of their dogs." It was difficult to find witnesses "competent to testify," in other words, a non-Native.

Mary Sadla Tunmer's petition was further complicated by a competing claim by the grown-up daughter from Ned's previous marriage to a white woman. Sadla was denied her widow's pension. With no means of support, she retired to a shack across the bay from the Fairmont railroad station.

Unsolved Murder

Nine months after the deposition, in an apparently unrelated incident, Mary Sadler Tunmer, age fifty-five, was murdered.

She was found dead in her smoldering cabin, her body singed beyond recognition. Her skull crushed in by a blunt object. The only clue, a glass pitcher of alcohol, drained and discarded on the dock. Nothing else was missing; there was nothing of value to steal.

Before the cabin was torched, both of Sadla's wrists were nailed to the floor. No one knows why. No perpetrators were ever apprehended.

38
Love and Survival
c. 1890

My mind reeled as I hastened from my grandmother's front door—contemplating the possibility that James Swan could be my grandfather.

If so, it explained one or two things—like why he insisted on helping me—but also raised as many questions. For example, if he was so attached, why didn't he claim us? Perhaps Swan was more of a conformist than I wanted to believe. In Port Townsend, marriage to a Native would have diminished his reputation. On the other hand, perhaps it was my grandmother Eliza III, with her noble lineage, who had refused to acknowledge him. I doubted that Seya would ever tell me the whole truth.

sk'ʷi?á?əm'

to be emotionally attached

On the Strait of Juan de Fuca—cradled in between the peaks of British Columbia, the Olympic range, and the Cascades—night descends without warning. The hike to our cabin was less than a mile along the shore. I knew I should hurry home.

Still I lingered. I lolled.

As I strolled homeward, the packet inside my skirt pocket crackled. A note from Swan, I assumed. Now that my curiosity had been aroused, I believed even the most straightforward letter might contain hidden imprecations.

I broke the seal. It was not the penmanship of the Judge, but an equally familiar hand:

FROM THE DESK OF
REVEREND PAUL WILLIAM MATHIESON

Dear Millie,

I just learned about the death of your father. I offer heartfelt sympathy. I loved Carl; a friend to all, except semonizing hypocrites. Allow me to raise this little glass of port to Charles Langlie, an ancient and modern mariner, who will forever be.

Back to reality. They say trouble comes in threes (though as a clergyman I should resist superstitious-thinking!) After I led my lost sheep through the winds of the financial gale, I hurried home. I learned that my daughter Edith had eloped with the actor. Next, I discovered my son Chris collapsed in a state of mental derangement.

Three blasts of the hurricane that howls! The next morning, treading hard on the heels of that awful night, Christopher, almost incoherent, informed me that you had fled, to be with your family in their hour of worst need. I concede that you did right.

They say that charity begins at home. I am that hypocrite your father abhorred for I failed to heed the lessons that I preached. Immersed in my congregation, after Adele died I allowed Christopher to handle all of my household affairs. I demanded his help, while withholding the help that he needed. This was wrong.

I cannot undo the past, but I can do better. You may be surprised to hear that I have resigned my parish to return to Scotland. There, Chris will receive treatment. At all times I will remain by his side, doing whatever I can to heal his mind and spirit. I have often observed that the determination to do the right thing often comes too late; not in this case, I pray.

Now, the real subject of this letter: three years ago your father and I agreed: In exchange for your services, I would ensure your education. Christopher's tutoring, though competent, was not sufficient to absolve me of my promise. Therefore, at the end of each month I set aside a fixed amount for college. All is in order; the Judge will withdraw the fund on your behalf whenever you wish.

I'm sorry that I did not tell you sooner. More than that, I'm sorry that I never shared this scheme with Carl. More than anything your fond father wished for you to flourish.

One last word: I don't know on what terms you parted with Christopher; however, I have an idea that it was not only Edith's rashly indecent behavior that has caused him distress. In the hours that followed, I begged Chris to tell me what happened prior to her elopement.

A fortnight before my daughter disappeared, Christopher offered Astor a substantial sum "to disappear." He did so without consulting me: I could never agree to extortion. Astor seemed prepared to agree to all of his stipulations, save one. According to Chris, Astor asked: "What about Millie? Is she off limits, too?" Chris said that he must never again contact you. Hearing this, the actor declined.

Thus, Chris surrendered his last opportunity to save his sister from disaster because he would not—could not—betray his devoted concern for you.

Millie, whatever your plans, think again! Book passage to Scotland! Do for Chris what you tried to do for Edith: heal him. Sacrificing oneself for the sake of others creates the greatest satisfaction that life can offer. In this matter and all else, let your affectionate heart, and a natural sense of what is good and right, guide you—

With my esteem,
Rev. Paul Mathieson

So, even in his delirium, what Chris had said was true. The Reverend, in lieu of past wages, had put aside funds to send me to college. What's more, inadvertently he communicated a detail that made the very idea of marriage to Hjalmer Henning—even for the sake of Annie and the children—unfathomable.

Astor did care for me. Enough to refuse Christopher's bribe. Enough to save his skin. But, if he did love me, then why elope with Edith?

With one hand he caressed me, while with the other he tantalized her. I found it hard to believe her delicate manners suited a salty rogue like Astor. She was lovelier but I was more vivacious. Jealously I wondered: How could he choose her over me?

From childhood I'd learned to perceive the world with two points of view at one time. In that case, could a person truly love two people at the same time? The flaming arrow I aimed at George in our scuffle at the top of the castle never hit its mark. Later that same night—I admit it here—I allowed the actor to explore unmapped, virgin territories. Let him? I cried out for it. Perhaps, like colonizing explorers, our passions are lawless. Our emotions lead us to adventure in various landscapes and climes. Maybe Astor loved us equally, but differently.

I could understand Astor's choice, but I could not forgive it.

I crushed the Reverend's epistle, and was about to launch it into to the Sound, when I spied this postscript:

P.S. Lately I learned, the fugitive couple decided to try their luck in San Francisco. The day they disappeared, two vessels—a brig and a schooner—departed from Port Townsend to the Bay City. One vessel hit the sandbar at the mouth of the Columbia. All on board the schooner drowned. Pray, Millie, with all of your heart, that Edith and Astor boarded the brig.

P.P.S. When I have news, I will write.

Edith and Astor, drowned? Like a sand dollar in the sun, my heart cracked.

Though it pained me to imagine Edith and Astor wound up in red satin in a dive hotel in San Francisco, it hurt me more to imagine their chilly embrace on the creeping floor of the Pacific Ocean.

For my spirit to thrive, I needed them to survive, especially Edith.

The Reverend was wrong: self-sacrifice was not the high mark of a woman's life. His only daughter deserved to experience the bliss of this world before moving on to the next one. Wasn't that precisely what she wished for me the day she packed me off to Alexander's castle? I pressed my palms together, to pray to God to save, not their souls, but their bodies.

That day, my affection for my two friends taught me to forgive.

I folded the letter, returned it to my satchel, and breathed in the warm seedweed breeze. I was ready to go home.

The Dungeness Massacre
Excerpted from Mary Ann Lambert

The blackened S'Klallams pounced upon the sleeping Tsimshians, killing all eighteen persons, or so they thought.

In reality a young woman, Nusee-chus by name, was pursued and hit on the head with a club. She fell close to the side of one of the canoes where she lay feigning death, scarcely breathing for fear of detection while the awful shrieks and screams of her tribesmen penetrated the night.

When Nusee-chus was sure the S'Klallam had departed, she cautiously rose, first upon her knee, then in a standing position, and looked around. A shudder crept over her as she looked upon the dead bodies of her tribesmen, which were strewn about the beach . . .

Contrary to general belief, the S'Klallams did not bury the dead enemy on the beach. Instead, the bodies were placed in the largest of the canoes, and in the bottom holes were bored. A strong southeast wind carried the funeral barge to the deep water of the Strait of Juan de Fuca, where it sank, bringing an end to this tragic episode.

James G. Swan, U.S. Commisioner, went to Victoria and arranged the matter as was supposed and understood, and upon the terms of settlement paid over a sum money and quantity of goods to agents of the Tsimshian Indians—

39
End of an Epoch
c. 1890-1900

So far, no one had noticed me. Except the duffy-grey mule munching on dried kelp. It lifted its head like a heavy boot, put out its lips, and nibbled my hair. Henning's ride. Like him, it had bad breath. I gave the old biddy a friendly shove.

Down the beach, Jake, in canvas trousers, was bent double over our weather-beaten skiff, scraping off the barnacles. Next to him, Julia, no longer a babe in arms but rather a curly-haired cherub wearing a pinafore, squatted to poke at a whirligig crab, better than a wind-up toy.

Jake lifted her up to dip her bare feet. She squealed. In her excitement, she tossed her skirt up over her head. Jake pinched her belly and held her up to reveal to her the mottled sunset. With tenderness, he pulled the skirt back down over her knees.

Annie peeled potatoes on the front step. She looked thinner. Her thick hair, in the past braided down her back, was now knotted on the back of her head. Her aspect had hardened: her forehead broader, cheeks and chin sharper.

On her pert knee, a pretty baby.

The alert infant was the first to notice me.

It shrieked.

"Millie," Annie called out. "You made it."

She didn't shout or leap up. She greeted me the same way she would a passing neighbor. Out of shyness, or something else?

What was I to her, anyway? A tangled net—a trap?

She stretched out both arms to show off the baby.

"James!" I exclaimed, greeting my youngest sibling. He smelled like fish oil and rosemary. I kissed his chubby belly.

Right off Annie noticed the dirty bandage unraveling from my wrist. She was too polite to mention it. Instead, she said, "Your dress. How pretty."

Inside, our cabin, though much the same, seemed homier. The kitchen now featured actual curtains, tied up to let the light in. There was a coiled rag rug under the table. The children still slept up in the loft. The bedraggled fox pelt still tacked to the hearth.

Carl had added a bedroom in the back. The threshold of the new marital quarters was topped by an arch. On either side, columns trailing vines. Above and below, a smirking Norse dragon. At the pinnacle of the doorway, a pair of stacked-up hearts, the one above a reflection of its partner below. Carl's carved vestibule, entryway to an intimate place: his Norwegian heart.

"How—lovely," I exclaimed.

Annie whispered, "Shh." She waved me into supper.

náč'

different,
strange

On top of the slab table, a steamy feast: bean soup, boiled potatoes, with assorted shellfish. Afterward we had blackberry oatcakes with nettle tea.

My brother returned from his new job at the mill, just in time. Julia crowed with delight. Charley, slightly fazed by his unaccustomed trial, tried to eat with the baby in his lap. However, her efforts to feed him tidbits with an oversized spoon made him put her down. A little while later, her sticky fists grabbed hold of my skirt. Using her belly for leverage, she catapulted into my lap. Edith's gown was ruined, but I didn't care. She made me feel like part of the family. Yet I couldn't help but notice that she looked even more like Jake Cook than Charley or James.

Jake filled in the details of our passage from Port Townsend, including the fever from my injury which forced us to camp at Dead Man's Point, delaying our arrival for three days. He didn't mentioned Charley's accident, or the healing ceremony that cured him. I, too, said not a word. Did she know what I knew?

After supper, as I dried the last dish, Annie remarked, "Carl was never anything but old, yet I never expected him to die. Charley put up a cross. Swan refused to read from Seya's bible. He called his friend 'eccentric,' 'odd' and 'unusual.' It's true, he seemed to attract predicaments. For example, fishermen are often are lost at sea, but who dies retrieving his net in a safe harbor? Late in life, Carl made a decision to settle down and protect our family until he was no longer able. Swan said he admired him, no, that he loved him, for that."

She sighed. "Wait until you see the beautiful carved grave marker. Charley's got a real talent for woodworking from his father."

Carl or Jake? I wondered. What comes from whom? I was discovering that in different types of people there was a disturbing amount of overlap that was hard to disentangle.

Suddenly, a rasping-grating sound, like the growl of an old dog chained to a creaky wagon emanated from behind the closed door. Annie gestured at the elaborately carved threshold of the new room.

"Hjalmar," she explained.

"What's he doing here?"

She smiled wanly. "Napping."

Annie opened up the pocket of her apron. Inside, a gob of candy wrapped in waxed paper. "Black licorice. It's the only thing that stops his hacking."

She handed Julia to me and disappeared into "the marital quarters." Just before the door clicked shut, I glimpsed their faded quilt, piled up on against the bedpost. I had to look away.

That night Charley slept on a pile of blankets next to the fireplace. I slept with the children up in the loft. Jake disappeared, where to I cannot say. Annie passed the night in the bedroom tending to Henning.

The next morning, despite a squall, while Charley served oatmeal to the children, I followed Annie through the marsh to the little marker on the hill by the water's edge. On a hill overlooking the Strait, a charming marker two-and-a-half feet in height. Despite the cold and damp, I knelt.

I felt nothing.

Not a twinge or a pang.

No tears.

Even if he was not my father, I still wanted to believe that Carl cared for me. Without Carl's love, to quote Hamlet, I did not "set my life at a pin's fee." Still, I felt nothing. What did it mean?

Annie folded her arms on her chest and looked down at the water.

The wind groveled.

I shouted, "I need to know. Was Carl my father, or not?"

Annie turned to face me and shrugged. "Yes."

I studied Charley's handiwork, simple yet stately. Annie had been right . . . he'd inherited a considerable talent.

Still, no tears.

I announced, "I want to marry Hjalmar Henning."

Her eyes widened.

For a full minute, she said nothing. After what seemed like an eternity, she smiled. "I didn't even know you liked him."

"How old is he, anyhow? Fifty? Sixty?"

She refolded her arms. "More like eighty."

A joke?

"I've thought it over. After he dies, I'll turn the property title over to you and the children—"

She stopped me. "No, thank you."

Annie knew—I knew it too—that my words, though brave, were empty. I could not marry the oxcart man. Not now, not ever. One year older than Annie when she married Carl, I could not emulate her noble gesture.

For I was still a child.

Hers.

She laughed and then turned serious. "The Reverend has set aside money to pay for college. Only a fool would pass up a chance for a real education. And, Millie, you're no fool." She paused. "Anyhow, I took care of it. I already married Hjalmar. Swan is in Port Angeles, filing the papers. It's too late."

Too late, a mantra. On the brink of her freedom, once again, Annie bartered her life for mine. There was nothing for me to say.

From out of my dress pocket, I retrieved the silver fish. I held them out to her. "Here," and added, "please."

Annie, after a moment, opened her hand. "You're right. The earrings came to me. It's up to me to make it right."

She dropped them into her apron pocket.

The carved cross, polished with a soft rag by Charley, gleamed in the sun-streaked rain. Still, I felt nothing.

Annie remarked, "He's not there." Before I could ask, she added, "I buried him in a tree."

In a tree? Was this her revenge? Carl had eschewed S'Klallam belief and prohibited their practice in our house. Was this way of getting back at him? Or, a sideways attempt to honor him?

Really, I was confused.

Swan remarked that in his lifetime Carl had a tendency to attract absurd situations. Death had dished up one last opportunity.

I asked her, "Did you love him?"

She replied, "No." Immediately, she added, "At least I didn't hate him."

Upside-down heart.

Annie said, "Let's go. I have things to do. Besides, I'm starving." A moment later she was swinging her arms to part the grass to clear a path to the cabin.

"Wait," I called out.

She stopped, and turned.

"What about Jake Cook?"

She shrugged. "Yeah, what?"

"Does he stay or go?"

It was her turn to act surprised. "It's not a bad thing to have a man around the place. Plus, I have three kids who need a father. Why not?"

"Because. He's a killer."

She turned away, swinging both of her arms as she moved through the wet, withering grass. "Well, everyone's done something."

Real life: at its best, a series of compromises; at worst a trail of tears leading to extinction. Holding my breath, I waited. For what? Redemption? A prayer? Forgiveness? For an instant, the earth stopped ticking—and then went on.

Together, we went in. To brew a pot of coffee and drink it fast. In my family, that's how we do it. The paradox that rules our lives: Too late to undo, but never too late to redo.

The next day Annie traveled to Port Angeles to secure the property that she had paid for with her life, not once, but twice. She planned to carry the marriage certificate to the land office and add her signature to the property deed. Meanwhile, Seya, now fully recovered, would mind the children. It was Jake, the unacknowledged groom, who would maneuver the canoe to the signing of a treaty that would legally bind her to Henning. Jake: a murderer, an invisible hero.

I was left behind to look after my new step-pappy. By dint of black licorice, I managed to put the crusty ox-herd to bed. I threw on Carl's big woolen shirt, my knitted cap, and went outside. Down by the water, a female goldeneye, attended by her partner with a white teardrop, bobbed in the shadowed grasses. Startled, they rose up, showering me with the rain from the tips of their spread wings.

The eye of the lighthouse blinked.

I let the bandage unravel onto the sand.

In the center of my palm, a red circle inside a black circle. The center opened up like the mouth at the center of a purple starfish.

With the water running over my bare feet, I stretched out my right arm, flexed my wrist at eye level, and peered through the hole in my hand, which suddenly burned with a searing intensity.

For the third and final time, I was visited by a vision of a vessel on the water:

"Heave," rasped out Lame Jack, the massacre's leader.

His unbuttoned shirt flapped. His big belly bounced. On the salted breeze I caught the scent of his body, which smelled of fresh fish guts and old whiskey.

Out of the shadows, about a half-dozen Native men, stripped to the waist, raised up a seafaring canoe. They carried it over the drift logs and shimmied it into the water without a sound.

Lame Jack staggered into the lead canoe. He turned to look back in my direction. His glare flinted and hit me squarely in the eye. "Are you coming, or not?"

Dream-like. Preposterous. Was it possible I had entered the vision so completely that *he* could see *me*?

"Why not? No weapon? Here."

He tossed me a twisted piece of rusty iron. I stepped to one side. The iron lump powdered the sand. I bent down to retrieve it. Was it even real? Just then, a lithe form passed by my right shoulder and scooped the makeshift weapon. The paddlers shoved off; the boy leapt from the shore. Thomas, his father, offered a hand. Together, they hunkered down in the canoe.

With his bone club, Thomas began to beat out a rhythm on the gunwale. His song: a call to action. His song: a wish to die. In less than one year, the one-sided battle at Dungeness would gratify that desire.

Jake swiveled to scan the shore. Searching for what? *Me*?

No.

He was staring at the mystic-silver light streaming from the bow of the canoe, a lit pathway with the power to reverse the flow of time.

"Leap!" I shouted.

It was not too late. If Jake would only listen to the phosphorescent murmurings underneath the current, he could absolve himself from a lifetime of bitter uncertainty. "Do it." But, if he did, he would forfeit his last chance to remain at his father's side, and to exhibit prowess as a warrior—sweet revenge for the raft of humiliation that would be his portion now and in the years to come.

"Jump," I urged. "Do it, now."

Next to his father's knee, Jake hunkered down, his gaze fixed on Dungeness.

Slowly, the vision misted. I cupped the moonlight in my palm. The pain subsided. My hand healed.

At last, I understood. The encounter with the legendary Aia'nl had imbued me with a special gift—to perceive the past, present, and future simultaneously. To locate what is lost and return it to its proper place. The memory of this mystic power would pour through my pen in the years to come.

With sudden clarity, I knew: If the Tsimshian girl had escaped, ransoming her life with a pair of silver earrings, then the mysterious eighteenth corpse had to be the leader of the massacre. Lame Jack—who was known as Nu-Mah the Bad to his own—had been shot and killed by a disgruntled kinsman in the melee. He'd been left to rot along with the massacred Tsimshians.

Thus, my tale concludes where it began. The way of things with my people. Redo but no undo.

With the pages remaining in this notebook, I offer this epilogue:

Edith and Astor arrived without mishap in San Francisco—having boarded the brig and not the ill-fated schooner. One year later, my mistress, sister, and friend succumbed to her illness. According to the actor, during the throes of fever, her eyes were alive with a feverish joy. Her final hour was helped along by morphine, injected by a hypodermic needle, a new medical tool, acquired by her desperate lover who no doubt used the same instrument to ease his own pain after she had breathed her last.

Ultimately, in fulfillment of Carl's wish, I would complete my formal education. At a liberal college for Natives and Anglos in Lawrence, Kansas the bereft Thomas Astor tracked me down. After two hysterical weeks in a hotel room, we married. With a new, well-respected last name I was admitted to the elite parlors of New York. Their disregard for the real challenges of real people confused me. It took two more years for me to realize that those in high society, with all of its luxurious distractions, were even more confused than me. In this atmosphere, Astor's better angel gave into addiction. The debased devil inside of him would stop at nothing to satisfy the need.

One night Astor, in a fit of despair, hit me. Afterwards he cried, collapsed on the divan, and passed out. I threw on my wrap to wander the cobbled streets of Manhattan. The next day I sold my wedding ring to a crooked jeweler. With a son and a daughter by Astor—of all of his gifts to me, the most precious—the next morning I booked passage for three on the cross-continental rail west to the Pacific Northwest.

In these pages I've fulfilled my pledge: to tell my own tale and the story of a region. What about the silver fish? Wait a bit. That will come.

George never came back to Dungeness. Though I have tried once or twice to find him, each time led to a dead-end. Whenever I felt lonely, on the teeming streets of New York City, and long after I returned to my home, I searched for him. Quite honestly, I still do.

After my third and final vision, Annie returned to Carl's cabin with two stamped documents: a marriage license and a property title. Grateful to her benefactor, or resigned to her fate. By spring, Hjalmar was recovered enough to help Seya out—gathering kindling, weeding the kitchen garden, and playing with the kids while Annie and Jake were off God knows where. This domestic routine, even with its apparent contradictions, suited Hjalmar. He brushed his teeth often.

In the autumn of 1891 Henning developed a sharp pain in one ear. Annie and the children were off at the wildflower camp fishing and hunting with Jake Cook. His minor ailment became intolerable. With a dollar and a half in his overall bib, he mounted his mule and set out for help. Though Jake searched the obvious routes, as well as the local hospitals, Hjalmar Henning never turned up. His final wish, to die in a proper bed with a devoted wife, thwarted.

Jake stayed, and though never legally wed, he and Annie settled into Carl's marital quarters.

The following autumn, Jake created an additional bedroom with one small window for my grandmother Eliza III. In all of the years that Annie lived with Carl, Seya refused to move into our house. At last, she agreed. Not because she liked Jake more than Charles Langlie. Of the two, she preferred Carl. In her own words, she agreed to move in to the plank house "because now it belongs to us."

Ten years after the events penned here, Swan, eighty-two, died of heart failure alone in town two days after he penned his last journal entry. My grandmother never acknowledged any particular affection for the man. She remained an active member of the Indian Shaker Church. Folks still talk about the ceremony in Jamestown, part wake and part potlatch, to honor her.

Like Annie in those first years, once in a while Jake disappeared. Now it was Charley who went to retrieve him from his broken-down shack in the woods. He'd find him lying in a heap of wool blankets next to a carved piece of wood and a manufactured bottle, empty. Most of the time Annie and Jake seemed contented, and the family thrived.

One September eve, not long after the death of James Swan, Charley discovered Jake's body in a column of rain that was illuminated by the Dungeness Light Station. Curled up on the sand in the exact spot where the fox fell. In the exact spot where the rescued infant, now a citizen of the world, had thrust her finger through a hole in the sky. His head was cracked open by the exploded shell of a hunting rifle at close range.

A long-postponed revenge killing?

An accident?

A suicide?

Like his half-brother George, he left no clues or signs to follow.

Why did Jake die?

Annie, who had witnessed too much death to indulge in eulogies, told me this: "If we had had a proper marriage—with feasting, gifts, and speeches—I believe that Jake would still be here. But, by the time he dreamed me up, there was no one left. No father to give me away, no villagers to host the groom's family, no real leaders to approve the marriage alliance. No neighbors and friends to witness the day, and recall it with us in the years to come. In one way, Jake Cook was lucky. Even as a youth, he knew who he was: a carver of canoes. Sadly, to others he remained invisible. No living person could actually see him. Not even me.

There was no official inquest into Jake Cook's supposed suicide. No shaman to help him cross over; no fleet of warriors to avenge his death; no woman to officially call wife and to mourn him. Each child received an indelible gift from Jake: Charley became a carver; Julia, a skilled tracker; James, a healer. Yet not one of these children legally belonged to him or recalled his Indian name.

Charley, with sand, scrubbed the damaged corpse. He polished his body with eulicon oil. Then Charley lifted his father's spent form, light as a child's, and placed it inside the elaborately painted seafaring canoe.

From inside her apron pocket Annie removed a little piece of flannel. Like the grieving Calypso—with her braids hanging down, bestowing gifts on her lover Odysseus as she set him free in the tide—Annie placed the fish earrings, along with his weapon, his paddle, and his carving knife, into the elaborately carved canoe with the notched bow.

Together the two waited for the tide to come in. Annie asked The-Current-Under-The-Water to deliver the craft to the coastal village of the Tsimshians. There, at last, his debt paid, Jake would receive a warrior's welcome.

As the Strait lifted up the canoe, the beam from the lighthouse raked its bright light over Jake's body, emaciated and scarred. However, this time he felt no pain.

His spirit had already moved on.

Afterword
November 1878-October 1966

*From my early years I have lived among the S'Klallam. I speak
their language I understand their way of life. I feel their side of the
struggle should be part of the history of Jefferson Country . . .*
—Mary Ann Lambert

This book was inspired by the life of the S'Klallam historian Mary
Ann Lambert. In her work she honored her Indian heritage, at the
same time sketching the daily lives of ordinary people in an epoch of
rapid change. Lambert told the stories of family, friends, and neighbors: Native and immigrant, who did their utmost to prosper, but
often struggled to survive. Her narratives describe the traditions of
her community and the impact, often negative, of white settlers on the
Indians. As one of the Strong People, Lambert realized the importance
of witnessing the past.

She was born in Port Townsend, Washington on November 13,
1879. Her father, Charles Luneberg Lambert, was a mariner-turned-farmer from Sweden. His family was Finnish, a pejorative for "peasant"
in Sweden at the time, according to Lambert's grandson Tom Taylor.

Her mother Annie Jacob, also of mixed-race ancestry, identified
primarily as S'Klallam. Annie was fifteen when she was given in
marriage by her parents to Charles Lambert, in his fifties or older.
Unhappy, she ran away from him numerous times but eventually stayed
when she became pregnant with Mary Ann who was born in 1879. The
couple had three more children: Cynthia, Charles, and Matilda.

When Mary Ann was six or seven the family moved from Port
Townsend to Port Discovery Bay. She attended the Old Mill School in
Blyn. A few years later, Mary Ann was sent to Port Townsend to board
with a family in order to attend secondary school. While she was away,
Carl died of septicemia from a minor fishing injury.

Shortly after, Annie Jacob Lambert, only twenty-three, but with
children to support, married Charles Lambert's best friend, Isaac
Barkhausen. According to Mary Ann Lambert's own account, Barkhausen,
already elderly and ill, developed "quick consumption" and died.

She then married the Chilean sailor Bartolo Reyes from Puerto Montt, Chile, shipwrecked on the Olympic Peninsula in 1889. In Lambert's account, the two met when Bartolo sold Annie a photo album as he peddled goods door to door. Bartolo was the love of her life. Annie Jacob Lambert, feisty and wise, never learned to read and write but was well-versed in family traditions, both S'Klallam and Swedish. She was well loved by her children, grandchildren, and great nieces and nephews until she died in 1946.

The teenaged Mary Ann Lambert completed her schooling in Port Townsend. She then attended college at the Haskell Institute in Lawrence, Kansas. Later she went to nursing school in Waterbury, Connecticut.

On the East Coast she met her first husband, a traveling actor named Thomas Maher. They had four children: Marion, Charles, Thomas, and William. Why Lambert left Maher is not a part of the public record. It probably ended in divorce. "Anyway, that's not the kind of thing we talked about in our family," remarked her great niece Sherry Macgregor. In the early 1920s Lambert, with her sons and daughter, returned to the Olympic Peninsula. A few years later she married Frank Vincent, a packer and jack-of-all-trades from Dosewallips.

In a Scrapbook of History, edited by Ida and Vern Bailey, Lambert's daughter Marian describes how her stepfather Frank taught her to fish and hunt. She learned to shoot while riding a horse. On one of their many trips over the Olympic glaciers, Vincent trapped a bear cub and presented it to her. Her oversized pet ambled after her, plucking out her hairpins. When Marian left Blyn to study at the University of Washington, she freed the bear but once in a while it would return to eat apples from the tree in their yard. Later on as a writer she would add to her mother's legacy of local history.

Her children grown, Mary Ann Lambert dedicated more time to her writing. Grandson Tom Taylor described how, in her middle age, she devoted herself to learning the local Indian languages. In the introduction to her first collection, Lambert describes what it feels like to listen to a S'Klallam elder tell his story: "His language is rich and full. He will express a phrase in a word, he will qualify the meaning of an entire sentence with a syllable, and he will convey different significations by the simple inflection of his voice."

Historian Jerry Gorsline, editor of *Shadows of Our Ancestors*, includes a number of Lambert's chapters in his anthology of primary documents of the period. Gorsline writes, "Mary Ann showed a fierce loyalty to her Native American heritage." To her family she made it clear she had no patience for those who disparaged others because of their race. She often asked her children, "Would you rather be Indian or stupid?" In a place where immigrants from every nation mingled with a tapestry of Indian peoples, Mary Ann Lambert could tolerate anyone and anything, except for a lack of curiosity.

As a child her great-niece Sherry Macgregor felt drawn to her. She recalls afternoons in the Blyn cabin off Chicken Coop Road, browsing in Lambert's famous scrapbooks with information on every subject. For a high school project, Mary Ann taught her how to make "Indian Ice Cream" using the dried Soap Olalla berry. At fifteen, Sherry moved to California, but the two remained close. When her great-aunt discovered she loved to drink tea, she sent Sherry her favorite tea, "one-third Darjeeling and two-thirds Oolong. Imagine that. My great-aunt was one of the few people in the 1950s and 60s living on the Olympic Peninsula who could easily discuss Eastern philosophies and practices."

"She wanted to know about the whole world." Sherry Macgregor, a scholar and a writer, searches for precise words to describe her great-aunt. "Mary Ann was a scholar in her own way. She even wrote letters from her cabin in the woods to people, often famous ones, to get answers to her questions."

According to Lambert's grandson Tom, she was "different. She was interested in everything. My god, what a mind." She had mental telepathy. When she needed to see me, she called me. I was working in the sawmill at three-thirty a.m. Bam! It hit me. Sorry I have to go. I'd come around Sequim Bay and sure enough the light was on. It's really an Indian thing. She didn't have it as strong as some."

Comprehension, compassion, courage—whichever word one chooses, Mary Ann Lambert had a gift she was brave enough to share. To her family she bequeathed a legacy: an outspoken manner, a love of place, and the ability to live in two cultures and with great pride.

Breakfasting with Mary Ann Lambert's descendants at Sequim's Oak Table offers up a platter-sized apple pancake, specialty of the house, and a reprise of her most outstanding qualities.

For example, the capacity to create a mesmerizing narrative, grandson Tom Taylor, her closest living relative, wears a big hat and a dungaree jacket with the sleeves cut off. He favors "Eggs Benny, Country Style," with mushroom sauce and sausage on the side, and he always pays the check for the entire table. The twinkle in his eye and the covert smile usually signify he's about to tell an insightful joke; most likely, at his own expense.

Great-niece Sherry Macgregor, also a storyteller, exemplifies Mary Ann Lambert's love of learning. She has a BA in Economics, an MA in Humanities and a Ph.D. in Ancient Near-Eastern Art and Archaeology. She's also a self-described Existentialist and Feminist, and, more recently, a Buddhist, because the practice "opens you up to a new world: the one immediately right in front of you." Likewise, the time spent on Inter-tribal Canoe Journeys has helped her "understand her Northwest Indian heritage." Currently Sherry is writing a book about *Past and Present Coast Salish Canoe Culture*—another female historian in the family.

Also, exemplifying Lambert's ingenuity and creativity is Cathy MacGregor, another great-niece. One of the first female winemakers in California, she is now in Sequim earning accolades and awards as a traditional weaver creating modernist baskets and bags of cedar bark and bear grass. Chatting in her sunny house overlooking Sequim, Cathy's warm sensitivity and humor made us feel at home.

I am honored to have a place at the table with this remarkable family: clever and curious, opinionated and open-minded, concerned with the past yet ever alert to the present moment. Mary Ann Lambert cherished the regional accounts of the people that surrounded her. Appropriately, her life and the experiences of her family are now a part of the greater narrative.

In 1960, historian Mary Ann Lambert was the guest of honor at a tea, held at the home of nineteenth-century merchant D.C.H. Rothschild, sponsored by the Port Townsend Science, Literature and Art Club, to commemorate the publication of *The House of the Seven Brothers.* Her second volume, *Dungeness Massacre and other Regional Tales*, was published a year later. She passed away in 1966, but her importance is acknowledged by the Jamestown S'Klallam Tribe and by members of her family.

"She is one of the most important recorders of her family and S'Klallam history," her great-niece Sherry remarked. "The Jamestown S'Klallam Tribe is very grateful to her, for her diligence in recording a people and a time in the past."

In the first decades of the twentieth century, as the Pacific Northwest became the West Coast of a great nation, Mary Ann Lambert increas-ingly dedicated herself to the preservation of the past. In her writing she strove to establish the rightful place of the S'Klallam. Lambert used her knowledge, skill, and empathy to document a way of seeing in accord with the environment. She captured the voices of the people, in their own words. Today, her works are an essential source of information for both white and Native historians. By chronicling the stories of the Strong People her voice resounds in the twenty-first century, clear and strong.

Key
Fact Versus Fiction

Honoring Mary Ann Lambert's real life and to gratify the curious reader, below I distinguish the facts of Lambert's history from the details in the story that are purely invented.

I played a bit with the chronology of Lambert's biography so that the fiction chapters might weave in and out of the history chapters, which develop chronologically.

The birth year of my main character, Millie Langlie, is 1876. Though documents vary, research by the family confirmed by the census identifies the year of Mary Ann Lambert's birth as 1879.

In real life, Lambert's father also died while she was away at school in Port Townsend, which caused her great grief. Charles Lambert also died from septicemia from a puncture wound. James Swan reported the death in an account whimsically entitled "Fatal Injury Inflicted By a Starfish," April 10, 1887. To preserve the fictional timeline of my tale, in the novel Carl Langlie perished from the same fate but three years later in 1890.

Both Mary Ann Lambert and my protagonist are believed to be one-eighth S'Klallam. Mary Ann's father, Charles Lambert, forty years older than her mother Annie Jacob Lambert, was a Swede of Finnish heritage, not Norwegian. I changed this detail to draw a line between the fictional family and the real one; the same reason I gave Millie a new name. I did borrow certain details from the tale of Charles Lambert's coming of age, which Lambert relates in *House of The Seven Brothers*.

Charles Lambert and Annie Jacob Lambert, according to the census, were married. In the fictional tale, Millie's parents are not. Many mixed-race couples, maybe even most, were not legally tied; I wanted to explore the legal status of Native widows with and without a legal sanction. In the archive of the Jefferson County Genealogical Society there exist reproductions of two marriage licenses for Charles Lambert and Annie Jacob, one recorded three months before Mary Ann Lambert was born, the second three months after. An archivist suggested initially there might have been some error; perhaps the second was a redo.

According to Sherry Macgregor, Lambert's great niece, family history that wends back nine generations, the first white European married into the family not long after Vancouver first explored the Strait of Juan de Fuca. In Mary Ann Lambert's accounts the matriarchs of the House of Chief Ste-tee-thlum in English are called Sally I, II, and III (in the fictional version Eliza I, II, and III). According to Lambert, Sally-the-First was indeed rescued from a sailing vessel of unknown charter shipwrecked in Ozette. Millie's red hair, in S'Klallam culture the mark of a royal lineage, is derived from Lambert's description of Sally I: blue-eyed, "tall and slender" with "very white skin and reddish hair."

In the novel I quote or paraphrase from a number of stories in Mary Ann Lambert's folios: the Hudson's Bay Company-commissioned massacre of 1828, the smallpox ship, the Point-No-Point treaty negotiations, and of course, the Dungeness massacre. In the retelling I have tried to convey the tone of her language. All of these stories, detailed and lively, are even better in the original.

Fictional Characters

Jake Cook and George Cook, fictional characters, bear no resemblance to historic persons. Though the Puget Sound Co-Operative Colony actually existed, the school teacher Delia Bright never did. The Mathiesson family is likewise invented. There are tales of scoundrels like ex-officer Daniel Smyth, however, in Dungeness the drunk who abducts the Native girl, Daisy, is made-up.

D.C.H. Rothschild

The Port Townsend merchant D.C.H. Rothschild, a distant relation of the Rothschild financial empire, owned a general store on the waterfront and a house on the bluff, now preserved as a museum. According to the curator, he probably perished by his own hand using a shotgun. His suicide may have resulted from financial stress. The house on the bluff, built for his bride as a wedding gift in 1868, is managed by the Jefferson County Historical Museum for the Washington State Parks and open to visitors.

Swan

The journal writer James Swan, the most famous figure in this account, for many years lived in Neah Bay just north and west of

Dungeness, and later, in Port Townsend. He knew Lambert's family. How well he knew them is unknown.

In his memoir *Winter Brothers*, Ivan Doig wonders if the journal writer, while serving as a school teacher on the Makah reservation, might have dispelled the gloom of the long, lonely rainy season with a Native woman named Katy. After Katy died, Swan covered her mound with daisies. Later, in Port Townsend, at age fifty-seven, without a doubt, Swan courted sixteen-year-old Dolly Roberts. He was rejected.

Ivan Doig ends his book by describing Swan's tagging of a bluff in Neah Bay in 1859. After visiting the spot, Doig recreates the scene:

> The deep-cut letters J G S are level with my eyes and above them the stone swan rides. Tail fluted high to a jaunty point. Neck an elaborate curve gentle and extended as a sailor's caress. Breast serenely parting the shadowed current of cliff . . . So clearly and intently did he sculpt that only the down thrust of the bird's head, where the beak and the eye would be, has faded with 120 years' erosion . . .

I refer to this passage from Doig to describe the carving of a swan on the outside of the front door of Seya's birdhouse shelter.

To experience a sublime wilderness with Swan and Doig, read *Winter Brothers: A Season on the Edge of America*. I could compare the study of Pacific Northwest history to a ride on a river raft. If so, then Doig's prose is the white water.

The Silver Earrings

The actual earrings from the Dungeness Massacre, fluted pendants with a bell-shaped cup on the bottom—not fish!—were extorted from the lone survivor Nusee-chus, sixteen years old and pregnant at the time of the attack. Did the instigator of the ambush, Lame Jack, aka Nu-mah the Bad, steal the earrings and leave her for dead, as Mary Ann Lambert suggests? The story is not confirmed. Years later, Joe Johnson, the youngest member of the raiding party, gifted the earrings to Lambert. Exactly how and when he acquired them is also unknown.

No member of the Lambert family was ever implicated in the massacre.

Where are the earrings now? According to Judy Stipe, the Executive Director of the Museum and Arts Center in Sequim, "That's the biggest secret in the county."

Opium Boat

Christopher Mathieson's boyhood tale of the leaky rowboat caulked with opium comes from a true story first described in the July 11, 1929 edition of the *Port Townsend Leader*. Retold two decades later, photographer Paul Richardson speculates the sticky goo he and the other boys used to fill the leak in the four-bit boat could have purchased "a fairly good yacht." Richardson's account is reprinted in Thomas W. Camfield's *Port Townsend: The City That Whiskey Built*.

Mary Sadla Tunmer

I learned of the incident from local historian Pam Clise after I revealed to her what seemed a rather extreme plot twist in my novel in progress, wholly invented by me or so I supposed, in which the creepy love interest Christopher Mathieson drives a nail through Millie's right hand. As Pam shared the details of Sadla's final moments on earth, I felt a chill. Later, when I learned that the incident took place not far from Lambert's childhood home, the eeriness redounded. Still, the real significance here lies not in the odd similarity between the two stories but instead in the sad demise of the S'Klallam elder Mary Sadla, disregarded by the legal system and then sadistically killed.

On the rights of widows, James G. McCurdy in By Juan De Fuca's Strait—an account that provided much useful fact and color in this account—describes how in court Emily Palmer Sconce, the widow of the murdered Ebey, won title to her husband's land, " thus establishing a precedent upholding widow's rights that was never after questioned in the commonwealth." Though possibly true for white wives, the frustrations of Katie Gale (the figure at the heart of Llyn Da Danaan's excellent account) and the sad story of Mary Sadla Tunmer belie that claim.

Notes

Part I: On The Strait of Juan de Fuca

Chapter One: The Aia'nl (S'Klallam Folklore)
Gunther, *Klallam Ethnography*, 293 – 294.

Chapter Three: Vancouver "Discovers" the Strait (1792) *Vancouver, A Voyage of Discovery*, 220 – 247.

Chapter Four: Swan Boat (1880)
1. Clark. *Introduction to Northwest Coast*, v – xxiii.
2. Doig, *Winter Brothers: Season at the Edge of America*, 18 – 24.

Chapter Five: Pestilent Spirit (19th Century)
1. Bancroft, *The Native Races*, 304 -307.
2. Bourasaw, editor. "S'Klallam and Chemakum Indian Tribes," *Skagit River Journal*.
3. Eells, *Notebooks Of Myron Eells*, 30 – 31.
4. Lambert, *Dungeness Massacre and Other Regional Tales*, 25 – 26.

Chapter Six: Shake Up (1881)
1. Eells, *Notebooks Of Myron Eells*, 427 – 440.
2. Keeting, editor. *Dungeness: Lure of a River*, 75 – 76.
3. Strauss, *The Jamestown S'Klallam Story*, 143 – 145.

Chapter Nine: Shaker Bells (1880)
Barnett, *Indian Shakers*, 11 – 40, 232 – 233.

Part II: School Days

Chapter Ten: Spirit Canoe Paddle (1884)
1. Eells, *The Notebooks of Myron Eells*, 409 – 412.
2. Jilek, *Indian Healing: Shamanic Ceremonialism*, 138 – 145.
3. Elmendorf, *Twana Narratives*, 57. 5 – 57.11, 194 – 198.

Chapter Eleven: The Winter Ceremony (1872)
1. Eells, *Notebooks of Myron Eells*, 397 – 400.
2. Griffiths. "Secret Black Magic," *Town Crier*, 10 – 37.
Acquired at the library at Little Boston.

Chapter Twelve: Siwash. (1886)
1. Keeting, editor. *Dungeness: Lure of a River*, 34.
2. Ibid, 57.
3. Ibid, 98 – 103.

Chapter Thirteen: Brave New World (1886 – 1900)
1. LeWarne, *Utopias on Puget Sound*, 15 – 54.
2. Chambers, *History of Clallam County*, 71 – 80.

Chapter Seventeen: In the Land of Salmon People (19th Century)
1. Everenden, *In the Land of the Salmon People, A Skokomish tale*. 87 – 88.
2. Strauss, *The Jamestown S'Klallam Story*, 3 – 5.

Part III. Zones In-Between

Chapter Nineteen: Steamboat Girl (19th Century)
Gunther, *Klallam Folk Tales*, 121 -122.
This story was told to Erna Gunther by Mrs. Robbie Davis of the Elwa S'Klallam.

Chapter Twenty-One: Between Life and Death (19th Century)
1. Eells, *The Notebooks of Myron Eells*, 343 – 346.
2. Leighton, *West Coast Journeys*, "Port Townsend, Washington Territory, April 4, 1869", 92 - 93.

Part IV. Whiskey City

Chapter Twenty-Seven: Two views of a Massacre (1828)
Gorsline, *Shadows of Our Ancestors*, 3 – 29.

Chapter Twenty-Eight: Port Townsend (1889)
Camfield, *The City Whiskey Built*, 89 – 90.

Chapter Twenty-Nine: Port Townsend (1889)
Camfield, *The City Whiskey Built*, 27.

Chapter Thirty-One: A Sunbeam in the House (19th Century)
1. Gorham, *Victorian Girls and the Feminine Ideal*, 49 – 59.
2. "Joy's Vegetable Sarsaparilla, " *Port Townsend Morning Leader*, Jan. 31, 1892. A-2.
3. Hardy, *How to be Happy Through Marriage*. The 1887 Edition (7tth ed.).
4. Hunt, *Bold Spirit*. Especially Chapter Eleven: "New Women's' Actions Old Victorian Attitudes," pages 137 – 149.
5. Seagraves, *Soiled Doves*, "Working Girls," 55 – 74.
6. "A Queer Freak," *Port Townsend Leader*, Jan. 28, 1892.

Chapter Thirty-Three: Good and Bad Indians (1854 – 1858)
On 'good" and "bad" Indians.
1. Leighton, *West Coast Journeys*, 150.

On Chief Chetzemoka.
2. Gregory, "The Duke of York" in *With Pride in Our Heritage*, 124 – 139.
3. Strauss, *The Jamestown S'Klallam Story*, 141- 145.
4. Swan, *The Northwest Coast*, 17. The first page of Swan's most famous account opens with an invitation to Port Townsend by the "Clalam" chief:

" . . . I had always, from my earliest recollections a strong desire to see the Great River Columbia, and to learn something of the habits and customs of the tribes of the Northwest... This chief, whose name was Chetzamokha, and who is known by the whites as the Duke of York, was very urgent to have me visit his people . . ."

5. "With Pride In Heritage," 124 – 131.
On the Point-No Point Treaty.
6. Gorsline, Part II: Point No Point Treaty" in *Shadows of Our Ancestors*, 33 – 70.
Reflections on the treaty from various viewpoints, including pieces by Governor Issac Stevens, his son Hazard, Chetzemoka's wife See-Hem-Itza, and Mary Ann Lambert.

7. Strauss, *The Jamestown S'Klallam Story*, 138-139.
On Chief Leschi.
8. Eells, *The Notebooks of Myron Eells*, 351 – 352.
9. Harmon, *Indians in the Making*, 92 – 94, 146 – 148.
10. Kaylene, *Judicially Murdered*, 268 – 306.

Chapter Thirty-Four: Swan Returns (1890)
1. Camfield, *The City Whiskey Built*, 91.
2. Christopher's tale of the "four-bit skiff" caulked with opium is based on the recollection of photographer Paul Richardson, as reported in the *Port Townsend Leader* (July 11, 1929), reprinted in Camfield's book, a whimsical collection of primary sources and essays.
3. Doig, *Winter Brothers*, 151 -156.

Chapter Thirty-Four: Cha-tic, The Painter (1818 – 1900)
1. Doig, *Winter Brothers*, 114.
2. Miles, *James Swan, Cha-tic*, 7 – 37.
3. Doig, *Winter Brothers*, 123.
4. McCurdy, *By Juan de Fuca's Strait*, 138 – 139.

Chapter Thirty-Five: What is Happiness? (1890)
1. Doig, *Winter Brothers*, 183 – 202.
2. Miles, *James Swan, Cha-tic*, 24 – 37.

Chapter Thirty-Six: Katy, Makah Slave-Girl (1865)
Doig, *Winter Brothers*, 96 – 97.

Chapter Thirty-Eight: The Murder Trial of Xwelas (1878)
Thrush, & Keller, "I See What I Have Done," 168 -176.

Chapter Thirty-Nine: The Magic Lotus Lantern (The Song Dynasty)
Yuan, Haiwang, *The Magic Lotus Lantern*, 83 – 88.

Chapter Forty-Two: The Celestials (19th Century)
1. Boardman. "The Saga of Bobby Gow, " *Leader, Summer Magazine*, 1987.
2. Clise. "Chinese Celebrate the New Year," *Peninsula Daily News*, Dec. 25, 2005.
3. Kannenberg. "Chinese in Port Townsend," Feb. 17, 1990. Jefferson County Archive.

4. Liestman. "Old Culture In A New Land," *Leader*, Dec. 7, 1994. D-1 sec.

5. Liestman. "Opium, Immigration Laws," *Leader*, Dec. 21, 1994. D-1.

6. Rice. "Chinese-Americans Share," *Peninsula Daily News*, Sept. 12, 1993. A-1.

7. "Three Chinamen in the Cooler," *Leader*, March 4, 1893.

8. "Townsend Again Visited By Fire," *Leader*, Sept. 2, 1900.

Chapter Forty-Four: The Play Is the Thing (1880 – 1890)

1. Campbell. "Play Houses." April, 1951. Jefferson County Archive.

2. Clise. "The Big Theater House Shuffle," 1999. Jefferson County Archive.

Chapter Forty-Six: "Sir, There Shall Be No Alps!" (Autumn 1890)

1. "Port Townsend's Own Railroad Was Inspiration for Boom Era," *Port Townsend Leader*, Summer 1969. 14 –16

2. "Prosperity Rides the Rails," *Port Townsend Jefferson County Leader*, Sept. 9, 1998. C-10.

3. "The Railroad Came," *Port Townsend Leader*, Summer 1978. 7 – 8.

4. Benton, Homer, "Port Townsend. Washington, Trolleys," *Electric Traction Quarterly*, Volume 4, Number 4, Summer 1966. 25 – 33.

5. Hermanson, James. "Did Fight Between Prostitutes?" *Port Townsend County Leader*, Weds., Oct. 19, 1994. C-13.

6. McCurdy, *By Juan de Fuca's Strait*, "The Railroad Comes and Goes," 287– 302.

Chapter Forty-Eight: The Only Safety Is in Marriage (1869)
Lambert. *The Seven Brothers*, 24 – 25.

Part V: Return to Dungeness

Chapter Fifty-One: Fatal Injury by Starfish (1890)
Swan. "Fatal Injury Inflicted," United States Fish Commission, Nov., 1887, Vol. 7: 33 – 48.

Chapter Fifty-Three: No Safe Haven (1906)

1. Clise, Pam McCollum. "Rich Family Heritage Runs Deep," *Peninsula Daily News*, Feb. 23, 2006.

2. Tunmer Dep. 869; 251, April 24, 1908. Jefferson County Historical Society Archives.
3. "Coroner's Jury Thinks Murder was Committed," *Port Townsend Weekly Leader*, Jan. 6,1909, 2.
4. "Woman's Mutilated Body Found," *Port Townsend Weekly Leader*, Jan. 6, 1909, 6.
5. "Tumner Murder Remains Impenetrable Mystery" *Port Townsend Weekly Leader*, Jan. 6, 1909. Jefferson County Archives.

Chapter Fifty-Three: The Dungeness Massacre (1868)
Lambert. *Dungeness Massacre*, 1 – 4.

Afterword: Mary Ann Lambert: "I speak their language, I understand their way of life." (November, 1878 – October, 1966)
1. Macgregor, Sherry. Personal Interview. Sequim, WA. Nov. 5, 2013.
2. Taylor, Thomas. Personal Interview. Sequim, WA. Nov. 5, 2013.
3. Bailey, Brinnon: *Scrapbook of History*, 52 – 56.
4. Gorsline, *Shadows of Our Ancestors*, 22- 23.

Bibliography

Alcott, Louisa May, and John Escott. *Little Women*. Newmarket: Brimax Books, 1995.

Bailey, Ida, and Vern Baily. *Brinnon: A Scrapbook of History*. Bremerton, WA: Perry Pub., 1997.

Bancroft, Hubert Howe. *The Native Races*. San Francisco: A.L. Bancroft & Company, Publishers, 1882.

Barnett, H. G. *Indian Shakers a Messianic Cult of the Pacific Northwest*. Carbondale: Southern Illinois University Press, 1972.

Boardman, Bob. "The Saga of Bobby Gow: Chinese Immigrants Discovered Freedom in Robust seaport Town." *Port Townsend Leader*, summer magazine, 1987.

Bourasaw, Noel V., editor. "S'Klallam and Chemakum Indian Tribes on Olympic Peninsula When Jarman Settled There in 1848-52," *Skagit River Journal*, Sedro-Wooley. http://www.skagitriverjournal.com/wa/olypen/indians1-sklallamchemakumjarman.html

Boyd, Robert T. *The Coming of the Spirit of Pestilence: Introduced Infectious Diseases and Population Decline among Northwest Coast Indians, 1774-1874*. Vancouver: UBC Press, 1999.

Campbell, Eva Bash. "Play Houses." Prize-winner of an essay contest sponsored by the Pen Club. April, 1951. Jefferson County Historical Society Archive.

Camfield, Thomas W. *The City That Whiskey Built*. 2002 ed. Vol. II. Port Townsend: Ah Tom Publishing, 2002.

Chambers, Craig. *A History of Clallam County, Washington*. 2nd ed. Port Angeles: Clallam County Historical Society, 2005.

Clark, Norman H. *Introduction to The Northwest Coast; Or, Three Years' Residence in Washington Territory*. Seattle: University of Washington Press, 1972.

Clise, Pam McCollum. "The Big Theater House Shuffle: An Overview." 1999. Jefferson County Historical Society Archive.

Clise, Pam McCollum. "Chinese Celebrate the New Year," *Peninsula Daily News*, Port Angeles, December 25, 2005.

Clise, Pam McCollum. "Rich Family Heritage Runs Deep," *Peninsula Daily News*, February 23, 2006. (Provided by the author September 15, 2012.)

Cobb, John N. *Pacific Salmon Fisheries.* Washington: Govt. Print. Off., 1917. Print.

"Coroner's Jury Thinks Murder was Committed," *Port Townsend Weekly Leader*, Jan. 6,1909, 2.

Doig, Ivan, and James G. Swan. *Winter Brothers: A Season at the Edge of America.* New York: Harcourt Brace Jovanovich, 1980.

Duncan, Kathy. "Dungeness Massacre," Jamestown S'Klallam Tribe, Sequim, WA. http://www.jamestowntribe.org/history/hist_massacre. htm.

Edwards, G. Thomas. "Terminus Disease," *Pacific Norwest Quarterly*, 70:4, October, 1979. 163 – 177.

Eells, Myron, and George Pierre Castile. *The Indians of Puget Sound: the Notebooks of Myron Eells.* Seattle: University of Washington, 1985.

Elmendorf, William W. *Twana Narratives: Native Historical Accounts of a Coast Salish Culture.* Seattle: University of Washington Press, 1993.

Everenden, Jeanne. *The Land of the Salmon People.* Wanda Hart, illustrator. Developed by the Skokomish Tribe. Portland: National Institute of Education, 1982.

Furtwanger, Albert. *Answering Chief Seattle, 13.* Seattle: University of Washington Press, 1997.

Gibbs, George, M.D. "Tribes of Western Washington and Northwestern Oregon." Contributions to the *North American Ethnologist*, Vol. 1. U.S. Govt. Printing, 1877.

Gorham, Deborah. *The Victorian Girl and the Feminine Ideal.* Bloomington: Indiana University Press, 1982.

Gorsline, Jeremiah. *Shadows of Our Ancestors: Readings in the History of Klallam-White Relations.* Port Townsend, WA: Empty Bowl, 1992.

Griffiths, FW. "Secret Black Magic," *Town Crier*, March 1935. Vol. 30 ; 10 - 37.

Gregory, VJ. "The Duke of York." In *With Pride in Heritage; History of Jefferson County, a Symposium.* First ed. Portland: Jefferson County Historical Society, 1966; 124 – 131.

Gunther, Erna. *Klallam Ethnography.* Seattle: Univ. Pr., 1927. 293 – 294.

"Klallam Ethnography "Welcome to Open Library!" (Open Library). Web, 293 - 294. 30 July 2010. http://openlibrary.org/books/ OL14178004M/Klallam_ethnography

Gunther, Erna. *Klallam Folk Tales.* Seattle: University of Washington Press, 1925; 121- 122.

Hermanson, James. "Did Fight Between Prostitutes Start Fire of 100?" *Port Townsend County Leader*, Wednesday, October 19, 1994. C-13.

Hardy, E. J. *How to Be Happy Though Married: Being a Handbook to Marriage*. 7th edition. London: Unwin, 1887. HathiTrust Digital Library. 20 Feb 2015. http://babel.hathitrust.org/cgi/pt?id=uc2.ark:/13960/t9377g53r;view=1up;seq=8

Harmon, Alexandra. *Indians in the making: ethnic relations and Indian identities around Puget Sound*. Berkeley : Univ. of California Press, 2000.

Hunt, Linda. *Bold Spirit: Helga Estby's Forgotten Walk across Victorian America*. Moscow, Idaho: University of Idaho Press, 2003.

Jilek, Wolfgang. *Indian Healing: Shamanic Ceremonialism in the Pacific Northwest Today*. Surrey, B.C.: Hancock House, 1982.

"Joy's Vegetable Sarsaparilla," *Port Townsend Morning Leader*, January 31, 1892. A-2.

Kannenberg, Bud. "Chinese in Port Townsend, WA," 17 February, 1990. Jefferson County Historical Society Archive, Jefferson County Genealogical Society.

Kaylene, Anne T. *Judicially Murdered*. Scappoose: Melton Publishing, 1999.

Keeting, Virginia. *Dungeness, the Lure of a River: A Bicentennial History of the East End of Clallam County*. Port Angeles: Sequim Bicentennial Committee, 1976. Reprint, Port Angeles: Sequim Bicentennial Committee, 1991.

Lambert, Mary Ann Vincent. *Dungeness Massacre and Other Regional Tales*. 2nd ed. Port Orchard: Publishers Printing, 1961.

Lambert, Mary Ann. *The Seven Brothers of the House of Ste-tee-thum*. Port Orchard: Publishers Printing, 1972.

LeWarne, Charles Pierce. *Utopias on Puget Sound, 1885-1915*. Seattle: University of Washington Press, 1975.

Liestman, Daniel. "Old Culture In A New Land," *Port Townsend Leader*, December 7, 1994. D-1 sec.

Liestman, Daniel. "Opium, Immigration Laws Target Chinese," *Port Townsend Leader*, December 21, 1994. D-1.

Macgregor, Sherry. Personal Interview. Sequim, WA. November 5, 2015. Unpublished.

McClary, Daryl C. "HistoryLink Essay: Dungeness Massacre Occurs on September 21, 1868." HistoryLink.org - the Free Online Encyclopedia of Washington State History. Web. 24 July 2010. http:www.historylink.org

Miles, George A., and James G. Swan. *James Swan, Cha-tic of the Northwest Coast: Drawings and Watercolors from the Franz & Kathryn Stenzel Collection of Western American Art.* New Haven, Conn.: Beinecke Rare Book & Manuscript Library, Yale University, 2003.

Miller, Bruce Granville. *The Problem of Justice: Tradition and Law in the Coast Salish World.* Lincoln: University of Nebraska, 2001.

"Port Townsend's Own Railroad Was Inspiration for Boom Era," *Port Townsend Leader,* Summer 1969. 14 -16

"A Queer Freak; Depravity Worthy of the Pen of a True Zola." *Port Townsend Leader*, Jan. 28, 1892.

"The Railroad Came to Port Townsend," *Port Townsend Leader,* Summer 1978. 7-8.

Rice, Randi F. "Chinese-Americans Share Hard Times." *Peninsula Daily News,* September 12, 1993. A-.

"The Rothschild Years," *Exhibit notes by the Jefferson County Historical Society.* Port Townsend: Jefferson County Historical Society, 1999.

Seagraves, Ann. *Soiled Doves: Prostitution in the Early West.* Hayden, Idaho: Wesanne Publicarions, 1994.

"Street Cars, Logging Railroads Fuel dreams," *Port Townsend County Leader*, Weds, Sept. 16m 1998. C-12.

Strauss, Joseph H. *The Jamestown S'Klallam Story: Rebuilding a Northwest Coast Indian Tribe.* Sequim, WA: Jamestown S'Klallam, 2002.

The Strong People: A History of the Port Gamble S'Klallam Tribe. Kingston, WA: Port Gamble S'Klallam Tribe, 2012.

Swan, James Gilchrist. *Almost Out of the World: Scenes in Washington Territory- The Strait of Juan De Fuca, 1859-61.* Seattle: Washington State Historical Society, 1971.

Swan, James G. "Fatal Injury Inflicted by A Starfish." *Bulletin of the United States Fish Commission.* Washington: 1887. Vol. 7: 33 – 48. http://archive.org/stream/analyticalsubjec00unitrich/ analyticalsubjec00unitrich_djvu.txt Retrieved 20 Nov 2012.

Swan, James Gilchrist. *The Indians of Cape Flattery: At the Entrance to the Strait of Fuca, Washington Territory.* Facsim. Reproduction 1964. ed. Seattle: Shorey Book Store, 1964.

Swan, James G. *The Northwest Coast; Or, Three Years' Residence in Washington Territory.* Fourth ed. Seattle: University of Washington Press, 1972.

Taylor, Thomas. Personal Interview. Sequim, WA. November 5, 2015.
Unpublished.

"Three Chinamen in the Cooler," *Port Townsend Leader*, March 4,
1893.

Thrush, Coll-Peter, and Robert H. Keller. "'I See What I Have Done':
The Life and Murder Trial of Xwelas, A S'Klallam Woman." *The
Western Historical Quarterly* 26.2, 1995: 168.

Tong, Benson. *The Chinese Americans*. 2nd Edition. Boulder:
University of Colorado Press, 2003. 19 – 66.

"Townsend Again Visited By Fire," *Port Townsend Leader*, September 2,
1900.

Tunmer, Mary S. Bureau of Pensions Deposition, 869; 251, April 24,
1908. Jefferson County Historical Society Archives.

"Tumner Murder Remains Impenetrable Mystery" *Port Townsend
Weekly Leader*, Jan. 6, 1909. Jefferson County Archives.

Vancouver, George, and John Vancouver. *A Voyage of Discovery to
the North Pacific Ocean and Round the World: In Which the Coast
of North-West America Has Been Carefully Examined and Accurately
Surveyed*. London: Printed for John Stockdale, 1801. Reproduced w/
permission: University of Washington, 1996.

"The Whaling Equipment of the Makah Indians"Internet Archive:
Digital Library of Free Books, Movies, Music & Wayback Machine.
Web. 12 Mar. 2011.

<http://www.archive.org/stream/whalingequipment00wate/
whalingequipment00wate_djvu.txt>.

With Pride in Heritage; History of Jefferson County, a Symposium.
Port Townsend: Jefferson County Historical Society, 1966. 124 –
131.

"Woman's Mutilated Body Found Amid Ruins of Isolated Home," *Port
Townsend Weekly Leader*, January 6, 1909, 6.

Yuan, Haiwang. *The Magic Lotus Lantern and Other Tales from the Han
Chinese*. Westport, CT: Libraries Unlimited, 2006. Print.

Karen Polinsky is a high school English teacher and writer from Bainbridge Island, Washington. Twenty years ago she drove to the Pacific Northwest from Boston with her three children in a beat-up Toyota station wagon. Not long after, she encountered the nineteenth century S'Klallam historian Mary Ann Lambert in a book of primary documents gifted to her by the director of the Port Gamble S'Klallam Cultural Resources. Her fascination with Lambert, a woman-of-vision, eventually turned into *Dungeness*, a revisionist-history coming-of-age novel inspired by her life. Also a playwright, she has had a half-dozen one-acts produced on Bainbridge Island and in Seattle, and has written scripts for two short films. Polinsky was recognized with the Patsy Collins Award for Environmental Educators in 2012.

CPSIA information can be obtained
at www.ICGtesting.com
Printed in the USA
FSOW01n1403210617
35441FS